When Love Evolves

by
Lonz Cook

ELEVATION
BOOK PUBLISHING

Published by Elevation Book Publishing
Atlanta, Georgia 30308
www.elevationbookpublishing.com

Library of Congress Cataloging-in-Publication Data

Cook, Lonz, 1960-
When love evolves / by Lonz Cook.
p. cm.
ISBN 978-1-943904-01-3 (pbk.)
1. African American businesspeople--Fiction. 2. Women-owned business enterprises--Fiction. 3. Organized crime investigation--Fiction. 4. Man-woman relationships--Fiction. I. Title.

PS3603.O5727W48 2011
813'.6--dc22

2011013635

Cover Design by Nederpelt Media.
Edited by April Michael.
Book Design by Rachel Trusheim.

10 9 8 7 6 5 4 3 2 1

Printed in America.

Acknowledgments

To all the wonderful readers who insisted on a sequel, this novel is dedicated to you. My hopes are that you enjoy the story continuation with the same enthusiasm you had while reading *Good Guys Finish Last*.

To my family, team of supporters, visionaries, and partners, I thank you. I pray to represent you well in the presentation of a dynamic novel. Without your guidance and feedback, this wouldn't have become a dream come true. I appreciate and admire each of you. For all you have done, I dedicate this novel to you.

My thanks goes to God for the many blessings and the given ability to write creatively. I'm grateful.

– Lonz

1.

Richmond

"Embezzlement, laundering! I can't believe Stefan would do such a thing," Simone said to Sabrina while driving from the lawyer's office downtown. Frowning, Simone pondered at how things had gone wrong over the years. She'd married her ideal man. Stefan turned out to be just that: an idea. He'd maneuvered his way beyond Simone's love and into her finances. It was over a year before Simone opened her life to him the way Rodney, a failed flame, had done for her. She had allowed Stefan access to her accounts out of love. Her eyes were blinded by her affection for a player, a man of few morals, who did not believe in true love. Stefan had seen a path to wealth, and it was the path he'd proudly traveled.

Stefan belonged to a group of people who played their luck on quick riches. He observed many men, comparing the lives of those who played the game of life fairly with the lives of those who cheated. It dawned on him repeatedly that good guys finished last and that immediate riches and wealth came to those who schemed their way to success.

It was like heaven when Simone crossed his path at the

annual city fundraiser. She wore an intricate designer ball gown, accented with diamond bracelets and a five-carat necklace. He made his way to her and pursued the challenge.

Realizing her huntress personality, Stefan stayed within her sight for the next few hours but never approached her. He masked himself with a cloud of mystery and led Simone with a blindfold of seduction. He intrigued her in a way she'd never experienced. Stefan began to flirt with other women in front of Simone, leading her into a rage of desire. His ploy worked and compelled her competitive nature. She fought hard to get his attention the entire night, to divert him away from the gorgeous women. Stefan played her like a man fingering the fiddle. His goal was entrapment, but Simone didn't see it.

Stefan never let on that he didn't ask anyone else to dinner or drinks that evening. He had, however, leaned on a few women and hinted at having such an interest, especially in plain view of Simone. With the night lingering, the cat-and-mouse game about to end, he postured himself as the hottest bachelor available and the winner… Simone! While in the midst of a crowd of beautiful women attending the fundraiser, his sudden invitation for her to accompany him to dinner came when her guard was down. "Yes," Simone said as she smiled triumphantly.

Dinner went well for Simone. She invited Stefan to her place afterwards, something Simone didn't do often with men she'd just met. It was the bad-girl move, a spontaneous adventure— one she'd have never thought of embarking on with Rodney. Stefan moved as if he played a song, plucking all the right notes, which encouraged Simone to fall into his arms. Once they arrived at Simone's mansion, Stefan smiled deep inside and visions of gold lingered in his mind. *I'm landing this one; this one's going to be my wife.* Stefan moved toward Simone and pulled her close.

"What are you doing?" Simone grinned and embraced Stefan's advances.

"It's what you expect me to do. I'm not alone here; you're ready for this." Stefan leaned in with a kiss, and then kissed her again. Simone savored his touch and forgot anything but her lustful thoughts. Since her Aunt Marge had passed away, she'd focused so much on managing her business and inheritance that she had never allowed outside influences. Simone never wanted to lose the money Aunt Marge had bequeathed, so she had concentrated on generating cash flow and building a successful company beyond her aunt's wildest dreams. Nothing gave her joy like seeing the numbers grow, and her financial background and training had aided her in her efforts. But at the moment, she only focused on Stefan. "I so want this," she said.

"I know you want this, just as I do." Stefan continued his advances and led her up the stairs, searching for a bedroom. "Take me to where you're most comfortable."

"Turn there," Simone said. Stefan turned into Simone's room where there was a queen-sized canopy bed, silk linens, and soft, white chiffon curtains. He guided her to the side of the bed, kissed her, and pushed her onto it.

Simone sat up and kneeled at the edge of the mattress. "Hold tight," she said, deciding to switch roles and take the lead. "Let me get you out of those clothes." Simone grabbed Stefan's shirt and pulled it over his head; buttons snapped as she ignored the restrictions. She pulled him onto the bed and then jumped and sat on his stomach while he lay on the cool satin sheets. She attacked him with outrageous kisses, but Stefan didn't remain powerless. He flipped her, laid her flat on her back, and massaged her body. He encouraged her to rise to the opportunity of seduction, preparing her for sensual pleasure. It was long coming as Simone hadn't allowed someone this close in ages. Her excitement built to a level beyond her control, and her moist flower gave Stefan indication of her will.

He placed his tie over her eyes and charmed her into submission. "Let me take you. Relax, darling, relax while I explore your lovely body."

"Oh, but I …" Simone said in a soft, excited voice. "I can't, no one has ever blindfolded me before."

"It's okay, trust me. Trust me and let me explore," Stefan said as he moved over to her side and touched her neck without touching any other part of her body. He touched her with his fingertips, barely grazing her as he moved down the curves of her breast, circled the nipples, and then down to her stomach. He kissed her stomach with no pressure, but full lips. Simone felt sensations, those nerve endings responding, like a brisk wind from a snow-covered mountain, thousands of feet above.

He jolted her with his next move—his lips touched the tip of her flower. He continued kissing her, from her toes and back, and surprised her when he finally made full body contact and thrust his manhood inside. It was enough to send blasting sensations up her spine and into her mind. Her body became rigid with pleasure, glorious pleasure. She grabbed her blindfold, threw it across the room, and grabbed Stefan as if holding on for dear life. She dug her nails into his back as he rode her like a bucking stallion, a colt being broken for the first ride. Stefan slammed her for minutes and took her for what seemed like hours as she reached her climax; ecstasy gripped her from the top of her head to the bottom of her toes. Her body shivered and he didn't stop, searching for yet another, and only slowing to grab her bottom, leveraging his balance for better control of his movements. He kissed her after bringing her to a second climax, and her body became limp from the intense sensations. He nibbled her softly on her lips, her eyes, and her nose and then whispered, "Aren't you glad you trusted me?"

"Um-hum," Simone said with her eyes half closed.

"Good." Stefan caressed her forehead. He cuddled her the rest of the night, feeling the elation of hitting the jackpot.

Stefan became her regular; he showered her with kindness and attention, yet still presented enough of a challenge to Simone's affection. He toyed with her ego to promote her admiration of him and fooled her into thinking she was the one who felt the thrill of victory. He established a strong character of wealth by posing as a rich man. Stefan impressed his ideas of living a quality life upon her and seeded the potential of a future business partnership in her mind.

Stefan had no wealth, nothing near comparison to Simone's financial situation. He rented nice cars to impress Simone, maxed out his credit cards while shopping with her, and surprised her with trips to exotic locations. Each time it was smoke and mirrors, a guise filled with deceit. Simone fell, and fell hard. She loved his attention, and his ability to captivate her was unmatched. Even his sly concentration upon other women encouraged her; she viewed it as the catalyst of challenge. Stefan borrowed to maintain the façade, and bank after bank, friend after friend, gave him loans. He managed to build a convincing paper trail of false companies, which elicited eager investors. The accumulated debt rose into hundreds of thousands of dollars, and still the image kept Simone at bay with excitement. He masked his reality and his profession with fake business meetings and friends who acted professionally in Simone's presence.

Simone fell deeply in love with Stefan. She couldn't wait to make him a permanent part of her life. She pushed for commitment, especially since so many other women seemed interested in him. When he proposed, she felt she'd conquered over and defeated the others and was filled with joy in her heart and mind. At last, Simone had found a partner who was sensual, witty, and complicated—nothing like her encounters with Rodney, who had always showered her with emotions. The carriage ride in the park, the dinner date, and the hospital were nothing in comparison to her adventures with Stefan. Sabrina, Simone's sister, had insisted, "You were crazy for not grabbing Rodney," but Simone still concluded, *I did well, really well.*

Stefan moved in with haste and embraced Simone's wealth. Simone was the CEO of Willingham Corp., the company she and her sister, Sabrina, had inherited from their late Aunt Marge. Since they'd inherited the small management company, Simone had grown it into a successful conglomerate. Stefan studied Simone avidly, waiting for the right minute to make his move. He managed to learn her business, one page at a time, and spoke to her as an advisor. He won her trust and admiration, as many of his ideas produced positive results. Stefan finagled his way into her financial accounts, and there it began.

Then, the happy Stefan, who was just as eager about marriage as Simone was, pressured her for a rush wedding. Instead of a large ceremony, he talked Simone into a quaint, simple event with few guests and whisked her away to Europe for their honeymoon. They trekked from the Swiss Alps to Naples, Italy in fifteen days, exploring the finer things each city offered. They visited Sabrina and James, her husband, in Paris, where the four toured the city for three days. It was a whirlwind of adventure for Simone, and Stefan moved strategically each day, gaining greater trust and love without Simone's slightest suspicion. Simone caught Stefan flirting with a few women along the way. *Harmless flirtations*, she always rationalized.

Months later, Stefan was under pressure to repay the debts he'd incurred while presenting his elaborate ruse. He devised a plan to dissolve his fake company and take over one of Simone's subsidiary businesses as a way of "contributing" to the household. "Simone, I need to talk to you," Stefan said on his cell phone from the empty office. He went on to feed her his ideas, and Simone agreed with him, as she always did. Stefan had rented an office suite as a front, with only a chair and table for furniture. Daily he lied to Simone as he ventured to the office "for work."

Simone remained focused on building an empire. She avoided checking on Stefan, as her interest was solely on the numbers his office produced. She felt that as long as the numbers were positive, there wasn't a need for supervision. Her greatest concern was the comfort in having a partner with whom she could share work over dinner.

Instead of going to the office, Stefan found entertainment throughout the city. He joined social clubs and fell in love with golf and tennis. Stefan often visited a coffee shop on the drive to a small beach town east of Richmond, where he'd found the perfect table facing the ocean. The distance from the city gave him the freedom to socialize during his hours away from Simone. Stefan lived the high life at Simone's expense, and as her spouse, he had no sense of guilt.

One day while golfing, one of his lenders pressed him for collection. Stefan agreed to repay soon, but over the next few weeks he didn't return the man's calls. One day, the man left a message on Stefan's machine, threatening to expose Stefan's scam to Simone. Stefan couldn't afford to lose the life he'd attained and promised payment by the end of the month. It was then that the wheels of deceit began rolling faster.

Knowing that his plan would screech to a halt if exposed, Stefan devised a serious plan to embezzle from Simone's company. As her husband without a prenuptial agreement, his access was immediate. Stefan wanted to prolong his lifestyle, manage his creditors, and keep them from Simone's knowledge. Day after day, he enjoyed a life of leisure and luxury while embezzling funds from Simone's investment business and her profitable accounts. The fraud was so smooth—it amounted to millions in business expenses over a period of two years. He cooked the books, threatened the accountants, and manipulated funds from Simone.

One particular deal Simone agreed to at Stefan's request was a merger with Thrust Funds Incorporated. Unbeknownst to Simone, this financial investment and insurance company was actually a front for laundering money for some of Stefan's shady friends and loaners. He created a deal to cover his debt and financed the scheme. Since the business made a profit, Simone didn't think to investigate her husband's operations. When numbers dropped, she only inquired about his active plan for returning the business to a profitable level.

She separated her business efforts from her relationship with Stefan to secure their marriage in the home and, as always, found it a challenge to keep Stefan from outside interests. Simone made him feel needed and appreciated at all costs. She was ecstatic with hope for the new effort, until the accountant approached her office with bad news.

"Ma'am, there is a problem," David, her accountant, said.

"Problem?" Simone asked. "What kind of problem?" He had her full attention.

"Thrust Funds Incorporated, one of our subsidiary companies, didn't make a profit as reported earlier. The company is actually *down* 2.3 million dollars. I can't find anything reporting achievements, and there is no evidence of output as the previous records indicated. The funny thing is, banking transactions show a cash flow, but nothing reflects concrete investments in any market, real estate purchases, or customer investment contracts. The biggest challenge is that the Internal Revenue Service will investigate. It is on their radar for audit. We have a real problem here, ma'am." David passed the folder to Simone and took a seat.

"Thank you for that report. I need to review the folder and make a few calls. Let me investigate your findings, and I'll call you with a plan. Thanks for the good work," Simone said to David. She excused him from her office, opened the folder, and began to analyze the contents. *If every account had large credits, why did he debit so much?* Simone played with numbers on her calculator. She took each major account, added them, and divided it per quarterly payout. The numbers were staggering. Thrust Funds Incorporated paid out over thirty million dollars in its short existence. Supposedly, the company showed six million dollars in profit, but it disappeared after David's review. *Where did it go?*

It had already been a long day, and Simone couldn't make sense of the inconsistencies. She set the file down and dialed her sister's phone number. Simone had managed to diminish her circle of friends, most of whom were very attractive women. When they were around Stefan, it made her quite jealous. Of course, Stefan's flirting didn't help the situation. Simone's closest friends decided to see her only when she was alone, but since she didn't like going to functions or events without her Stefan, the women had dissipated. Sabrina was Simone's only sounding board.

2.
Rodney's Excursion

RODNEY, DAN, AND GAIL stood over a bottle of champagne and glasses. Rodney smiled and raised his arms in celebration. "We did it!" he said. "Another successful year for the firm!"

"Yes, we did," Dan said. "We have been together for years and never in my dreams did I imagine we'd get this far and achieve such success." He took the glass of champagne that Gail held out to him.

"You two really are great partners," Gail said as she handed Rodney his glass of champagne.

"We're the best of friends too." He bumped his fist against Dan's closed hand. "To our success and many years of continued growth," Rodney said while raising his champagne for a toast. The three followed suit and sipped in celebration. Rodney moved over to the window and pointed across Richmond to the area where they'd first opened their firm. "Dan, remember our first office years ago? I wonder who owns the building now."

"I'm not sure, but it was practically a dive." Dan began chuckling. "Most of our clients didn't want to come to our office because it was in the cargo port warehouse. We had to meet at their office or on the road. Gail, let me tell you, if it weren't for this guy's ideas and creativity and my execution, we wouldn't be here today."

"I've heard this story, guys. You two aren't going to reminisce again, are you? It takes *so* long. I think you should start looking toward the future and not dwell on the past."

"The past made us who we are today," Rodney said.

"Yes, but I have ideas for the future, and it's not all business."

"Rodney, that's my cue to give you two some privacy. I'll call you later after visiting Richmond City Parks and Recreations. They want us to market the park jazz concert season," Dan said as he walked to the office's door. "We have to talk about our Los Angeles office. Give me a call when you're available." Dan closed the door as he left.

"Are we going down this road again, Gail?" Rodney asked.

"We are, and I feel it's important that we do. We met nearly two years ago and have been dating for almost just as long; I'm not getting younger, and you're not getting any richer before we settle down. Besides, I think you have made enough money to live comfortably for years to come and have a family. I'm sure we could raise children on the money we make from the business today without problems. I mean, we'll live quite well."

"Gail, I'm just not ready for a family. I'm not ready for that kind of commitment. Not that I don't love you, it's just that I'm not yet ready to get married and have a family." Rodney grabbed her in his arms and held her. He whispered in her ear, "I do love you and our time is coming. It isn't right now, but you'll be the second person to know when. Please give me a little time to love you the way I should before I make that commitment to you, to us, and to our future kids."

"You know it's what I want, Rodney." Gail kissed him on his neck as she laid her head on his shoulder. "I want all of you, heart and soul. I love you so much."

"Then love me and give me a little time to match your determination for our future within my own heart. I'm not going anywhere." Rodney kissed her deeply as they stood in the middle of his office. The desk phone buzzer rang, breaking the passionate moment. "I need to get this, babe," Rodney said as he released her and walked behind the desk. "Can we continue this tonight?"

"Yes, please, we need to settle this, Rodney," Gail said as she left the office. *That man is going to marry me. I'll make sure of it*, Gail thought on the way to her hair appointment.

"Did I call you at the right moment?" Dan asked.

"You sure did. Man, I have no idea how to avoid that conversation much longer. I keep putting it off."

"You know, we've been partners for a long time. Gail is a keeper, a good woman, and gorgeous. I know you fell hard for Simone, but you have to let her go. I mean, *really* let her go and give Gail a chance."

"I know, Dan, I know. You are right. Gail is the only woman who has consistently been with me over the years and allows me to breathe and build my love for her. I never let others get so close. If I keep putting her off, I'll lose her."

"Exactly right, you'll lose her. Besides, I can't keep interrupting these conversations between the two of you. If she ever finds out I'm your diversion all the time, she'll kill me. I don't want my future sister-in-law to be mad at me."

"You are my true brother. I never tell you how much I appreciate you. Man, I really appreciate you. Now enough of the mushy stuff—come back to the office and let's talk about Los Angeles."

"I'm on my way."

It wasn't two minutes after Dan arrived back in Rodney's office when the desk phone buzzed. "Yes?" Rodney answered.

The executive assistant's voice spoke over the speaker. "Sir, it's Carl Starzinsky from Network Galaxy."

"Please patch him through," Dan said.

"Sure thing," she said as she connected the call.

"Starz, how are you?" Rodney asked.

"I'm doing great, love this place. Moving to Los Angeles has been awesome."

"I'm glad you love it. Say hello to Dan."

"Hi, Dan."

"Nice hearing from you, Starz," Dan said.

"What can we do for you?" Rodney asked.

"I have a tentative proposition for you and wanted to see what your schedule looks like for the next quarter. I want your firm to be our marketing agency. I don't have a large capital budget just yet, and I'm still tying up some loose ends before we get started on the production, but you know I'm always good for whatever we agree upon."

"Yes, we know. It's why I put you through ahead of everyone else." Rodney laughed.

"We love you, man," Dan said, and the three laughed before returning to the serious discussion.

"Your firm's work has been remarkable. I mean, who takes an unknown company and makes them a common household name in three-quarters of the civilized world; and not do it once, but three times? That is remarkable work and pure genius. Plus, you did an amazing job with the market-ing of our last play when Network Galaxy was still based in Richmond."

"I have an office and staff available in Los Angeles. I trust those people; Dan and I placed them ourselves. We're quite confident—"

"I'm quite confident in your ability to choose adept em-ployees too—hell, I even 'stole' one of them from you!" Starz chuckled. "However, I'd still be more comfortable with the idea of one of you veterans taking the reins on this one. I'm telling you, this play is going to be a hit."

"Hey, Starz, we love the idea of being your marketing firm. Instead of my representative coming to your office, how about we travel down memory lane? One of us will head to your lo-cation and give you a personal touch."

"I'd like that. Besides, you owe me a bottle of brandy. I haven't forgotten you drank the bottle purchased from my vacation in Poland years ago. It was supposed to be my celebra-tion bottle."

"I thought you were already successful. Besides, it was a long time ago, but you surely have lots of bottles of brandy. I owe you and always pay my debts, but are you positive it was me?" Rodney chuckled.

"Yes, it was you, Rodney," Dan and Starz said together.

"The bad thing was I never got a sip, and I hear it was the best," Starz said.

"It was good. I admit, it was really good." Rodney laughed again. "We'll send you our travel itinerary if you give us a win-dow of your availability."

"Great, just like old times," Dan said.

"Okay, I'll talk to you soon then," Starz said.

"Always a pleasure, Starz." Rodney selected the flashing number from the multiline desk phone and looked at Dan, "Are you sure it's okay for you to travel to L.A.? I don't want June to be upset with you being on the road. I promised her you'd be home for a while."

"It's been forever since I packed a bag. I'm ready, besides she isn't due for another month. I'm sure she'll be fine with me heading out there."

"No, no, no, I'm a man of my word. We'll send Gail; she's worked with Starz before."

Rodney, who was happy with Starz's call, headed to the art gallery to find a moment of solitude, a moment to reflect on his history. It was at the art gallery where he'd met Simone years ago. It was there that he had left Simone with Sabrina years earlier, yet still the gallery led him down a path of comfort and grace. *I love this place*, he thought while walking from painting to painting.

The gallery staff knew him very well from the multiple purchases he'd made over the years, and they never interrupted his visits. Rodney sent paintings to his closest friends, decorated his marketing firm's Richmond, Norfolk, and L.A. office locations, and saved a few for his home. Yet, no painting would ever erase the pain he'd finally succumbed to over losing Simone. But earlier today he faced Gail's demand. She was a woman of great energy and beauty beyond his wildest dreams. She was truly the definition of a great partner. He was skeptical about completely freeing his heart for a commitment, and here at the art gallery he pondered the probability of success in relationships.

It was a little less than three years ago, right after Ms.

Marge's memorial cruise when Rodney threw himself into the firm. It was his way of dealing with the horrid pain of rejection. His ego was crushed, and the only way he could handle his emotions was by focusing on business, creating new accounts, building partnerships, and staying busy. Rodney also had begun stressing his body with extreme and grueling physical training. He ran longer distances, swam greater lengths, and biked for hundreds of miles. He kept emotional situations with women at bay, even avoiding casual conversations with the opposite sex outside of work.

After a year of fighting his internal battle, educating the firm's staff, and improving productivity, Dan suggested that Rodney take a vacation or an extended weekend. Rodney agreed, and before long he left for Napa Valley to escape his emotional and physical letdown.

His journey started with a flight to San Francisco, where he rented a beautiful convertible and drove the two plus hours to Napa Valley. It was his way of releasing the anguish caused by Simone, his unrequited love. Yet, he also came to acknowledge that loving a woman without confirmation of her affection had been a mistake. Rodney's dreams of a future with Simone had just been a fraction of thought coupled with a wish. His drive through the countryside and scenic rolling hills was just the medicine he needed to clear his head.

Further on the drive, he stopped to watch some kids playing soccer. He envisioned trampling the idea of his dream girl with the many little feet running up and down the field. He felt the pressure inside him release with every kick of the ball. His imagination released his ideas of love and partnerships, and he accepted a reality of pain and agony. As the kids kicked the ball into the net, Rodney decided to never fall for anyone so hard again. It was his wish, his ego seeking protection against the storm of broken-hearted emotions.

He first encountered Gail at the hotel in Calistoga. Gail had arrived at the hotel counter minutes before him; she and June, a girlfriend, giggled excitedly about the suite they'd just received. Gail spoke first, just as she turned and saw Rodney in line waiting his turn to approach the desk clerk. "Hi," she said to Rodney.

"Hi. Seems like you're set," Rodney said.

"Yes, we are. Enjoy your stay." Gail smiled as she and her friend left. As Rodney turned to pick up his bag and move forward, he noticed Gail's eyes on him. She smiled again and continued her journey. Rodney waved and turned to check in.

Not long after a nap, Rodney found himself exploring the city strip, walking the main drag and observing people, deciding on a restaurant, and just enjoying the solitude. He passed Gail and her friend June dining by the window at a popular place where a man was playing blues guitar on stage. The place had a larger crowd than any of the other restaurant pubs around. Like any loner, Rodney entered and sat at the bar. It was the singles section, and everyone else seated near Rodney also sat alone. It was fine for him, as his thoughts were to escape the very essence of having a companion. He talked to the guy on his right, who struck up a great conversation about the valley's history. The man gave Rodney advice on which wineries to visit. They talked through the entire dinner. An hour later, Rodney's dinner mate left for the evening and there Rodney sat, alone again.

Gail, energetic and observant, identified Rodney to June and asked if they should join him. June assessed Gail's condition after a night of drinking. "Are you sure you want to right now? Maybe you should wait till you're sober."

"No, I want to," Gail said. She stood up. "Let's go."

"I guess we might as well; you've gawked at the man nearly all night. Hurry up though if you're going to, we have a spa appointment early tomorrow."

"Okay, we'll go." Gail stood and walked in a straight line to Rodney. Her eyes, reddened from wine, locked on him like a prizefighter on a mission. She emanated a hazed look in the soft light.

Rodney noticed Gail's gaze and stood to greet the two. "Hi, again," Rodney said as he pulled out a chair on his right and then the left as June approached.

"Hi, yes, again," Gail said. June nodded and smiled.

"I see we're staying at the same hotel," Rodney said to start a simple chat.

"We are. I saw you checking in," Gail said with a slur.

June grimaced. "Sorry, she's a little tipsy. We drank two bottles of wine and had a shot of whiskey. I hold my own a little better than Gail."

Rodney turned to Gail and extended his hand. "Hi, Gail, nice to meet you."

Gail returned the handshake. "Nice meeting you."

June leaned forward and extended her hand as well. "I'm June, and you are?"

"Oh, that's rude of me. I'm Rodney, and it's a pleasure meeting you two ladies. Please, sit down."

"I thought you'd never ask," Gail said.

"Don't mind her, even though it was her idea to come over here and talk to you."

"I don't mind. Did you enjoy the music?"

"We did," June said. "It was pretty good for a small town."

"From what I heard, it was. I'm surprised it ended so soon."

"Soon? It's nearly eleven thirty and the place closes at midnight."

Rodney looked at his watch. "Oh, I must have gotten a late start this evening. I'd better ante up and pay my bill before everyone starts trying to close their tabs." Rodney waved for the waiter. With the waiter's attention, Rodney signaled for the check. "I'd offer you both something to drink, but you're right, the place is closing soon. Besides, I have spa treatment in the morning."

"Spa treatment for a man? I don't want to sound mistaken, but are you gay?"

"No, not at all, and I don't mind you asking. I think a man should rejuvenate every once in a while."

"Are you meeting someone tomorrow?" asked Gail. "You seem pretty nice. Not to mention handsome. Usually the good guys are taken. Are you involved?"

"Don't answer her if you don't want to. I mean, it's her prying questions that always get us into so much trouble!" June said.

"It's okay. I'm here alone for a weekend getaway. The spa treatment came with my hotel reservation."

"Alone?'

"Yes, alone. You know, sometimes we need to clear our head of things, and why not here?"

"You made a good choice. I can see you are using your time here wisely," June said. She stood up and moved over to Gail. "All right, I have to get this philly back to the hotel."

"I can help. We are going the same way. I don't mind."

"Okay. Gail, let's go."

"Is he coming with us?" Gail asked.

"He's at the same hotel. He'll walk with us and make sure you don't get blasted by some car."

"Okay," Gail said to June. She wobbled as she turned to Rodney. "I like the way you look."

"I'm not sure how to answer that tonight. I'll answer when you're sober."

"I'll remember. I never forget anything. Are you ready, June?"

"I'm waiting on you."

"I'll stand on the opposite side of you and be there if she needs someone to help her stand up," Rodney said to June.

"Good, let's go." The three exited the restaurant and headed towards their hotel. Rodney didn't speak much on the walk; besides, it was Gail who wanted to talk to him. June was kind enough to follow. Within a half hour, they arrived at the hotel and, upon entering the front door, split their separate ways. *Interesting, very interesting*, Rodney thought as he settled in for bed. *Tomorrow's a new day.*

"Good morning, please remove your robe and lay face down on the table," the masseuse said.

"Sure thing." Rodney followed directions and relaxed. "Whenever you're ready?"

"I'll be right there. Give me a moment as I extend the divider screen."

The massage therapist completed preparation and returned to Rodney. He started the massage process and Rodney began to relax. Within minutes, Gail and June entered the room for their massages on the other side of the divider. All three laid in silence during their therapy.

After an hour, Rodney got up from the table and followed his masseuse to the hot springs tub. The man instructed Rodney to enjoy it and then added, "This is supposed to last for thirty minutes. Please relax, but remember this is a unisex environment."

"Sure thing," Rodney said and he entered the water nude. *Right now, I really don't care. If anyone joins me, I'll ignore them and move on to the next part of my plan.* Rodney slipped down into the water and closed his eyes.

Ten minutes later, Gail and June walked in the pool area. They dropped the towels that covered their bathing suits, stepped in, and found a comfortable position. "We meet again," Gail said.

Rodney looked up in surprise. "Well, yes, we do."

"How did you like your massage?" June asked.

"I enjoyed it. Is this water hot enough for you?" Rodney asked while the jets pushed strong currents against their bodies and bubbled enough to mask Rodney's nudity.

"It's wonderful," June answered as she lay back and enjoyed the comfort of the added massage.

Gail didn't say a word, but she sat observing Rodney. She watched him close his eyes again, lie his head back on the pool's head cushion, and relax. Gail examined Rodney's facial features. She imagined him being next to her in a lustful predicament. Her imagination led to touching her breast in small circles, barely embracing her nipples, and with her other hand she followed her midsection to her groin, then to her legs. Rodney's lips appealed to her. His fine bone structure and sculpted shoulders were exquisite, sparking her erotic imagination. It was his voice, the first time he spoke, and last night's gentlemanly support that made the fantasy of his touch so irresistible. She moaned as the jets massaged her clitoris. Her roaming hands helped matters. Her imagination went further as she noticed Rodney's chest, toned arms, and fine chest hair, barely covering the middle area between his pecs. Gail moaned again, and in an instant June spoke to her. "Gail, are you okay?"

"Huh?" Gail jolted back into reality. "Yeah, I'm okay."

"Whatever you were having, I'd like a little."

"You—well, I'll tell you later."

"Oh, I get it," June said and giggled.

Rodney lifted his head up and opened his eyes. "You girls having a nice time?"

"I, well, we are enjoying the stay so far." Gail attempted to regain her composure.

"You seem to take good care of yourself," June said. "Do you work out?"

"I try to work out at least six times a week."

"I thought you were an athlete. What sport do you play?" Gail asked.

"I'm in marketing, not an athlete."

"Marketing and you advertise quite well." June winked.

"I think that was a compliment. If not, I'll take it as one."

"It is very much a compliment."

"Thank you. I appreciate it." Rodney smiled and sat in silence. He thought about trying to leave but couldn't figure out a way to do that without embarrassing himself or the ladies. He decided to wait a few minutes longer, hoping they'd finally sit back, close their eyes, and find a relaxed state. Minutes later the attendees appeared with cold cloths for everyone's foreheads. Rodney took his first and the women followed suit.

Just as silence returned and the attendants left, Rodney

stood and exited the tub. He robed quickly. "You ladies enjoy your day," he said, and without waiting for a response, he left the area.

After his exit, Gail and June peeked from their cool cloths. "That man is *fine*," Gail said.

"Yes, he is, he definitely is," June said.

Rodney walked into the first winery on the Silverado Trail. He looked at the winery trinkets, and the bottles of wine, while listening to the counter salespersons spilling their pitch. He later approached the counter and asked to taste a few flavors. He, being the novice, didn't discard the wine he tasted and consumed it instead. He exited the store and sat on a bench under the shade of a large oak tree. *That was different,* he thought while reading the wine country map. He plotted a few wineries on the route and waited for his dizzy spell to settle. When he felt a little better, he took off after confirming his destinations. He planned to visit a few more of the wineries that the man at the pub mentioned on the first day of the trip.

On the third stop of the day, Rodney ran into Gail and June. They were at the tasting bar in conversation with a couple of men. Fortunately, neither of the ladies noticed Rodney as he passed them after making his order and shipment request.

By his fourth stop, he decided to have lunch. Since he didn't have breakfast, he settled for a winery with a deli. The place was packed with visitors with the same idea. The store had a smorgasbord of carts outside serving all types of foods. Inside was a full deli with snacks, trinkets, wine, and other cold drinks. Conveniently located off the main highway, this winery attracted busloads of tourists.

Being alone, Rodney selected a bottle of wine, ordered a

barbeque meal from a vendor, and ate his lunch as he observed the others. He watched multiple couples enter and exit the store—happy families and young lovers sitting in the veranda as if no others were around. He recalled the stroll with Simone in the city park, and then his memory flashed to dancing with her under the stars. He and Simone had laughed as the couple sitting at the next table did. Rodney forced his mind into silence and blocked all things around him, fighting his memory of Simone, fighting his inclination to analyze couples, conversations, and his environment.

Rodney shook his head and began focusing on his next event. He grabbed his map and studied his routes to the next few wineries. Within moments, he finished his lunch, cleaned his mess, and walked towards his car. On the route, he noticed a picturesque water fountain with a peculiar flow. The water flowed from six angles top to bottom and displayed fresh flowers at the very top. It was a piece of art to behold. Rodney took a picture. After he put his camera away, he took a coin from his pocket and threw it in the bottom of the fountain. *I hope this gives me good luck. I sure need it.*

It was his last winery for the day, and upon entering, he again crossed paths with Gail and June. Gail recognized him first, and she approached him. "Hey," she said.

Rodney reached out to shake her hand. "Hi, nice seeing you again."

"Is this your last winery for the day?"

"Yes, it is. I'm pretty wined out. I never drank so much in my life and didn't know there were so many types and flavors."

"It's your first time."

"Yes, it is. I was a virgin until this morning."

"Virgin," June said, grinning as if she'd had too much wine.

"I guess you two look out for each other," Rodney said, remembering Gail's tipsy night at the pub.

"It's what friends do."

"That's what they say."

"You sound bitter, like no one has ever looked out for you."

"I…" Rodney hesitated to answer because Dan always looked out for him in every case. "I have a great friend. He's more like a brother. I think he saved my life one day, but the doctors think differently."

"Oh, really? How did he save your life?" Gail asked.

"It's a long story, and I'd like to get to my wine. I appreciate the interest, but I have plans for the evening and would like to keep on schedule."

"You mean you came here with plans?"

"Plans, he said. Didn't you hear him?" June asked.

"I heard, June. Here—drink this." Gail handed June her glass of wine to pacify her while Gail talked to Rodney.

"Yes, I have a cooking class tomorrow morning."

"You cook?"

"Yes. Well, I try every once in a while. I can make a great meal when needed."

"I bet you could." Gail smiled as if opening a door for an invitation.

"Well, I have to get going. Enjoy your stay, and I'll probably cross your path again." Rodney walked to the wine counter and started the tasting process.

June peeked over her wine glass. "I guess he's not interested."

"He's interested enough, he just doesn't know how much," Gail said.

Rodney returned to the hotel without incident. It was amazing that he'd stopped drinking with enough time to minimize the wine's effect on his driving. He never took chances driving intoxicated and felt a little guilty for taking the chance this time after consuming so much wine in one day. After everything he'd reflected upon that afternoon, it was also an emotional drive, and Rodney looked forward to reaching the security of his hotel room and unwound in his room for a while. Then he changed into swim trunks, grabbed a bath towel, and headed to the pool for an evening swim.

It was early evening and the heat of the setting California sun warmed the pool's water. The pool's temperature was not quite as hot as the hotel Jacuzzi, but it was warm enough not to shock the body. Rodney dove into the deep end and swam to the stairs at the shallow end. He swam four laps before exiting the pool to sit on a poolside recliner.

He put on his sunglasses and sat back. Rodney was one of three people using the pool that evening; the other two were an elderly couple reading books for their contentment. He struggled to resist another memory of his dreams for a future with Simone. *Growing old together and a lifetime of stories to tell.* Rodney fought another memory of pain, a punch of agonizing failure. He closed his eyes and concentrated on his business and his ventures. Thinking about work was the only way he knew how to distract himself from his painful memories.

Although he tried to think about work, he continued to ruminate over his failed attempt at love with Simone. Suddenly, an image of the water fountain he'd admired earlier sprang to mind. He pondered why it had made such an impression upon him, and realized that it was the awesome reflection and analogy the fountain represented. It was a choice, he realized, to rejuvenate and recycle his psyche, taking on a twist of security, and building a wall to protect the heart.

Darkness settled as the sun disappeared over the horizon and Rodney returned to his room with a book for entertainment. It wasn't a fiction novel; he read his marketing advisor, which he'd begun to read regularly. He studied the motives of the writer, matched marketing campaigns to the book's message, and found ways he'd modify the commercials the firm created to generate better public response. In the middle of his read, there were two knocks on the door. Without thought, Rodney answered, "Just a minute," while opening the door.

"Hi. We want to know if you'd come with us for dinner?" June asked.

Rodney looked down the hallway, trying to figure out how the women had guessed his room number. "Thank you for the invite, but I'm staying in tonight. I hope you two have a wonderful time."

"We thought we might have a wonderful time if you'd join us," Gail said, "but I hope you enjoy your night. We'll catch you around tomorrow. If you change your mind, we're headed to the Mexican Calabash."

"I don't think I'll change my mind, but thanks anyway. I appreciate the invite," Rodney said and closed the door.

Mid-afternoon found Rodney in the middle of his cooking lesson. He'd checked out of the hotel a day early, packed his things for the road trip to the San Francisco Airport, and enjoyed his class. It was a soothing experience and one meal he'd surely repeat the next time he cooked for a lady, not that he actually had any plans to have a woman in his life at that point. Though he'd recognized Gail and June's attempt to ignite something, Rodney had decided not to welcome their advances.

The trip to Napa Valley succeeded in helping him forget and forgive his failures with Simone. It worked so well, it had even helped him ignore the opportunities with Gail and June. He found resolution to his objective and ended the weekend with a sense of comfort. It was a feeling of achievement, letting go.

Rodney's drive back to San Francisco was just as soothing as the road trip to Calistoga. He encountered little traffic in the roadway, the sky was sunny, and he found the ideal radio station for comforting music. He left Calistoga with great motivation to get back to work. Rodney spent his last night of his getaway in San Francisco. He explored, as any tourist would, visiting Chinatown, having dinner at the Fisherman's Wharf, and enjoying a great night's sleep. The next morning, he returned his rental car, bussed to the airport, and caught the morning's flight heading east. His emotional release from Simone, as he saw it, was final. Rodney enjoyed his first night home and finally slept with a content heart. He woke early with greater energy and a new outlook on life and his profession.

3.
Investigation

SIMONE HEARD THREE KNOCKS on her office door. There'd been no announcement of visitors from the receptionist, the executive assistant, nor the building's security. Three men in black suites entered. They were led by a tall, dark-haired man, who spoke first to Simone as she stood behind the desk. "Hello, madam."

"Who are you? How did you get in here?" Simone asked.

"Doesn't matter, I'm here to make a few suggestions for your business. I enjoyed doing business with Stefan, but he's a small fish. I need the support of a whale to make things work."

"What are you referring to?" Simone picked up the desk phone and pushed for the intercom.

"There's no need for that, I sent everyone home, so there are no witnesses to our conversation. It's safer for us that way, and for you."

"Why are you here?" Simone gripped the edge of her desk as she sat in her desk chair.

"As I said, I need a whale to take on my next operation. You provide the perfect setup, and since Stefan mingled my business with yours, you understand what I need to get on the map."

"I have no idea what you're talking about."

"You mean, you're a CEO of a major company and you have no idea what your subsidiary units do for business?"

"You mean Stefan's business."

"Yes, I do. Since he's dropped out of the business, I expect you to pick up my transactions."

Transactions? The accounting report. "We don't do your type of transactions." She stood again in an attempt to drive her reluctance home.

"You will carry out my transactions, and you will ensure their security," the man said as the other men reached into their coats as if they were about to pull out guns. "And you'll do exactly as we ask, with enthusiasm too, since I'll bring you a lot of business. We'll keep the same financial agreement I had with Stefan. You'll be happy I came once you see the numbers."

"What kind of transactions are we talking about?"

"You get with Stefan; he'll make sure you understand. I'm planning to start tomorrow. Will this be a problem for you?"

"Tomorrow is kind of soon. Can I at least talk to Stefan before I give you my answer?"

"You can talk to your husband, but we're starting tomorrow. I won't take no for an answer. If you don't comply, there will be hell to pay." The two men pulled out Uzis, flashing them in Simone's view. She pushed herself against the back of her seat. "Can I at least get a name?"

"Chameleon. Talk to your husband. He'll fill you in on the process and who I am." The man pointed to the door and his two counterparts vacated the office. He turned when he reached the office doorway. "Talk to your husband, and re-member, I'm a man of my word. He'll know."

Simone stood still in her office for several minutes after the men left. Her fears began to consume her as she played out the possible scenarios in her mind. She picked up the phone receiver and called Stefan. There was no answer from the house phone, so Simone called his cell. *Pick up*, she thought while waiting for the fourth ring.

"Yeah," Stefan answered.

"Are you okay?"

"Of course I'm okay. But can I return your call in a few minutes? I'm in the middle of something."

"Do I have a choice? This is kind of important." Simone paused. "I had a recent visitor, a business partner of yours."

"Hold on." Stefan placed his hand over the receiver and looked around the room. "Can you guys give me a few?" Stefan's crew of acquaintances left the card table. "Okay, you have my undivided attention."

"Good. Three well-dressed men came to my office. They were business partners of yours. They said you did a good job for them and want me to do the same, but at a greater scale. What on earth did you get us into, Stefan?" Simone questioned. *Damn*, Stefan thought as he scrambled to find a way to explain his actions. "It's nothing big. We made trade transactions for Chameleon. He'd deliver the products, and we'd store and move them for a fee."

"What type of products?"

"Whatever he shipped to our warehouse. We need to talk about this in person. The phone is too dangerous."

"Dangerous!"

"We'll talk about it when you get home. Just get there soon."

"I'll get there," Simone said and rushed out of the office.

Stefan hung up. *Those bastards*, he thought as he paced around the card table. *If I call him, he'll kill me. If I let him get next to the wife's business, I could be put in jail. If she discovers the laundering, I'm doomed.* Stefan pondered as he imagined his next action. *I'll call him and ask why he didn't talk to me. What happened between us that he had to go to Simone?*

Simone arrived home one hour after ending the call with Stefan. *He had better be here.* She exited the car and headed for the front door. Upon entry she announced her arrival. "Stefan, I'm here and this had better be good!" No answer. She walked to the kitchen, dining room, den, living room, and office and didn't find Stefan. She then walked upstairs to the master bedroom. She searched every room she could think Stefan would use or had used in the past. There was no sign of her husband in the house. Simone ran downstairs, headed for the garage. "Stefan, are you in there?" She waited, but there was still no answer or sign of her husband.

Stefan's absence fueled her anger; she stormed into the house and headed for her office, where she kept her notes and mementos of her past. She kept a hidden picture of Rodney taped under the main drawer. *I should have listened to Sabrina and Aunt Marge. Damn it!* Simone thought as she heard noises from the office closet. She shoved the picture back under her desk and ran to the closet. "Stefan, are you in there? Why on earth would you hide from me?" she asked while opening the closet door. To her surprise, Stefan's mouth and hands were taped, and bloodstains were on his shirt from where he'd been beaten. It was evident that whoever did this to Stefan didn't want to kill him but wanted to scare him. "What the hell is going on?" Simone removed the tape from Stefan's mouth.

"It's a long story. We have to get out of here!" Stefan looked up at her with his eyes as open as the swelling allowed. "We have to get out of here. Give up the business, turn it in, and maybe we'll live."

"Damn it, you bastard! You've gotten us into something big. I trusted you with my business, to make it work as you've done with your own, and this is what you do?"

"There were no others. Look, we don't have time to argue. If you want to live, we have to get out of here."

"What? I don't understand, and I can only imagine what is going on with that guy in my office. You know more than you're telling. What did you do?"

"I'll explain as we leave."

"I'm not leaving. So you'd better tell me now!"

Stefan released his feet just after Simone freed his hands from the restraints. "You don't understand. These guys are extremely dangerous. I can't control or save you from them. I don't know what to do. I tried talking to them to keep you out of it and this is what I got."

"I figured they're dangerous. No one has ever pulled a gun on me to enforce a business decision. I'm not sure if I should call the police or not. David found mistakes in the books from your company. I was reviewing the report when this guy walked in my office."

"That wasn't just some guy, he's the boss. He heads the entire region from Canada to Mexico, all on the East Coast. You'd better listen to him—his connections are global."

"He's a *mobster*?" Simone cried. "You got us mixed up with this guy. Why?" Simone sighed with her hand over her forehead. "Why on earth would you do something so stupid, when you have everything in the world?"

"I don't have everything like you do. Besides, I wanted to make some money with my ideas. When I tried it straight, nothing happened. Once I figured a way to meet my objectives, it was on. The money flowed without effort, and it was easy."

"Easy. I'm not a fan of easy. It takes hard work to make it. Why the hell didn't you tell me your ideas weren't working?"

"Because you wouldn't have listened. It would not have made a difference," Stefan said while moving towards the front door.

"You're still leaving."

"Hell yeah, I'm leaving. I suggest you do the same. It's better to leave than to face those guys. They will kill you."

"They didn't kill you. When I wasn't involved, they didn't kill you. They didn't kill me either."

"They didn't because they want something from you. I'm sure they would have if you'd told them no."

"I didn't get a chance to respond. The directions were to talk to you, and you're leaving. I can't believe you're leaving me and running like a spring chicken."

"Not running, being wise in the interest of my life. They're threatening to kill me. I think you should leave too."

"I can't leave. You are so stupid. What a meek man."

"Meek and alive, that's my motto. I'll see you in another life."

"Don't you dare! Damn you. It's because of you I'm in this crap, and you're leaving?" Simone watched Stefan get in his car and fought back tears. She stood on the porch, not trying to stop him from driving away. "I can't believe you're still leaving. Stefan, before you go. Let's have a farewell drink."

"You've really lost your mind. I'm not wasting one minute." Stefan drove off, leaving Simone standing there. She watched as the car's tail lights disappeared. She called Sabrina on the house phone.

"Hey," Sabrina answered.

"Sis, you're not going to believe this. I've gotten mixed up with the mob."

"Say that again?" Sabrina sounded as if she'd just woken up.

"I'm dealing with the mob. Damn, what should I do?"

"What?! You should call the police."

"Don't you think if I call the police that those men will kill me?"

"They'll kill you if you don't. Where is Stefan?"

"Screw that weak man, he left me. I'm here dealing with this crap alone."

"I'll come to you. I'll get on a flight as soon as possible." Sabrina got out of bed. "I think I can get to you in a couple days."

"A couple days? Where are you?"

"I'm in Africa on a shoot, and James is a freaking dog. I'll tell you later. Let me look for flights, and I'll get back to you."

"Do that. I want you here to help save our company."

"Save our company? I thought the mob was involved with you."

"It started with Stefan. He did some illegal things with them and now they want us to handle the larger transactions. One of my accountants, David, found a trend, couldn't support his findings, and came to me. I tried to call you when I was reviewing the report, but you didn't answer. Then, those mobsters marched into my office. I bet Stefan used the company as a front for something to help them. I'm afraid to guess. I'll call David tomorrow. Right now I need to find Stefan and get him to explain what happened."

"Didn't he just leave?"

"He did, but he'll be within reach. I know he will … he's my husband."

"You have faith in the worst guys. I'm sorry, but it's the truth," Sabrina sighed. "Next time you'll follow my advice."

"He's my husband, and I still love him."

"He's your husband who's gotten you into deep crap."

"I'll cancel his credit cards, and he'll come crawling back."

"That would be a sign of his greed, not love. Anyway, if he's involved with this, don't you think he's probably sifted cash from you over these years?"

"I don't know, David found some discrepancies with Stefan's subsidiary company, but it could be a mistake. He'll want to work this out. I'm sure of it."

"Okay, sis, I'll be there in a few days. Let me know what's happening. Right now I suggest you go to the police."

"I will, but first I have to do a couple things," Simone said.

The next morning, Simone called an emergency staff meeting. She ordered all the books from Stefan's subsidiary business operations, records of financial transactions, records of phone calls, and surveillance tapes that recorded his visitors. She contacted a private investigation firm she'd dealt with from earlier business dealings.

After collecting all the information from her staff, she reviewed each record to understand every transaction, reviewed the accounting report she'd received earlier, and realized there were large sums of money missing. She looked further and saw that the last account transaction directed funds offshore, with a startling name on the ledger. Stefan had transferred ten million dollars to an offshore account.

"That bastard!" Simone stood up and began to pace her office. She picked up her cell phone and dialed Stefan's number. He didn't answer and it went to voicemail. "You bastard, you fucking bastard, you were money laundering. You jeopardized my company for personal gain. All the money my aunt invested and all the work I've done. You bastard! After I'm done with this I'm going to kill you…"

Simone's executive assistant entered with an IRS agent. "Did I walk in at a bad time?"

"Who the hell are you?" Simone asked the man.

"Ms. Simone, this is the IRS agent who came by earlier when you weren't available. I tried to stop him, but he insisted, and it's quite urgent."

"Thank you," Simone told her assistant. "Please sit, Mister—" Simone said as she caught her breath.

"Williams. Call me Agent Williams."

"What can I do for you?"

"You were pretty heated there. I don't hear people threaten others very often. Is there a problem, and can I help?"

"You may actually be here for the same thing I discovered. I'm going to have to call the police too."

"Your numbers don't add up, and you owe the IRS 1.7 million dollars. I'm here to investigate how you managed to hide the transactions and not pay the IRS. I wanted to talk to you before launching a large investigation."

"I'm discovering this myself. That phone call you walked

in on was with my husband. He's the one who did this.'

"You mean he ran the company?"

"No, ah yes, well, he ran a subsidiary company to this organization. It was doing fine for a while, and then David, my accountant, walked in with a problem he couldn't explain. Then I...I need to call the police."

"I think you should, and do it now." Simone called the police and waited for their arrival. She and Agent Williams discussed her findings. The agent took notes on each discovery and concluded that the subsidiary company had run without controls. David's insight to do the right thing for the company may have saved it from the mob's takeover. "You have faithful employees," Agent Williams said as he looked over the documents on Simone's desk.

"I'd say so. Yesterday they all left me alone in the building when I had dangerous visitors."

"Everyone left but you?"

"Yes, that's correct."

"Say no more until the police get here. I'm sure they'll want to hear this and that way you won't have to repeat it a second time." Silence fell in the office as the two continued reviewing documents. The trend was clear to the IRS agent. Soon after, Simone received a call from her assistant. "The police are here to see you."

"Please send them in." When the police walked in, Simone exchanged greetings with them and asked them to review her explanation of what happened. She then presented a timeline to both the IRS agent and the local police.

Simone explained to the police what she'd found after her meeting with David and her thorough research. The police and IRS agent continued taking notes. It was an hour into the conversation when Simone finally acknowledged that her husband was the person who'd started it all. At the last moment, she suggested that perhaps he didn't know what was going on.

"Are you kidding me?" asked the police officer. "This is well organized, and I'm sure the mob approached him."

"They were here yesterday."

It was an hour into the conversation when Simone's cell phone rang. Simone picked it up and looked at the number. It was Stefan. "Excuse me for just a second," she said and walked into the hallway.

Simone answered the call. "Why did it take so long for you to call me? I'm really pissed but worried. Are you okay?"

"I'm fine, but don't call me again. I'll call you. I need money. You froze my accounts, and I need money. Bring me a few thousand so I can get myself on the way. I'm at this motel on Pendleton Drive. You know the place; we drive by it all the time on the way to our cabin."

"I'm dealing with the police and IRS. I'll call you when I'm on my way."

"Be careful who you're talking to. Just because they are who they say doesn't mean they are straight."

"It's a chance I'll take. I have to run. What room are you in?"

"215. Hurry." Stefan ended the call.

4.
Back to Work

GAIL AND JUNE RETURNED HOME to Richmond after their weekend. It wasn't long before either of them spoke of Rodney. "He had to have been gay," Gail said. "I feel so stupid, being aggressive and rejected. Is this how guys feel?"

"I'm not sure, but you were pretty strong willed. I know you wanted to have a great time, but you weren't yourself. And you got negative results."

"I don't think he was open to having fun with women. I bet he's gay and didn't want us to know."

"I don't think so, I think he either wasn't impressed or maybe it was just bad timing. I'd say bad timing, because he was still courteous to us."

"Let's go with timing. Besides, I'll never see him again anyway. My aggressive tactics scared him. I told you that coming on so strong doesn't work."

"It works, Gail, it wasn't effective on him, but with some guys it works."

"Maybe this experience will guide me another time. Right now, it's back to my norm. I have a meeting with Starz for the upcoming show."

"I hope it goes well. Every time you guys get a play on the road, I find more ways to save on your travel. I'm so glad you chose my agency for travel arrangements."

"It was a no-brainer. Besides, my best friend is the owner."

June smiled. "Yes, I am."

Rodney returned to work, strengthened by his refreshing trip and feeling motivated to apply the tips he'd learned in the marketing advisor to his firm's ventures. His renewed zest aided him in hitting home runs with the projects he'd contracted just before leaving for Napa Valley.

Word of the firm's latest success spread, and a little over two months later, Carl Starzinsky, who most people knew as Starz, called and proposed that Rodney, Dan, and their team create and execute the marketing plan for Network Galaxy's latest stage production. After reviewing the script and consulting with Starz on his vision, Rodney and Dan agreed that they would be happy for the chance to take on the project. It was their first venture with the company, and Starz needed a campaign to bring in the numbers. Network Galaxy had a great reputation, and Rodney knew that landing this first project with Starz would prove lucrative. He was also determined to create a marketing scheme that would raise Starz's profits even more. After a long day at work, Rodney headed home.

After dinner, he went to his desk to brainstorm ideas for selling Starz's play. Rodney went through every scenario and contemplated the variants that would allow him to construct a successful marketing plan for it. Surprisingly, he had nothing. The play was about love, and the theme had touched a little too close to home for Rodney, who'd resolved not to let such strong feelings overtake him again. *Think Rodney, think. Work has always been your outlet—you can do this.*

Sighing, he decided he wasn't going to get anywhere with his plans that night. He looked at his desk and saw his camera sitting next to his stapler. Grabbing it, he hooked it up to the computer to upload the forgotten photos from his trip to California. Rodney scrolled through and saw the photos he'd taken of winding roads and grapevines from the winery. Then, he came to the picture of the water fountain. A memory of the analogy he'd formed came to mind, and he had an epiphany: the marketing plan for Starz's play could be built around the ideas the fountain had provoked. Rodney knew it would be the perfect way to present the theme of the production.

Eager to get started on the new marketing idea, Rodney arrived at the office two hours ahead of anyone in the company the next morning. He started right away on his design, his drawings, and organized all his ideas that stemmed from the fountain at the winery. He drew line after line, sketching his idea, creating the masterpiece with everything he'd read and learned from his marketing advisor. It was hours into his morning when everyone arrived. He called a meeting, passed his ideas along to his staff, and set quick turnaround guidelines. Later in the day, he called Starz to coordinate a meeting and presentation.

Dan entered Rodney's office a day before the meeting with Starz for their routine review of the presentation. They looked over drawings, logos, and handouts to ensure quality and consistency between the play's theme and Rodney's ideas.

Like the successes in the past, the partners chose the best

members from the team and wrote a presentation script. Dan and Rodney called Stanley to the office and awarded him with the presentation. Stanley had designed the best logo and distinctly created the campaign Rodney had in mind. It was Stanley's chance, and the aggressive young man took it with vigor.

Later, Rodney and Dan called a staff meeting and announced Stanley as the lead for the campaign. They instructed the staff to follow his guide as appropriate. Stanley took control and led the design staff with his script. His group took Rodney and Dan's idea to a new level. The youngster actually taught a couple senior executives a lesson in marketing. It made the two realize the importance of talent, and the importance of having Stanley a part of their team.

They were well prepared to give Starz a solid presentation. The rehearsal proved Stanley's leadership with the staff; he created the path of success, highlighted the way the fountain idea would tie into the play, and complimented the firm members on their good work. Rodney felt great about Stanley and the marketing campaign.

It was 10:00 a.m. on Friday, and Rodney's team arrived at Starz's office. They performed the preparation suited for an executive sales presentation, reviewed the script one last time, and motivated one another for a good showing. Rodney and Dan were elated at the preparation, as it seemed their selection of Stanley was paying off. It was only a matter of time before they landed the account.

"This guy is good, really good," Dan said to Rodney.

"Who hired him?" Rodney asked.

"I think he was an intern a few years ago, and you said to

hire the best guy. I placed him under our right-hand man. He's done well with us, and it's only his second year."

"He is good, really good. After this let's talk to him about running the campaign."

"You said it, so let's expect it," Dan said, acknowledging the directive.

Starz and a few members of his staff entered the conference room and began the meeting. He introduced his party and asked Rodney to introduce the firm members. Without pause, the team went into action. Stanley followed each person, adding unscripted comments to the piece. As they delivered their pitch, Starz's head nodded in agreement. Stanley played on the positive reaction and jumped with initiative to close the deal.

It was a shocker to Rodney, as he never expected someone outside of himself or Dan to land a major deal. "Starz," Rodney said, "Stanley is your main contact for this project. Dan and I will be there with him along the way and add direction as needed."

"Starz, you're in good hands," Dan said.

"Your firm carries a great reputation of delivering. I researched it well enough to know the backbone of the organization is you two. I trust your judgment. Stanley is it?" Starz asked.

"Yes, sir. It's Stanley," Stanley said with a youthful grin.

"I'll make sure you're in contact with my deputy director. You two will work well together. She isn't here at the moment, but I'll call you with the contact information, and she'll set a meeting. I'd like you to bring her up to speed."

"I'd love to, sir."

"Good." Starz stood and reached for Rodney's hand. "You have a deal," Starz said.

"Let's get together and talk numbers."

"We will. Are you available now? What's on your agenda?"

"Let's talk now," Starz said. "Please, come to my office."

"I'd be glad to." Rodney followed Starz. Rodney knew if the invitation to settle was offered, it would be better to take it and commit before leaving and to get everything in writing while things were fresh.

Dan sent the team to the firm and congratulated them on a job well done. He waited for Rodney with Starz's staff members. He chatted and networked in the background just as a strong team member would. Dan and Rodney worked so well together that it was never a boss–subordinate type of situation but equal partners and brothers. Dan gathered information about Starz's deputy director from every angle. He found the information about her very interesting as an executive, and also confirmed that she was single.

Starz led the contract negotiation with Rodney and surprised him with numbers that were much higher than expected, and for good reason, as the dates were aggressive. "If this works out, I have an idea that we'll be coming to your firm for future projects … something to think about," Starz said.

Just as Rodney and Starz stood and began to shake hands, Gail walked in.

"Hi, Gail." Starz smiled and released Rodney's hand.

"Hi, I hope I'm not interrupting anything," Gail said.

"No, you are just walking in on the last part of our agreement. This is—"

"Rodney, we've met." Gail extended her hand to Rodney.

Rodney's eyes widened as he returned her handshake. "I'd

say we have. I mean, we spent a weekend together. Nice seeing you again."

"Ah, well, I don't need to know the details," Starz said, "I'm glad you two know each other." He looked at Gail. "We hired his marketing firm and I saw their campaign for the play that was inspired by a water fountain."

"A water fountain?" Gail asked Rodney.

"Yes, it was my vision to reflect your play and its theme via an analogy of the fountain's water flow. My team actually made it work, and work extremely well."

"Really? I'd love to see it."

"You will. I'll have you in contact with their campaign representative, Stanley," Starz said.

"Yes, he'll be in contact for sure. I'm your secondary contact and Dan is third. I'll introduce you to them both," Rodney said.

"Good deal," Gail said. "Nice seeing you again, Rodney. Starz, I have the tour travel arrangements to conclude. I'll get with you after I confirm the play's tour locations."

"I look forward to seeing you," Rodney said as Gail left the office."

Dan met Rodney as he left Starz's office. "How did it go?"

"It went great," Rodney said. "The schedule is more aggressive than we expected, but it's doable."

"Man, did Stanley drive this one home!"

"Yes, he did, and I met Gail, his deputy director."

"You know, from what I hear she's a very dynamic woman. Everyone admires her work and go get'em attitude. She is also—"

"Single. I know. We spent the weekend together in Calistoga."

"You did what? You didn't mention meeting a woman."

"I did, I met her and her girlfriend, June. I didn't follow up with her after I left to come home though. I had no idea she worked for Starz."

"You let Simone get in your head again."

"I actually decided to not allow her to have an impact on me again. It's been over a year, Dan."

"Sounds like a broken record, repeating exactly what I've told you."

"You are right, it's time I moved on. I can tell you, I didn't make an everlasting impression on Gail in Calistoga. She's gorgeous, Dan, drop-dead gorgeous."

"And you didn't want to meet her?"

"I did say we met. I mean, not well enough, it was a night of her over-indulgence of wine. We, her friend and I, walked Gail to the hotel together from the restaurant."

"And you followed up with a night cap?" Dan smirked and crossed his fingers for a positive answer that would indicate Rodney had moved on from Simone.

"No, I had to get up early the next morning."

Dan frowned. "Okay, so what did you do with her?"

"We had a massage, sat in the Jacuzzi together, and toured wineries. Well, it was more of crossing paths instead of actually sharing the experience. She seems really nice."

"I heard she is focused and doesn't date."

"Are you kidding me?" Rodney asked, remembering how forward she'd been in California.

"No. As a matter of fact, the word is she hasn't dated in some time now. She was forced to take that weekend off and not to have her cell phone with her."

"Oh, no wonder she seemed out of practice."

"Out of practice?"

"She was pretty aggressive or seemed that way."

"Maybe she was really interested, or perhaps she just wanted to just let her hair down. You should know 'being out of practice.'"

"I know, Dan."

Gail moved quickly to her office, closed the door, and dialed June's cell phone number from her personal cell. "You are not going to believe this," Gail said.

"Go ahead, tell me. You know I'm not good at guessing games," June said with a sigh.

"He owns the marketing firm we hired for the play."

"Who?"

"Rodney. Remember the guy we met in Calistoga? The guy who saw me drunk, aggressive, flirtatious, and was even there when I masturbated in the Jacuzzi? Oh God, he was there when I masturbated in the Jacuzzi!" Gail shook her head and put her hand to her forehead.

"That guy? I bet you were shocked," June said.

"I'm shocked all right. I'm quitting my job. How embarrassing!"

"I wouldn't go there. Do your job as you would normally, and I'm sure you'll be fine."

"He was okay; didn't say anything to Starz."

"What would he say about you to Starz? You did nothing unprofessional while he observed you."

"No, I didn't."

"No one else knows what you and I know about the weekend, and he didn't seem interested enough to be involved."

"No, he didn't."

"Then why are you worried?"

"Maybe because he's a fine, handsome man, and I'd still do him."

"Get your mind out of the gutter and think professionally. Even though, it is time you got some."

"You know I'm professional. I am in need, but I'm patient enough to start something and not jump into anything to satisfy a physical desire."

"Stay professional. It's all I'm saying. Stay professional."

"No sweat, June. I'll let you know how it goes."

"You sure will." June ended the call.

Stanley approved of Starz's deputy director, Gail, when he met her in his new office. Dan moved him in the day before Gail arrived. It was a promotion, a feeling of accomplishment, and his peers applauded his rise through the ranks. The initial meeting between Gail and Stanley was formal; they strictly focused on campaign work. Gail reiterated the company's demands and aggressive timelines and reminded Stanley of his position and her seniority as a very important client. Stanley took it with a grain of salt and admitted that Rodney would be available to her when needed. *Man she is hard, really hard*, Stanley thought.

It was a plan they expected to execute without any hitch. Gail called Stanley daily for updates and changes. She submitted so many changes to the original campaign that it nearly lost the water fountain theme. Gail argued that her view as the deputy director was important and that her vision was exactly what Starz wanted. Stanley couldn't take the changes in stride and requested a meeting with Rodney and Dan. Because the account was important to the firm, both cancelled their meetings and focused on Network Galaxy as requested.

It was early Tuesday morning when the three gentlemen met. "I'm in big trouble, and I need your help," Stanley said.

"How do you think you're in trouble?" Dan asked.

"I know you can handle the team, and the client," Rodney said, encouraging Stanley toward success.

"It's Gail. She's changing our idea quite a bit. We're losing the theme that Starz liked. If we continue to change, we won't meet our objective. It will delay the show, and we can't afford to do that. There is too much happening to get behind. She doesn't listen to me; I've already suggested not changing so much."

"I see. I'll call Starz and set up a meeting," Dan said.

"No, I'll talk to Gail to see what she wants and how she envisions the campaign. I bet Starz doesn't know about her vision," Rodney said as he dialed Gail's number.

"Then I should continue with the plan?" Stanley asked.

"Hold off until I get an answer. I'll have it for you within a few hours. Have your team continue with the basics."

"No sweat. Just let me know when to move forward." Stanley stood, waiting for acknowledgment from Rodney.

"Okay, you do that and push as needed when I give you the word. Right now I have to get Gail on the phone."

"Do you want us to hang around for the conversation?" Dan asked.

"No, you guys continue with your day. I'll handle Gail and get back to you."

Dan and Stanley left Rodney's office. Rodney dialed Gail and waited for an answer, but he got her answering machine. "Hey, Gail, it's Rodney Witherspoon, please give me a call at your earliest convenience. I need to talk about the project, and it's quite urgent." He hung up. *I hope she calls right away. I'd rather talk to her than inform Starz of a potential delay.* Rodney planned for the worst and best outcomes in maintaining the original look and feel of the campaign.

5.
New Beginnings

GAIL WALKED DIRECTLY out of Starz's office and called June. It was their day for lunch together.

"Are you going to be there or will I have to wait?" June asked vice answering with the traditional hello.

"I'm leaving the office now. I'll be there," Gail said as she walked out of the office with her purse in hand.

"I know how you can get sidetracked. I pushed a couple clients to have lunch with you today. It's important we chat."

"Why is it so important?"

"I met this wonderful guy, and I need to tell you about it. I mean, it wasn't intentional, but we talked. It was amazing." June giggled.

"Did I hear you giggle?" asked Gail.

"Maybe."

"There you go, moving so quickly and jumping to a conclusion."

"I didn't jump, it's just already there. He feels the same way I do."

"With the sexual parts and not your brain or heart?"

"See, I can't wait to smack you up side your head for that comment. And I'm not violent at all."

Gail laughed. "I know you aren't, that's why I said it. I'll be there shortly." Gail ended the call and got into her car. *This is going to be interesting*, she thought as she backed her car out of the parking space. Although it was Gail being the aggressive one in Calistoga, normally June was the one who fell deeply in love. Even when it was nothing but infatuation, she'd fall head over heels without a conscious thought of relationship success.

Gail was the different player. It had been months since she dated, and the weekend away didn't help things. It actually ruined a good chance with a great-looking guy... she wished she could have met Rodney on better terms. After twenty minutes of driving, Gail arrived at the restaurant.

June was inside with a table, waiting for Gail to enter. Her anxiety to share was overbearing. Why? She'd found a perfect guy who seemed promising. He was a dream of a guy who paid strict attention to her comments and didn't pressure for more. He was perfect in her assessment. Gail sat at the table just after entering the restaurant.

"Let me tell you, he's perfect," June said. "Well, he's perfect *so far*."

"You said the last guy was perfect," Gail said. "What makes this new man so different?"

"He's totally awesome. He's smart, gorgeous, funny, and has a smile to die for."

"Oh my gosh, are you talking about *Mickey Mouse*?"

"No. Stop being silly."

"He's tall, dark, and handsome, right?"

"Well, he's not so tall. He's not so dark, but he truly is handsome. Didn't I say smart earlier?"

"Okay, he's smart. You gathered this from one question?"

"No, it was a series of questions, and in conversation he hit on a few things that made me think."

"You're a businesswoman. You are a woman of today. I'm sure you ran across a special interest, but it's easy to get a newspaper. Like some newspapers, guys are a dime a dozen."

"You'd think so, but he's not common. He's very unique and different from all the other men I've dated. Mostly, he's always interested in me, and willing to assist. I didn't let things go badly during our few conversations. I kept them pretty interesting."

"What if he decides on the subject?"

"Give me a subject he won't enjoy." June smiled with confidence in her new guy's wit.

"But what if he brings up something you can't discuss?"

"He changes the subject so I can have input. I experienced it the other night when we spoke."

"I honestly don't want to spoil your great impression of him. Remember, I'm on your side and always look out for you."

"As I do you, and right now, well, I'm glad you're giving feedback. I think he and I will be fine. It's so exciting."

"Exciting. I can see you're definitely excited about him. I'll be here for you for whatever. When's the next time you two are going out?"

"I hope the weekend."

"Hope?"

"We didn't make plans, and I didn't pressure him to get together.

"So he's not eager to see you?"

"I didn't let him be. I took his number and haven't called. So, it's up to me to open the door. I'll call him today, and I'm sure he'll ask me out this weekend."

"It's good being in control. You know exactly what you want to do."

"Yes, I do."

The girls ordered lunch and started on a different subject. Gail told her story of meeting Rodney and Stanley. "I was shocked to see Rodney in Starz's office."

"Are you kidding? The same Rodney from Calistoga?!"

"Yes, he was standing there, looking as handsome as the first time we saw him at the check-in counter. I was stunned, but I had to hide my surprise."

"You mean as a professional?

"Yes, I had to represent Starz."

"Yes, you did. How did he respond?"

"Very mellow, but he let the cat out the bag that we'd met earlier."

"Did he seem upset seeing you, or was it strictly business?"

"I guess he was just as embarrassed, but he played it well. He called me before lunch. I agreed to meet him about the marketing program for Starz's play. I like their idea, but I think it could use some changes. So, I guess he and I will discuss them."

"There you go again. Taking charge and control; careful, I think Rodney is going to be your match."

"I'm his customer. He's got to keep me happy or he'll not have us as a client."

"Happy? You should think of the word happy in a different light. Think personal this time when you talk to him. Remember, it's been a long time since you've dated."

"I don't think I can mix the two. Since he's working on the account, I have to keep my head on business first. Happy is with business and not my personal life. But, maybe if the scenario were different I could think of myself," Gail said while placing her thumb on her chin and forefinger on her cheek. "Maybe I can persuade him to do everything I want while still being professional. A little cat-and-mouse game could work wonders with him."

"I don't think so. Remember, he's not after the mouse. He proved that in Calistoga."

"A challenge is good though. I'm the director with awesome persuasion skills."

"Are you thinking of dating him then?"

Gail took a sip of her water. "I might be."

The waiter set their lunch on the table and left. Gail and June chatted about June's new interest, creating a scheme for her next phone call. Gail made simple suggestions to June for their next dates.

"Either way, it's going to be fun," June said. "I like him and he'll be fun to be with. I just know it."

"See, you're right in line with me. Don't forget, you're a businesswoman. Treat him as you would treat a job opportunity."

"Job opportunity?"

"Yes, because you take on a new client and learn as much as possible to keep him."

"I move fast enough. Remember, you told me earlier?"

"I do, but if you think he's worth it so early on, then I'm trying to make it last for you."

"You know, it's my time for a long-term relationship. I'm so tired of the mismatches I've gone through."

"The door is cracked, go open it, but be careful along the way. If you think I'll help, just ask."

"I don't think I have to ask, you'll be there. It's what friends do. And don't forget about Rodney. You're so focused on me; why not give him a chance?"

"I doubt very seriously he's interested, especially since we're working together now."

"Am I hearing you back out of your initial thought?"

"No, you're right. I'll wait and see. If opportunity knocks, I'll be there."

"Now you're talking." June smiled in her reply. It was a smile of encouragement, as she knew Gail could get over the embarrassing weekend.

"Look at the time; I've got to get going," Gail said as she placed her tray on the side of the table and retouched her makeup.

"You look fine. I'm heading out myself. I'll let you know what happens with my guy. He'll feel excited when I call. Trust me."

"I'm sure you two will have a wonderful time. Let me know what you have planned."

"Great, I will." June stood and grabbed her purse, then placed a tip on the table. "I got the tip. Call me later after your meeting with Rodney. I want to hear it all."

Gail grabbed her bag and put her things away. "I will. Talk to you later."

"Looking forward to it," June said as she walked to the exit.

Gail exited the restaurant just after she watched June disappear. *Am I ready for this?* Gail pondered as she walked to her car.

Rodney waited for Gail's call. He planned to address her concerns, but he knew he would enjoy watching her squirm during their meeting. *She's going to finish out the Calistoga weekend with her attitude. I have the upper hand in this case, and if she's smart, she'll make compromises early. I'm sure of it.* Rodney felt confident as he plotted their next conversation. Soon after, his office phone rang. He answered, "Yes?"

"Sir, Gail Hill from Network Galaxy is on the line," his assistant said.

"I'll take it, thank you," Rodney said and clicked over to the call. "Hi, Ms. Hill, how are you?"

"Doing well, Rodney. I'm available for the next few hours. Are you able to meet me?"

"My calendar is open for you. When can you get here?"

"I'll get to your office within, let's say, twenty minutes."

"Fine, I'll look for you in twenty-five to thirty minutes." Rodney contemplated the time for her to arrive and come into the building.

"I suggested twenty and you added ten minutes. Why?"

"Time for you to get from car to office. It's no big deal; I'll be waiting for your arrival."

"Okay, see you soon." Gail finished the call. *Wow, he's a detailed person*, she thought.

Rodney called Stanley to his office to review the changes once again. He wanted to ensure his strategy for the conversation. Stanley arrived in his office moments after the request for his presence. "Yes, sir?" Stanley said as entered Rodney's office.

"Hi, Stanley, can you give me a list of the changes Gail requests, please?" Rodney asked.

"I sure can. Do you want it in e-mail or hard copy?"

"E-mail is fine. I can review it with her when she comes in. The sooner I have it, the better. And what was the greatest modification?" Rodney turned to his computer to review the original schedule and scheme for Starz's play.

"The change from the original theme, which throws our timelines off and of course takes us nearly back to the drawing board."

"I see. I'll get back to you after my meeting with Gail. I may need you to come in, so don't go too far."

"I'll be around and will be available at a moment's notice."

"Good. That's all, and don't forget to send me that e-mail."

"Will do, boss," Stanley said, quick to follow instructions.

It wasn't long after Stanley left Rodney's office when the receptionist announced Gail's arrival. "Sir, Gail Hill is waiting for you."

"Please send her in." Rodney moved from behind the desk to the entryway to greet Gail. Just as she entered, he extended his hand for a welcoming handshake. "Hi, Gail, nice seeing you again."

"Hi, Rodney," Gail said as she shook his hand. "I know you want to discuss the campaign. Did Stanley fill you in on the changes?"

"Please have a seat. Yes, Stanley gave me the scenario, and it's why I wanted to meet with you. The changes you're requesting are moving away from the theme of the campaign. I think if we stick to the core part of the theme, we can create a win–win with your changes."

"No, the importance of my changes is to get away from the core part and create a better vision for the play. I think the fountain idea is nice, but not quite what I had in mind."

"Okay, do you understand the impact of what you're asking us to do?" Rodney leaned across his desk, looking at the printed material Gail had set down. "It's why we asked for feedback from Starz before starting the campaign."

"I don't mind the extra effort you guys have to make. I want it a certain way, and Starz will approve. He always does."

"Okay, well, can you share your vision with my group, or is it specific ideas you want changed?'

"The fountain analogy is nice, but I don't think it fully embodies the theme of the play. Here's what I was thinking…"

Rodney and Gail discussed the play and determined how Gail's proposed changes would affect the marketing plan. Gail knew what she was doing, and Rodney was surprised to find himself nodding his head in agreement. Gail had some insights into the play that would create a selling angle for an even wider audience. After talking for a while, Rodney said, "I think we're on the same page here, but I'm a visual guy. Do you mind if I call in one of my artists?"

"No, please, if it helps us with our ideas."

"And Starz will go with the changes and push off the timeline?"

"I know he'll go with the changes, but we can't afford to push the time out. The show has a committed start date."

"First, let's get that artist in. Afterwards, we'll address changes and time." Rodney moved towards his desk phone and pressed for his assistant. "Please send Alfred to my office. Have him bring a sketch pad."

"Sure thing," the assistant answered.

Rodney continued his discussion with Gail. "I see you have a creative mind. Have you run a few campaigns, or is it your eye for other people?"

"Eye for other people?" Gail asked, not quite understanding.

"Yes, you provide a viewpoint that makes others take notice. It's not a learned talent, it's mostly natural."

"Oh, I thought of your comment differently," Gail said. *He got out of that one. I thought for sure he'd say something of that weekend in Calistoga.*

"I'm starting to see your point about needing to tweak the plan for marketing the play, but I'll have to get a visual of what you have in mind. When Alfred arrives, please give him your idea and let me chew on it."

"Chew on it? Rodney, we have to move on it without hesitation."

"I understand your wishes, but we have to make sure the changes are feasible. We signed on to deliver one thing with Starz, and this is a different approach. I'll have to communicate with him on our agreement. Besides, you can present him with the idea you have. Didn't you say he'll support you?"

"I'll handle Starz. I know what he likes and wants. Also, if you're worried about cost, don't. If I were you, I'd worry about the time you need to get things on the market."

"I thoroughly understand, Ms. Hill. If cost is not a problem, then doubling my staff will help. I'm sure we'll get the campaign completed as you'd like."

Alfred arrived at Rodney's office and knocked on the doorframe. "Hi, Rodney, what can I do for you?"

"Alfred, this is Gail Hill. She has ideas that I'd like to incorporate into our marketing plan for Network Galaxy's production. Can you please spend some time with her and sketch her vision? I'd appreciate it."

"Sure," Alfred said and sat next to Gail.

"I'll leave you two for a few while you work on the sketch. Alfred is great, and fast; just explain things to him, and he'll have something on paper within minutes." Rodney exited the room and entered Stanley's office down the hall. "Stanley, here's what I'm thinking. We'll incorporate her idea into our scheme, but we don't have to change the plan completely. How long will it take to add her ideas to our original one?"

"Depending on the changes, it may not take too long if she approves it right away."

"She'll approve. Leave that to me."

"Yes, sir, I'm glad to."

"Good. I'll let you know what I have in mind once I see Alfred's sketches."

"I'm standing by for directions." Stanley took his seat behind his desk and reviewed how much the team had already accomplished and questioned the impact of the coming changes.

Rodney returned to his office as Alfred completed his sketches of Gail's ideas.

Gail gazed at Alfred's drawing. "You're good," she said.

"Yes, he is," Rodney said as he moved around his desk. "Thanks, Alfred, perfect as usual."

"You're welcome, Rodney," Alfred said as he left the office.

"I'll get Stanley right on this," Rodney said to Gail. He called his assistant. "Can you please have Stanley come to the office?" he asked.

While they were waiting, Rodney turned back to Gail. "You're quite the creative person. Are you sure you haven't worked in marketing?"

"I have taste for what will work with most things. Well, I slip up from time to time, but not often." Gail noticed Rodney's attitude had shifted to a relaxed state.

"I'm sure you have great taste. I guess once we get the campaign started we can chat about the progress. I mean, Stanley is still your key contact, but I'm always available. Isn't that right, Stanley?" Rodney asked Stanley as he entered the office.

"Yes, Rodney," Stanley said.

"Great. Let's review Gail's ideas so we can get to work on the campaign. I'll let Gail start with her view that Alfred sketched, and I'll add my comments after she's finished."

As Gail reiterated her ideas to Stanley, he soaked in the key points and felt settled on not losing the firm's idea but adding hers. It was a good accent to the current plan—he hadn't seen it earlier when Gail wanted so much changed. Now they'd reached a compromise.

Gail seemed happy with the discussion after Rodney had added his thoughts. It was as if the two had worked on many campaigns before; one thought sparked another, and Stanley couldn't believe his ears as he heard laughter from the two as if they shared inside jokes. When Stanley had a full understanding of how to move forward, he headed to his office. Rodney and Gail were left in the room alone, as the day seemed to slip into early evening. "Oh my, where did the time go?" Rodney asked Gail.

"Time always flies when you enjoy what you're doing, and this is no different. It seems I enjoy working with you, Rodney," Gail said.

"Yes, it was interesting. Working with you today reminded me of how I got started in the business when Dan and I took off. Thank you for the wonderful afternoon."

"Well, it's getting late, and I should be going. I don't have to rush to anything, but I'm sure you're a busy guy."

"I don't have anything on my calendar. What are you doing for dinner? I mean, would you care to join me? I don't normally ask a client to dinner, but maybe we can discuss the campaign some more."

"Rodney, before I answer I have to apologize for that

weekend in Calistoga."

"You don't have to. I should, because it was horrible for me to be distant to such a lovely woman. Please accept my apology for not being open to you."

"I'll only accept the apology if I get to choose where we're having dinner." Gail smiled.

6.
Safe House

SIMONE RETURNED TO THE OFFICE where the officers were waiting.

"You'd better come with us to the precinct."

"I can't just yet. I have to meet my husband. I'll get there after I see him."

"At this point you know it's dangerous to leave our custody. We can't force you to go, but we can advise you to go into protective custody. If I'm correct, the boss was notified the moment we walked in your building. It's unsafe for you to leave. You should come with us," the police officer pleaded.

But driven by her heart, Simone demanded a visit with her husband. "Maybe I can bring my husband with me for protection."

"That will work; he's vital to identifying the leader. We'll get him in the office and negotiate a bargain for his testimony."

"What if he doesn't come?" asked Simone, knowing how hardheaded Stefan could be. "I'm going to talk to him. I'll return as soon as I can. I'll see you at the western precinct," Simone told the officers.

"I'll wait to move forward with your case and report to my

superiors that it's under investigation with the local police," Agent Williams said.

The police officers agreed to escort Simone to her vehicle. They searched the car for explosives or any other object that seemed out of place.

"You guys are taking this too far. I'm fine, and I'll be to your office after I visit my husband. Just in case, he's at a motel off Pendleton."

"Thanks for the info, and please be careful and observant. I still think you shouldn't go for your own safety, but I can't hold you."

"I'll be okay." Simone entered her vehicle and drove off with the police officers watching. She looked in the rearview mirror and observed one officer entering the police car while the other went inside. The explosion rocked the buildings as the officers' car went up in flames. Shocked and shaken, Simone drove faster to get away from her building. *Why would they blow up a police car? I've got to get to Stefan before something happens to him!*

She traveled for miles without incident. Simone was observant along the drive and didn't recognize any suspicious cars or anything that seemed out of place. Within minutes, she reached the motel and found Stefan's car. She parked, walked in, and while passing the check-in counter, she spoke to the desk clerk. "Hi," she said. Simone smiled, as if nothing bothered her.

When Simone arrived at room 215, the door was partially open and she heard no sounds within. *Damn it. He already left.* Simone opened the door. "Hello?" She looked about the room and saw no one. "Stefan?" There was no answer, but she noticed his coat was still on the chair. She turned, looking for a missing ice bucket, or any sign indicating a reason for Stefan to have left the room. Everything seemed exactly in its place, except for the jacket and creases on the bed where someone had sat. Simone looked around the room and suddenly noticed a turned over chair near the bathroom. It was over. She knew there had been a struggle. When she looked in the bathroom, she saw Stefan facedown in blood on the floor.

Simone's gut leaped to her throat. She took two steps backwards and ran back through the corridors. She passed the clerk without saying a word. She jumped into her car and her wheels screeched as she spun out in her immediate escape. In panic and disbelief, she realized Stefan was dead.

The clerk ran upstairs to see what had startled Simone. The clerk saw the floor immersed in blood and immediately called the local police. When they arrived, he told his account of seeing Simone go upstairs and then run out in a panic. He hadn't initially made any assumptions about Simone's reason for being there, but when he'd seen Simone run out, it had made him very suspicious.

Simone made it home. She called Sabrina to tell her not to visit and explain to her what was going on, but there was no answer. Simone hung up and rushed to her room, grabbed a few items, placed them in a bag, and returned to her car, only to find a vehicle pulling in behind her. It was IRS Agent Williams. "Going anywhere in a hurry?" asked the agent.

"I'm heading to the police station. Why are you here?"

"Don't ask questions. Just listen, and do as I say," Agent Williams said. "Go back into your house and call this number." He handed her a piece of paper with a phone number written on it.

Simone took it and ran into the house. She went to her home office and nervously dialed while the agent observed.

As the phone rang, Simone watched the agent look around the house as if he was waiting for someone to arrive. Finally, a man answered the phone. "I thought you were smarter than the average person," a voice said to Simone.

"I am, but who is this?" she asked.

"I'm the investigator you hired. Agent Williams is a cover to protect you. We figured out that a man is after you and your business. Now, here is what you do. Leave your car and drive with Williams to a safe location. I called the police, and they'll have an officer chat with you about yesterday's meeting and your husband's involvement."

"My husband's dead."

"Sorry to hear of his death. It goes to show—you have to move, *now*."

The call ended and Mr. Williams reached out to Simone. "Come, we haven't much time."

Simone followed his directions. The two got into the car and headed to the airport. "One thing we've learned is security amongst the city dwellers is better than being out in the countryside," Agent Williams said.

"I believe you. How did you guys figure out what was going on?"

"Your accountant, David, filled us in. He actually did call the IRS, but they aren't supposed to show until tomorrow."

"What about the police? I saw the car blow up when I left my office."

"I suspect one of them is working for the mob, but I can't confirm it. I will tell you that the guy I'm taking you to is well known as being a straight cop. He'll do the right thing."

"I surely hope so." They drove in silence, and Simone let her emotions overtake her and started crying.

"You'll be okay, just stay with us. You need to trust us. We will be at the airport soon." Both Simone and Agent Williams boarded a plane heading to Los Angeles.

After the flight, it was an hour's drive into the heart of L.A., which seemed an eternity to Simone. Agent Williams drove to Market Street, where a number of renovated old storage and office buildings were now apartments and condominiums. It was a perfect setting for a safe house, as it limited traffic and gave perfect visibility of the entry. Police were waiting in the corner apartment on the twelfth floor. When Simone and Williams arrived, a suit-coat-wearing detective greeted them. "I'm glad you made it safe," the detective said. "I need to speak with Simone in this room. Will you please follow me?"

Simone followed the detective. On the way, she observed her surroundings, noticing the layout of the apartment. She entered a room where the detective had put together a make-shift office. A large file was spread across the table. He lifted a folder, handed it to Simone, and said, "Okay, here it is—this is why you're here in our protection."

Simone took the folder and sat as she opened it. Inside she saw pictures of herself and Stefan, on the beach, walking in the park, at a fine restaurant, and at the airport. They were pictures of their lives, and obviously under surveillance. Later in the folder, the pictures changed to Stefan with the mobsters who'd visited her. Simone let out a sigh, shocked and saddened to see Stefan laughing with them. She recalled the image of Stefan immersed in blood at the hotel and the horror she'd felt. Tears fell on her face as she looked at the detective. "Why was my husband killed?"

"He's dead? How do you know?"

"I saw him facedown in blood."

"Anyone see you there?"

"No." Simone then realized she was wrong and said, "Wait—yes. The clerk saw me."

"As long as no one else saw you, we're okay. Let me tell you what's going on. Your husband was laundering money for these guys. He started with a few dollars and ended up moving millions. It was a remarkable process, and we fell upon it just as it stopped. We didn't get enough evidence to close the operation. We'd lost until the moment the boss walked into your office."

"He was the boss? He wants my company to work for him."

"He has a lot of power, unfortunately."

"Yes, I've heard. And I understand he has police officers on the take. I saw one blow up the other when I left to meet my husband."

"He may have, but that was a fluke accident. The car blew up because of a gas leak from an earlier event. When one of the officer fellows threw his cigarette on the ground, it caught the fumes and *ka-boom*."

"No officer on the take?"

"Not that I know of."

Simone sat in silence for a moment as she recalled all the actions of last week, including when she'd learned of the accounting error. Things didn't add up as she continued to create a map of events in her mind. It was exactly as she thought—the laundering started when Stefan took over the subsidiary company. Simone recalled Stefan's regular disappearances. *All this time I thought it was women. All along, it was the mob.*

Sabrina's flight landed in Richmond two days after the missed call from Simone. She took a cab to her sister's house, only to find it dark and empty. Since Simone hadn't answered Sabrina's calls, she assumed Simone was just in meetings. Sabrina called her sister a few times, but Simone hadn't called her back. Now Sabrina felt a spark of worry. *Why hasn't she called?* It was later in the afternoon, just before rush hour, when she made it to Simone's office. Once inside, Sabrina asked for Simone. "She is supposed to be visiting you," the woman said.

"No, I was told to come here. Does anyone know where she is?"

"I'm told to inform people to call this number if there are persistent questions of her whereabouts." Simone's assistant handed the number to Sabrina.

"Thank you. I'm going to use her office." Sabrina went inside Simone's office and sat behind the desk. She looked around for any sign of Simone's whereabouts. Sabrina began to feel increasingly scared and frustrated. *Where the hell is she?* Sabrina dialed the number from Simone's desk phone.

"Hello," a male voice answered.

"I'm looking for Simone—"

"Who are you?"

"I'm her sister, Sabrina. She's expecting me. I expect you to put me through."

"Not so fast," said the officer. "Where were you within the last week?"

"Africa."

"What is your husband's profession?"

"He's a photographer."

"From whom did you inherit a business?"

"This is getting annoying. Where is she, where is my sister?"

"She's in good hands. I'll text you the location and travel instructions. When you arrive, get a cab and meet me at Fifth and Main Street, and I'll escort you to her."

"I'll be there."

"Make sure you come alone, it's important."

"Can I talk to my sister?"

"Sure, when you get here. You two can catch up. Make sure no one is following you."

"Who would follow me?"

"You'd be surprised."

The two ended the phone call. Sabrina received a text message instructing her to take a cab to Shockoe Bottom on Main Street, wait for Richmond cab services car 107, and drive through downtown Mechanicsville on the way to Richmond International Airport. The text included a specific flight to Los Angeles with a connection in Charlotte.

Once she arrived, Sabrina took another cab to the corner of Fifth and Main Street. She exited the cab and observed a few people walking in and out of traffic, some dressed in office attire and others who were dressed casually. A homeless person approached her and asked for change. She reached in her pocket and handed him a few coins. "Thank you," he said. The homeless guy winked as he walked away.

Someone touched Sabrina on the shoulder and before she turned, he said, "Come with me."

"Okay," Sabrina followed. She traced her steps and watched a few people along the way. She saw a few men manning the parking lot, a couple of building workers, and more homeless people all aligned around the building they entered. "Is she here? This is very unusual," Sabrina said as she continued to follow the gentleman.

"This is for her protection," The man pressed the elevator call button. They waited in silence for the elevator, and when it came, he held the door while Sabrina entered. Sabrina and the man road up the elevator as Sabrina fumed over having to go through so much red tape just to see her sister.

As soon as the door opened, Simone jumped at the chance to hug Sabrina. "I'm glad you made it," Simone said with a tear.

"What's going on?" Sabrina asked.

"I told you part of it over the phone before other things happened. Stefan is dead."

"What? What happened?"

"He was killed, and I'm here under protection."

"Some place for protection. What happened to Stefan?"

"I found him dead at a motel. It was horrible. Then I got back home and a detective was there waiting for me. They brought me here for protection from the mob."

"I'm so sorry, sis, I really am." Sabrina hugged Simone. "Did they catch the killer?"

"No, I'm scared they think it's me."

"Why would they think so?"

"I ran and never told anyone what I found."

"I doubt they think that. If the mob is involved, they'll find it logical that it wasn't you."

"I don't know sis, it's messy and unclear. I know the protection is important because I didn't give the mob a decision. The IRS is investigating too. This is where you need to come in. I'm not running the company right now, and you need to step in."

"Step in? I know nothing of running a company. I'm still modeling."

"You have to step up, or we'll lose everything."

"I suggest we talk to our lawyer. He's been there for us through everything. I'm sure he'll have insights to what we should do with the company and how Stefan's dealing and death will impact it."

"Are you sure?"

"Yes, I'm sure. Who else can you trust?"

"I wish I'd listened to you about Rodney."

"Don't bring that up, it's entirely too late. You had a chance with him and didn't listen."

"Hindsight is really clear. I bet we could be on top of the world had I listened to you. But no, I'm here in protective custody from the mob. FROM THE MOB!"

"I hear you," Sabrina said as she hugged Simone. "It's going to work out. I'll go to the office. Just let me know what you want done. I'll try to stay in touch with you every day."

"That sounds good, but we have one problem: if the mob comes in and tries to push their muscle, you have to get out of there right away."

"Don't you think the office is under surveillance? I'll be okay. You didn't accept his proposal, right?"

"No, no way. I called the police instead."

"Then the mob will not go after the company. Instead, they'll find another business to do what they want. It's too risky for them to try to work with you now."

"Then why am I here? How long will I be here?"

"I have no idea, but maybe someone will be able to answer that for you soon."

"Stay the night here and tomorrow you'll start on the job. You can go to my house afterwards. I'm sure there will be police to protect you. I'll find out when I can join you."

7.
Love and the Future

STANLEY AND GAIL WORKED for three days to get the ideas on paper and new sketches ready for Starz to view. Rodney let them work as he managed with hands off; however, he kept in contact with Gail. At their dinner days earlier, they'd had a wonderful time. It wasn't personal or professional; it was a combination of the two. Gail managed to win Rodney's confidence and she offered to keep him abreast of every step in the campaign. Rodney fell hard for her idea, as it complimented his own. It seemed that the two were in sync and could do a lot of good together. His opinion wasn't propelled by personal interest—he was genuinely impressed by her ingenuity. Yet, Rodney stayed true to his organization and allowed Stanley to continue running the campaign.

On Friday afternoon, Rodney received his end-of-week brief. He, Dan, and Stanley were the last in the conference room when Gail entered. "Hi, Rodney, can we have a minute?" Gail asked.

"Sure. It's quitting time, and I haven't anything else scheduled."

"I'll talk to you tomorrow after the picnic," Dan said to Rodney as he moved to exit.

"Dan, can you also stay, please?" asked Gail.

"I guess I can. This must be pretty important since you're asking us both to stay."

"I think it's important," Gail responded. "Let me start by saying that Stanley and I have done great work these past days. We've discovered a chance to show Starz more with your marketing firm. I wanted to give you two a heads up on my conversation with Starz. I'm going to suggest to Starz that we continue working with your firm for future productions. I'm really impressed, and Stanley is a prize, really a prize."

Stanley was still gathering his things and overheard the conversation. "Thank you, Gail," he said. "You're a charm to work with."

"I like what I'm hearing; what do you think Starz will say when you tell him your thoughts?" Rodney asked.

"It's going to be a tough conversation, but I know he'll be pleased with the work we've done here. Plus, he values my opinion as his deputy director. Since I've had the privilege of working with you all, I know that your work is top-notch, and I can't see why Network Galaxy should bother trying to find other marketing firms for future productions."

"Wow, that's very kind of you. Isn't this inside dealing?" asked Stanley.

"No, it's business," Gail said as she started for the door to exit. "And good business if you asked me."

"Yes, it is," Rodney said. "Ms. Hill, can you wait for me in the other room for a few minutes? I'd like to talk to you after a quick conversation with Dan."

"Sure, I'll be out in the lobby."

"Good. Thank you so much," Rodney said. Gail and Stanley left the conference room. "Man, isn't she hot?"

"Oh, wow, I see it. She's getting to you. I remember the last time I saw that enthusiasm. What happened?"

"We went to dinner the other night, and she's really a nice lady."

"Isn't she the Calistoga drunken woman you avoided?"

"Yes, she is, and now I'm thinking I shouldn't have avoided her. What do you think I should do now?"

"Are you kidding me? You're asking me what to do, and all I've ever done is push you to get out."

"I know, but she isn't just anyone, she's a smart business-woman with good qualities."

"You're impressed. Then do what you want. But don't let her get away without getting to know her personally."

"I'd better, huh?"

"Go now before she gets bored waiting for you. I'll call you after the picnic tomorrow."

"I wanted to ask you about that. Quick, what's her name?"

"June. I'll tell you about it later," Dan said as he rose to leave the conference room. "Don't let her get away," he whispered as he and Rodney walked into the hallway.

Rodney walked to the office lobby and stopped short of Gail. He noticed her legs, which were slender and sexy, and he de-fined her rightly as a woman who took care of her body. He re-called his impression of her in California. *Did I miss something then?* He walked up to Gail. "Thank you for waiting."

"I don't mind." Gail smiled. "Is there something important you wanted to ask?"

"Yes, there is. Actually, we can walk and talk on the way

out. I don't want to hold up others." Rodney opened the main entrance door for Gail to exit first. *A fine woman,* he observed as she walked ahead of him. "I couldn't wait to share my thoughts about dinner the other night. I enjoyed it so much that I thought we could do it again soon. This time no business and purely pleasure."

"Are you really asking me out? Isn't there a client-relationship clause in your contracts?"

"Let me see." Rodney looked upward as in searching for an answer and then said, "No, I own the company, and if there is such a rule, I can make the exception."

"That isn't good, changing rules to suit owners."

"People do it all the time."

"Yes, I know."

"I guess the answer's 'no' then?" Rodney stepped back waiting for confirmation of his assumption.

"Actually, I'd love to. Which car are we taking?"

"You mean now? You don't have anything else going on tonight that you need to cancel?"

"Nothing going on tonight. Are you sure you want to go?" Gail wondered if he had something else planned.

"I'm driving. We can pick up your car afterwards." They walked towards Rodney's car.

"A decisive man; where are we going?"

"I thought we could have drinks and dinner at Panache."

"You don't have reservations. It takes a month to get in there."

"No worries, the owner and I go back a ways."

"Nice having connections."

"Yes, it is."

It wasn't long before their dinner conversation led to a discussion about past relationships. Both Gail and Rodney started to explain their hang-ups on the types of people they'd chosen.

The owner of the restaurant had set them up at a table near the window overlooking the city. Panache, a swanky restaurant on a hill, had a five-star rating that was well deserved, as every menu item was prepared excellently, the service was to die for, and the wine list was among the best. When Rodney arrived with a date, the owner followed his lead. What both failed to mention to Gail was that Rodney was a partner of the restaurant.

After his momentous event with Simone years ago, Rodney's effort gave the owner ideas and they hit it off quite well. Rodney put Panache on the map by continually impressing upon the romantic at heart: "It's the place to go for all occasions." It was his marketing and coordination efforts, and eventual partnering with the owner, that helped earn the restaurant's place as one of the "Top Five Restaurants on the Eastern Shore." The campaign went so well, Rodney gained 45 percent ownership of the restaurant.

Gail had no idea of Rodney's involvement with the restaurant and enjoyed him with eager enthusiasm. It was only her third time at Panache in three years. The reservation list was a mile long on any given month. The restaurant's reputation of being 'the place to be' made it very special for a date, and this was a first real date with a gorgeous man. "Thank you for asking me out," Gail said to Rodney.

"My pleasure. I hope this is appropriate for you."

"Now that I know you've had as horrible taste in women as I've had in men, it's perfect, and getting better with every minute."

"I finally let those bad choices become bygones."

"I look forward to new endeavors."

"Why, Gail, is that a come-on?" Rodney smiled as he tilted his wine glass towards her.

"I think you could take it either way, but please, take it as a yes." Gail smiled and touched his glass with hers. "You seem to catch on without me having to push for clarification. I've never met a guy so keen."

"There is a first time for everything, as I've met a beautiful woman. Let me be honest, when I saw you in Calistoga, I thought you were gorgeous. But let me tell you, after my open-minded transition, you're extremely beautiful."

Gail blushed. "I'm so embarrassed about Calistoga."

"Don't be. I was in the wrong frame of mind. You were funny but beautiful."

"I'm glad you think so."

The waiter arrived and asked for their orders. "Rodney, are you having the usual?"

"No, I'll wait for the lady to order, and then I'll let you know."

"The usual?" Gail asked.

"I come here quite often. What are you going to have?"

"I'm having the lamb."

"Awesome selection," the waiter said as he took notes.

"I'll have the same," Rodney said to the waiter, "and bring a bottle of the Chablis wine, please."

"Sure thing, Rodney." The waiter walked away.

"You come here quite often, and people know you as a regular?"

"I come here at least once a quarter but sometimes monthly."

"You must have vested interest."

"I do, actually. I had the restaurant as a marketing client."

"It must have been a great campaign; people all around know of the place."

"It was, really good for both my firm and the restaurant. I'm proud of our work."

"You know, your firm is—"

"I don't want to interrupt, but we agreed, no business tonight."

"Yes, we did. I'm sorry, I got carried away."

"Tell me more about yourself, Gail. Where did you grow up, and how did you get to be this dynamic woman?"

"I'm the middle kid from a traditionally structured family. I was a drama major in college. My talent never developed on stage, but I mastered behind the scenes."

"Oh, so that's why you're working with Starz."

"Yes, after a year of not making casting calls, even for openings that were supporting roles, I figured acting wasn't my talent. I decided to try to make it by coordinating and establishing the stage. It became a challenge with each show, but I got through it. Now, Starz uses me as much as possible for every event."

"I see; it's always good having a right hand. I know I'd never be here if it weren't for Dan."

"You guys work so well."

"He's not just my business partner, he's like a brother."

"Enough about me. Tell me about you!"

"I'm just a regular guy with a similar background. I grew up with a normal childhood, without anything exciting, attended a traditional college, and found work in my hometown with a marketing firm. Then I started my own after a few events. It was interesting, but my parents were supportive, very much so, and allowed me to explore many majors in college. However, they finally forced me to choose and I did. I was actually a business major and arts minor."

"I'd never know." Gail started laughing. "If you were hiding your major, you don't do a good job of it."

"Hiding? Never. I'm pretty much a book ready for reading."

"This I can agree with," Gail said with a smirk. "You are pretty open about things, and yet I'm still intrigued. I have a feeling there's a lot more I'd like to know about you."

"Well, you are definitely kind with that comment."

"Why hasn't a lovely man like you moved on to a wonderful woman yet? And I'm curious as to what type of woman you'd enjoy having as a partner?"

"Which do you want me to answer?" Rodney took a breath and pondered on the best answer while looking at the city lights below. "First, I see a lot of qualities I'm looking for in this woman right in front of me. I see you as my type because you're talented, witty, gorgeous, a great conversationalist, and outgoing when needed. All those traits make for a perfect mate. Which leads to your second question; I'm curious to learn about the inner you, that lovely spark of passion I'm sure you possess—for a man, for affection, and eventually for love. But, I don't like using the 'love' word too loosely. When I say 'love,' I mean beyond the lust, when you give your heart and soul."

"I knew you'd answer the question. Just like a man with class."

"Oh, you call a guy's character early."

"I have my ways of reading."

"Am I that obvious?"

"No, remember we've been together for over a week. Well, not together but interacted well enough for me to observe you. I've seen you in action."

"That observation's from watching me in a professional setting, and perhaps professional and personal are quite different." Rodney paused for a moment and thought of a way to explain that difference. Unfortunately, he couldn't decipher between the two because his personal life was pretty stale. He'd dated a few times since Simone but never anyone as interesting as Gail.

Gail included herself in the same category as Rodney without admitting it. "It's pretty much the same. I'd think you are very good to people both personally and professionally," she said as she gently touched Rodney's hand.

"You could be right. I mean, I enjoy being treated as I'd treat anyone. For some reason I feel the need to treat you especially well."

"I agree, you should." Gail looked into Rodney's eyes. It was a message of desire, and a break from their professional interests. She thought back to the moment of lust for Rodney in the Jacuzzi. She felt her body warm, and before she knew it, there was heat between them. "Is there something on your mind?" she asked, as if she knew Rodney would insist on being alone.

"Yes, but now isn't the time. I mean, I figured we'd go out on the balcony and have our drinks after dinner."

"It's a lovely view from here. Sitting by the window gives us a gorgeous view."

"Wait until you see from the balcony. I have to show you," Rodney said. He knew the view had a good chance of setting the stage for what was on his mind. It was a moment for

Rodney to make his move without thinking of any recourse. Yes, actions to forego business temporarily for pleasure. *If she goes for it, I'm good. If not, I'm in trouble for next week. But what the hell, I like this woman and she has to know,* Rodney thought as he estimated his next move. "Shall we have dinner boxed for takeout instead so we can go to the balcony now?"

"Sure, let's take our wine with us though."

Rodney waited for the waiter to arrive. He calculated the time it would take to package the meals and drink another glass of wine. "Can you please package this for takeout?" Rodney asked the waiter. The waiter poured the wine as other waiters assisted him with the meals. "We have something important to address."

"Yes, sir," the waiter said. "We'll have it for you shortly, sir."

"Thank you so much." Rodney smiled and took a sip from his wine glass.

"Yes, something very important," Gail said.

"Very important, for sure." Rodney gazed upon Gail and couldn't wait to whisk her to his place. "I mean, it's not my usual course of action, but…"

"I suggest we skip the balcony."

"I agree." Rodney turned to see their dinners delivered. "Put this on my tab, please," he said to the waiter.

"Sure will, Rodney."

"Thank you so much." Rodney stood and waited for Gail to rise from the table. He guided her to the exit of the restaurant. "We'll be at my place in no time."

It was a ride with small talk, a glance, and a sparkle between the two. Silence fell as each pondered the probability of a negative outcome. Rodney drove with ease, and selected love ballads on the car's entertainment system. He smiled from warmth and anticipation of a lovely evening. "I hope you like this music," Rodney said as he drove.

"Actually, I do. How far do you live from here?"

"Not far. Not far at all. We'll be there in a few minutes; probably before the second song on the CD ends."

"Good, because I have a confession."

"You'd prefer to get your car. Is that your confession?"

"No. Nothing about my car, it's the ladies' room. I drank the wine pretty fast and am feeling it, but mostly it's time I use the ladies' room." Gail giggled.

"Oh, wow. I'm way off the mark. I'll have us there in no time. Unless it's an emergency?"

"No emergency, but do get there soon."

"I will. Oh boy, will I."

"Meaning?"

"I'm excited to get you to my place. Honestly, I've thought of the moment when I can see you all over."

"You saw me all over. Remember Calistoga?"

"Yes, I remember Calistoga, but you wore a bathing suit. I'm dying to see all of you. Every inch of your body, every crack, I want to see all of you."

"Okay, I'm a little afraid now." Gail frowned. "Do you always tell your women you want to see every crack of them?"

"No, I mean every inch of you. Forgive me; I'm a little out of practice."

"Out of practice? Does this mean you need me to show you how to make love to a woman?"

"No, not make love to any woman; I want to know how to make love to you."

Gail fell silent for a moment to ensure she had the right

response. It wasn't long before Rodney pulled into the garage when she finally said, "Good, a bathroom." She intentionally left without responding, leading Rodney to assume her agreement or will to share an intimate moment.

I guess it's up to me to try, and if she changes her mind it's just as well, Rodney thought as he opened her car door. "The bathroom will be the first door on your right," Rodney said.

"Sorry. It's funny; you know when you have to go it's normally horrible timing." Gail said as she walked into the condominium. Rodney pointed to the bathroom just as Gail rushed in.

"I'll be right out." Gail closed the door. *I hope he doesn't think I'm avoiding him. I do want to be with him.* She heard music, soft sounds of rhythm beyond the bathroom door. The voice singing was one she recognized, and it made her feel welcomed. Gail walked out of the bathroom and into the living room. "You have exquisite taste in music. I think you have it all." She viewed the condo's layout. His decor had a hint of the style of a bachelor but also included fine collections of art, furniture, and classy colors. Gail had no idea Rodney was such a connoisseur of fine things. "Wow, you decorated your condo well," Gail said to Rodney as he handed her a glass of wine.

"Yes, thank you. I try to keep things within my idea of quality."

"You've done a great job, Rodney. Great job."

"Thank you. Please join me on the couch." Rodney waved his hand in invitation. "I'm glad you came. It's been quite some time since I've had a guest."

"Really?"

"Yes, really. I normally work and go home. The time you

saw me in Calistoga was my escape. It was a time for change and rejuvenation."

"Like we said before, we were on the same path."

"Yes, I remember saying it before dinner."

"Dinner, you did bring in the lamb, right?"

"Of course, I placed it in the fridge." Rodney looked puzzled at her for a moment. *Is she nervous or not serious about being with me?* They sat quietly on the couch for a few moments and listened to the music. "Why don't I fix the lamb for us if you're hungry?"

"No," Gail said, "I was just checking. I'd hate to ruin a good meal. I'm sure we'll be hungry later."

"Okay, well, it's as if you've changed your mind about being next to me."

"I haven't changed my mind; just remember it's been quite a while since I've been with a man."

"Don't worry; it's like riding a bike. I promise to go slow. Stop me any moment you feel uncomfortable."

Rodney moved closer and embraced her. He touched her gently, kissed her neck, then paused for any response. *Nothing yet?* He followed with another kiss on the neck, just behind her earlobe. *This spot?* Rodney waited for a response. *This spot is it,* Rodney thought as he kissed her ear, and finally, in the corner of his eye, saw goose bumps on Gail's arm. *Yes, this is it, do it again.*

Gail broke the embrace and placed her wine glass on the coffee table. Without thought, she moved her lips right to Rodney's. It was the kiss she'd imagined in Calistoga at the spa. It was her chance to explore Rodney, the way she'd envisioned. She took over and pushed Rodney on his back, jumped on top of him, and positioned herself to feel his passion. He aroused her as his manhood rose to the occasion; it felt like a rod of steel through his garments. Gail smiled as she maneuvered and danced to the rhythm. Rodney responded, moved as if a dancer following a lead, and managed to find a pleasing spot with his hand. She felt the joy of his touch, moaned, and found his lips once again.

Rodney was pleased with her interest, her aggressive nature, as he had long imagined this moment with Gail. She stood, grabbed and pulled him to sit straight, and found a way to pull his shirt off of his body. Then she pushed him down on the couch again and pulled his pants below his knees.

Gail followed her urge to strip and indulge the rod as quickly as possible. She grabbed the condom from her purse, unrolled it on his manhood, and smiled. She then stripped nude and yanked Rodney's stiff erection to her moist channel of pleasure. She took her breath and embraced the sensations of ecstasy. She exploded on the third stroke, with the combination of Rodney's roaming hands.

Keeping pace, Rodney continued moving his muscular body, climbing towards a climax he desperately needed and desired. He held her tight and moved with quick strokes, keeping Gail positioned to feel everything. He had one focus: one spot, one sweet pleasure point. Without allowing his body to convulse, he stopped mid-moment as she shivered with passion. Rodney stood still inside her and repositioned her underneath him. He held her head in a lock with one arm, and with the other hand, he pressed her ass against him, leveraging the pressure to give depth with every stroke, a plunge for a brighter future, new emotions, and the wish to release that mound of old emotions towards relief.

It was minutes into his effort, and they orgasmed

simultaneously as Gail screamed, "Rodney!" at the top of her lungs. "OH MY GOD, Rodney!" Gail collapsed like a rag doll under him, totally limp from pleasure and exhaustion. It had been a long time since Gail had released such pressures of joy, inhaled the life of a man, and allowed herself to journey beyond the end of the earth. She'd finally allowed herself to let her apprehensions go. She let the strictly professional thoughts of him leave and didn't question why. She felt the goodness of desert rain, the first swim of summer, and the first bite of seasonal fruit. She didn't fight it with logic but decided to embrace it, as the experience was greater than she'd imagined. "I'm so glad that's over," Gail said.

"Over?" Rodney wrinkled his brows. He realized they'd probably moved a little faster than he'd planned. "I didn't expect it to be like this," he said. "I expected we'd make out on the couch and later move into the bedroom."

"We did exactly as I expected we would after we left the restaurant. I've wanted you for awhile, and I'm just glad we finally had our first time."

"Do you think making love to you was my only motive?" asked Rodney.

"Yes. It was, right? Honestly, it was mine. Aren't you glad we did?"

"Yes, oh yes, I am. Very much so, and want to know if you'd do it again. Like five minutes from now." Rodney laughed.

"Five minutes. It takes you that long to have interest again?" Gail teased.

"Well, it doesn't, but I'll make the five minutes worth your wait." Rodney took Gail by the hand and led her into his bathroom. He turned on the shower and adjusted the water to a perfect temperature. They entered and he took control, kissing her, caressing her with soap and massaging her entire body. Rodney explored every angle of her body, cleaned and rubbed every crevice, and entered her with his fingers. He found her spot of arousal and massaged it, turned her to face the glass wall, and held her in his arms.

Her back to his chest, she moved like a mambo dancer pressing back to him. She pushed her rear and moved it, enticing the growth of a newly found friend. Rodney responded and rose to the command of her moving rear. The heated water pressed her imagination, and she became moist with the excitement. He pumped as her body ordered; the friction touched the inner walls of her intricate nerve endings—the pulsing throbs of sensations.

Rodney found those exciting spots and she pressed back, harder, faster, deeper. Gail squirmed, and again found a moment to remember. Rodney, pressing her body on the glass and not stopping, expired once again. He stopped, turned her around, and kissed her as if the joy of tomorrow existed in the moment. Rodney felt that he'd opened a new door of chance and possibility, and he was thrilled about it.

They robed and exited the bathroom and lay on Rodney's bed. Gail relaxed and faced Rodney. "I really needed this, I needed the connection; it's exactly what the doctor ordered."

"'I'm glad we got it over with.'" Rodney laughed.

"Are you mimicking me?"

"Yes, I am. That line threw me a curve. I was lost for words."

"You don't seem like the type to ever lose a thought. I had you." Gail touched Rodney's chest.

"I'll admit, I'm usually not one to stop short of sharing my thoughts or feelings. But tonight, you had me."

"I'm good."

"Good, you definitely are."

The connection between the two moved them into a comfort zone, a time of contentment as if they had been lovers and friends for years. They moved to embrace each other in bed, and both fell into a deep sleep after talking the night away. It was the conversation of dreams, visions, and deepest desires. They both aspired to one day have a family. Gail loved his responses and ideas, and she took the night as an indication to the chance at a wonderful future.

8.
Dan and June

JUNE ARRIVED AT THE PARK with a satchel of goodies. She'd planned her picnic idea when conversing with Dan days earlier. It was their third date, a time of reckoning with excitement and reality. When she found a spot between a large oak tree and the pond, she called Dan.

When he answered, Dan was within a block of their meeting point. He too carried a basket of goods, mostly as June had directed. Dan took his cell phone out of his pocket when it vibrated and answered the call. "Hey, June," he said as he walked.

"I'm over by the pond, near that large oak tree," June said.

"You found a great spot. Good," Dan said, "I know exactly where you are. I'm just over the ridge from you."

"Great. I can't wait to see you."

"Me too. Be right there." Dan snapped his cell phone closed and put it away. He remembered so many events in his life that had taken place at the park. He'd taken a few dates to the very spot at which June was waiting. He'd climbed the oak tree as a kid on family picnics, carved his initials on a limb near the top, and lost his virginity under the tree in the midst of the night. He knew the spot well, very well.

June sat waiting as she took out the blanket and placed heavy objects on the four corners so the wind wouldn't take it away. She took out additional items and set them in place so when Dan arrived there were only a few things he had to prep before totally focusing on her. June knew exactly what she wanted to do and say. She'd rehearsed it in her mind a few times since their last date. It was time, in her mind, to start living again, and Dan was the spark she needed. Their time together felt effortless; each date had gone quite smoothly. Dan impressed her with his quality of character, security, and persistence in being active. He was exactly the kind of guy she sought after. He'd played the field, as he'd admitted during their last date, but never pressed her to give herself sexually too early. This alone warranted the picnic. It was June's suggestion and invitation.

Dan was eager to get out in the sunshine on his day off and enjoy the scenery of the park. He'd followed June's instructions and purchased every item she'd suggested. He hoped for a perfect third date. Yes, the door of opportunity.

June was happy that Dan was a true gentlemen and not overly aggressive. To her, it seemed as if Dan was her match made in heaven. She smiled as Dan approached. "Hi." June rose to greet him.

"I made it." Dan smiled and placed the basket on the blanket.

"Are you hungry?" June asked. "I'm starved. I skipped breakfast and waited for our date."

"I'm not famished, but I can eat. Actually it's a great time for me so I don't eat much later."

"Are you on a diet?"

"No. I watch my intake so I can one day turn your head on

the beach. You know, have that 'beach body' women die for."

"I think you're okay now." June smiled again.

"Glad you think so."

The two helped themselves to fruit, wine, cheese, and crackers. Soon after, June pulled the potato salad from the satchel. "I didn't think you'd want this so soon, but since we're snacking so much maybe it would be better to eat the main courses."

"What else did you bring?" Dan asked, as he was told to bring wine, water, and cheese.

"Turkey and salmon. I hope you like at least one of them."

"Good deal. I actually like them both. Whatever you select, I'll have the other. I'm not choosy with my meals."

"Good man. I like a man who is flexible."

The two ate their lunch with little talk of the last two dates. The major conversation piece was Dan's vision for the future. She wanted to know if he wanted a wife one day or wanted to continue playing the field. June maneuvered her conversation well, quizzing him on finance, beliefs, parents, parenting, and the ultimate question or point: love. She dug hard for facts with Dan as if looking for a life-or-death decision. She smiled with charm during those rough questions and giggled flirtatiously with erotic inquiries.

Dan felt under pressure. The fire in her questions made him pause, but he let her know that if the right woman entered his life, he was ready to live with her forever. He had realized months earlier how lonely it was dating multiple women. He'd finally arrived at a point of wanting to embrace emotional opportunities. He desired to have feelings for and just focus on one woman. Financially, it was a smart move; emotionally, it was a greater move, and fortunately for him, June was fun.

He could tell from the first date. He felt that the probability of June becoming his woman was a ten out of ten.

After three hours, two bottles of wine, snacks, and a long conversation, Dan asked June, "Would you come to my house? I'd like you to see more of me."

June hesitated for a minute before answering. She looked around for a sign of encouragement. She wanted to go but wanted to limit herself from being overly eager. "I'd love getting to know you."

"Great." Dan stood and packed the basket with all the items, discarded their leftovers, and grabbed the corner of the blanket.

June watched in amazement as she realized Dan was ready to leave. "You meant now?"

"Sure, I thought you understood that; unless you want something different."

"I'd like a walk to think about it. At least give a lady a chance to build confidence in her decision."

"Confidence in your decision? What a throw-off."

"I know we aren't young, but I don't want to rush into something."

"Are you having second thoughts?"

"No, I'm just not sure what you wish to show me. I mean, is it sexual or personal?"

"You wanted to know everything about me, and I thought I'd show you another side of me. Like my kid pictures, photo albums of my past, my writing, and other things."

"Are you sure? This isn't a take home with the expectation of me sleeping with you, is it?"

"You can be skeptical, but I am at least honest in my

response. If we're supposed to happen, we will. If it happens, we're consenting adults, and life goes on."

"So it's your intention."

"Not my intention. Are you afraid it's your idea, and you don't want to admit it?"

"Are you kidding me?"

"No, I'm not actually. I bet it's your way of trying to throw my focus."

"Not even interested in throwing your focus if it's not your intent. Listen, I'm not ready to sleep with you. I'm interested in you, but not ready to move so quickly to your place and lie in your bed."

"Well, I don't want you to feel uncomfortable. I guess we can meet at the coffee shop on a different day, and I'll bring my photo albums with me. I want to know you, bring you close to me, and maybe share some of my life with you."

"You don't give up easily, do you?"

"You are a different woman, and believe me, I've dated a few in my time. I'm intrigued by your character and your wit, motivation, and fun personality," Dan said while moving the blanket and basket to his shoulders. "It's like I've known you for so long, and yet I don't. You've excited me by just being you. I like that about you."

"You've said a mouthful. I guess we can meet at the coffee shop. How about today? I'll wait for you."

"You mean the shop around the corner from Memphis Avenue?"

"Yes, that's the one. Is that too far for you? Shall we make it another location?"

"It will take some time, but I'll be there within an hour and a half. That is, if I leave now."

"We're leaving. I can read a few things while waiting."

"I'm glad you feel better this way; I'd rather you're comfortable than be nervous in my house."

"You have a house?"

"Yes, I purchased it years ago. Since my best friend Rodney and I grew our business, it's been a wonderful investment. I'll have to tell you about it one day. Right now, let me retrieve my photo albums. I'll only bring two. I call them 'The Early Years.'"

"It's so cute that you titled them."

"Yeah, it keeps them in order, and me organized. I shall return." Dan entered his car. Within seconds, he placed his basket in the front seat, secured his seatbelt, and drove off the lot into traffic.

June entered her car and headed for the coffee shop as agreed. It was a quick drive, and when she arrived, the place was crowded, with no available seats. She decided to order coffee and sit in her car waiting for Dan. The weather was still awesome and being outside made her feel extremely confident, warm, and capable of standing her ground.

Yes, she'd thought of going to Dan's place, but strongly decided against it. It was her way of not being taken as an object. Even though the afternoon was magical, and Dan surely played into her expectations, it was a move to keep the flame burning for another day. June made the decision not to get close physically, to hold all the cards, and maintain focus on building a relationship. It was her second time dating where her feelings were strong toward the idea of a long-term relationship. She really liked Dan; every outing showed her something more attractive. The latest was his eagerness to share his past. It was something she didn't think men did quite often, especially sharing information from childhood. June sat in the sun, listened to music, and watched people interact while waiting. It was a very nice pastime she'd learned to enjoy while being alone.

Dan arrived at his apartment within moments of leaving June. He parked his car, ran to the front door with the basket, blanket, and whatever else from the front seat. He unlocked the door and went about his business putting things away. His idea to have June follow him had sunk like a World War II battleship. It actually bruised his ego, as not many women in his life had ever turned him down. *Who in their right mind would not love being with me? She is the first to say no to me. I bet she didn't want to wait. I just bet.* Dan continued to grab photo albums as planned. He picked up the two books, looked around the house, and then exited. He locked the front door and ran to the car in haste, as he couldn't wait to return to June. *She had better be there,* Dan thought as he drove the few miles to the coffee shop.

Before long, he arrived and saw June's car parked in front. The coffee shop was still crowded and, fortunately for him, he found a decent parking space. It wasn't next to June's, but he parked close enough to get her attention. "Hey," Dan said. June didn't respond. "Hey," Dan said a second time, a little louder. June still missed the voice as she listened to her radio. Dan walked over to her car and tapped on the driver's door side where June was sitting. "Hey, I'm back."

"Oh, hi," June said.

"Here." Dan handed her the two albums, and without saying a word, he looked around for places they could sit instead of the car.

"You were quick. I didn't expect you for another fifteen minutes."

"Would you like me to go away and come back?"

"No, silly." June giggled.

Dan looked in the coffee shop for seats and saw two individuals moving away from the lounge chairs in the corner. "I'll get those lounge chairs before someone else snags them. Can we move in there?"

"Good idea." June moved from the car while Dan grabbed the seats. She entered the shop and onlookers immediately took notice of her beauty.

Two guys stood as she walked by, and Dan noticed the attraction. It was as if the guys knew her and invited her to sit with them. He watched June smile and continue to the lounge chairs. It was a happy scenario for Dan; the scene reminded him of June's desirability. *My goodness, if I don't do this right I'll never forgive myself,* Dan thought as he watched June get closer to the chair. His imagination went to their second date. The glowing candlelight had grazed her smooth skin. He'd stared at her beautiful brown eyes, the smile of warmth, and the body that could make a man boast for just being in her presence. She was fine and beautiful. Dan stood as she approached and waited until she took her seat before relaxing in the chair. "I'm not the only one noticing how gorgeous you are," Dan said as he moved closer to the end table and grabbed one of the photo albums.

June shrugged. "I think men love women. Well, all women are beautiful, and boys will be boys."

"You said it, 'boys will be boys,' but you're wrong in every sense. I'm a boy, and I know there is a difference when we see a beautiful woman. And my God, you are truly stunning."

"Thank you, Dan," June said as she looked at him. "Are you

going to show me the pictures or are we going to chat?"

"Oh yeah, the albums. I'm going to show you these pictures, but before we start, can I get you another cup of coffee or a drink?"

"No, I'm fine, but if you want one I'll wait for you."

"I'll order one. Be right back." Dan left for the counter and, after ordering his coffee, he noticed June looking at the first album. *I hope she enjoys my pictures*, Dan thought as he waited for his order. He then observed others around the shop and set eyes on another beautiful woman. Before meeting June, he might have thought to venture over to the woman for a quick conversation, in hopes of creating an opportunity for later interactions, but he quickly focused his sights back on June. It was a breakthrough for Dan, as he realized his motivation for only her and wanted to get back to her right away. With his coffee in hand, Dan approached their table. "What do you think so far?"

"It's darling. I see you smiled a lot as a child."

"Yes, it's a sign of a happy childhood. Didn't you smile a lot as a kid?"

"I guess so," June said and turned another page. "You were a Cub Scout?"

"Isn't every little boy a scout at one time or another?"

"I'm not sure, but this is the first time I've seen a guy's photo album before being in a relationship with him. It's a nice change."

"Change, I know the feeling." Dan thought of how different things already were with June. "If you think I was cute then, wait until you get to my high school years."

"Teenage years mean so much. I remember my high school years. They weren't as much fun."

"What? Are you kidding me? Those years were great."

"Not for everyone, Dan. I'd rather forget those years. I didn't really have fun until my last year of college."

"Okay, what changed?"

"Changed? I think I actually found myself and didn't rely on others to make me happy, or define who I am. I took control."

"It was a group thing in high school, right? I can understand fitting in was important."

"I was accepted. I did all the things most girls do. It was just so much pressure. I had friends, but most of those friendships were a little shaded with conceit."

"You were an 'it' girl and didn't like it? I'm not surprised."

"I didn't like it, not really. It took so much to stay a part of the 'in crowd.' In college, I found the transition to be quite easy. I gave up the cheerleading, and drama club, and just found myself interested in business. I then realized my destiny, and that acceptance was is in my hands and not determined by the opinions of a few so-called friends. I have one great friend now who is like my sister."

"Really. I didn't realize you were also a cheerleader." Dan smiled and envisioned June in a cheerleading outfit. He smiled again, and this time June noticed.

"I'm never wearing one of those outfits again." June looked at Dan with a frown.

"Not even when we're married and attending a costume party?"

"Not even then. Never again. And who's getting married?"

"Forgive me, I don't usually talk about marriage, it just slipped. I used it as a figure of speech to make a point."

"It's okay. I'm joking with you. The future is as it will be, you never know what will happen," June said and turned the next page.

"I agree, you never know what the future holds." Dan stared at June. *What on earth is up with me?*

It was Saturday afternoon when Gail jumped from bed and ran into the bathroom. Rodney moved more slowly when he rose. He grabbed his robe, tied it after putting it on, and went into the kitchen to make coffee. It was his routine for a Saturday, and with Gail being there, he knew she might enjoy a nicely brewed cup of java. He returned to the bedroom to find Gail putting on the robe he'd given her the night before. "Good morning, lovely," Rodney said with a smile. "Coffee will be ready in a few. I hope you don't mind me making a pot."

"No, I don't mind. This is your place, Rodney. You can do what you like."

"I know, but you're my guest. I thought maybe if you didn't like coffee, I'd make you tea."

"Coffee's fine. What else do you have available for breakfast?"

"The usual breakfast foods—bacon, eggs, cereal and milk, Danish, and bagels. You are welcome to anything you'd like."

"I'll cook breakfast for you. You've been so kind."

"No, not here, you're my guest. I'll have no such thing happen. Give me a minute, and I'll cook to your order. I'm just going to clean up and I'll be right there." Rodney moved to get dressed. Gail walked to the kitchen and found cups after her quick search. She poured a cup of coffee and sat on the stool in his kitchen. It gave her a few minutes to reflect on the previous night. *I had a wonderful time and Rodney is surely an exciting lover. I needed this.* Gail smiled with both hands around the coffee cup she sipped from. *I could get used to this.*

When Rodney entered the kitchen, Gail had just poured her second cup of coffee. "I'll get started with your breakfast if you tell me how you like your eggs," Rodney said as he pulled items from the refrigerator.

"I'd actually like an omelet with cheese. Toast would be nice, and any side breakfast meats like bacon or sausage." It had been some time since a guy had actually waited on her. The last guy she dated never took the time to make her breakfast. This was a novel moment, and she watched Rodney move into action. Rodney glided through the kitchen with enthusiasm, cutting, slicing, mixing, and then setting the pans on the stove for cooking. He moved like a skilled artisan. "You should do this professionally," Gail said as she moved closer to him over the stove.

"I enjoy doing this. It helps me zone out on a bad day or give me light for a new day. Cooking is soothing."

"I see you enjoy doing it. You're a surprise of a man."

"Thank you, I guess."

"It was meant as a compliment."

"Thank you for sure. I guess we are two of a kind. You are a very surprising woman."

"You don't say, how so?"

"Need I go there?" Rodney smiled and winked in response to Gail's comment.

Gail touched his back and kissed him. She then left to get cleaned up for breakfast. She showered and dressed while Rodney cooked. After her shower, Gail realized there were no clean clothes available. Wrapped in a bath towel, she walked into the kitchen. "Do you have something clean I can wear?" she asked.

"Yes, I do, as a matter of fact. If you look in my closet on the shelf, you'll see a pair of my sweats. You are welcome to them. I think they are quite comfortable."

"I'll look for them. Thanks," Gail said and returned to Rodney's bedroom. She followed his instructions, but instead of sweats, she grabbed a dress shirt. The blue dress shirt covered her like a sexy dress; it was just long enough to cover her key areas but short enough to show off her legs. *Perfect*, she thought as she looked in the mirror.

Rodney set the table and poured coffee and juice, just as Gail returned in his dress shirt. "Wow," Rodney sighed as he watched her walk towards him. "You are beyond beautiful. It seems anything you touch becomes a vision of pure beauty. You are gorgeous."

"Thank you. I see breakfast is ready," Gail said as she sat at the table. They said grace and started eating. They enjoyed small talk during the meal, and when they were finished with their meal, Rodney moved plates to the dishwasher.

Gail became excited watching him. She moved like the swift panther on her strike. She led him to the bedroom for another session of intimacy, and they found the joy of seclusion from the world. They spent a full day together, deepening their connection, embellishing the foundation they'd built for a successful relationship. Gail and Rodney didn't separate until Sunday afternoon. Rodney returned Gail to her car and there they parted. It was a heart-moving experience for Gail, as she'd never been with a guy who was so easy to enjoy for nearly an entire weekend.

Monday morning, Dan and Rodney met for a quick brief to go over the activities of the coming week. They sat in Dan's office and reviewed what they'd accomplished last week, the previous two weeks, and concluded on which things they should achieve next. They realized how close Starz's project was to completion. Dan heralded Gail for collaborating and Stanley for being persistent in managing his team. The team dynamics kept the project on schedule, even with the multitude of changes. It was a total accomplishment on everyone's part, and Rodney decided to call for a quick meeting with the rest of the team.

After Dan called his assistant and instructed her to coordinate the meeting, he spoke to Rodney about June. "I had a great weekend. Let me tell you, I went on a date with this woman for a third time. It was a picnic in the park, and later we looked at my photo albums."

"What?" Surprised with the photo album comment, Rodney responded with an explicit grin. "You mean there is a woman who impressed you well enough to actually let her in? I've never heard you talk about doing that since we've known each other."

"This one is impressive, beautiful, and smart. She has her own business, and is very kind and high-spirited."

"She hasn't slept with you."

"No, she hasn't, and I'm taking my time getting to know her first."

"This is getting serious. Who else are you seeing?"

"I dropped everyone but June."

"Oh yeah, you'd mentioned that was her name. That's funny, the woman Gail was with on our trip to California was named 'June,' too. Maybe it's the same person."

"It may be, but I don't know. We're just moving slowly."

"I'm shocked, but at the same time I'm happy for you. I

haven't seen you excited for one woman in years. Actually, I've never seen you crazy about one woman."

"Yes, it's funny, but I'm enjoying her. She's different and interesting at the least. She's a take-home-to-mom type of woman."

"Stop, Dan, you're scaring me. I can't believe I just heard those words from you."

"I'm serious, Rodney. I'm surprised myself. So you know she has to be awesome."

"Has to be!" Rodney tapped Dan on the shoulder as they walked out the door. "I'm proud of my brother, graduating from dog academy."

Dan laughed. "Dude, you're funny."

The team assembled in the conference room. Stanley sat at the middle of the table. Gail was just arriving as the last of the team members entered the room. "Hi, all," Gail said to everyone as the meeting was about to start.

"Hi, Gail," many team members said.

Rodney began the meeting. "I'm not going to take up much of your time, but I gathered you here to share my impression of you folks doing a bang-up job. It seems Stanley and Ms. Gail are pushing you in the right direction, and you'll be on time with your delivery. This means you've given us 150 percent of your effort. Dan and I truly appreciate your work and commitment. I'm sure Starz will be happy as well. Please keep up the good work. Thanks, guys. Before I leave, is there anyone with a question?" Rodney waited for a few moments but no comments were spoken. "Okay then, if you need us for anything, please contact us through Stanley. I'm sure we'll respond accordingly."

"In that case, we need a raise," one team member said.

"Hell, so do I." Rodney laughed. "I'm joking. Of course you'll receive part of the profit, as you always do for every project. Good work is well rewarded in our company." Rodney smiled and headed out of the room.

"You folks have a wonderful day and stay motivated with an eye on the prize," Dan said, following Rodney.

The team returned to their respective work cubicles and focused on continuing to achieve the marketing campaign goals. Stanley walked into Dan's office and closed the door. "Are you guys always like this?"

Dan hesitated. "Umm, yes, we are actually. Why do you ask?"

"It isn't the norm for me. I'm surprised at how well you guys treat everyone."

"We've been in your shoes and vowed to always let people know where they stand, how they contribute, and the importance of being in our firm."

"I love it," Stanley said. "I just wanted you to know that the team appreciates it."

"You guys continue doing fabulous work, and we'll show you more. Remember, it's never done without the team." Dan led Stanley to the door. "I have some things that require my attention. Anytime you want to chat, my door is open."

"Thanks, Dan," Stanley said as he returned to his office. He found Gail waiting there. "Hi. I'm glad you could make the team meeting," he said.

"So am I. Have we completed the first display for Rodney and Dan to review?"

"Yes, it's waiting for your final approval."

"Good, I think they'll love it." Gail knew the display met

all objectives and would be the key milestone to completing the campaign. "I know Starz is going to really like the results. He's excited to see it."

"I'm sure. Let's finalize the display and move on to the rest of the items."

"We can. I'm sure they'll love it. I'd bet my life on it." Gail followed Stanley to another work conference room.

"I'd bet your life too." Stanley smirked.

9.

Stefan's Plight

THE POLICE SHOWED UP at the motel on Pendleton Drive. The clerk led the police to room 215, where they saw Stefan holding his head and sitting at the desk. The clerk swore she'd seen him dead in a pool of blood. "What happened to you?" asked the local officer.

"I slipped. My head hit the tub, and I'm waiting for the ambulance," Stefan said as he held a bloody towel against his head.

"How long ago did you call?"

"I guess a few minutes ago. I'm fading in and out, so I'm not sure."

"I'll check," the second officer said as she stepped out into the hall and radioed dispatch. "Find out the ETA for the ambulance heading for the Strike Lucky Motel off Pendleton." She received confirmation from dispatch that an ambulance was headed to the building and would be there soon.

Stefan continued telling his story to the officer. "It was early afternoon when I called my wife to meet me here. I came in and looked around, leaving the door open so I could have a quick escape if someone was in here. I slipped in the bathroom and fell. Oh, my head." Stefan grimaced but continued with his story. "I've been out since. When I woke, there was all this blood on the floor and my head was throbbing. I called the ambulance."

"You didn't see a lady come to visit you?" the clerk asked. "I assume it was here where she visited. I saw her run out of the motel in a state of shock."

"I didn't hear anything. Was my wife here? I guess she saw me there and assumed I was dead."

"I did the same thing."

Two emergency medical technicians entered the room. They brought a rolling stretcher with them and performed the medical evalution of Stefan. His injury was evident; gushing blood still spewed from the split on his head. The technicians took action. They stopped the bleeding and started intravenous therapy as they placed him on the stretcher. "Is there anyone you want us to call?"

"Yes," Stefan said with his eyes closed. "Call my wife."

"Is there a cell on you?"

"My coat." Stefan fell into a deep sleep while the EMTs transported him to the nearest hospital. One of them picked up the cell phone and called the first number he found, but he reached a voicemail. Unsure if he'd reached Stefan's wife, the EMT asked for a return call. He tried calling a few different numbers, and left messages without releasing any detailed information. The EMT did everything in his power to contact Mrs. Stephens as trained. He turned over the phone to the nurse's station when they reached the hospital.

After the ambulance rolled Stefan into the hospital, doctors took over his care. Because he'd suffered a head injury and had lost an extreme amount of blood, they decided to keep him in the hospital for observation and further medical attention. After two days in the hospital, no one was able to contact Simone to inform her of Stefan's whereabouts. The nursing staff and patient services continued to call her home number. On the third day, Stefan went into a coma due to the brain swelling caused by the impact. Before long, the hospital suspended the search for Simone, as they'd left multiple messages to no avail. Even the police station, who held Stefan's car, failed in contacting Simone. The officers simply impounded the car for security reasons.

It was five days after Sabrina landed in her hometown, and being in the office certainly made her very uncomfortable. She reviewed the documents that incriminated Stefan and also monitored the activities of Simone's other subsidiary companies. Sabrina realized how much she didn't know about business and began to gain interest. That day, Simone called to catch up. "How's it going?" she asked.

"It's not bad. I made a couple marketing decisions outside of your norm. How long have you had a relationship with this firm? I found them hard to work with."

"Don't change anything until this mess is over."

"I'm surprised at you. Come on, didn't you ask me to run things while this blows over?"

"Sabrina, I said to run things, not change them. Just don't make any rash decisions."

"I'm just hoping to generate business. Don't we need to change something? I see potential here."

"Since you're insisting, draw it up and let's talk about it tonight. I'll look it over, but don't make any changes. I know you have a stake, but remember not to do anything. I don't interfere with your modeling career."

"This is different."

"I'll look at your ideas. Are there any messages?"

"Not here, but at the house there are quite a few. I didn't listen to them."

"Let them stay on the machine. I'll check them when this is over. I hope it's over soon, and they'll release me under surveillance instead of holding me here," Simone said. "I haven't heard you once speak of James. Are things okay?"

"Your situation is more important, sis; let's not talk about mine until things here are settled."

"There is something going on. Tell me, it will take my mind off of everything for a few."

"Let's just say things aren't as rosy as they seemed. He's an ass. We were in Africa and I caught him with three models in a provocative situation, and no one had a camera—if you know what I mean."

"He was cheating on you?"

"Yep. I knew he was messing around when we were in Paris, but not with my fellow models. This time he crossed the line, and it was *so* embarrassing."

"I'm sorry. Maybe you too have regrets about the past."

"We can talk about this some other time. I'm not focused on James or my past. I'll let the situation simmer for a while."

"As you wish. I wonder what he's doing now?"

"Simone, let's drop it. I want to focus on this marketing strategy."

"Focus, sis, I'll be around if you need me. And I'm glad you're here."

"Love you, sis."

"Love you too," Sabrina said as she disconnected the call. She tried to get back to work, but her call with Simone had forced her to relive what had happened with James. *That ass caused me to lose faith in our marriage. I'm so through with him.* Her mind flashed to when she'd seen James in a compromised position with the other models. He was nude, with one girl on top of him, while the others flanked him in a king-sized bed. Sabrina had stormed out of the room and hadn't spoken to James since. She'd returned to her hotel, checked out, and moved to a different one. She'd needed and wanted space to think clearly. She'd been alarmed but relieved to have a distraction when Simone had called and asked Sabrina to assist her.

It was the right escape from a soured mixture of events. Sabrina felt embarrassed and hurt. It was the final straw, and what timing! She'd run into Lorenz in the city just before discovering James's misdeeds. She'd only spoken to Lorenz for a moment, just long enough to see how he'd changed into a fine-looking and dynamic doctor. It was a brief moment in passing but long enough for Sabrina to learn that he was in Africa volunteering his services. Sabrina explained that she was there with her husband, and that yes, she was still married. They'd parted and Sabrina had watched him disappear amidst the crowd. Sabrina had thought of that moment with Lorenz through the entire flight to Richmond, as if it were a movie recorder stuck on replay. Over and over, she watched Lorenz once again walk away, leaving her. Just like the last time, it was her decision to go separate ways.

Over the next couple weeks, it was a lifesaver for Sabrina to focus on the challenges at Willingham Corp. instead of thinking of what James had done to her. She pressed forward with developing the business and learned more about managing such a large corporation in Simone's absence. Sabrina didn't let the IRS investigation hinder the company's effort in continuing to grow. They had employees and a board to consider, and she hoped that profitable results would keep the company above water. Sabrina wanted to experience business success for the first time and felt she had the knowledge and desire to achieve it.

Finally, the police agreed that it was safe enough to let Simone go home. They had trained her to watch out for potential threats and planned to keep her home and business under surveillance. Simone was eager to get out of the city and back to Richmond. She missed her bed, her things, and her life. Simone was relieved but still saddened about Stefan's death. She found it funny that no one had contacted her about it. The blood around Stefan's head was etched in her memory. It was time to go to that small town near their cabin and inquire to what had happened to Stefan's body. Simone arrived home in an undercover police car. She stepped out and walked to the front door. Sabrina opened it just as Simone touched the door handle. "Is it ever good to see you," Sabrina said and smiled.

"Hey, sis. How's everything?" Simone asked after she hugged Sabrina.

"I think it's pretty good. Things here are quiet. How on earth did you manage to sleep in such a huge house? I forgot how large this place is."

"It's easy."

"No, I haven't gotten there just yet. I'm not sure if I'd ever get there." Sabrina walked to the kitchen and grabbed the many letters that came for Simone while she was gone. "I'm sure you want these."

"Yes, I do. Thanks."

"You should listen to all these messages on your answering machine. I haven't checked them."

Simone nodded, and Sabrina pushed the "play" button. The machine took over the silence of the house. "Voice mail received Tuesday, June 21st at 8:30 p.m. Sabrina, it's James. Call me, I know you're angry. I still love you."

Sabrina pressed for the next message on the answering machine. "Ignore him."

Beep, the machine went to the next message: "…received Tuesday, June 21st at 8:45 p.m. Please call 804-555-2134. This is Meg from Martha Jefferson Hospital, in Palmyra. I'm calling about Stefan Stephens. Please call 804-555-2134. He's in the emergency room. Please call."

Simone was confused at hearing from the emergency room of Martha Jefferson Hospital. She'd thought for sure Stefan was dead, yet someone called about him from the emergency room. "It can't be. I saw him dead," Simone said as she held her face with each hand on her cheeks. "It can't be."

"I guess he's not dead, he's at a hospital." Sabrina grabbed Simone and hugged her. "He isn't dead! This is good news."

"I'm happy, but how can it be?"

"Why bother the small stuff. He's *alive*! We should go, NOW."

"No, let's listen to the rest of the messages." Simone moved towards the machine.

"Okay, don't get mad at me, but that's your husband, and we need to go to the hospital."

"But what if he's involved with the mob and playing a game now?"

"He's still your husband. Besides, we need to know what he did so the IRS can finish their investigation. He's alive, so let's go get him."

"Not so fast—what about the mob? Do you think he's still involved with the mob? If we go get him, it could be a trap for us. I don't want to go into hiding again. I can't handle not living."

"Now you bring up a very important point. We'll take those police officers with us to get Stefan. I'm sure they'll protect us."

"Nice idea, but I'm not so sure I want him in this house." Simone frowned with anguish. "He is such a jerk for putting us through this."

"Good point again, but you need answers from him and so does the police. They'll want to have him identify the mobster."

"I can turn him in to the authorities and have him out of the company for sure. I like that idea. Let's listen to the rest of the messages. I'm sure he's not going anywhere." Simone pushed the message button again and the machine continued to play, "Mrs. Stephens, it's vital you call us immediately. It's in reference to Stefan Stephens. You have to call 804-555-2134 right away."

"I think you should call that number. It's been left a few times and each one says it's vital."

"I'll call it." Simone picked up the receiver and dialed the number. She listened to the recording and followed the instructions on the other line.

"Hello, Intensive Care Unit," the on-call nurse answered.

"I'm Mrs. Stephens, and calling about Stefan Stephens."

"Yes, can you give me your first name, please?"

"Simone. Why do you ask?"

"What was your husband last seen wearing? Where was your husband when he sustained his injury? What is his identifying mark on his body?" The nurse asked these questions for identification and security reasons. She was trained to screen callers and ensure that the person calling actually knew Stefan.

Fortunately for the nurse, Simone answered each question correctly. "Listen, can I speak to my husband yet?" Simone asked. "I answered all your questions, now I'd like to talk to Stefan."

"I'm sorry, but you'll have to talk to the doctor first. I'll page him for you." The nurse placed Simone on hold and paged the doctor.

Simone held the phone for minutes on end until, finally, a gentleman answered. "Simone Stephens, I'm Doctor Smith, I'm a neurosurgeon and I operated on your husband. He's stable at the moment and in a coma. Yes, coma. After the operation to reduce the swelling in his brain we hoped he'd wake, but his condition deteriorated and he hadn't awakened."

"He's alive?"

"Yes, I'd hope so. He was when I made my rounds. I'm sure you'd know if he had gotten himself killed."

"No, but I'm going to when I get there."

"Please come, as I think you're voice could strike him and help him wake from the coma."

"ICU, right, Doctor?" Simone asked. She took notes to the hospital directions, talked about the medications Stefan received, and answered any medical questions the doctor had. She then went to her office and grabbed her security photo of Rodney before going to the hospital. *Stefan's not dead. I wouldn't be going through this had I not been so stupid.*

"Who is that picture of, Simone?" Sabrina had walked into the office.

"No one."

"That is a big 'no one.'"

"Give me a minute, will you? I need a moment alone. You can tell the officers out front we need them to escort us to the hospital."

"I can do that, but you're going to tell me who is in the picture."

"I can't, not right now. You'll find out another time."

"Well, whoever it is, he must be really important to you."

"I'd say becoming more and more all the time," Simone said and waited for Sabrina to leave the office before placing the photo in her safe place. *He's becoming more and more important.*

An hour and a half later, Simone and Sabrina arrived at the hospital. During the drive, neither had spoken of Stefan being alive and in a coma. The conversation centered on Sabrina's ideas for the business. Simone thought it best to focus on the business instead of Stefan's health since she couldn't do anything to influence the outcome of Stefan's condition. As Simone always did in the past, she focused on work to keep herself grounded. They conversed on all things pertaining to marketing, products, and management. Both women avoided mentioning that the last time they were at a hospital it was to see Aunt Marge; not a nice memory for either of them. As they approached the hospital, the two began to feel anxiety and remorse. "I wish he'd died," Simone said without thinking.

"Why would you want him dead?"

"Because we'll have to explain what happened to the IRS and the police about the money laundering, and embezzlement."

"What happened between you two? I thought you loved each other."

"I loved him, but enough is enough. I'm imagining what the hell I'll have to go through before things settle again. I'm not into this, sis, really I'm not," Simone said as they parked in a visitor's spot at the hospital parking.

When they saw a police car parked in front, it reminded them both of the still-possible danger of the situation. Simone didn't want to take any chances, as she remembered the hypothetical scenarios that the police explained to her during her safe house stay. The girls exited the car and looked around for anything out of the ordinary, anything suspicious. Simone moved towards the hospital doors first; Sabrina then followed as if they coded a military security formation in a combat zone. Sabrina looked over her shoulder for observers.

They arrived securely into the hospital and checked the directory for the Intensive Care Unit. They took the elevator up to the third floor and walked to the nurses' station to inquire about Stefan's location. The nurse informed Simone that the hospital had moved Stefan to a lower deck since his condition had stabilized. Simone and Sabrina followed the nurse's directions to the second floor. Once they arrived at the secured double doors, they noticed an intercom voice box on the wall as a passing point of entry. Simone pushed the button to speak and said, "We're here for Stefan Stephens, room 21B."

A nurse responded through the intercom speaker asking, "Are you a family member?"

"I'm his wife and with me is his sister-in-law."

"Please step back so the doors can open. They will swing towards you." A buzzer sound filled the hall and the doors swung open, allowing the girls to enter. Once at the nurses' station, Simone and Sabrina displayed their identification cards and the nurse pointed out room 21B. "Just go right in. We recently changed the sheets—and ignore the feeding tube, it will stay with him until he wakes."

"Okay, thanks." Sabrina said as she followed Simone. It was a quiet room, with the bare minimum, and simple tools for the feeding and observation. Stefan lay on his back, his face blank in color, as if limited blood circulated his face. There was a window, but it was at the foot of his bed. "He looks fine."

"Uh-huh." Simone moved over to Stefan's bedside. She didn't have a sympathetic tear in her eye. She was frozen with a memory, one where she'd visited the hospital years ago. The hospital reminded her of death, when they'd lost Aunt Marge, and the pain of losing visited Simone's heart. This time it wasn't loss she felt though, it was anger. Simone placed her purse on the side of the bed, moved closer to Stefan, raised her hand in the air and with a tight fist slammed it down on Stefan's chest. "You're an ASS."

"Simone, what are you doing?" Sabrina asked.

"He's an ass, and I wish he felt it," Simone said to Sabrina and then turned back to Stefan. "I've taken a lot of crap from you. I watched you play with other women, learned long ago about your business acumen and imitation wealth, and allowed you to disrespect my house, family, and now my business. You're an ass and I hoped you were better so I could physically beat the living crap out of you. How could you do this to me? Your wife, your support, and a woman who loved you, cared for you, and gave you everything. How could you open my business to the mob? How could you leave me with so much crap to deal with, and threats to my life? What a waste of a man, you hear me! A waste of a man! I hope you come out of that coma, and they lock you in prison. I'm not letting you get away with this and I'm not taking the fall for you in the laundering; and since I'm your wife, I can't even charge you with embezzlement! I know you did it."

"Sis, he can't hear you."

"He can hear, but he's too chicken of a man to respond. I should beat him again."

"No, don't, it's not good and makes no difference. He won't feel it."

"Feel it? Feel it? I feel the pain he's caused me, the asshole."

"You should sit for a minute," Sabrina helped her sister over to the visitor's chair. Simone sat in tears; one fell right after the other. "I was so stupid, Sabrina, stupid with my selection of men."

"Me too, sis, but now is not the time to think of it. You have a husband you still love. Help him get better, get healthy again."

"No, I'll not help him be in my life. After he's out of here, I'm divorcing this man. He'll be in prison. I hope he's in prison."

"I hear you, but remember we all make mistakes. Don't be hard on yourself, we all live and learn. Now you know. Just leave it at that, knowing is half the battle to understanding what you want in life."

"I know what I should have wanted, but I was too damn stubborn when I had the chance."

"Let's not go there."

"I've gone there from time to time over the years. It was right in front of me. Damn it!"

They sat in silence observing Stefan for nearly an hour. Neither sister wanted to discuss their marriage situations, as it was a painful slap in the face to acknowledge bad decisions and to accept the deceit of their husbands. It was nearly a spiritual situation as both simultaneously came to realize their poor choices in men. Their eyes met from time to time, filled with the hardships they'd endured with the men they chose,and with recognition of the mistakes of letting go of the good guys they discarded. "If I had known what was ahead of me…" Sabrina said as she stood and looked out the window.

"…you'd not be here and neither would I," Simone said. They both had somber looks. "At least we still have the business," Simone said.

"So far we've got it, unless the IRS finds something else damaging."

"I don't think they'll find anything outside of this asshole's laundering."

"I really hope not."

A patient representative walked into the room. "Hi. Mrs. Stephens, I'm the patient rep and need Stefan's insurance information. Can you walk with me to administration? We have lots to share about the care he's receiving and the cost of it."

"I'll go with you. Sabrina, are you coming along?"

"No, I'll wait here for you."

Simone followed the representative down the hall. When she arrived at the office, a young lady named Cill asked her to enter. "Hi, can I help you?"

"Sure. I'm here for Stefan Stephens. I'm his wife, Simone."

"Of course, please come in and have a seat. I'll explain the current status of your husband's medical bill. I think you'll be happy to know we've taken great care of him."

"I'm sure, this is a fine hospital," Simone said as she looked at Cill's desk of cluttered papers. "How much is the cost so far?"

Cill pulled Stefan's medical report from the desktop

computer and a hardcopy file from the multiple papers on her desk. "Let's see…" She opened the folder and her computer opened to the hospital database file, where red numbers flashed on the screen. "Oh my, no wonder I called you. Stefan hasn't paid one dime to his care, and we're in collection mode, so it's important to get this taken care of before the next step."

"And the next step is?"

"Moving him to the state-supported facility. We're at our limit for non-payment of insurance information."

"How much are we talking about?"

"So far it's one hundred and forty-five thousand dollars and growing."

"What? That is a large amount of money."

"He's been here for quite some time. We've done our part to communicate with you, and it's been weeks. His treatment is the best we offer and since he's stable, the room cost is twelve hundred dollars per day. This adds up, of course."

"I see. Here is the insurance card, and let's start there for the coverage. I'm not so sure about continued care at this hospital."

"He may not need to stay because, according to this report, there isn't much we can do. It's a condition he'll have to adjust to by himself. According to the doctor's last report, there isn't much to do but observe."

"I'll have to take him home."

"Mrs. Stephens, you can do that as long as I know 80 percent of this bill is covered."

"Yes, the insurance company will cover that, I'm sure of it. So can I take him out today?" Simone asked in haste, she did not want her dollars to go to waste, especially for Stefan.

"I'll let you know what the insurance company says. You'll

have to speak with the doctor once more, but when he says that Stefan can be moved, it's up to you where."

"I have a plan for him. I need to know if I can discharge him today."

"I don't think that will be a problem, just check with the doctor first. Again, I'll get the insurance company involved and once things are settled, I'll get him discharged."

"Thank you," Simone said as she rose to leave Cill's office.

"You are very welcome." Simone and Cill shook hands and parted their ways, leaving her insurance card for Cill's use.

Simone returned to the Stefan's room and spoke to the doctor, who provided information, and the head physician who had directed Stefan's treatment. "Doctor," Simone began, "do you think we should keep him here? I'd like to take him home if it's feasible."

The doctor responded, "He can go home once we're certain that the brain swelling is down for good. I'd like to keep him here until I'm sure he's out of trouble. So far, he's doing well, other than being in a coma. You can take him soon. I'll let you know."

"I have a place for him. I need his release before doing anything else. I'll get him in a stable environment and get him the best care."

"Good, I'll have no problem releasing him once I get the approval and he shows improvement."

"Thank you much, Doctor."

"You are welcome, Simone. I'll keep in touch." The doctor stood and exited Stefan's room. Moments later, Sabrina looked at Stefan. "Be glad you are loved by a wonderful woman."

Simone turned to Stefan, frowned, and said to Sabrina, "Keeping him here will drain us. Medical insurance will run out before long. If we move him home, the cost will drop by half."

After Cill informed the doctor that the insurance company covered Stefan's bill, Simone had another short briefing with the doctor, who told her that she could probably take Stefan out of the hospital for in-home care in a couple days. It wasn't long before she returned to Stefan's room. "You're an ass," she told Stefan, then turned to Sabrina. "Let's go home."

"Is everything okay?" asked Sabrina as she walked behind Simone heading out.

"It's fine. I'm not expecting anything to change, but I'm not spending our hard-earned money on his ass. As soon as he's well enough to move, he's out of here. We can keep him at home and hope for the best."

"I agree. Medical bills are expensive and especially since he's embezzled from the company, we should treat him as he treated us. We shouldn't use our hard-earned money to pay his medical costs."

Simone and Sabrina gathered their things and began to exit the hospital.

10.
Love Finally Comes

IT WASN'T LONG BEFORE Dan followed his instinct and ascended on June's place. He hadn't intended to, but he managed to follow and observe her routine for a typical day without her detection. He'd never felt this way before and wondered if he'd become obsessed with June. It was the first woman he'd not won quick intimacy with, and he found the challenge quite intriguing.

In his younger years, he'd have considered the non-activity as her loss and moved on, but being a mature guy, he now recognized June as the total package. He'd found himself beyond the norm, beyond the search for a quick thrill; it was the increased pounding in his chest driving his actions. It was the rhythm of desire, a beat uncontrolled by logic, and it ran purely on emotions. This behavior was new to Dan. He managed to see June daily for two weeks. He created scenarios for moments when she'd cross his path. Dan felt the desire and wanted more of her whenever she left his side.

Dan's obsession increased, he wanted to hear her voice, explore every opportunity to share quality time and build on her emotions. He didn't want competition and didn't expect any, but he had to know if June had others interested in her. Dan couldn't help himself and continued to observe June. It was an adventure, and the reconnaissance would lead him to feel secure in freely letting his heart go. This was Dan's first time having such deep feelings for a woman.

It wasn't Dan who made the first out-of-character move but June. She unorthodoxly practiced the art of reverse psychology to win his heart. She resisted her normal behavior, as she'd realized it never worked. Before Dan, she would throw herself into the life of her interest. This time, she consciously made an effort to see and entertain other men, or at least have coffee with them if nothing else. This confirmed in herself her feelings for Dan but also kept the door open to other men in case he failed to impress. She figured her actions also helped refrain herself from giving too much too early. It worked. Every time she turned around, there was a message or evidence that Dan was around. Happy with her actions, June felt comfortable about Dan and was sure she was doing the right thing by not being too eager.

On Thursday afternoon, June went to visit Gail at her new location. It was the marketing firm that Dan worked at and partially owned. The name didn't quite ring a bell for June, so she acted as usual when entering an office complex. June stepped to speak to the receptionist and asked for Gail. The receptionist asked, "I'm sorry, who are you looking for?"

"Gail Hill, she's with Starz and Network Galaxy, really attractive lady who dresses well and works with the marketing team."

"Madam, this entire company works with the marketing team."

"Can you announce her name over the loudspeaker?"

"No, we haven't a speaker system; however, I'll call the executive assistants to see if they know someone by that name."

Dan was leaving the office for an appointment when he walked by the receptionist's desk. Seeing June stopped him in his tracks. His heart fluttered as if June had come to visit him, and without thinking he asked, "Are you okay?"

"I'm fine," June said while looking over a list of employees the receptionist provided. "Oh! Hi, Dan, I didn't know you worked here. Well, I knew you worked for a marketing company, but I didn't realize you meant here," she said.

"Hi, June." Dan smiled. "Can I assist you?"

"Yes, actually, I'm looking for Gail Hill. Do you know her?"

"Of course I know her. She's an extraordinary woman. She's working with Stanley. How do you know her?"

"She and I are best friends. We've been friends for almost ten years."

"Great. You're welcome to go back and see her," Dan said to her. He motioned toward the receptionist. "You'll have to sign in and get a visitor's badge."

"Thank you so much, Dan. I'll remember this."

"I hope so, and I'm glad you came by. I have to leave for an appointment. I'll call you soon," Dan said as he left for the front door.

"What a nice man," June said to the receptionist.

"A great boss too."

"That's good to know," June said as she signed the visitor's log and received directions to Stanley's office. She stopped short of arriving to her destination just in time to see Dan's name on a door. *He's someone's boss for sure*, June thought as she continued to Stanley's office. She arrived and tapped on the open door while looking at Gail. "Hey, I hope I'm not interrupting things."

"No, you're not," Stanley said.

"Hey, girl." Gail smiled and spread her arms to hug June. June reciprocated the effort and met Gail halfway. They hugged, kissed cheeks, and released contact. "I'm almost done here for the day. Can you give me a few minutes?"

"Sure. One question, is that Dan's office a few doors down?"

"Yes. Do you know Dan?" Stanley asked.

"Yes, quite well I must say. Although, I never knew he worked here."

"He's our COO and part owner of the firm."

"Are you serious? This is your Dan?" Gail asked.

"Yes, it is. I'm as surprised as you."

"Excuse me, ladies. Gail, can we get back to this and then we can call it a day for your part?" Stanley was eager to finish the project, and they were so close.

"Yes, we can. June, I'll be right out. Can you wait in the lobby or text me where you'll be so I can meet you?"

"I'll be in the lobby. Take your time, I have nothing planned for the afternoon," June said as she walked towards Dan's office.

"Okay, I'll buzz you when I'm ready," Gail said as she returned to her focus.

It wasn't a minute later when June entered Dan's office. She opened the door and walked in, looking at the many objects on the wall, the multiple framed pictures, and the awards well placed and balanced around the room. June walked behind Dan's desk to look at his desk pictures. She saw photos of young kids, a dog, and two cars. No other woman seemed evident in his life. June's findings made her smile as she assumed the children were his siblings', nephew and niece, or friends' children. She thought it was cute that an attractive businessman would display children that weren't his own on his desk. June got bolder and looked in his top desk drawer. She saw that Dan was a very well-organized man. She'd fulfilled her investigation and decided to leave Dan's office. Just as she closed the door and walked five steps down the hallway, Gail spoke behind her. "Hey, June."

"Hey, Gail."

"Are you ready?"

June nodded.

"How do you know Dan?" Gail asked.

"We met and I told you about it. But I didn't know this Dan is the same one that you work with. I walked in today as he was headed out. It shocked me—he'd told me he worked for a marketing firm, but I'd have never guessed that he's the COO."

"How did you meet again?" They walked through the door towards the parking lot.

"It was interesting. Remember how I told you about when I went out three weeks ago?"

"I remember, but not how you met Dan," Gail said as they approached June's car.

"It was that Saturday afternoon after shopping in the clothing district." June unlocked the car doors with the keyless entry. She entered the vehicle and placed her seatbelt over her torso. "I wanted to explore with this pattern I'd read in a magazine. I got hungry and walked down a side road of Seventh Street, going to Sixth Street. I found a quaint shop with various types of desserts and drinks. I walked down the stairs below the sidewalk to enter. Café Blue was so cute, a darling setup with a nice atmosphere; the owner was a young gentleman with real style, and his café reflected such taste." June started the car in reverse, cleared the parking space, and took off toward the main street.

"Some of those shops are so neat," Gail said.

"Yes, they are. Well, the tables were suited for four people and the bar seating was limited to four, which I found unique. The place wasn't too crowded, but business was good. Sitting at one of the three tables for two was Dan. I took a seat at a table for four next to him. That table selection was practical because of my bags. He looked handsome, so I spoke to him and asked if he'd been there before. My question interrupted his reading and we started a conversation. Things started from that point. We shared a dessert and talked for hours—three hours went by before we looked at the time. It was the easiest time meeting a man. That night we ended up going out to a bar, had drinks, and danced. We found another late coffee shop and talked more. It was so easy to be with him."

"Did you?" Gail smiled. "Come on, I know you, June. You're such a free spirit."

"No, I didn't," June answered while driving. She turned at the next corner heading north. "He's really special, and I want this to work differently. He's nothing like those other men in my life. You know, the ones that rush into things and push. He never mentioned anything sexual the entire night. It was comforting to know a man doesn't want to rush into something physical."

"Nice, I know what you mean."

"We ended up spending the rest of Sunday together doing things. It was simply beautiful."

"He seems really nice at the office. He and Rodney

founded the firm."

"Rodney. So he's Dan's best friend, right? The same Rodney from Calistoga?"

"Yes."

"Dan speaks highly of him."

"I'm sure he does; they're like brothers."

"Remember how you came on to him?" June asked. "You were so forward. I'm glad you were able to get past that so you could work together."

"Actually we … we spent some time together."

"The same Rodney who didn't want anything to do with us in Calistoga."

"One in the same; he's awesome. He's gentle, kind, considerate, and fun. He asked me out again. I spent the entire weekend at his place."

"And you talk about me being fast," June said while turning onto a busy four-lane street.

"You *are* fast. Remember, I know your dating history… if you want to call it 'dating.'" Gail snickered.

"Yes, you know it well. This is different for some reason. Dan isn't like any man I've met."

"I don't think either of them is anything normal," Gail said as she looked at the tall building next to the street. "Where are we going?"

"Lunch. It's a place I know you'd enjoy."

"Okay."

"Dan is surely a catch. I just feel it, so I haven't slept with him yet. It's been a few weeks since I met him."

"You think not sleeping with him will get him interested?"

"He's interested, and I want to, but it's better to play this one for long term."

"He is a great guy and the people who work at the firm love him; just as much as they love Rodney."

"I wonder if other women saw in them what we see in them?" June turned the car into an old warehouse parking lot.

"Is this it?" asked Gail.

"Yes, this is a great place. Wait until you see the inside."

"Nothing like a fancy restaurant for lunch."

"No, nothing like it at all. So tell me more about Rodney."

"He's a classy guy, just as you described in Dan. I think they both have those qualities. I'm surprised neither of them is married or seriously dating."

"You know why Rodney isn't dating or wasn't dating. We thought he was gay. Remember?"

"I remember, but trust me, he isn't gay. Or, if he is, I've never enjoyed a gay man like I did last weekend!"

"You lucky girl; it was that good, huh?"

"'Good' isn't the word," Gail said as the two entered the restaurant. The hostess escorted them to the table and took their drink orders. 'I'll have water," Gail said.

"Me too, water is fine," June added.

"I'll stop talking about that for a moment, but Rodney probably had to get over someone at some point, as he seems quite the sincere type," Gail waited for the hostess to leave the table. She continued, "But I heard Dan was a player, so you'd better be careful."

"He may have been, but I'm a player too."

"A match made in heaven."

"Yes, a match for sure." The girls laughed.

The waiter returned with their drinks. "I'm Wilbert and will be taking care of you," he said. "Are you ready to order?"

"Yes, I am," Gail said.

"So am I," June said. Gail motioned for June to order first, so she continued. "I'll have a turkey ruben, and vinaigrette for the salad."

"Very well, madam," the waiter said as he wrote the order. "And for you, ma'am?"

"Lunch-size cordon bleu, please."

"Excellent choice," the waiter said. "Is there anything I can get for you in addition to your lunch?"

"No, it's too early for wine, and appetizers are out of the question. Thank you much."

"Great. I'll have your orders right out."

"Thank you," the ladies said in harmony.

Gail took out her notebook and pulled the campaign pamphlets from her purse. "I bet you can guess what this design resembles."

June took the pamphlet and scanned it. She examined it far from her face and smiled. "It's the water fountain in Calistoga."

"Yes, it is. It was Rodney's vision."

"I'm sure you had something to do with it."

"Yes, I did. I added a few things, but these guys are really gold. It's the best marketing material I've come across in my few years in the business. I mean, the campaign will take Network Galaxy to new levels."

"Do you think the firm will grow too?" June asked, pondering a future with Dan.

"No doubt, I can bet it will grow. They've grown over the years and went from the two of them to a staff of over 200 in four cities."

"Wow. They are good businessmen. So how does the operation work?"

"Like your travel agency, they all work together. Dan is,

as I said earlier, the COO and handles the day-to-day things, and Rodney is the CEO and makes the larger decisions. I'm telling you, these two are really smart and interesting. I'd bet whomever gets close to them will have a wonderful life."

"One I'd envy." June sipped her water. "I'm telling you, Dan is one hell of a guy."

"Are you falling for him, June?"

"I find myself actually falling for him," June said. She felt her cellular phone vibrate. She grabbed it from her purse and pulled it from the case. "See, he's the sweetest guy. He just sent a text saying that he's thinking of me, and he complimented me on looking great at the reception desk. He's wishing we have a wonderful lunch."

"He's a sweet man. I know he is if he acts as you say and from what I've seen of him in the office."

The waiter brought their lunches to the table. "Is there anything I can get for you two ladies?" he asked.

"No, that's it, thank you."

"I'll bring water to refill your glass."

"That will be great," June said. The waiter left the table and June resumed the conversation with Gail. "Have you been in Dan's office?"

"Yes, once or twice."

"Did you see any pictures of women anywhere? I went in there and didn't notice any at all."

"He didn't have any when I was in there. I remember seeing a few kids, but that's it."

"Good, I'm just checking," June said. "Do you think the four of us could have dinner?"

"I'm sure we can. I'll have to ask Rodney."

"I know Dan will go; he'll do anything I like or want."

"A well-trained man. Good for you." Gail laughed.

June snickered and took a bite of her lunch. "Yes, I seem to influence his decisions lately, and I did it without intimacy!"

"Are you proud of not going there yet?"

"It's funny, as he's quite a character and we have such a connection. Nothing like I've experienced before."

"You sure about what you're experiencing? I mean, come on June, I know you. It's like one of the other guys you dated a few months ago. You were so crazed over him and that didn't last. What gives with Dan?"

"I changed my ways with this experience. Dan is different, and I'm so sure he's my catch. I can't explain it, but it's him."

"You couldn't explain it with the other guy either, or the one before that." Gail laughed as she reminded June of her earlier proclamations.

"No really, I know I've said it before, but this time it's real. I mean, the dynamics between us, it's awesome."

The two stopped talking long enough to enjoy a bite or two. June looked at Gail and said, "I know it's kind of funny, but, Gail, the man lingers on my mind like an obsession. I want to know more about him. So you have to tell me as much as you can from now on."

"Are you asking me to spy on Dan?"

"No, not spy, just get to know as much as possible and share it with me. I mean, do it without being noticed."

"I don't know. Maybe we should do the double-date thing and see what happens after." Silence fell at lunch as Gail contemplated her future actions. *Should I actually spy on Dan for June?* Gail looked at her friend across the table. "You know, he's a great guy, and I don't think I need to spy on him. I think we should definitely go out this weekend though."

"After all these years and being the best of friends, you're not going to do this for me?"

"I'll share whatever I find out, but I'm not snooping. I can't do that again."

"Again?"

"You forgot about the guy you were so into, and I nearly got caught tagging him?"

"That was different." June laughed. "He was a hot guy, that Toney."

"Hot or not, I'm not going to do it. I'll share with you what I find out naturally. Again, I'm telling you Dan is a great guy. I can feel it."

"Okay, I got it. A double date it is. I'm serious about him, this is the guy. I'm telling you, Gail, Dan is the one."

"Remember, Toney was the one too." Gail gave June a serious look. "But please, don't play on Dan; he's really a great guy."

"I know, but Dan's not like any man I've ever dated. I'm serious about him, I'm not just playing games. So we're on for this weekend in our minds?"

"Yes, we are, and I'll talk to Rodney and Dan when I return to the office," Gail said.

Lunch ended and Gail returned to the office, smiling about the information she'd learned. She couldn't wait to corner Rodney and share her discovery and introduce the idea of the four going out together. It was also an opportunity to inquire about how much Rodney knew about Dan's private life. Gail knew Rodney and Dan were the best of friends, and that sometimes guys share those private things most girlfriends never know.

As soon as she was inside the office, Gail searched for an opportunity to chat with Rodney. Rodney and Gail had agreed to keep their relationship outside of work as much as possible, so she needed to speak with him privately. Gail entered Dan's office. Rodney and Dan were conversing as she stood just inside the door. When silence fell between them, she spoke. "Hey, you two have a minute?"

"Yes, we were just finishing," Rodney said as he looked at Gail.

"Sure, come on in," Dan said.

"I have a couple of questions for you two." Gail smiled as she closed the office door and then sat next to Rodney on the office couch. "Well, I had lunch with June."

"I saw her in the lobby and wanted to ask you about her. How long have you known her?"

"Are we talking about June from Calistoga?" Rodney asked.

"Yes, and she wants to know about you, Dan."

"Dan, June's the woman you spoke of, right?"

"Yes, she is. I want to take this chance slow. She's nothing like others I've dated. Nothing like them at all."

"She's into you, Dan, no doubt, so I was hoping the four of us could go out together. Since we're all friends, maybe we can find time this Friday night. What do you think?"

"You'll have to talk to June. I'm game, though. You didn't tell her anything silly, did you, Gail?"

"This is June's idea, so I'm sure she'll go. Anyway, what is there that's silly for me to tell?"

"Oh, nothing silly at all." Dan whistled as he blushed.

Laughing, Rodney said, "Nothing to tell for sure."

"Then why are you guys laughing?"

"It's a guy thing, Gail. I know you girls have inside jokes. This one is a guy thing."

"Oh, okay. I hope you two don't do that when we go out together."

"We'll be on best behavior. I really like June; I mean, she's a serious catch."

"You and I have to talk, Dan. I'll catch you later, Gail, but we're on for Friday. Let us know the details since it's you girls' idea." Rodney stood from the couch and left the room.

Dan turned to Gail to speak with her more about June. "I'm nervous with her, Gail, I haven't been nervous with any other woman in my life, but with her I'm making an effort to do the right thing. Did you talk to her about me? I want to know."

"Yes, Dan, we talked about you. She likes you, and it's kind of cute the way you two are acting like teenagers. You have nothing to worry over; she's already in your corner. Trust me," Gail said. "I'll have her call you with Friday night's details this evening."

"Okay, it's good that she'll call. No, I better call her."

"Yes, you call her. I'm heading back to finish the project with Stanley. I'll call her later. Remember, Rodney wanted to see you."

"Gail, thanks for the news, and it's nice having you here. It's really nice."

Gail started to leave the room. "I like being here. But Dan, remember June is my best friend and if… well, she really likes you so do your best with her, will you? I mean do your best at making her happy." Gail left without waiting for Dan's response.

Dan entered Rodney's office shortly after Gail left his. "You wanted to see me?"

"Yes," Rodney said. "Dan, why didn't you let on that you liked this girl so much?"

"I'd planned on telling you for sure once I knew where I wanted the relationship to go."

"Did I hear you say relationship?"

"I'm serious, man. I'm really serious with this one."

"No more hit and run, then find another?"

"I haven't hit this one yet. I mean, I'm waiting for the right moment. Man, she does it for me. I can't place my finger on it, but she does it. I love her smile, her mind, and her humor. She's fun to be around, and always interesting. We talked for hours, laughed until the sun rose, and enjoyed each other at every moment."

"You've dated for a few weeks now? Is that what I hear?"

"Yes, we've dated quite a few times, and I'm not even worried about sex with her. I mean, I do want her, but it's not my priority right now."

"It's your game, right. Remember, I've known you for years. It is your serve, setup, slam, and match. I know the process."

"Honest, Rodney, honest, she's much more to me than my game. I'm serious here, she's truly impressive, a doll, and a joy much greater than I've ever experienced."

"You've taken the time to get to know her. Are you using your reserve for a backup when you get to that exploding point?"

"No, not at all. I've managed to keep June in my mind and want to explore her character. I'm so intrigued with her it's unreal."

"Exactly, it's not real at all. I hear you, but I'm shocked at you, Dan. Finally, someone has your number. I have to meet this girl again. She's the woman who got Dan to give up his single lifestyle and settle. So we're on for Friday night?"

"Gail said we were. How long have you been seeing her?"

"You mean Gail?"

"Who else invited us to a night out?"

"A few weeks now. She's pretty nice too. I mean, going out with her was unexpected, but I'm enjoying it."

"There you go; we're on the right path. Why not enjoy what is given to us?"

"Yes. Why not?" Rodney grinned as he took his seat. "Why not," he repeated. "Because it's actually time we became men, involved men for a change. It's time."

11.
The Presentation

THURSDAY MORNING ARRIVED with a splash. Stanley indicated to Rodney and Dan that the last phase of the project was going to be completed ahead of schedule. Rodney was pleased and concluded that the early completion was in part because of Gail's influence. She'd designed the variation from Rodney's earlier agreement. Her changes led to a shortened timeline for developing the marketing program. With her insight and knowledge of what Starz needed, it was a snap for program success. Rodney requested a total review of the campaign by Friday morning. He wanted to evaluate the campaign and provide objective advice to Starz during their next weekly meeting.

Stanley walked into Rodney's office again by three in the afternoon. "It's ready, boss, just as you asked. We reviewed it, rehearsed, coordinated the sketches, and recorded the transcripts for air waves. I'm confident you'll like everything we've done."

"Thank you, Stanley. Let's move to the conference room, then listen and view the screening within the hour. Make sure the entire team is available."

"Sure thing, I'll coordinate it now." Stanley left the handout material on Rodney's desk and returned to his office. He executed Rodney's instructions as directed. Rodney called Dan. "Hey, it's time."

"Gotcha," Dan said and headed for Rodney's office. On the way, he passed Gail in the hall. "Are you going to review this with us?" he asked.

"No, I have to get home tonight. Since tomorrow night is going to be interesting, I should take care of a few things. Tell Rodney it has my vote of confidence."

"I'll do just that. See you in the morning."

"I'll call June when I get in the car. I'm sure she'll be thrilled about tomorrow night," Gail said as she turned to exit.

"I hope she is," Dan said. *I really hope she is.*

Rodney and Dan knew the final presentation routine. It was something they'd perfected during the business's growth. They would rehearse the presentation for hours on end, until it was second nature. It was their perfectionist ploy for every business effort. The precision in timing, their speech, hand speed for gestures, and hand-off coordination kept their presentations seamless. This process had landed them multiple contracts over the years. It was now their standard for key team members to do the same type of presentation. Though the two would be in the audience for assurance reasons, they now chose to allow firm employees to take the helm. Even with the idea that Starz might change a few things, Rodney felt comfort in knowing Stanley was the main spokesperson. It was his project, and he'd earned his place. Rodney walked from the bay window in his office to behind his desk when Dan appeared.

"Is this the handout?" asked Dan.

"Yes, it's the latest and greatest," Rodney said.

Dan took a hard look at the handout while taking a seat in one of the many chairs in Rodney's office. "Hmmm, this is good, Rodney. I wouldn't change a thing."

"I figured it's almost too perfect."

"Seems like the best we've done so far. I know you had gut feelings earlier, but I don't think Starz will change any of this. Remember, he sent us Gail to ensure we didn't have rework on the campaign."

"I remember. She's a great lady, but that's what bothers me with my gut feeling. Maybe we've been had?"

"No way, don't get paranoid. That's my position." Dan laughed. "Besides, you know her very well. Let's not think negatively."

"It is good. I couldn't find a flaw in it. If this is anything like the commercial clip and radio tape, we're really in there."

"I agree. What time do we start?"

Rodney looked at his watch before answering, "Within the next half hour."

"Good. I'm anxious to see the team's presentation." Dan placed the handout down. "Are you ready for tomorrow night?"

"Dan, I'm as ready as any guy can get. It's just hanging out with a couple girls. We've done this a hundred times over the years."

"Not like this time. I can't get June off of my mind whenever I'm not focused on something. Every free moment, she comes up. Did you know she's dated a few guys since I met her, but never takes them to her place? Nor has she joined anyone at their home. I know this is the one."

"You *followed* her?"

"I followed her. I know, I know, I know. It isn't like me at all."

"Let's just say it's obsession, pure obsession."

"I'm long gone, and I have no control, Rodney. I'm gone and can't get it back. Not that I'm trying, but I'm pretty much gone."

"I agree. Gone!"

"Dude, it's no laughing matter, I'm gone."

The team rehearsed their presentation of the project like a well-oiled machine, tuned for performance. One person stood, spoke, pointed, and just as he sat, another stood and followed the presentation as planned. It was nearly flawless. The only objection Rodney made was the speed of speech from the gate. He knew that speech speed sets the tone for the presentation. Rodney didn't want to lose this contract after so much work. He mentioned the speed, had Stanley start over, and the team followed. After a second pass, Rodney and Dan both stood and applauded the team. The two execs then left their seats and headed for the door. Before exiting, Rodney turned and said, "Great job. We'll move up the presentation to tomorrow. I'm really impressed." He turned again, leaving the room.

Stanley took control of the team and spoke to them with distinction. "Great job! I knew you guys could do great things. I'm happy we gave them a solid presentation. Let's work over the last part of transitioning to the tape review."

Rodney and Dan returned to Rodney's office. "They are good. I'm calling Starz to see if he has time tomorrow. I don't think we'll wait until next week," Rodney said.

"You're right, Starz was adamant about the short timeline, so we should get this out as soon as we can."

"Agreed." Rodney dialed Network Galaxy.

"Hello, Carl Starzinsky's office," answered Starz's executive assistant.

"Rodney Witherspoon for Starz."

"Hold, please."

Rodney held while standing behind his desk. He looked down at the city through his bay window.

"Hi, Rodney," Starz said on the other end of the line.

"Starz, how are you?"

"Doing well, my man, doing well. I hear you guys have a great campaign. I knew you could do it. I liked everything from the beginning. When will it be ready?"

"That's exactly why I'm calling. What's on your agenda tomorrow? Do you have any time?"

"Let me see," said Starz. "I have three hours open. How much time do you need?"

"We're looking at an hour. Unless you have comments or changes, we'll finish within forty minutes."

"Three o'clock is fine. I have you reserved for one hour. If we finish early, great, it's Friday."

"Yes, I'll buy the first round." Rodney turned and held up three fingers to Dan. Dan then left the office and explained to his assistant to set up a quick rehearsal for tomorrow morning, and to make travel arrangements for the team to Starz's location on the other side of town in the afternoon. He instructed her to gather all the equipment necessary for the presentation, and then to call Stanley and give him marching orders so the team would be ready and in place. Dan returned to Rodney's office. Rodney had completed his call moments earlier.

"Everyone will know about the meeting within the next fifteen minutes," Dan said.

"It's why we're so good, Dan. We've done this with team-work from the beginning. It's awesome."

"You know it. We aren't just friends, but we're great business partners."

The next morning at the office, most of the team was rehearsing by the time Dan arrived. He noticed the conference room doors were closed, but multiple voices were behind them. He peeked in and observed the team reviewing lines in small groups. Dan then entered his office, placed his briefcase next to his desk, and went to the break room for his morning coffee. Gail was there pouring a cup. "Hi, Gail," Dan said.

"Oh, hi, Dan. Did you see the team rehearsing?"

"Yes, I did. I'm surprised—it's before nine o'clock. How did Stanley get them here so early?"

"He asked them, from what I heard. So, I understand we're on with Starz this afternoon."

"Yup. We're going to knock 'em dead. You did a great job with the group."

"Thank you. It was easy with you guys and, of course, Stanley. He's something else, that Stanley. I thought we'd bump heads the entire time during the project, but he's a special guy, easy to work with and gets along with everyone; actually, he's a combination of you and Rodney."

"I knew he was good, but wow. You gave him a glowing review just now. Are you comfortable he can run an entire office?"

"Honestly, I think he'll be in his own business as your competitor before long."

"He really impressed you. I'm glad he's with us. I had a gut feeling when we hired him that he'd shine."

"Shine he does, without a doubt."

"Great," Dan said. "I'll remember your comments when we review his performance report. Oh, by the way, we're still on for tonight, right?"

"I thought you'd never ask." Gail took a sip of coffee. "We're on, and June is really excited. She kept asking me if you'd like dancing or did you want a quieter time?"

"I'll leave it to you ladies to decide."

"What about Rodney? Do you think dancing is best?"

"He'll go for anything as long as you're there."

Gail giggled and then walked to exit the break room. "Sure he will," she said as she left.

At noon, Rodney held his motivational meeting with the team. He spoke to them as if it were the beginning of a world champion sporting event. He made jokes, got serious with his last review, and prepared them on what to expect from Starz. He asked the team to arrive no later than 2:00 p.m. He also asked the technical members to ensure that all tools and equipment was working at least fifteen minutes before the meeting. Rodney smiled as he exited the conference room and walked into Dan's office. "These guys are really excited. I haven't seen a group so well prepared since we were doing it."

"I said the same thing this morning when I came in."

"I'm proud of them. Man, Stanley is on the ball."

"We hired a great guy."

"Are we driving together tonight?"

"I thought we'd drive together. It will give me a chance to get June to take me with her tonight."

"Back to your old self, I see."

"No, I need a strategy just in case."

"Where are we going tonight?"

"The girls said dancing, more than likely."

"I don't mind, just as long as we have fun."

"We'll have fun, no doubt, we'll have a blast." The guys took off for Starz's office and decided to grab a bite on the way. They talked business along the ride. It was like the old days, rushing to a presentation but different in that they were going to observe the presentation instead of give it this time. When Rodney and Dan pulled into Starz's office parking lot, most of the group had arrived. A few firm members sat in the building's coffee shop, promptly waiting to go to the twelfth floor. Rodney and Dan went right to Starz's office and found Gail en route. "Hey, Gail," Rodney said.

"Hi, Rodney. Dan."

"Hi," Dan said.

"You two are right on time; Starz is expecting you. Go right into his office. You know where it is, right?"

"We know. Hey, are we set for tonight? Do we have a plan or is it ad lib?"

"No solid plan, but we're definitely on. June will meet us after we close shop. I told her we could start with an early dinner. Is that okay?"

"Okay with me," Dan said. "Is Starz in a good mood?"

"Great mood," Gail said as she walked away.

"Starz, you young man, you—never aging a day." Rodney grabbed Starz's hand for a strong shake.

"I'm doing great, never felt better. How the hell are the both of you?"

"Great," Dan answered reaching to shake Starz's hand.

"It's a great year, and you're making it better," Rodney replied.

"I am? Oh yeah, the campaign. Are you guys ready? I mean, really ready?"

"What does 'really ready' mean?" Rodney asked as he looked at Dan. It was their glance to one another when unexpected things surfaced.

"If you guys are ready with the campaign, we can move quickly. We need to build interest and run the ad two weeks earlier than planned. I mean if we're 'really ready,' we can. If not, we need to cut corners and get it out there within that window."

"We're fine with releasing two weeks earlier. I thought you were talking about a change to the fountain theme."

"Oh, Gail loves the campaign theme. It's my time schedule with investors. They feel two weeks earlier will give us a competitive edge in the first city. I need you guys to hit it with a vengeance."

"As we always do," Rodney said.

"You are going to love it, and it's ready for production," Dan said while moving toward the office door.

"Good news. I like it; you're ready before being asked."

"We pride ourselves in delivering on time."

"I appreciate being on budget too. Speaking of budget, I don't owe you guys any additional funds for the changes Gail made, right?"

"We'll review the hours and get back to you. Are you ready for a great campaign presentation?" Rodney asked.

"I'm as ready as I'll ever get. Let's go see this." Starz led the way to the conference room. To his surprise, the marketing team was in place and waiting to start.

"Hello, sir," Stanley said as Starz entered the conference room, followed by Rodney, Dan, and Gail.

"How are you?" asked Starz.

"I'm doing well," Stanley said, "nice seeing you again."

"Nice seeing you too, Stanley. Are you ready?" Starz took a seat at the head of the table.

"Sir, we are prepared to dazzle you with an outstanding campaign. First, allow me to introduce the team." Stanley introduced every team member and kicked off the presentation. Just as rehearsed, he set the tone and all followed. The presentation took thirty-five minutes to complete. Each person highlighted their presentation skills, and Rodney and Dan couldn't believe their eyes. Not one person required a correction or input. It was flawless.

Starz watched with the intensity of a cat watching its prey. At the end of the presentation, Starz stood from his seat, frowned, and began clapping. "That was awesome, truly awesome."

"Thank you," Stanley said.

"When can you have the commercial in production?"

"We need to finalize the video with a cast member of your choice, and we're ready for production."

"Outstanding. Great job, Gail, I like it. Rodney, Dan, please commend your team. I'm happy with the campaign."

"We aim to deliver," Rodney said as he stood. "Great job, guys."

Starz looked at his watch. "There is a bar one block east from here. First round is on me. See you there in thirty minutes."

"Thank you, Starz, we'll be right there," Rodney confirmed. He looked at Gail and winked, tapped his watch, and waited for a response.

Gail nodded as if to say, "It's okay, right on time."

"Okay, guys, you heard Starz. First drink's on him," Dan said. The team rose to pack up the presentation materials. Dan hoped to get things moving so he could get to the double date with June.

12.
The Fight for Survival

Sabrina and Simone drove away from the hospital. They started the journey with small talk, exhausted with anxiety and anger from visiting Stefan. Simone lamented over her stupidity in falling for him and falling for a man she knew so little about. Somehow she'd found him more appealing than a man of better quality whom she'd pushed away. "I am an ass," Simone said while focusing on the road. "No, *he* is the ass!"

"Yes, he is," Sabrina said. "Let it out, sis, it's good to let your frustrations out."

"Oooh, he pisses me off. Just think, this could have been different had I opened my eyes."

"You aren't going there, not now. You need to focus. Focus on what we're going to do with the company."

"What if we can't save it? What if we lose Aunt Marge's money, our inheritance, what if?"

"It's not going to happen. We'll think of something. Trust me." Sabrina looked out the window at the wooded roadside. She watched tree after tree, fallen branches, and the leaves in shades of green, browns, and reds. It was mesmerizing—she imagined a clothing line composed of such natural colors.

Sabrina pulled out the mini sketchpad she kept in her purse. She grabbed a pencil and allowed her imagination to run rampant. She drew sketch after sketch while Simone drove in silence, contemplating where things had gone wrong.

Simone continued driving in a daze, yet careful enough not to cause an accident, as if the car was on autopilot. She continued driving until Sabrina broke silence. "How much longer?" she asked.

"What?" Simone broke from her reverie.

"How much longer? I can't remember how long it took us to get there. You've been so quiet on the ride."

"Yes, I'm just thinking of how much I invested in Stefan, both emotionally and monetarily. I gave too much too fast."

"No, you did only what a woman in love would do. You loved. That isn't bad; it's just learning more of life's challenges. I did the same with James. I should have known."

"You and I made horrible selections in men. Why did we, sis? Why did we select such jerks?"

"I wish I knew. Especially now, I can imagine how our lives would be had we not turned the good men away," Sabrina said. "I know for a fact, had I not been silly with fantasy, Lorenz and I could have had a great relationship."

"We both overlooked the obvious and followed men who took advantage of us. I can't believe I let it effect the business too. I don't know how I'm going to recover from this. It hurts, really hurts." Simone sighed.

The girls were quiet for a moment. "You know what?" said Sabrina as she sat up. "We will bounce back in no time. I know if Aunt Marge were here, she'd tell us to stand up, brush off, and get back to being smart women."

"You're right. She'd also tell us to get back to business. I wish she were here. I miss her so much."

"So do I. So do I."

Simone took an unexpected turn towards the city. "Where are you going?" asked Sabrina.

"We should stop by the office first. I want to look around."

"Is there something you want?"

"No, nothing in particular. I'm following a gut feeling."

"I know the feeling. I should have followed mine years ago."

"There is no time like the present to start."

Minutes later, the sisters arrived at the office building.

When the two entered, the security clerks at the front desk stood and addressed them. "Good afternoon, Mrs. Stephens."

"Good afternoon," Simone said as they walked to the elevators.

"I'm interested in seeing how far the investigation has gotten," said Simone as she leaned back against the elevator's walls. "I bet they uncovered more."

"I'm sure they did." The two arrived at their floor and exited the elevators.

It seemed like a typical work afternoon until Simone's executive assistant approached. "I have bad news for you. The IRS invaded your office. They took everything away in boxes. I couldn't stop them."

"It's okay, Sheila. I appreciate you watching my office. Did they take anything that will impede the continuation of our current projects?"

"No, I don't think so. Since you haven't been here, most of the ongoing project folders are in Sabrina's new office. But they took everything from yours. I think they took everything off the wall too. I had to let them in your wall safe. They had a warrant."

"You said the IRS and not FBI, right?"

"The guy showing the warrant was IRS; however, I heard the FBI was around too. I can only vouch for what I read on the warrant."

"I suspect the FBI took the office apart looking for evidence or clues. Thanks again, Sheila."

"You're welcome, Miss Simone," Sheila said just as a plainclothes FBI agent walked into the room. The agent wore jean pants, a non-collared shirt, and a soft, multicolored sports coat. He walked up to the women and spoke, "I'm Agent Wilkes," then showed his identification. "I need to speak with you two. I have good news."

"What news can be good now, after learning that my husband was dealing with the mob and that I'm facing the potential loss of my company?" asked Simone.

Agent Wilkes's face remained solemn. "We confiscated your things and found no evidence of your involvement."

"Of course you didn't. My involvement with the company is strictly honest and legal."

"Exactly what they all say; we had to be sure."

"Well, what's the next step?" asked Sabrina.

"I'm only here to thank you for your cooperation and let you know that your names have been cleared. With your help, we've gotten enough to put Stephen away and that syndicate boss who visited you earlier."

"You mean Stefan?" asked Simone.

"Stephen Craig, alias Stefan. He is notorious for conning gorgeous women, using their money or organization, and setting up laundering operations or embezzling. Remember when you met him, Simone?"

Simone reached behind her in an attempt to find a chair. "Yes—yes, I do. It was remarkable. He was a man with a mission, had his own money, and had an impressive business. He was my equal."

"Those companies were fronts."

After Sabrina pushed a chair behind her, Simone collapsed in the seat. "They couldn't have been. I dropped him off at his office all the time. He seemed like such a dedicated worker. It was part of my decision to marry him."

"That's what baffled us. You married him. Marriage is not his usual MO. He normally lives with a woman and then uses their money to support his efforts with the mob."

Simone exhaled. "You mean he's done this many times?"

"Yes, he has, but with your help, we've gathered enough evidence to put both Stephen and the mafia boss away. I have to go now. We'll have your things back in the office after we've collected our equipment. Sixty percent of your assets are frozen due to the connection your company had with Stephen's activities. Once the investigations are settled, they should become available to you again. It's a good thing you didn't allow him to move in as the COO as he suggested. We're arresting him now."

"Good thing." Simone held her head in her hands as she sat behind the desk.

Agent Wilkes left the building.

The office fell silent, as Simone and Sabrina sat in surprise. They looked at the empty walls, the bare office, and found themselves shocked at the recent news. Tears fell upon

Simone's face. A swell of emotions and memories overtook her as she recalled the last two years with Stefan ... Stephen Craig.

Sabrina got up from her seat and closed the office door, then moved to console her sister. "It's going to be okay. Simone, it's okay. You're better off without the heartache."

"I know, but it still hurts. I can't believe it." Simone sniffed. "I don't find it ideal, having a husband or man deceive you from the very beginning. I feel such a fool."

"You should be happy it's over." Sabrina moved closer to Simone and hugged her. "It can only get better. Trust me, your life, and our business, can only get better."

"Our business? Who can think of business right now when I'm in such pain over a man?"

"Sis, you're right. I think Stefan or Stephen, whoever he is, happens to do us a favor. He's gone, out of our lives. This gives us the opportunity to reinvent the business."

"There you go again, with business. What about my heart?"

"Good women take the heart and twist it into whatever gets them the love they want. Unfortunately, only a few men will do the same. So you and I are back to square one." Sabrina pulled a tissue from the container on Simone's desk. I think you'll do well bouncing back without any man in your life."

Simone and Sabrina sat quietly, digesting all the information. Simone started writing, scratching one thing and another. She took out a calculator. *Click, click, click,* and then she scribbled on a notepad. Simone stopped for a moment and turned to view the skyscrapers across the way. "We'll have to close so much of the business with these frozen assets. So many people involved. "

"You're right, I think this investigation is going to take some time to conclude," Sabrina said.

"Yes, I think so too. Sis, we're going to have to restructure our business and try to save as many jobs as possible. The only thing is, I'm not sure how."

"I have an idea to get us on the right track, but before I show you, are you sure you're over the pain Stefan caused you?"

"No, I'm not over it, but keeping busy is a way to get me sidetracked."

"I agree, but before we move forward, maybe we should call Phil and ask how long it will be till the divorce is final. I think you're a free woman. I'd hate to create something Stefan can return and take from us."

"Great point, I'll make a note to call Phil. But for now, I'd rather hear what you have planned."

"I think we'll do fine if we work the idea out right. If there's one thing I'm good at and secure with, it's fashion. I have these design sketches you should review." Sabrina took her sketchpad over to Simone. "Let me know what you think."

Simone reviewed each page. "I'm getting the picture, but I'm not sure about funding the cost to get a new clothing line going."

"It's not going to be too expensive, and I have savings; I'll throw every penny into it. It's an idea that will work, and work well."

"I'm listening."

"This project will help us keep some of the employees you were worried about losing. Plus, once the line gets off the ground, I know we will make a profit."

"I'm following you," Simone said, "but tell me more. Where did this idea come from?"

When we were driving from the hospital, I took in the

earth-toned colors outside. I remembered the styles I saw in Europe and Africa," Sabrina said while moving closer to Simone.

"I noticed your designs are very different, yet something most people can wear."

"Exactly. Well, my idea is to create both male and female lines and market them collaboratively with a production."

"A production?"

"Yes, we can have a showcase of clothing and market the pieces during a stage play around the country. We can gain notoriety through actors wearing the clothes. Instead of costumes, we'll have a catalog as a handout, like a playbill."

"Sounds interesting and unique, but where are we going to find a production that fits? Surely you don't want to fund a play too?"

"I have a playwright in mind who we might be able to work with. Plus, he has connections to a production company that is known for great shows. I think we can piggyback on his effort. That is, if you think it can work." Sabrina turned towards the door. "I'll be back in a few minutes."

Simone pondered on the idea and examined each drawing. Page after page, minutes went by while she looked at Sabrina's sketches. *I'm getting it. This just might work.*

Sabrina returned and looked at Simone. Simone stretched in her office chair. "It's a great idea, but only if you have contacts in place. I'm starting to love your designs. They are practical enough for everyday wear. As I look at this design, I see a typical day shopping, and this one," Simone turned the page to show Sabrina, "I see a guy going for a date. And you know what I like about it all? The collection is in earth-toned colors.

We could spruce it up as needed. I see big possibilities. There is only one thing out of our hands: marketing."

"Let me speak with my contact on the matter. I'll have an answer by the time we reorganize the company. Man, freezing 60 percent hurts. Can we get Phil involved to see what we could do to release those assets? Especially since you've proven that you weren't involved, those assets should be available."

"I'll call Phil and see what he thinks. Besides, we need to know where we stand with protecting ourselves from lawsuits. God knows what Stefan has done to hurt the company. Money laundering, embezzlement, and whatever else is going to put a strain on the company's business relationships; thanks to Stefan, the great lover, my husband."

"You mean former husband."

"We'll know of that too when I talk to Phil."

Agent Wilkes's team joined forces with Agent Williams and the local police; they finally cornered the mafia boss at an office building around the corner from Stefan's business front. Wilkes had his team of agents shut down the communication and movement of the mafia group. Williams took down the key players who supported the boss, and in one swipe, they moved in on the target. When the mafia boss appeared outside in cuffs, it was a celebration. The final bust was successful, and the two-year investigation ended with one king pin in the hands of justice.

Early one morning, two days after Simone had reviewed the sketches, Sabrina woke remembering a conversation with the playwright she'd met. It was at an event in France where James was on his rampage chasing young models.

Patricia approached Sabrina and nodded toward James, alluding to his behavior. "I don't know how you do it."

Embarrassed to reply, Sabrina glanced at the wall opposite of James, took a breath, and said, "I can't explain."

"A beautiful woman shouldn't endure this type of disrespect. I can tell you love him."

"I think that was a compliment."

"Yes, it is, and I'm sure he's a lucky man."

"Oh, he's lucky all right. I knew this before marrying him. It's partially my fault."

"No, nonsense. I think the heart knows what is best, yet it's sometimes deceived into naively thinking that all is good for the greater end."

"'Good for the greater end'—now that's a line. What do you do?"

"I'm a playwright, producer and have created an ideal show. I'm just waiting to get the right business partner."

"Oh, really, what have you done recently?"

"Nothing on Broadway, or off-Broadway for that matter, but a little show here and there; I assisted in a few big-name productions. I'm just waiting for my break."

"I get it. What's stopping you?"

"Funding, I need funding."

"Well, one day, I'll have to listen to your story. Right now I have to get my husband before he really embarrasses me." Sabrina stepped towards James, then paused and looked back at her new acquaintance. "What's your name?"

"Patricia," she replied and handed her card to Sabrina. "Nice meeting you."

"Nice meeting you, Patricia the playwright." Sabrina stepped along.

Looking now through her luggage, briefcase, and bags, Sabrina searched for Patricia's card. She thought a call to Patricia would put her idea to save the company in motion. She continued to dig to no avail. It wasn't until Sabrina heard Simone move around the house that she made the decision to call her soon-to-be ex-husband, James. Finding Patricia's number was important enough to break silence. Reluctantly, Sabrina took her cellular phone with her as she left her bedroom for the kitchen. "Good morning," Sabrina said to Simone.

"Hey, want a cup of coffee?" Simone asked as she reached for a cup from the counter rack.

"Yes, sure. I've looked everywhere for this playwright's contact information. I can't find her card anywhere. I was thinking I might have left it in the hotel room in Africa, so I was thinking of calling James. But at the same time, I'm not too motivated to."

"Then don't call. We'll find a different production here."

"This Patricia would be great though. She seemed hungry for a chance." Sabrina sat at the kitchen counter and smiled at Simone when she handed her a filled coffee cup.

"Well, you know how I feel about trusting your gut," Simone said. "Although, I suppose we shouldn't have trusted our guts when it came to our choice in men."

"Come on, sis, I know this, but we should lighten up a little. We have to focus on moving on with our lives. Let's get rid of the bad memories and move towards a new day."

"I agree," Simone sighed. "I just didn't think we'd be here talking like this."

"Neither did I, neither did I." Sabrina looked away from Simone towards the nearest window. She imagined sitting with James at a quaint café, on a morning like this one.

"Okay, let's talk about your vision again. Do you think this playwright's work fits in with your plan?"

"Well, I haven't read her work yet, actually," Sabrina said, "but after meeting her, I went to one of the plays she worked on, and it was fantastic. I just know my plan will succeed. Do you know how many contemporary shows reflect people in great clothes? I'm sure we can pull this off if it's with the right story."

"I think you're onto something. I slept on it, and it excites me. Maybe you should find that number after all, but you'll have to get strong before you call James. You'll have to, or you won't be able to talk business."

"I'll look around, reach out to some friends, and use James as my last resort."

"That is a better idea." Simone stood. "Well, I have to get to the office. I'll also set an appointment with Phil."

"Okay, I'll see you later. I need to keep designing the line and find a way to contact Patricia."

"Let me know if you need my help. Remember, before you sign any contract, let's talk about it first. Not that I don't trust you, it's—"

Sabrina put her hand up. "I know, it's business and we need to communicate everything."

"Sure thing."

Simone left the kitchen and headed for her bedroom to prepare for the day. *Saving employees, how the heck am I going to do it? I'll have to bring the board together and solicit ideas. Meanwhile, I hope and pray Sabrina's idea hits home.*

Sabrina finished her coffee, and headed to the home office. She remembered unloading her briefcase of papers and notes from modeling events, business meetings, and contracts she'd created to support James. She sat at the desk and sorted through every item. Her search sent her back into the past, bringing with it memories of her failed relationship. Sabrina shook her head and forced herself to concentrate. "My dream, it's my dream," she repeated to motivate herself. Sabrina thought again of Patricia. *She's the key, I just feel it. As Simone said, sometimes a gut feeling tells you to do something. Although, I should have stayed with Lorenz, but no, I needed excitement…* Sabrina allowed a tear to fall down her cheek.

Her search seemed pitifully in vain. Sabrina found all sorts of interesting notes, documents, agreements, and ideas, but nothing with Patricia's information. Not even the playbill for *Her Last Hoorah*, which she'd kept as a souvenir, had Patricia's information on it. The production company's name and address were on the playbill though, and Sabrina realized they might have the information she needed. It was a start, and Sabrina smiled at her discovery. She got online and researched the company, finding contact information. Sabrina copied the production company's phone number from the website with a feeling of triumph.

Sabrina was relieved that she wouldn't have to call James. She pranced her way upstairs to get dressed. It was a mood shift of good fortune; Sabrina felt one step closer to her dream. She left the house with a spring in her step and headed to the office.

She stopped at a major intersection and observed her surroundings. She envisioned other drivers wearing a piece from her clothing line. Sabrina was hopeful that her idea would help save the company her sister had managed over the years; she wanted to be a part of fulfilling Aunt Marge's dream. The light changed and Sabrina returned to focusing on her drive.

Simone sat in her office, working the numbers, pressing her accounting skills to all end, and then focused on revenue streams. *How the hell am I going to do this? I'm so glad I didn't allow Stefan to touch every part of the company. At least the property management operation is still productive. If anything else, we may have to give up a building or two. Aunt Marge would turn over in her grave if that happens.* Frustrated, Simone set her pen down and decided to call Phil. She dialed Phil's office and got his assistant. "Is he in?" asked Simone.

"No. He isn't in at the moment. I can take a message or set up an appointment," the assistant answered.

"This is Simone Stephens."

"Okay, I'll pass on the message that you called. I suggest you set an appointment, as his scheduling is pretty busy these days. I have an opening tomorrow morning as someone cancelled earlier. Is ten o'clock good for you?"

"Yes, but still have him call me today. Please, it's very important."

"You're set and I'll give him the urgent message to call you."

"Thank you," Simone said and ended the call. She continued her attempt to come up with a new plan for the company. *I know there has to be a way to keep going without biting off more than the company can chew. There's always creating new partnerships, but I don't have much to offer. Who will want to collaborate* with a company with 60 percent frozen assets? Simone called her assistant into the room. "Hi, Sheila, can you come here for a moment, please?"

"Sure," Sheila answered and stepped into the office's entry. "What can I help you with?"

"I need you to contact the board of directors for an emergency meeting. I have to share this information with them. Can you schedule the meeting for two days from now?"

"You know we'll have to fly some of them in. Is there an alternate day if they can't make it so quickly?"

"No, this is important and stress emergency. You have to stress EMERGENCY to them. I'm counting on you to get them here. Our company depends on it, Sheila."

Sheila saw the concern on Simone's face; the same stress she'd recognized when the FBI and IRS investigation began. *Poor Simone.* "I'll get them here as if my life depended on it."

"Good, because your career just may depend on it," Simone said and returned to her work. Sheila left the office and made contacting the board her priority.

13.

Double Date

DAN, RODNEY, AND GAIL headed to retrieve June, as they'd decided to drive together for dinner and dancing. It was a marvelous idea that would allow the four to really share in the evening. Dan, the excited one, boasted how lucky he was to meet his dream woman. He glowed during the ride to June's house.

"My, you are serious about June. I never thought it would be so obvious," Gail said as she turned back in her seat.

"Obvious?" Dan asked.

"*So* obvious. I knew you liked her, but you've only dated her a few times. June is a fantastic woman, but my goodness, you have it bad. I think it's cute." Gail snickered.

"Cute is a good thing though, right?" Rodney laughed.

"You two know it's new to me," Dan said. "Maybe for once I'll have the feelings I've seen Rodney have for a woman."

"You've been in love before, Rodney?" Gail asked as if it were news to her. Rodney didn't respond. "Well, aren't you going to answer?"

"Yes, I've been in love before. Well, let's say 'lust.' It wasn't reciprocated."

"Oh, he's traveled the road of love. He fell hard. It was some time ago. I'm glad he's over it," Dan said with a serious look.

"Thanks, my friend." Rodney turned into June's driveway.

"We're here, let me call her," Gail said.

"No, I'll walk to the door. It's the gentlemanly thing to do," Dan said as he exited the car.

"You were in love. I bet she was a lucky woman," Gail said once she and Rodney were alone.

"She didn't think so." Rodney watched Dan walk up to June's front door.

"What happened?"

"It's a long story. Let's just say I was too far gone and it wasn't reality."

"I guess we can talk about it another time."

Dan knocked on the door and stood, anxious with anticipation. He felt like a teen on a first date. The jitters had overtaken him. *Nerves; got to get my nerves under control.*

"Who's there?" June asked as she stood at the door looking through the small window.

"It's Dan."

June opened the door with a smile. "I'll be right there; let me get my purse."

"Sure," Dan said as he stood fast on the porch and waited for June to exit. June grabbed her purse, peeked in the hallway mirror and touched her lips, cleaning the lipstick at the corner of her mouth. She stepped outside and smiled as she approached Dan. "Hi, you look nice."

"You beat me to it! You look gorgeous."

"Thank you. We're taking one car?" June noticed Rodney and Gail in the front of the waiting car.

"Yes, it's easier for us. Don't worry; I'll take you home later."

"No worries." June moved in the backseat as Dan held the door for her. "Hi, guys," she said.

"I'm glad we're finally going out together," Gail said as she turned sideways in her seat to face June.

"Where are we headed?" Dan asked.

"Gail suggested a place that's full of life a few minutes from here; nice crowd, classy joint," Rodney said as he drove towards the major intersection. "Nice place, I'm sure we'll like it."

"You will," Gail said.

"I'm glad you know these places. Dan and I have been looking for new places to go." June leaned against Dan in the backseat.

"Dan, I'm pretty sure you've been to this club. Why haven't you taken her there?" Rodney asked.

"Honestly, it's because I wanted June to myself on every opportunity."

"I think that is so sweet," Gail said while grabbing Rodney's hand. "I know the feeling, Dan."

"Well, there's still nothing wrong with exploring new places once in awhile," June said.

"June," Dan whispered as he looked at her, "we'll have lots of time to explore."

June smiled as she gazed at Dan. It was a message she once dreamed of hearing, but she was still hesitant to show her true emotions.

Minutes into the drive, music filled the air as Rodney played a few smooth songs from his MP3 playlist. It was a nice drive.

The sunset displayed its majesty and the skyline stood behind the pinkish evening glow. Most of the glass buildings reflected the sun, giving the four a beauty to behold. They rode, listening to the music and holding their interest's hands. Shortly after, Rodney drove up to their destination's entrance for valet parking. "This is it," he said as he exited the car.

The other car doors opened as valet members escorted each person out both sides. When handed a valet ticket, Rodney replied, "Thanks," and placed it in his pants pocket. With his other hand, he reached for Gail to walk with him. Dan reached for June in a similar manner but put his arm around her waist. The two couples walked to the entrance and the men allowed the women to enter the building first. Rodney approached the hostess's podium, "Reservations for Rodney Witherspoon, please."

"I'm sorry I don't have reservations under that name." The receptionist said after searching her list. "Is it under any other name?"

Gail stepped up to the counter. "Gail Hill," she said.

The hostess looked at her clipboard. "Here you are. Follow me." She led them to a table and set four menus down. "Donna is your server, and she'll be right with you."

"Thank you," Rodney and Dan said. The guys pulled seats out for Gail and June, and took their own once the women were settled.

"Sorry, Gail, I forgot you'd planned the date tonight. I'm so used to being the one to take the lead," Rodney said.

"Sometimes I like to take charge." Gail winked.

Rodney smiled. "Isn't that the truth?" He turned to Dan and June. "What's the menu like?"

June opened the folded menu and started reading. The

others followed suit and opened their menus just as the waitress approached. "Hi, folks, I'm Donna and will be serving you tonight. Let me share our specials with you," she said and explained three specialty dishes. "Can I take your drink orders while you decide?"

"Yes," Dan said. He turned to June and asked her to order first. "What are you having?"

June looked at the waitress. "A glass of white wine; house brand is okay."

Gail then gave her order. "I'll have a vodka and cranberry."

"I'm driving, so I'll have a glass of iced tea," Rodney said.

"And for you, sir?" Donna asked.

"Tom Collins sounds pretty good right now. Oh, and please bring four glasses of water," Dan said.

"Sure thing. I'll return with your drink orders soon."

The restaurant was a popular place and it began to fill shortly after they arrived. There was a band coming in and setting up for their set. Donna brought drinks to the table and took their dinner orders. The background music then changed to a more aggressive Latin sound. The seductive candlelight cast shadows upon their faces, and the music had all four tapping their feet on the floor, entranced with the rhythm.

"This is very nice," Dan said as he scanned the room.

"Do you Latin dance, Dan?" June asked.

"I do if you do."

"Don't let him fool you, June. Dan is a great dancer. He moves to all types of music."

"The question isn't just for Dan, Rodney, it's for you too," Gail said.

"I'll dance to anything."

The four continued listening as the band started their set.

The band played smooth love ballads; the lead singer's svelte voice cooed over the microphone, enough to tingle every nerve in the body. He sang three numbers before changing to a more upbeat song. The meals arrived, and the four talked about jobs, economy, fitness, and (of course) dating. It was thirty-five minutes into the dinner and all were satisfied with their meal. "That was excellent," Dan said while he wiped his mouth with the dinner napkin.

"Yes, it was. I'm ready for another glass of wine," June said as she lifted her glass for the last sip. Dan raised his hand towards Donna for her attention.

Rodney touched Gail on the hand. "Are you okay? Would you like another drink or something?"

Gail made eye contact. "Just you."

"Wow, you stole my line."

"I mean it." Gail blushed as the candlelight accented her face.

Donna arrived at the table and asked for a dessert order or order for more drinks. Dan ordered the glass of wine and asked for the check. "Also, can we move to a booth closer to the dance floor?"

"Sure, I'll find you a spot after I bring your drink and check."

"Great, thanks." Dan's arm touched the back of June's chair. He pulled a brown leather wallet from his pocket and placed it on the table. "I have this one tonight, my friend," he said to Rodney.

"I hear you. Thanks," Rodney said.

June observed Dan's gesture. *He's a keeper.*

Donna returned with the check and drink and then pointed to a booth just shy of the stage. "There is your new booth. I can take more drink orders when you're ready." She took Dan's credit card just after he placed it in the check folder. "Thank you," she said before leaving.

"You guys want to change tables now?" Dan asked.

"Aren't you going to wait for your card?" Rodney asked.

"No, she'll bring it to our booth. I'm sure of it."

"Okay, let's go." Rodney stood and pulled Gail's chair out for her while she rose from the table. As they got seated, the band started a new song. It had a nice salsa beat, one that ignited the desire to move.

"Excuse me," June said, "I have to take Dan to the dance floor." Dan followed June to the middle of the floor.

Donna returned to their new table and asked Rodney and Gail if they would like anything from the bar. Rodney reached in his pocket and pulled out his wallet. He handed a credit card to Donna and asked her to start a tab, and indicated that she should leave Dan's card at the table. "He purchased dinner, I've got this."

Donna nodded. "Sounds good. I'll get your order."

June grabbed Dan by the hand. "Are you ready to have fun?"

"I'm not sure you want me as your partner."

"Why not, we're here, aren't we?"

"Yes, but I'm not so good at this type of dancing."

"Don't worry, just follow my lead." June began to move her hips without moving her torso. "Mimic me if you can."

Dan moved with June even though it was difficult to maintain focus on moving his hips alone. Dan felt the music reverberate through the floor, and suddenly he had the urge to move his feet in rhythm. It was nothing like a salsa dance, but move he did and coordinated it with his hip gyration. "Is this it?" he asked.

June giggled as she kept moving and placed her hands on Dan's hips. "Here, step like this."

"Like this?"

"One, two, three, and step." June gently persuaded Dan to move in her direction. "Yes, just like this. Don't forget to count with the song, one, two, three…"

Dan smiled and looked appreciatively at June. "You're good," he whispered.

"It's fun and you're doing great. Just keep moving." June took his arm, held it high over her head and twirled. "Keep moving, one, two, three…"

They danced for three songs, and Dan began to get the hang of it. Rodney and Gail enjoyed watching the two work their magic, moving as a team. "They look great," Rodney said. "You know, Dan and I have been friends for years, but wow, I've never seen him so interested in a woman."

Gail nodded. "You told me this before. Dan must impress you with his feelings for June. Is that jealousy I suspect?"

"Jealous, no. I'm genuinely happy for him. I think those two are amazing. He's pretty content to be in her life. I can tell."

"I think you missed the point. What are *you* feeling?"

"I get it, but that isn't my focus today. I'm supporting Dan and his new love. Me, I need to step back for a moment and let him enjoy the spotlight."

"He doesn't need the spotlight from everyone else, only June. I don't see June focusing on you."

"I get it, babe, I have you." Rodney looked into her eyes. "I really have you. Can you dance salsa?"

"I thought you'd never ask."

"I'm not the greatest, but I can step with the best."

Rodney slid from the booth and held his hand for Gail.

She followed and they both proceeded onto the dance floor. Within seconds, they moved as if they had had rehearsed for competition. When the song was over, the band stopped and changed to a slow ballad just in time for June and Dan to rest.

"What timing," June said while heading for the booth, grabbing a tissue to wipe the moisture from her forehead. "That was fun."

"Yes, I enjoyed it," Dan said as he took his seat next to June.

June laughed, remembering Dan's eclectic moves on the dance floor, but then she grew serious. "So what's next?"

"Would you like another drink?"

"No, I'm talking about us. What's next?"

"I'm glad you asked. I've never felt so strongly about a person in my life. I can't say it's love because I have no idea what that feeling is like, but I sure crave you."

"Crave?"

"Not that way. Well, not *only* that way; what I mean is, I crave being around you and learning more about the things you enjoy. I find myself wanting to be the reason you smile or laugh, or just being a part of you."

"The feeling's mutual, Dan. I see a future for us."

"Really? 'Us,' what a lovely word—new to my vocabulary." It was true; Dan had been single for most of his life. He had focused on work and play and never acknowledged the possibility of a serious relationship. Things changed when he met June. Suddenly he'd found himself thinking of her throughout the day, evenings, and nights. Dan took June's hands in his. "June, I'm crazy about you, really crazy. I don't know how to explain it."

Gail and Rodney returned to the booth. "You two seem to be having a wonderful time," Rodney said.

"Yes, we are," June said.

Dan nodded in agreement. "It's the first time I've danced salsa. I had no idea it was such a workout."

June laughed and patted him on the back. "You were great. Not bad for a first time."

Gail took a sip of her drink as Rodney sat down. "I think I'm going to run to the ladies' room. June?" June grabbed her purse and slid out of the booth with Gail.

Once they were out of sight, Rodney turned to Dan. "Hey, this is real, dude."

"Yes, I know. I'm ready, Rodney. This is the one. I told you earlier, and it's confirmed right now. I'm in love."

Rodney sat back after hearing Dan's profession. He held his drink close to his lips and paused. "Are you okay? Really, I want to know because I need you to realize what you're telling June. All jokes aside. I know what you've done to women before, but it's not a game, and I think she's falling for you."

"I'm serious. Really, I am. I've never felt this way, even when I liked a woman so much, it wasn't like this."

"Okay, I just wanted to make sure this isn't just some ploy to get her to spend the night with you. This isn't the Dan I've known."

"It's not to spend the night, even though that wouldn't be bad. But yes, I'm serious. I know this isn't like me, Rodney. I haven't felt this way, and it's freaking me out! But it's good."

Dan nodded towards the girls, who were approaching the booth. Gail approached within arm's length and without a word led Rodney back to the dance floor. June did the same, and the four danced as if it was their last night on earth. The music went from salsa to merengue, and samba to bachata.

A slow number began, and June moved towards Dan in one step, grabbing his sweaty body and feeling the heat of their desire. She laid her head on his shoulder and allowed her body to move whichever way Dan compelled his motion to flow. The two swayed on the floor and danced through two songs, and didn't break from each other when a fast song resumed. Dan held on, and barely moved as he looked into June's eyes. It was the moment he'd anticipated. He tilted his head and moved closer to her lips, and without touching, he held her close. June didn't move at first. Just feeling the warmth of his body and his lips so near hers sparked her desires. She moved, finally sealing the gap between their lips as if a humming bird landed on a flower. They kissed, not for a moment but for minutes on the dance floor. She never pulled away, and Dan didn't nudge to release her.

Rodney and Gail maintained their interest in one another without showing concern for Dan and June. It wasn't until Donna returned with the final bill, as the club was starting to close, that they realized how late it had gotten. "Wow, we've been here all night. It's nearly four in the morning," Gail said.

Rodney looked back to the dance floor. "I should get them. Wow, and they're still at it."

"Honestly, they haven't stopped. Are we dropping them off somewhere?"

"It seems that way. You didn't expect them to come with us, did you?"

"No. We'll drop them off at Dan's."

Gail moved closer and placed her lips on Rodney's neck. She grabbed his thigh, pulling it closer to her. Rodney reciprocated the touch by turning his head towards her and kissing her lips. Just as the two broke their passionate moment, June and Dan finally returned to the table. Before they took a seat in the booth, the club's overhead lights turned on. The bright lights indicated that it was time for all patrons to leave the premises. "I guess that's it for tonight," Dan said as he grabbed June's purse for her.

The four exited the building and walked to Rodney's car. Rodney unlocked the car doors. "We're heading to your place first, Dan. I hope you don't mind."

"Not at all, as a matter of fact, it's one stop for the both of us."

Rodney helped Gail into the passenger seat, and Dan opened the door in back for June to scoot in. Dan eased in after her and sat toward the center of the backseat. June reciprocated and scooted closer to Dan and placed her head on his shoulder. They rode in silence to Dan's apartment. On the drive, Rodney played soft music and held Gail's hand. Minutes later, Rodney pulled into Dan's driveway.

Dan jumped out. "It was a fun night, you two. Thanks for driving, Rodney, I'll call you tomorrow or…" he looked at June for a moment, "maybe not." He closed the door and walked to open June's car door.

Just as it opened, June stepped out. "It was fun, we'll do it again I'm sure. Night, you two."

"Night," both Rodney and Gail said. Dan led June to his front door. As he shuffled his keys, they were both silent; no words needed to be spoken. When Dan unlocked the padlock, they both reached for the doorknob. June's hand landed across Dan's and both felt a spark travel through them. The door opened and before June could enter, Dan grabbed her close to him, and with a step inward, he kissed her with all the passion they'd felt through the evening.

They stepped through the apartment door as they embraced and kicked it closed. They maneuvered to the couch and continued kissing, caressing, and without words, stripping their clothes. June stopped just as he got to her panties. She moved across the room to Dan's bedroom door. "Come here, sexy man," she purred. Dan moved towards her and jumped with one pant leg still on his body. Mesmerized by June's womanly features, he stepped and fell to the floor. June watched helplessly, and then giggled, covering her smile with her hand. "Oh my gosh."

Dan got up, grabbing his pants in one hand and shoes in the other. "I was too excited." He laughed.

"Are you always like this when you're excited?"

"No, I'm usually a bit smoother than this." His face turned somber. "Listen, June," he said while approaching, "it's the first time I've felt this way for a woman. I'm trying to put it in words, these feelings I have for you."

"I think I understand." June pulled Dan to the bed. "I see something different in you that I haven't seen in other men."

"Then you know it's our turn." Silence fell as both Dan and June looked into each other's eyes. Neither one moved. Dan had never shared such an intimate moment before sex. June hadn't either, as she would have usually pressed a man for details, trying to open the door for a long-term relationship. Tonight, neither found themselves compelled to follow their long-standing habits.

In one gesture, Dan moved to kiss her gently on the lips and then pulled her into his arms. June responded with intent; she succumbed to his effort and let Dan take her in the moment. Dan proceeded to explore June's body; he kissed her from her forehead to her shoulders, then laid her flat on the bed and continued his exploration. Every so often, he would pause in kissing her to massage her erogenous zones, the points of pleasure. He drove June to the heights of her sensations.

He touched, caressed, and kissed along his journey, taking time to note June's responses. His excitement peaked when June shrieked from pleasure. He moved to join her, slid himself to a point of entry, and began moving, setting up the moment to thrust. Dan moved with passion. He eased himself into her and didn't allow his excitement overcome his desire to make this moment last as long as possible. June responded, kissing him with fervor, pulling him closer and tighter, as if inviting him to plunge deeper inside. Yet, she felt Dan's gentle touch and relaxed to his control. They'd finally connected, and they made passionate love for hours on end. The two fell asleep mid-Saturday morning.

On Monday morning, Dan was already in his office when Rodney arrived. "Hey, you're early," Rodney said as he stopped at Dan's office door.

"What's up?" Dan said. "I'm on time like usual."

"True, but I thought you'd be a little late after a great weekend."

"That's a plan in the making, my friend. June and I are working out details for a weekend together. I know we'll have a great time."

"I'm excited for you. I see June means a lot to you. It's your time, dude."

"I'm excited about her. I had a great time the other night.

The best thing is that it continued until this morning. To be honest, I didn't want to leave her, but I knew how important our campaign is to Starz. I kind of told her that, if I work hard this week and get things going, we'd have a long weekend. She agreed, so it's why I'm here. I think she's doing the same so we can leave Thursday night."

"All you had to do is let me know. I'll cover you Friday. Heck, I'll even cover you for the rest of the week. It's not like you haven't done it for me."

"I know and appreciate it, but June and I planned this well. So, I'm okay and thanks for the offer."

"Okay, Dan, I'll catch you later. This is it; I see it all over your face. June's it."

"Yes, she is. I'll admit it again and again."

Rodney left for his office. When he arrived, there were messages on his phone and paper notes on his desk. He picked up his desk phone and listened to his messages. Just as he wrote the last detail, Dan walked in. "Have you heard anything from Stanley or Gail about their progress today?"

"No, they've both been at Starz's office. I haven't heard from them."

"Hmm," Rodney said, "I'll get Gail on the phone and ask her for an update." Rodney dialed Gail's number and got her voice mail. He left a message for her to return his call. "I'll call you when I find out what she has to say," Rodney told Dan.

"Sure thing," Dan said and left the room. The two men returned to their busy schedules.

The day lapsed into evening, and after awhile Gail returned Rodney's call. "Sorry I missed your call earlier today. I spent most of the day with Starz working on a script."

Rodney winced. "Is it going to affect our ad campaign?"

"No, it's a new script. Don't worry, Stanley's still chugging along with the ad campaign for the current project."

"Oh, okay."

"Yeah, Starz was pretty excited about this new prospect. It's a play by Patricia Dugan."

"Oh? I hadn't heard him mention that name."

"She was one of Starz's underwriters not long ago. She was a dynamic playwright and added just enough to his last play to make it a success. It's actually the reason that Starz profited enough to fund the company's upcoming move to the West Coast. Patricia isn't with us now though, sadly. She passed away not too long ago."

"I'm sorry to hear that. So, what prompted Starz to have you look at this play when everyone's so busy with the current production?"

"He heard from someone who was searching for Patricia. I guess it sparked sentiments with Starz, so he finally read Patricia's scripts. She left them to him when she died."

"I'm surprised at the sudden interest, but I can now understand why."

"I'm not sure I understand the concept he's pitching to me, but I'm sure he'll elaborate in the morning. Any plans for us tonight?"

"Of course there are plans for us. You just show up to the condo and see how things are planned."

"I'll be there."

"Great. See you soon." Rodney shifted his thoughts back to business. He phoned Dan to inform him of Gail and Stanley's status and suggested they have a meeting in the morning.

It was two hours into the evening when Rodney arrived at his condo. Gail was there waiting, as she'd arrived minutes earlier. Rodney smiled as he met her at the door. "Hey, gorgeous."

Gail smiled. "Hi, my guy." She went to the kitchen to open a bottle of wine she'd brought with her. "I'd guess you had a nice day."

"I did. I was surprised to see Dan at the office first thing this morning."

"Why would that surprise you?"

"He's not himself. Usually when he'd found a new fling, he'd do extraordinary things to impress her. Not coming in on Mondays was his way of extending the fun."

"I don't think he's just having fun with June."

"You and I are suspecting this one is real."

"It is for June. Like I told you before, she's really into Dan."

"I bet there is more happening here. I'm so proud." Rodney moved to the kitchen and took the glass of wine Gail poured. He took a sip and commented on the taste, "Hmm, pretty nice."

"It's another of my favorites."

"The more you show me, the more I like."

Rodney went to his bedroom to change into a more relaxed outfit. Gail followed and watched him as she spoke about her day. "It was kind of strange this morning. I was in my office when Starz called me. I thought it was something important from the tone of his voice. When I got there, he had this manuscript in hand, on a specific page. He handed it to me and directed me to read it. I read it and was so moved."

"You were moved? That had to be some manuscript."

"It was; Patricia was a serious writer. I didn't understand why Starz took so long to read it."

"Will he take it as his own?"

"Starz isn't that way at all. He called Patricia's mother and shared his ideas."

"Wow. That's kind of him."

"You'll learn Starz is really a fair man."

"I respect him already, but he just gained a few brownie points in my book." Rodney continued changing. "Are you going to change clothes?"

"Yes, I'm going to. I was going to ask, what's for dinner?"

"I have dinner covered. Come to the kitchen after you've changed." Rodney left the bedroom for the kitchen. He pulled multiple items from the fridge and cupboard and began his preparation. Rodney chopped, seasoned, and seared as Gail changed into something comfortable. She had a few items at Rodney's place, just as he now had multiple items at hers. They spent so much time together that it became natural to create a comfort in each other's places.

Rodney continued cooking as Gail approached the kitchen. She set the table and poured wine, giving one glass to Rodney as she placed the bottle on the table. "Smells great, Rodney. How long before it's ready?"

"It will just be a few minutes."

"Good. I didn't realize I was so hungry until I smelled the aroma. I'm *really* hungry now."

"A sure way to your heart," Rodney wiped his hands with the dish towel.

"As if you needed an invitation or a compass," Gail said as she moved closer to Rodney, pulling him to her and placing a gentle kiss upon his lips. Rodney finished cooking and prepared their plates. Gail took her seat at the table. They began eating in a contented silence.

"You know, Starz is planning on moving to L.A. as soon as

we've completed this project," Gail said.

"Mm-hmm." Rodney had a mouth full of food.

"I figured I'll wait until everything's set to tell them that I'm going to join your firm."

"Join my firm?"

"I'm giving Starz my notice as soon as we get the campaign initiated. I'm not needed there anymore. Besides, he's moving to California, and I don't think that is a good idea for me to go. Face it, I just found you."

14.
Patricia

A WEEK BEFORE Gail and Rodney's conversation, Sabrina had arrived at her Willingham Corp. office and grabbed her sketchpad. She called and solicited advice from her designer friends that she'd met while modeling. It was breathtaking how a couple of them actually enjoyed her designs without critique. Sabrina felt great receiving validation from reputable professionals.

Later in the day, Sabrina dialed the number for the production company, Network Galaxy. While talking to a company rep, Sabrina learned that the director for *Her Last Hoorah* had Patricia as his assistant and second writer. Happy to learn how involved Patricia had been with the play, Sabrina was sure that collaborating with Patricia's own production would be a perfect partnership. Sabrina dialed the number that the company rep had provided her. "Hi, this is Sabrina Clark. I'm looking for an assistant director of a play you once toured. Her name is Patricia."

"Yes, you mean Patricia Dugan," said the woman on the other end of the line.

"Yes, I believe so, Patricia Dugan. Is she the one who's a

playwright as well?" asked Sabrina. "Recently toured France and Germany?"

"Yes, one in the same. Unfortunately, she's not with us anymore. Is there anything I can help you with?"

"Sure there is. I need to get in contact with Patricia. Can you pass her information to me, please?"

"Let me just take down your information and see what I can do. What did you say your name is?"

"Sabrina Clark. Tell her we were in France together, and I'd like to help sponsor her next play."

"Okay. Can I get your cell phone number, please?"

"Sure." Sabrina smiled as she gave the assistant her contact information. "Make sure you add 'sponsor your next play.'"

"Yes, ma'am."

"Thank you."

Sabrina moved around the table and looked at the walls scattered with her pinned-up prints. *What an accomplishment this morning!* She went back to her desk to refine her list of possible clothing manufacturers. She wanted to make sure she found a manufacturer that was affordable but that still put out quality pieces. Sabrina wanted to show Simone a full presentation to win her trust and confidence. Besides, it was her turn to participate in running their conglomerate, even if it was only a small piece of the business. She couldn't fathom having Willingham Corp. collapse, especially since it had started by a woman with a great heart. Inheriting such large assets and sums of money also came with big responsibilities. Sabrina gathered her new data and headed downtown.

Sheila entered Simone's office. "I've confirmed the attendance of all board members for the meeting."

"Good, very good, Sheila, thanks," Simone said without looking up to respond. She continued scribbling numbers and ideas.

"You're welcome," Sheila said as she returned to her desk. Sheila disregarded Simone's preoccupied behavior and instead noticed her concern and focus. It wasn't Simone's habit to be so distant, but since learning of the company's frozen assets, she'd been clearly worried.

Sabrina approached Simone's office door. "Hey," she said.

Simone heard Sabrina's voice and paused to look up at her. There were papers scattered all over her desk. "Hey, what's up?"

"If I didn't know better, I'd swear you were cramming for an exam."

"I feel like it," Simone said while she went back to writing.

"I was hoping you had a minute to talk." Sabrina walked closer to Simone's desk and handed Simone a copy of her presentation. "You aren't the only one who's been cramming. I'm excited about this. Give me a few minutes, and I'll explain."

"Are you sure it can't wait? I'm trying to get ready for the board and my conversation with Phil."

"Please, sis? Let me distract you for a few minutes. You can add this to the board meeting. Trust me."

"Okay." Simone stopped her writing and looked at the presentation.

"Remember when I told you about my idea? Well, this finalizes it. The numbers are there and our initial investment estimate is included. We can afford this without impacting the company."

"Everything we do impacts the company. There is no space

for mistakes, especially right now. I saw your idea and thought it would work. But this number…" Simone pointed at the very top of the page, "is greater than we can afford. I thought we agreed to an inexpensive project."

"I know it's costly, but it will bring jobs and could help stabilize us. My plan is to have an economical partner for the first round of manufacturing. Later, we can then have our company take on that part. It's worth a try."

"Still, the numbers are greater than I'd like to spend."

"I know, but no gain, no pain. We need to keep building."

"Building, not spending. We can't spend anymore of our money on new investments."

"We only invest in ourselves. I'm willing to take half of my part of the inheritance and worry about the return later." Sabrina reflected on the multiple accomplishments Simone had under her belt. "Come on, sis, you've done a lot and during a challenging time. I bet we can do this."

Simone continued to look through Sabrina's presentation. At first, when Simone saw the numbers, she had wanted to give the presentation right back to Sabrina. However, with sisterly love she continued reading and felt compelled to believe it was possible. *It's a wildcard of a chance, but maybe.* "Okay, let's give it a try. I can run it by the board tomorrow and see if they think it will work."

"What do you mean, 'run it by the board'? I thought you were on my side?"

"I am, but let's be realistic—those numbers are high and we can't afford research and development. Not on the company's money. I can't see where we'll get the money."

"Like I said, I will put some of my own money into this. Plus, I think some of my designer friends were so impressed that they might be willing to invest in my efforts. It will work, and if you think it won't, you're crazy." Sabrina crossed her arms in disgust. It was her motivation to get this project out and give the company a new direction. "I get it; you want me to fight harder."

"I want you to believe in this with everything you have. Even when I saw your idea earlier and liked the clothes, I didn't think you'd come up with a real plan."

"I have a plan."

"A costly plan; yes, you've done well. Now I don't have the budget. If you use your money for the upfront cost before investors, we can do it."

"What about the company's money? You're not going to invest in this at all?"

"I'm not so sure."

"That burns me."

"How do you think we've gotten this far with the business? I put my money into it earlier while you were with James. It's how we got here."

"So, this is your company?"

"No, that's not what I'm saying. I took a chance on it and made it to this point. I used my inheritance and never asked for your assistance. I think if you really want this, you'll fund it. Even if you want investors, you'll contribute more. It's yours, and when I see it moving, you have my support. But right now, it's a dream we can't afford on company dollars."

"I see, business-sister-CEO, I see." Sabrina took the presentation board to her office, placed it on her desk, and left the building. She went to a tapas bar to unwind and thought of her conversation with Simone.

She's right. Like all things when we were kids, she's right about my investing. My modeling career took time and work, and so will this. I get it. I'll invest in myself, that's her message.

Simone had her assistant retrieve Sabrina's presentation and reviewed it further. As Simone played with numbers, she began to reconsider Sabrina's proposal. With the current state of the company, it might not be a bad idea to start fresh with some new business goals. Still, they needed funding in order to meet Sabrina's estimated budget. *Maybe I was a bit hasty. If we can generate interested investors, it may work. No, I'm sure it will. My genius little sister.* She continued computing and segmented the cost into a chart. Later, she compared her projections with Sabrina's and saw a remarkable recovery effort. *It's all here. If we can find investors, we're in. It's exactly what the company needs to stay afloat.*

Simone packed up her belongings and finally headed home.

Morning came, and like the close sisters they were, there was no residual animosity between them from their disagreement the day before. They met in the kitchen for coffee and breakfast, just as they did any other morning.

"Hey," Simone said.

"Morning. What time did you get in?"

"It was nearly eleven."

"Did you go anywhere after leaving the office?"

"No, it was all work and no play. I reworked your plan, and if we can find funding, it fits perfectly. We can get back to standard operating levels in six months."

"Are you serious?"

"Yes. I'm serious. If we get enough investors, it will save you from using your money."

"No, I'm using my money."

"What?"

"I'm using my money. I thought about it, and you're right. I had to work hard and make sacrifices to be a model, and this is no different. I never thought I would fulfill my dream as a designer. Now, I have the money, and I'm using every penny."

"Let's not get crazy, not every penny is needed. But I get it."

"I'm glad you do. Where do we start?"

"Well, first thing this morning I have to meet with Phil. I have a meeting with him at ten o'clock. Can you make it? It might be a good idea to fill him in on your plans so he will be aware of the upcoming paperwork."

"I'll come. I think it's a good idea for me to make this meeting."

Both left the kitchen and headed to finish preparing for the day. It was 9:00 a.m. when they emerged from the front door. "One car?" Sabrina asked while exiting the house.

"Yes, why not?" Simone said in agreement as she locked the door.

"Great, let's take mine."

"That old thing? It's been in the garage forever."

"I drove it yesterday and it runs. I don't mind."

"Of course you don't, it's your car. Why don't you get another one?"

"Because I have money to invest in bigger things." Sabrina opened the passenger door and gestured for Simone to get in. Simone entered the car and secured her seat belt. *I pray we make it on time*, Simone thought as she settled in.

The sisters arrived fifteen minutes early to Phil's office. They waited for him in the lobby and had coffee and tea. After ten minutes, Phil arrived. "Hi, Simone, Sabrina," he said.

"Hi, Phil," the women said in unison.

"Right on time. Your aunt taught you well." Phil smiled. "It's nice seeing you both. It's been a while, Sabrina. Welcome back from Europe."

"I actually left Africa to come here."

"How was it?" Phil asked as he led them to his office.

"It was very nice. But not as nice as being home."

"It's good she's here," Simone said. "Let me get to the chase. We wanted to meet for two reasons. One is to find loopholes in accessing the company's frozen assets."

"Yes, I heard about your recent misfortunes. When you called for an appointment, I had my staff research your options. Unfortunately, there's nothing we can do to get the assets back right away. The only thing we can do is finalize your divorce so you can testify against him when needed."

"Bad and good news in one statement, let's get the divorce going then."

"Will do. Now the second point you wanted to discuss?"

"Well, I have an idea to help save the company," Sabrina said. "Since the assets are frozen, and we need a new venture, I designed a clothing line. I know with the right marketing it can take off."

"I looked at the numbers and all we need is a little help," Simone said.

"You mean you need money, an investment for this clothing line."

"Yes," Simone said, "if we find investors, I was hoping you could draw up the contracts."

"I can do you one better," Phil said. He leaned forward. "Given the prior success of Willingham Corp. since you've taken over as CEO, I'm certain that this is a good business decision. Your family's money helped get my law firm off the ground when I needed investors, and it would be my pleasure to return the favor."

"You mean you want to invest in my idea?" Sabrina asked.

"Yes, that's exactly what I mean."

"Thank you so much, Phil," Simone said as she stood from her chair, reaching to shake Phil's hand. Sabrina smiled and moved behind the desk to hug Phil just as he let go of Simone's hand. "Thank you," she whispered with a tear on her face. Sabrina then moved near the office door and waited for Simone to exit.

"We'll work out the logistics. Any advice on the new business effort?" Simone asked as she walked closer to the door.

"I'll have more ideas once you send me your business plans. I know we shouldn't make another subsidiary of the company. If you want to save the company, you'll have to make it one of the major products. Legally, it shows a rebirth and doesn't have to cross any red tape or cause major adjustments."

"Good," Simone said. "Thanks again and I'm glad you're on board."

"Me too," Phil said as he ushered them to the door. "You two have a great day."

Sabrina worked diligently to refine her plan. She recruited staff members to support her effort that Simone would have otherwise had to lay off. Sabrina assigned one person the task of finding Patricia Dugan, and also created a marketing group and asked for their ideas. At the end of the day,

Sabrina felt confident that her vision would work. With Phil and Simone's help and guidance, she knew it would be a win for the company and herself. She felt proud to focus on a new endeavor without James' involvement. It was one more step in achieving emotional independence from her estranged husband.

The next day, it was time for the board meeting. Board members arrived as scheduled and gathered at the large conference room on the executive floor. Simone packaged her discussion kits with attention to detail and orchestrated her slide presentation. She'd perfected boardroom etiquettes during her reign as chief executive. It was her steadfast ability to adapt and her stern love of the business that got her involved in Aunt Marge's company. She was proud of how far she'd come with the help of the board she'd created. Their multiple talents and input aided her in making profitable decisions and creating positive results. A successful story until now, but she had to share the horrible news with the group and seek advice.

The board members took their seats for the meeting. Simone stood at the white screen against the wall. "Welcome everyone," Simone said. "Thank you for attending this emergency meeting. As you may have heard, there was a huge investigation with the company. The findings were embezzlement and money laundering by a major player in our corporation. He's been removed from the business, but the impact is great. If you turn to the first page of your booklet, you'll see the findings." The slide projected on the whiteboard with the same information. Simone pointed to the chart. "Sixty percent of the company assets are frozen until the investigation is complete. The risk is never recovering those assets, or receiving them years from today. With such a risk, I devised a plan and need your input."

Simone continued to speak to the group and explained her ideas. The board discussed every aspect of the presentation. Just as Simone suspected, she dealt with anger from the members. So many of them had invested in the business and expected a secure return. The board then agreed to explore the effort to take on new ventures. Simone sprung into action, selling Sabrina's idea. It was going well until finance came into question.

"With money and assets frozen at 60 percent, how in the world are you going to pay for this new product?" one member asked.

"We have new investors. The best thing is, we'd be gaining revenue to return a profit in a reasonable amount of time," Simone said.

"Does that mean we'll receive buyout payments with this investor?"

"No buyouts are on the table. I hope you folks hang in there with me while I rebuild the business."

"Rebuild the business. It's going to be quite challenging."

"No different than we've done before."

"But before, your hands weren't tied with the government holding your assets. Will they touch any new development from this company?"

"I have my lawyer looking into it, but so far the answer is no." Simone stood in silence waiting for another comment or question. She scanned the room as many of the members spoke amongst themselves. After a few minutes, Simone asked, "Do I have your buy-in?"

"With reservation, you have ninety days to have the first

line up and running. If there isn't any return after six months, we'll pull our money from the 40 percent and expect full payment by the end of the year."

"Six months? I don't think that's long enough. Can we double the time?"

"Not even an idea at this point. Six months is what the board agrees. If I were you, I'd get moving, as the time is non-negotiable."

Sabrina's team member who searched for Patricia approached her with bad news. "Patricia is no longer available. She died six months ago."

Sabrina gasped. "Oh my gosh, that's terrible! Do you know what happened?"

"The woman I spoke with said she didn't know Patricia well but did know that she'd died from an eating disorder. Bulimia."

Simone recalled Patricia's stellar appetite despite her taut figure. Being a model, Sabrina was accustomed to conversing with thin people, but she was surprised that she hadn't considered the thought that Patricia might have a problem. She recalled Patricia's trip—alone—to the bathroom after the dinner they'd had the night Sabrina went to see *Her Last Hoorah.* "Wow," Sabrina said while shaking her head, "I wish I had known. Maybe I could have helped."

"It's unfortunate, but I do have some good news to go with the bad, actually."

"Good news?"

"The good news is: Starzinsky remembered you and would like to talk with you. He worked closely with Patricia and still possesses her work, and he thought you could provide some input to her last manuscript. He was under the impression you were close to Patricia. I didn't deny it, as I have no idea to your past relationship. Here's his number." The employee passed Sabrina the note.

"Thank you, fine job," Sabrina said as she took the piece of paper.

15.
The Commitments

IT WAS WEEKS into the campaign and all activities were aligned. Stanley impressed Starz with his coordination and his eye for detail. He was a master at grasping and applying techniques in any environment. Working closely with the Network Galaxy team was no different, and Stanley made it his opportunity to shine. He spent extra hours around the Network Galaxy office and seemed to expand his knowledge of the production company's functionality. Stanley loved the arts, he loved marketing, and because he spent so much time at Starz's office, Stanley interjected his ideas for the production when his creativity struck him, and modified the marketing scenes according to the play it depicted.

The marketing effort seemed to be a success; the idea hit a home run with every evaluation group; Starz's response was overwhelming, and he credited Stanley with the achievement. Starz realized that Stanley had not only put his touch on the campaign but had somehow slightly changed the production for the better. Starz felt excited with the work Rodney's firm completed and noticed Stanley's tendency to speak. Since

Stanley had begun working on the project, he rarely visited the marketing firm office. One day, Starz asked his staff to explain the current progress of both the marketing and play productions. Before Gail could answer, Stanley gave an accurate assessment of each. Gail, unsurprised, didn't fight to speak and realized it was her opportunity for an exit strategy.

Meanwhile, Starz followed his intuition for talent and relied on Stanley for information and input on many business decisions. Starz also maintained a connection with Rodney's marketing firm and applauded the project they delivered. As they met the final milestone, Starz reached out to Rodney with a telephone call. "Hey, guy, how are things?" Starz asked Rodney.

"Pretty good. How are you, Starz?" Rodney asked.

"Great. Let me tell you, the campaign is a hit, and I'm ready to put this on the road. Your firm has done it for us. The package, campaign, and people have delivered, just as we agreed. And speaking of people, I'm going to be sad to lose Stanley and his input."

"Stanley is a great guy, and I can understand why you'd miss him. He's a valuable employee."

"Did you know he has a knack for the arts?"

"Not really, but his creativity is partly why we hired him. Okay, Starz, what are you telling me?"

"I'm not telling you anything you don't know about Stanley, but I wanted to share one thing with you. He's a keeper, one guy worth every dime you're spending."

"I'm happy you are pleased. He is a strong part of this firm, so I see it as a reflection of us. I believe he represents the firm and the quality work we deliver."

"Awesome, you guys are awesome. You'll receive payment

today, and I added a bonus for early delivery. I'll remember you guys for my next production." Starz went silent for a moment. "You're okay with me, Rodney. Stay in touch."

"Sure thing, Starz, sure thing. Call us for anything." The two ended the phone call. Rodney wasn't surprised that Starz would compliment a guy like Stanley. Rodney called for his assistant.

While he waited, he recalled his conversation with Gail the night before. *I've certainly enjoyed working with her and she's contributed immensely to the team, but working with someone you're dating is often a challenge.* Rodney paced the room. *She's proven herself in the workplace, but what would that mean for us personally? Will she expect us to move in together next? Wow, what am I getting into?* Rodney moved behind his desk and looked outside as if searching for an answer. *If Gail is my match in life, why not see how it goes each day? This is the test of all tests, either we'll build a great relationship or fail quickly and learn it won't work.*

Rodney's executive assistant walked in his office. "You called?"

"Yes. Can you please have Stanley come in?"

"Sure thing," the assistant said and left the office.

Rodney called Gail's cell phone. She answered, "Hey, how are you?"

"Hi, I'm good. We need to talk," Rodney said.

"I agree. Where should I meet you?"

"How about this evening, at the office?"

"I have a better idea, why not at home? That way we don't have to leave, and I can fix dinner. It's my turn to cook." The phone went silent as Gail waited for an answer. "Are you there?"

"I'm here. Let's get coffee and take a walk in the park. I'd like to show you something."

"I guess so. Are you okay?"

"I'm fine. Meet me at Maymont Park at six o'clock this evening. I'll be waiting."

"I'll be there."

Rodney ended the call without his usual sweet words. Gail knew something was up. *He is never that short in conversation unless someone interrupts him. But I heard nothing in the background. It's only a conversation, why should I worry? Knowing the type of guy Rodney is there has to be a surprise.* With that thought, Gail's outlook changed from doubt to excitement for the evening.

There were two knocks on Rodney's office door. "Come on in," Rodney said.

Stanley entered. "You wanted to see me?"

"Yes, please have a seat." Rodney walked to take a seat in a comfortable chair near Stanley. "You did a great job for the firm with Starz."

"Thank you. I do my best."

"And you do just that, deliver your best. You did it so well that I think Starz wants to hire you."

Stanley froze for a moment and considered his response. "I think it's great our firm has the quality people that others wish to have in their organization."

"Yes, it's why we hired you. I wanted to tell you personally how proud I have been to have you in my firm. I'm telling you there are no limits for you—shooting to the stars. Thanks for a great job."

"Thank you, Rodney. I guess. I mean, I'm thankful for your acknowledgment. There's nothing like having a boss who looks out for his people."

"I'm sure you'll feel it in your bonus. You make it easy. I've been pleased with our decision to make you a key player on my team."

Stanley rose from his seat. "I appreciate the bonus."

Rodney stood and reached his hand forward. "Again, thanks for your hard work. You'll do well, no doubt." They shook hands and Stanley left the office.

Within minutes of their meeting, Starz reached out to Stanley for dinner plans. Starz wanted Stanley to relocate with his company to California. Starz felt it was the best way to put things in motion, and he made Stanley an offer he couldn't refuse. Starz did nothing halfheartedly—not only did he offer full relocation, a sign-on bonus, and vacation perks, but a paid-for home on the coast. Stanley never thought he'd live near the ocean on his salary. Now, it was a dream come true. At dinner, Stanley made his decision on the spot after hearing the offer. He and his wife were quite happy with the change. The next morning, Stanley gave his two weeks' notice to the marketing firm.

Right after Rodney and Stanley met, Rodney wrote Dan an e-mail explaining his gut feeling about Stanley and what Starz had exclaimed. Within minutes, Dan arrived at Rodney's office door. "I'm not happy about losing Stanley."

"You know it's to our advantage to have one of our own on Starz's team. My gut tells me that Stanley will be our contact for future projects with Starz. You know he's leaving for California. If I'm right, when Starz needs a marketing firm, we're going to be his right hand. No questions asked, because Stanley has loyalty."

"I hope you're right."

"I am."

"I'm going to congratulate him on a job well done."

"Do that and we'll talk later."

Dan left the office and had a long conversation with Stanley about his stellar performance.

It was 5:55 p.m. when Rodney arrived at the park. He looked around for Gail and remembered that he hadn't told her exactly where to meet. He called her.

She answered after one ring. "Hi, I'm here."

"Hey, where is 'here'? I'm near the pavilion."

"I see you. Turn around," she said and ended the call.

"Why didn't you just call me?"

"I wanted to see how long it took you to look for me."

"All right." Rodney smiled and grabbed her hand. "Let's walk."

They took off for a stroll around the park. Rodney didn't say much at first. He recalled how much the park had changed as he'd grown up. "This is where it began. I rode my bike as a child over there," he said as he pointed. "It's now a street. I have fond memories of this park."

"Is this why you had me meet you in the park?"

"No, but aren't you enjoying our stroll?"

"Yes, I am, but something is on your mind. Tell me what it is."

"That's what I like about you. No fluff, get to the point. Okay, I'll do that. Starz called me today and asked about Stanley. How long did you know he wanted Stanley?"

Gail pondered. "Last week at the end of the meeting he asked me if I'd relocate to California. I told him no, so you may be onto something. Starz likes Stanley, as he reminds Starz of Patricia's enthusiasm, and he'll need someone to take my place. It makes perfect sense."

"Did you resign from your job?"

"Not yet, but he knows I'm not moving."

"Okay, since you aren't moving, you'll need a job. I feel as if I have to put you on my payroll in order for us to stay together."

Gail stopped Rodney in his step and faced him. "You don't have to hire me to be with you. I'm a big girl and can find a different job. I don't want you to make the assumption that I'm to be taken care of. But, with that said, I do think we can work well together. You know I carry my own weight, and I know business."

"You don't have to sell yourself to me. It's why I wanted to talk to you tonight. Out here where there is no chance of a different influence." Rodney hesitated in his next comment. "I, ah, um…" He coughed.

"Rodney what are you saying?"

"I want you to work with me."

"I can do that, but I thought we'd already decided that, unspoken but understood. At least I thought so."

"Well, unspoken yes, but I needed it out in the open. I know we have these feelings for each other, but I have a concern."

"Concern?" Gail looked down and then looked at him in a flash. "Concern about…me being too close to you all the time?"

"Sort of," Rodney said as he grabbed her hand again and started walking, guiding her along. "I'm worried about being together day after day in two capacities. I mean, home and office; don't you think it's a little much for the two of us?"

"Rodney, people do it all the time. Are you afraid of being with me?"

"No, just setting parameters, keeping our office and personal lives separate."

"Okay, so you're worried you won't be able to separate our relationship with business because you love me so much."

"What? I knew you'd slip in the emotion talk, Gail."

"It's true or we wouldn't have this conversation."

"Right, right, you're right. I love you. I mean, on one hand I'd be happy to have you work with us, but on the other hand I'm not sure if it'll work unless we set parameters."

"Since you put it that way…" Gail smiled and moved closer to Rodney, "I'm listening."

Rodney explained his ideas about how they should work together and he promised no favoritism. Gail listened to Rodney and realized how secure he was in his business. Her decision was to go along with every rule Rodney laid out in his conversation. She was happy because he'd professed his love and will to be together. Nothing could ruin the moment, not one thing.

A few months passed and Gail integrated well into the marketing firm. One day, Dan and June walked into Gail's office. June smiled as she approached Gail and pushed her left hand forward. "Isn't it beautiful?" she asked Gail.

"Wow, Oh my GOODNESS!" Gail covered her mouth in surprise after shouting and moved to hug June.

"Yes, it's what you think!" June said with her arms open wide.

"When is the day?"

"We think it's soon, and I want to know what's on your calendar."

"Soon?" Gail moved around her desk and looked at her

desk calendar. "Well, you know I'll clear anything I have planned for my best friend's wedding!"

"I'll give you ladies some time to chat." Dan smiled and walked to Rodney's office. Upon approach, Dan spoke to the executive assistant and asked, "Is he busy?"

"He may be, but he's not in a meeting, and there's nothing on his calendar."

"Good," Dan said as he opened Rodney's door. "Hey, dude."

Rodney looked up. "Hey, man, what's up?"

"June and I are engaged." Dan smiled as he stood next to Rodney's desk.

Rodney rose from his desk and reached for Dan's hand in a congratulatory manner. He patted his best friend on the back and then pulled him in for a hug. "I'm happy for you. I told you she was the one."

Dan reciprocated and then stepped back. "That you did. It happened last night."

"You didn't tell me about your plans! I thought you'd let me know before you did it."

"I didn't know myself, but I purchased a ring before I had even made up my mind on when I was going to propose. It just so happened I popped the question after dinner."

"Smooth, I bet."

"Not really, but I guess she'll remember."

"As if any woman forgets when they're asked to marry." Rodney looked around the office. "Why aren't you two spreading the news together?"

"She's in Gail's office. I wanted to tell you alone."

"Okay, well, let's go get the soon-to-be bride."

"Wait—I wanted to ask you something. I'd love for you to be my best man at the wedding."

"I wouldn't have it any other way, Dan. I wouldn't have it any other way."

After Dan had left Gail's office, June had closed the door. "I'm in a hurry to get this wedding over," she said.

"Dan loves you, and he's not backing out."

"Not because of that. I know he's not backing out. He does love me."

"Then why do you want to rush? You can have a nice wedding if you give it time."

"I'm okay with a simple wedding, but we need to get things moving."

"Excited, are you?"

"No, well, yes, but that isn't the reason why." June smiled and Gail finally caught on.

"No! You *aren't*."

"Yes, I am! I took the test yesterday, and he doesn't know."

"You mean he asked you without knowing you're pregnant?"

"What timing, huh? I'm not going to share it with him until later, I'm worried he won't want to get married right away anymore when he finds out."

"Come on, Dan is a great guy. He'll be fine with the news."

"What news?" Dan asked as he and Rodney entered the office.

June looked up in alarm. "We set a date and wanted you two to agree."

"When are we talking, maybe in a few months?"

"I'm thinking two weeks."

"Two weeks?"

Rodney raised his eyebrows. "That's fast, really fast."

"Don't you think we can have a better wedding if we planned it for at least a month out?" asked Dan.

"Yes, we would have a lovely wedding if we planned it out that far. But why?"

"Who's the wedding for? Isn't it for you two?" Gail said in support of June's effort.

"Yes, it's for us, but I'd like my family and friends to be there."

"How about a nice cozy wedding and a romantic reception?" June moved closer to her fiancé to influence his response.

Dan pondered. "Hmmm, I can buy that. What do you think, best man?"

"You know I'm with your decision," Rodney said.

"I think it's a perfect plan." Gail put her arm around June's shoulders. "Then we're set for two weeks?"

"I think so," Dan said. "That is, if June really wants a cozy wedding."

June nodded with enthusiasm. "I want cozy."

"This is cause for a celebration; why don't we celebrate your engagement tonight?"

"I'm game," Gail said. "Let's do something."

"We'll do that, but right now we're off to get the license," Dan said as he grabbed June's hand. "Since we're saying in two weeks, we need to get things going. I'll—um, we'll catch you two later."

The wedding was a hit with nearly twenty close friends, a few relatives, and anyone available from the firm in attendance. It was a wedding that most women would love having. Dan felt accomplished in his new role as a husband. At the reception, he jumped at the opportunity to toast to his bride. He raised his glass of champagne and looked into June's eyes, "You are the gift I've waited to receive my entire life. I'm so grateful we met and that you shared your heart with me. I know I've done the right thing in my life, taking you as my wife."

Everyone cheered, and the two kissed. As they sat down, Dan pulled the champagne bottle from the bucket of ice and started to pour June a glass. June stopped him short and whispered, "I can't have it. I want to toast to us, but I can't have it."

"Baby, you've lost the weight you wanted, so why not drink a little bit of champagne with me?"

"I'm okay without it. Just let me drink the juice. No one has to know."

"All right, if you insist." Dan continued celebrating their wedding. They danced at the party and did the traditional cake cutting, dinner, and toasts throughout the night. It was a successful event. When they arrived at their hotel suite, Dan took her to the master bedroom. He kissed her, but before he could lay June comfortably on the bed, she jumped to get out of his arms and ran into the bathroom. She lurched towards the toilet and made a gurgling sound.

Dan, shocked at hearing it, rushed to her and rubbed her back. "Are you okay?"

"I'm going to be fine."

"It's okay, this is our first time being together married. I'm nervous too."

"No, Dan, it's not because of the wedding. I'm not nervous about being married to you. That is a dream, finding you is my dream come true."

"Then I guess everything we had tonight must have hit you pretty hard. Why don't we get you in bed and you can relax. I'll see if I can find some ginger ale for your stomach."

"No, Dan, that isn't it either."

Dan looked at June. "Then what do you think is the matter? I can't think of any reason…" His eyes widened. "OH MY GOD! You're…?"

"Yes *we* are pregnant." June smiled and wiped her forehead.

Dan was shocked to learn his marriage was already a family in the making. Then, he realized he was having a baby with the love of his life. He jumped from June's side. "Wow! We're expecting."

"I think we're almost six weeks along."

"You don't know for sure how long?'

"I called the doctor, and she said to come in to find out."

"How did you hide it for so long?" Dan asked.

"Because you leave earlier than I most mornings, so you haven't seen me get sick. I only started getting sick recently. It's been a couple weeks, just after we announced our engagement."

"You kept it secret. Why?"

"In case I was just late and not pregnant. I didn't want a false alarm, and then when you asked me to marry you, I didn't want to add a reason for it outside of love."

"I'm happy," Dan said as he lifted June from the floor in front of the toilet. "I'm happy, but I'm not kissing you right now." He laughed.

"Don't worry, I wouldn't either." June laughed with him.

16.
Fingers Crossed

SABRINA CALLED THE NUMBER she took from her clerk. She was curious about Starz's intentions for the future of Patricia's manuscripts, but also wanted to speak with him about her ideas. She realized that as the CEO of a major production company, he was the key to getting her designs on stage. Patricia had mentioned Starz, but not enough for Sabrina to know much about him. Sabrina waited as the phone rang.

"Thank you for calling Network Galaxy. May I help you?" answered the receptionist.

"Yes," Sabrina said. "Starz, please?"

"May I ask who is calling?"

"Sure, tell him it's Sabrina, a friend of Patricia's."

"Please hold."

Sabrina held the phone and wrote a few points to mention on a pad. She wanted to ensure her comments to Starz included her ideas. She felt more confident in her plan after her first pitch to Simone, and hoped her conversation with Starz would be just as effective. When he answered, it caught Sabrina by surprise. "Hi, Sabrina, this is Starz, how are you?" he asked.

"I'm doing well, thanks for asking. How are you?"

"Good. The reason I wanted to chat is I heard you were a friend of Patricia's."

"Yes, we met during one of my photo shoots in France. I'm sorry; she was a very nice woman."

"And a dynamic writer. Have you read her last play?"

Sabrina hesitated a moment before answering. "No, but she told me she had some great ideas. I was thinking we could incorporate my idea of an interactive fashion show…" Sabrina paused and then continued, "by incorporating my designs into a production."

"I can see where it may fit into Patricia's repertoire."

Sabrina interjected, worried that she'd lose her chance. "It's why I searched for her. She inspired me with her ideas, so I designed a clothing line to support her play. I originally called to present the fashion line, presentation, and see what she thought. Too bad I missed the opportunity."

"Hmmm." Starz went silent for a moment.

Sabrina held her breath, nervously waiting for a response.

"Well, an opportunity may still exist," Starz said. "Patricia entrusted me with her work when she passed, and after reading it I was so impressed that I've been contemplating using it for my next production. I'm happy to hear from you and would love to discuss your ideas in person. When can you come to L.A.?"

Sabrina held her smile. "I can get there as early as two days from now. When is best for you?"

"I'll have my assistant contact you with my schedule. I think we may have something, even though Patricia didn't quite include your idea. I can see where it would coincide with one of her manuscripts."

Sabrina again fell silent, holding her excitement. "I'll be there, just tell me when."

"Good, my assistant will call you." Starz ended the call and sent for his assistant. He informed the assistant to coordinate a meeting with Sabrina the coming week. Starz thought more about Sabrina's idea, and it was hitting home. The more he thought, the greater he envisioned it. *That Patricia was brilliant; and what are the chances, having Sabrina Clark call me about Patricia's play? A fashion show and stage play all in one. Never happened, but wow, I can see this being huge.*

Sabrina smiled from ear to ear, left her office, and sprinted right into Simone's. "Hey, you're not going to believe this. I just spoke to a big-time producer, playwright. He wants to meet and discuss my ideas."

Simone looked up. "What?"

"Yes, he wants to talk and see my sketches. He's in California and his assistant should call me. Dang, I didn't leave any information for the assistant to get in contact with me. I better call him right now." Sabrina started walking towards the office door when Simone asked, "Who's the producer?"

"Starzinsky!" she said and scurried to her office. Simone recognized the name as a producer who she'd known to be based in Richmond, but she realized she didn't know much about his company. She took a moment to research him online and was impressed with her findings. She learned that Starz's production company had grown so much that he'd moved his main base to Los Angeles. Her excitement grew at the thought of Starz's potential involvement. *Oh my,* Simone thought as she continued reading. She realized Starz's reputation might have a positive impact on the board of directors. *Hopefully, if*

Sabrina lands the deal, the board might give an extension on the turnaround deadline. Simone scrambled for Sabrina's office, hoping to discuss her travel plans to California. Simone arrived at the office door as Sabrina was ending her call. "I'm in." Sabrina smiled.

"You have a date?"

"Yes, I'm there. Woo-hoo!" Sabrina jumped up from her chair. "You didn't want to go, did you?"

"No, this is your puppy. But, before you leave, we need to get you prepared. I know it's your idea, your clothing design, and you did all the legwork, but it's the company's livelihood and the money we inherited that's on the line. You have to nail this, or we're in the ditch."

"No worries."

"Worry." Simone frowned. "I know you. Don't take this lightly, or we'll be out."

"Listen, I know how important this is. I'm not that college kid who would run to Aunt Marge for help anymore. Nor am I that silly sister on safari with a deadbeat husband. I'm ready to make my mark."

Simone moved closer to Sabrina and touched her shoulder. "I know you understand, and forgive me if I'm nervous. There's just a lot at stake here, and I want to show the board they made a good decision in their investment in us. I know you can do this, sis."

Starz walked around the office as if waiting for an answer. It was his ritual before making a decision, especially one with a costly impact. He recalled his business lessons from earlier shows and assessed the profitability of this new idea. He regretted that Patricia wasn't there to see her play come to light, and he wished she was there to strategize with. Remembering Stanley's creativity, Starz asked his assistant to call Stanley. In minutes, he arrived. "Hi, boss, you called?" Stanley asked.

"Yes, have a seat. I want you in on this meeting with a lady who knew Patricia. She is coming in from Richmond. Do you know Sabrina Clark?"

"No, but I wasn't really a socialite either. I can find out about her if you'd like though."

"Naw, that isn't my point. I just wanted a little more information before she arrived. I was under the impression she and Patricia were close, but my phone call with Sabrina leads me to believe she didn't know about Patricia's last manuscripts. I think she may be just meeting us in hopes that we'll review her idea for a new production."

"Why did you think she'd read Patricia's work?"

"Maybe you should read this. There are holes in her story requiring an explanation, and I'm thinking Sabrina could help with that." Starz passed the manuscript to Stanley.

"I'll read it right away."

"Good. Meanwhile, get the date for the meeting with Sabrina from my assistant and make sure you're available. I'll need a second opinion."

"I'll be there," Stanley said as he rose to leave. He walked towards the door and before leaving said, "Starz, thanks for the chance."

Starz didn't look up from his desk. "You're welcome."

Sabrina and Simone worked all week on the presentation; Sabrina rehearsed her delivery and continued to revise her clothing line after consultations with fellow designers. The night before Sabrina's flight, Simone coordinated a good-luck gathering; she invited their closest circle of friends and business associates.

Phil bestowed his investment check to Sabrina, as a gesture of confidence and positive wishes for her journey. Sabrina circulated the room and shared her plans with members of the board. Recognizing her potential for success, the board agreed to an extended delivery time and continued support, contingent upon Starz's involvement.

After the party, Sabrina retreated to her room at Simone's and considered the added pressure for her success. *I have got to make this work. It's up to me; this is bigger than having a great shoot, this is greater than anything I've done.* "Aunt Marge, are you there?" Sabrina whispered. "If you are, please tell me things are going to be okay. I'm so scared for tomorrow. I know I can do this, but it's just so important. Practice just isn't enough, and when you were here, this would be nothing. I mean, every time I doubted myself you gave me confidence. Aunt Marge, I need your vote of confidence." Sabrina held her head with her hands while lying on her bed. With her eyes closed and hands covering her eyelids, she felt complete darkness, and silence filled the room. She remembered Aunt Marge's voice and serene image: *Things are going to be fine. You go out there and break a leg. Isn't that what they say to models?* Remembering how Aunt Marge would laugh, tears fell upon Sabrina's face.

The chauffer opened the passenger door for Sabrina to exit. "Ms. Clark, they're waiting for you right up those stairs. I'll be here waiting for you. I was instructed to take you to your hotel after your meeting, so I'll be outside when you're ready."

"Great, thank you," Sabrina said as she exited the limo. Still a little anxious, she walked briskly into the Network Galaxy building. Starz's assistant met Sabrina as she walked in. "Hi, Ms. Clark, how was your flight?"

"Call me Sabrina, please. The flight was nice, very nice. I didn't expect such VIP treatment."

"Starz insists that we put our best foot forward for visitors."

"That you did, and I appreciate the limo too. It made all the difference."

"We'd hoped it would. Please come this way."

Sabrina followed and observed the building's décor along the way. There were paintings on the walls, and production posters, including posters of shows she recognized. They reminded her of Starz's esteem, and she felt her stomach jump to her chest at the thought of the magnitude of this meeting. *We'll have a poster right along those walls*, Sabrina assured herself as she continued to follow the assistant. Just as the two arrived at the conference room, Sabrina paused. "Is there a restroom and somewhere that I could get a coffee or hot tea?"

"Sure. Just go down the hall on your left and there you'll find the ladies' room. I'll be glad to bring you a hot tea. Would you like honey and lemon with it?"

"No lemon, but honey would be great, thanks. Will Starz join us in a few minutes?"

"He's inside waiting for you."

"Oh, he is?"

"Yes, you'll learn Starz is a very prompt person, he likes being early to most meetings."

"Oh, I see. I need to set things up. Is there an overhead projector available?"

"This is a state-of-the-art facility. Everything is in the room. All you have to do is plug in your flash drive or insert your CD if you have one. If not, I can help you with your handouts and project it on the overhead."

"I have a disc, thank you."

"No problem, I can get the disc ready while you visit the ladies' room if you'd like."

"Great." Sabrina retrieved the disc, handed it to the assistant, and then headed to the restroom. As she washed her hands, she looked at herself in the mirror above the sinks. *I'm ready, I'm going to knock the socks off Starz*. She smoothed down some flyaway hairs and dabbed on some lip color. *Showtime.*

Sabrina entered the conference room and counted four people in attendance. Starz sat at the head of the table. When Sabrina entered, he stood. "I gather you're Ms. Clark, how nice meeting you. I'm Starz." He offered his hand in greeting.

Sabrina took his hand. "Yes, please call me Sabrina. Nice meeting you."

Starz introduced the rest of the attendees. "This is Stanley, Mike, and Elaine." Each member raised their hands and greeted Sabrina with a hello.

"It's nice to meet all of you," Sabrina said. "If you don't mind, I'd love to get started." She moved around near the wall projection and in an instant distributed a leaflet of her presentation to everyone. "You can follow me with your handout. Please feel free to ask questions at any time."

Before she could begin her presentation, Starz asked, "How well did you know Patricia?"

Sabrina paused before responding. "I'll be honest, not very well. We only met on a few occasions. I saw *Her Last Hoorah* and was impressed. After the play, she and I shared a dinner together and met once or twice after that. We were only acquaintances, but we seemed to click."

"Good answer. I'm glad you are an honest woman."

Sabrina took a mental sigh of relief. "Yes, honesty is my policy."

"How long did you walk the catwalk before getting married to the photographer?" Starz asked.

Sabrina balked at Starz's mention of James. She didn't remember telling Starz anything about her marriage. Finally, she said, "I'm not sure where you're going with the questioning?"

"My team and I would like to know who we're dealing with before moving forward. We did a little research on you, and the company your sister developed. We know about the investigations and your brother-in-law's dealings with the mob. I'm trying to avoid as much of that as possible."

"Then why did you invite me to come out? I guess you could have cancelled this if you thought there is a threat to your business."

"Yes, I could have, but I wanted to see what you knew of Patricia's work. And since you haven't much information, I'm not sure why we should continue." Starz rose in an effort to vacate the conference room.

Sabrina had to think quickly; she wanted this to work and knew that so many others were depending on her to get the deal. "Sir, please give me a chance. Patricia and I may not have known each other long, but I believe we would have produced something great together if we'd had the chance. I told her about my life, my modeling career, and she expressed a sincere interest in working with me for her next play. I know she's gone now, but if you want to follow Patricia's wishes, you will at least hear what I have to say."

Starz turned. "And you said you hadn't read her last manuscript?"

Sabrina was confused. "No, I already told you, I haven't.

But we talked for hours, and it's why I tried to find her. I figured out a way to enhance her work. This is why I'm here. I'll bring a piece of realism to the show, something never seen in theatre." Sabrina clicked the remote and the first slide appeared.

She then explained as rehearsed, "The benefit of combining the play with an actual fashion show is that we can entertain an audience while also creating an avenue for further revenue. This concept is audience-centric and unlike most fashion shows. Why? Because it allows people to see the clothes in action, how they'd relate to real-life events. The concept is to showcase all sizes and shapes, so the common person can purchase the pieces. This interactive concept enhances audience experience, especially when combined with a stellar play. Purchases are taken during intermission and after each show." Sabrina paused and looked in Starz's direction. She was delighted to find that he was sitting back down.

She changed slides and continued. "Here are sales estimates," she said and pointed to the screen. "Based on your normal city tour, the probabilities are in line with industry trends." Sabrina paused and waited for any response from Starz or those in attendance, and then switched slides again. "Here is the actual product, which are my designs. I believe they will collaborate well with Patricia's aesthetic. It's a partnership in sales, a collaboration in style, and capitalizes on the idea of spontaneous purchase. We can draw up a distribution deal with retail as well, and we'll surely capture every corner of America." Sabrina took a deep breath. "Do you have any questions?"

"I have a question," Stanley said. "How do you know the play will successfully integrate your designs?"

"As I mentioned, I think Patricia and I have, um—had, similar style. Plus, my line is meant for everyday wear, so it would fit with any modern script. Instead of costumes, I'd encourage use of my designs."

"I can see the potential," Mike said and Elaine agreed by nodding her head.

Sabrina nodded. "It's sure to be a hit with our partnership. The key is to have two strong products—a quality play *and* great clothes. The biggest challenge I anticipate is the marketing. I have the contacts for market distribution, but we're going to need a top-notch marketing team to promote this new concept. Starz, this is where I need your help or specialty. I mean, aside from producing the play."

Starz waited to respond. He looked around the room and noted his team's approval of Sabrina's presentation. "I think I know of a marketing team that will be able to handle this project well. My question is: are you available to be deeply involved in every aspect of this project? If we go through with this, you need to be involved in everything—your line, the play, and the marketing scheme. Is that something you can commit to?"

"I'm available, and I'd love giving my input to the play."

"I mean the entire campaign. You have to be involved with every aspect of this project." Starz insisted in her availability. He knew Sabrina's participation would be vital for the play he had in mind.

"I'll be here and do whatever it takes to make this a great partnership."

"Well then, I think we can do this. Thank you, Ms. Clark; I'm sorry, ah, Sabrina." Starz smiled and stood. "We can work out the details later. Stanley will be your point of contact. Have your folks send the contract, and we'll look over it. If the numbers are okay, I'm sure we have a deal." Starz extended his hand as he approached Sabrina.

Sabrina's eyes widened and a smile spread across her face. She worked to retain her composure. "Thank you," she said as she took his hand in agreement.

"What are you doing tonight? You aren't leaving right away, are you?" Starz asked.

"No, I'm not leaving until tomorrow, but I have no plans."

Starz winked at his assistant and said, "Make it the usual, around seven o'clock."

"Will do, boss," she said.

The others stood and complimented Sabrina on a fantastic presentation. "We think you'll do well working with us. We like the clothes," Mike said as he moved toward the door.

Elaine pointed to one of Sabrina's designs. "I could see myself wearing this to a nice dinner."

"I can understand why. The line is practical and the best thing is it's inexpensive—not like most fashion show items. I wanted this to be everyday, anytime wear."

"I'm sure it will be easy to market. I think Starz and I already have the firm in mind," Stanley added as the three finally exited the room. Starz's assistant explained to Sabrina that a car would pick her up at her hotel before dinner. "Oh, and just a tip, Starz likes to make deals in both casual and business environments, so be ready to make a gentleman's agreement," she said.

"I guess I should say thanks for the warning."

The assistant returned the presentation disc to Sabrina and escorted her to the waiting limo. "Thank you, you are so kind. I appreciate your assistance," Sabrina said. She walked to the opened car door and took a seat inside. Sabrina took her cell phone and dialed Simone.

"Hey, how did it go?" Simone asked as she answered her cell.

"Like a charm. It was kind of interesting though—Starz knows all about the investigation, Stefan's causing it, and even about my marriage to James. I didn't know we were national news."

"We aren't, but remember, he's a successful guy. So be honest with him about everything. You stretch the truth and you're out."

"Don't you think it's a little late for that advice? I *was* honest, and that's why he didn't walk away. We have him interested. He shook my hand and said if the numbers are right, he's in."

"Oh, that is wonderful, Sabrina. Wonderful news! Are you going to fly out tomorrow morning?"

"Yes, but I didn't tell you about tonight. I have no idea where we're going, but Starz wants a dinner meeting."

"Damn, a dinner meeting can be dangerous. I didn't prepare you for that. It's going to be tricky, because even though it's a 'friendly' meeting, business is still on the table. So here's what you do…" Simone started explaining the different conversations usually spoken during dinner. She explained that dinner meetings were often a showdown of wit and skill, a decisive chess game. "Do not make any promises you know we can't keep. I don't care how good it sounds; always say you'll get back to him after the drinks wear off."

Sabrina took in every word and recorded the information to her memory. The car stopped and she finished her call, "I'll keep you abreast, sis, just keep the faith."

Sabrina stepped out of the car to a lovely five-star hotel that overlooked the ocean and was shadowed by Hollywood hills. *Wow, now this is the life.* Sabrina maneuvered to the front doors. "Everything is set, Ms. Clark," the chauffer said. "I'll come for you around six o'clock."

"Thank you so much. I'll be here in the lobby." Sabrina checked in and made it to her room. The room was nothing fancier than she'd experienced before, but this time there was no James and no other models walking around her suite. It was purely her own. Sabrina made herself comfortable and took a nap.

17.
More Than a Show

IT WAS 4:00 P.M. when Sabrina rose from her slumber. She jumped to her feet, quickly dressed in her training gear, and headed for the hotel's gym. On the elevator, she watched the numbers decline until it stopped at the fourth floor. Sabrina exited and walked to the gym, and using her room key, she entered. There were six others in the gym: three working on cardio machines and three using weight-training equipment. Sabrina went to the corner with mats and began stretching. Moments into her stretch, a gentleman approached. "Hi," he said.

"Hi," Sabrina said and kept stretching.

"I noticed you when you entered. Do you remember me?"

Sabrina stopped for a moment and gave the gentleman a good look. "I'm not sure. Where did we meet?"

"I'm Mikel Shores. We worked together on the East Coast. We had dinner and discussed a program to help raise money for a children's club. You were dating this great-looking guy. "

"You mean Lorenz. Yes, I remember the dinner. What are you doing here?"

"I'm visiting someone who is remarkable in show business.

He goes by the name Starz."

"Wow, I just met him today."

"He's the best producer. Have you seen the advertisements for his latest show? It's going to be a wonderful production. I can't wait to see it."

"Why are you meeting him, and when?"

"He worked with a friend of mine—"

"Patricia," they said in unison.

Surprised, Mikel smiled. "How did you know Patricia?"

"It's a long story, but let's say we had similar interests." Sabrina moved towards the treadmill.

Mikel followed, continuing the conversation. "I knew her from childhood. That woman was so creative. I can tell you a lot."

"When was the last time you spoke to Patricia?"

"It was a month before she passed. She had this idea, and usually when she wrote a rough draft she would send me a copy and later talk about it. I was her sounding board."

"Small world," Sabrina said while huffing during her running. "Are you going to dinner with Starz tonight?"

"Yes, as a matter of fact."

"Meeting him at seven?"

"A car will be here in another hour and a half. I'm supposed to be down in the lobby at six."

"Funny thing, so am I. Let's continue our conversation later tonight. I'm sure we have lots of notes to share." Sabrina faced forward and began running a little faster.

"Oh yeah. Sure, you models have to always workout. I'm sorry. I'll see you in the lobby." Mikel left the gym. Sabrina got lost in her thoughts while running, *So tonight isn't just a business dinner with me. That changes Simone's strategy. Maybe* not—it could be just a way to really see what Patricia had in mind. Sabrina continued her exercise regime. She stopped thinking about the coming meeting until she was in her room. *Tonight is going to be great. I don't have to sit there with Starz alone, and I can still use Simone's advice. I can close this deal with anything he throws at me. I can close this deal.*

Mikel stood next to the concierge table when Sabrina approached the front exit. "Hi," he said.

"Hi again, I see you're ready for tonight."

"My, you look marvelous."

"Thank you, that's kind of you to say." Sabrina blushed.

"Did you two get married?"

"Who? Oh, you mean Lorenz. No, we didn't," Sabrina said. *And that was a mistake.*

"During those days, I would have bet on it. I wonder what he's doing these days."

"I haven't heard." Sabrina moved as she noticed the limo out front. "I think the car has arrived." Sabrina walked to the chauffer she recognized from earlier. "Hi, are we including another person?"

"Hi, Ms. Sabrina, yes, as a matter of fact, we are. I told the concierge."

"Thank you so much, we have to get moving, or we'll be delayed."

Sabrina entered the car and slid to the far sidse, and Mikel joined her. Sabrina gazed out the car window, observing traffic and the scenery. She noticed the large buildings of downtown L.A., which reminded her of a shoot she'd done on a rooftop. Sabrina and the other passenger engaged in small talk; they enjoyed a discussion on scenery, city landmarks, and history.

When the limo stopped, the chauffer had parked before a beautiful restaurant entrance. The chauffer opened Sabrina's door and assisted her exit. Mikel slid across the limo, exiting through the same door Sabrina had used. The two walked to the front, where Stanley waited for their arrival. It was so organized, Sabrina felt like royalty and then questioned all the attention. *How nice but weird*, she thought as Stanley led them to a table set for four.

Starz rose to his feet as Sabrina approached. "Hi, glad to see you again," he said as he pulled out Sabrina's chair.

"Nice being here, thank you," Sabrina said with a smile. The other two gentlemen took their seats and a waiter arrived with a bottle of wine.

"I hope you don't mind, Sabrina, I took a chance and ordered this wine." Starz took the bottle from the waiter and insisted on pouring everyone a glass. He took each glass, poured, and said, "It's nice having you join me for dinner, I appreciate each of you for sharing the evening with me. Let me get started on why you're here. Stanley is my right-hand and has the ability to see things, kind of like what Patricia did. Mr. Shores is here because he was close to Patricia and was the last person to interact with her about her ideas. Ms. Clark is our guest, whose partnership will put Patricia's manuscript over the edge. See, we're a group of people with one focus: this manuscript." He reached into his briefcase and took out a copy of Patricia's last script. "Patricia was onto something. Before I get into this, I'd like you to make your dinner order. That way, once we start, there is no interruption."

Starz waved for the waiter. Each person took the menu and listened to the specials of the night. The waiter patiently waited for someone to start the order. Starz insisted that the

waiter take Sabrina's order first. Then, one by one, they ordered. Moments after the waiter left, Starz picked up his conversation right where he'd left off. "As I said, Patricia was onto
something; and this, my friends, is it. I must admit I didn't focus on it when she was alive, and now I'm paying for it. I know
Stanley read it, Mikel read it, but Sabrina, I was surprised to
learn this afternoon that you hadn't read it yet."

"No, actually we discussed ideas and I gave her insight to a
few questions she had, but I didn't read anything new of hers."

"I think you'd better read this." Starz handed her the
manuscript. Sabrina took it and turned to the synopsis. Her
eyes grew, as she'd had no idea what Patricia had written. She
snapped the manuscript shut and covered her mouth, masking
her surprise. *Oh my.* Sabrina looked away from the table. After
a moment of silence, she rose. "Excuse me for just a minute,"
she said and walked to the ladies' room. Once there, she called
Simone.

"Hey," Simone answered, "Why are you calling me so late,
you know it's three hours later here. I'm sleeping."

"You have got to get up. I just saw the synopsis of Patricia's
play. It's us," Sabrina said. "Patricia wrote about us in her play.
It's our lives."

"No way." Simone sat up in her bed. "She didn't even know
you that well, and I never even met her."

"It is making sense…now it's making sense why Starz
wanted me to come out."

"I guess this is to our advantage," Simone said. She was
now fully awake. "That is good, Sabrina. Now go back and tell
him you're in, or just listen to his idea or what he needs from
you."

"I don't know if I want our lives showcased to the public."

"I'm sure Patricia didn't say it's about us directly without our approval or agreement. A story is a story; let's not care about it until you are sure."

"I'll do what it takes to save the company." Sabrina reminded herself of her main reason for the visit. "You're right, we need this and I'll deliver. Don't worry."

"Good. Now go close the deal." Simone ended the call and returned to bed. Sabrina looked in the mirror, recomposed herself, and returned to the table. She apologized to the men. "I'm sorry, guys, the story kind of grabbed me."

"That's what I want from the public, Sabrina," Starz said. He took a sip of wine. "I actually thought you knew."

Sabrina shook her head.

"Patricia was my best friend. We watched you two for years, before your Aunt Marge died. I attended the memorial cruise, and so did Patricia. She thought it was marvelous," Mikel said.

"Excuse me?" asked Sabrina. "You mean Patricia knew of me before I met her?"

"She was a distant relative to your Aunt Marge, the family who didn't accept her when she married your uncle."

"Wow." Sabrina sat in awe, surprised at the information she'd just received. She tried to gather her emotions. "Why am I really here?"

"You know more of the story than anyone at this table. You can provide insights that nobody else can. When you presented your fashion show idea to us, it made sense. It's why I asked you to come and really dive into making this a success," Starz said.

"You could have asked my sister instead of me."

"No, that wouldn't work, because Patricia was fascinated with your work as a model. It's the ending, a major part of the story, that makes the manuscript so emotional. But I'm not in the industry, and why have an advisor when you can have the actual inspiration for the character involved? What do you say, Sabrina, can I count on you?"

Before Sabrina could answer the question, dinner arrived. The waiters came with four entrees and placed them on the table after Sabrina removed the large manuscript from the table. She looked at her dinner and found herself too engaged in thought to eat. Dinner sat there staring at her as if providing advice. *You should answer yes,* her steak was saying, and her potato added, *Hurry, before Starz changes his mind.*

Sabrina looked at the others who were chatting about the meals. "I'm in, but only with our business agreement. I'll add my focus to the story, but the fashion show must be included."

"You know what's funny about the fashion show part, and what makes Patricia so amazing, was that your character ends up designing clothes in the manuscript."

"What? Are you kidding me?" She recalled her conversation with Patricia in France: *I want to design my own clothes for a change.*

"Patricia told me she wanted to do something for you and your sister, Simone. She felt guilty about how the family treated your aunt," Mikel said.

Starz directed his gaze at Sabrina. "When you called, I thought you and Patricia must have discussed the piece. I was surprised you hadn't."

"I see, it's all coming together."

Stanley remained focused on business. "Except one thing, we have to create the buzz for it. I'm sure it's going to be great, but building the public's motivation is very important."

Starz chuckled. "That we do, Stanley, that we do. I'm sure

you have someone in mind."

"Starz, you know exactly who I'll call."

Starz nodded.

Dinner continued and the discussion managed to move from shock to planning. Stanley, being the well-organized guy, quickly took notes on the discussion and set the stage for contract negotiations.

Sabrina left dinner with motivation and doubt; she felt bombarded with this new information and wasn't sure how to process it. Then she felt guilty for not getting to know Patricia better when there was opportunity. The limo ride to the hotel was silent, neither passenger spoke, and when they arrived at the hotel, Mikel exited first and reached to assist Sabrina from the car. "I bid you a great night and farewell. Safe flying tomorrow," he said.

"Aren't you heading out tomorrow?"

"No, I'm going to stay here and work with Starz on some parts of the manuscript."

"Oh, okay. Thanks for the well wishes, and it was nice meeting you."

"We'll see much of each other in the future. I'm sure of it."

"Yes, we will," Sabrina said.

Sabrina's flight landed right on time. She scurried out of the plane and headed to the main terminal. There, Simone was waiting with a huge smile. "Success," she said, "we got the deal."

"How? So fast! I have no idea, I don't know what you said or did, but we have the deal and the numbers are exactly as you presented. If this works, we're on the road to recovery."

"I'm still not so sure," Sabrina said as they walked to Simone's car. "I'm not so sure I want our story told publicly."

"Do we really care? It's not like we've hidden anything or have done things to be ashamed of."

"Patricia was Aunt Marge's relative."

"What?" Simone stopped before entering the car. "Did I hear you correctly?"

"Yes, you heard me. Aunt Marge's relative." Sabrina repeated the story she'd heard at last night's dinner. The two drove to the office as Sabrina dove into explaining the manuscript and what she'd read the night before and on the flight. "It's a great story. I cried in the middle and smiled at the end."

"I can't explain what I'm feeling now," Simone said. "Are you really okay with this?"

"Funny you ask. That's what I asked you last night."

Simone felt her reservations intensify. " I know it's to save the company, and you'll make your clothing design a reality, but are we sure we want people to know about our lives?"

"Face it, sis, we're unique, but our situation is like many others. People will be able to relate to our story." Sabrina paused a moment to gather her thoughts. "And besides, we loved Aunt Marge, and this gives her the respect that's long overdue."

Simone kept driving towards the office and didn't respond to Sabrina's last comment. As she turned the car into the parking lot, she finally spoke, "I hope my love life isn't in the story. I need to read the manuscript."

"It's not, well, not totally. The manuscript is in my briefcase." Sabrina reached for the large document. "I'll warn you, it's really good."

Sabrina exited the car. She walked to the office building and didn't realize Simone hadn't followed. Sabrina looked back and saw Simone reading in the car. With work on her mind, Sabrina focused on the task ahead, getting every aspect of the clothing line in production. There was too much to do, and not enough time to do it. She rallied the troops, called a meeting, and explained the importance of the newly acquired contract.

Simone finally made it into the office; she'd read the first few pages and stopped before the manuscript consumed her attention. Once in her office, she turned her focus to the faxed contract from Star, and connected with Phil to ensure that all the legal aspects were covered. It was a day of success for the sisters. They applauded the win yet were skeptical about endorsing the play. Pushing their reservations aside, they remembered their objective to keep the company afloat.

During the first week of rehearsal, Sabrina traveled to California. It was heartbreaking to watch the first scene develop. She viewed the scene that depicted Aunt Marge's childhood, which relayed the fact that she was the lovechild of a wealthy man. The gentleman had seduced Marge's mother, kept her as his mistress, and later supported them. It was a love story, until the mother tragically died. Patricia had written that Aunt Marge's mother was murdered, but in real life, Sabrina recalled Aunt Marge saying it was cancer. Sabrina indicated her approval, noting that Patricia probably changed the occurrence for dramatic effect.

As she continued to watch the play, Sabrina focused on where she could introduce the clothing line in the production. She recalled the later parts of the play, about her journey into fashion and Simone's battle as a young executive. Sabrina marveled at how well Patricia had been able to piece her segmented knowledge about the family into such a compelling production. Sabrina had discussed her life with Patricia during their few interactions, but Patricia's attention to detail was astonishing.

The entire week, Sabrina followed scene after scene, adding input where she could to depict Aunt Marge as accurately as possible. When the story got to Sabrina's parent's death, when she and Simone moved in with Aunt Marge, it too was close to home. Sabrina cried and left the theater. She ran into the ladies' room and sat in a stall. She remembered feeling helpless—it was the most horrible experience. She sat in silence and ignored any activity outside of the stall. She wept as if it were yesterday; the play was bringing so much pain to the surface. After getting herself together, Sabrina returned to the rehearsal and managed to maintain her composure through the rest of it. She wondered how Patricia knew so much, so well about Aunt Marge and her life.

Starz interrupted Sabrina's thoughts. "This is where you pick up with your fashion show," he said. "I'm having the writers create a scene showing your development in the fashion industry."

"I'd like to keep it simple," Sabrina said, "if you don't mind."

"I think you and the writers will do a bang-up job; nothing like having your input to your own story."

"I agree. Thanks again for this, Starz." Sabrina smiled. She worked with the ghostwriters to incorporate the extra scene. After a long week, she headed home with the new scene in tow, hoping to get Simone's input.

After the script was finalized, Sabrina started her casting for extra models. She traveled to Vegas in search of her ideal models, all of different sizes, shapes, and ethnicities. For the first time, she really felt as if her dream was coming true.

Starz walked into Stanley's office cubicle. "How do you like the temporary office?"

"It's okay. I can do a job anywhere. I don't mind it at all," Stanley said.

"Good, because I want you close to the set. How do you see things coming along?"

Stanley paused. He knew Starz had been keeping his own eye on the set's progress. "It's going great. Sabrina had some hesitation about a few parts, but she's on board and everything's been finalized now."

"She'll be fine, I'm sure of it. Since we're right on schedule with most of the show, we now have a solid product. I think it's time for our marketing group."

"I'll get right on it. I'll reach out to Rodney and set up a meeting."

"You know what? Let me give them a call with you," said Starz. "I mentioned the potential for a new project to them earlier, and I want to let them know that we're moving forward with it."

"Sounds great," Stanley said.

18.
The New Campaign

RODNEY AND GAIL FINISHED their coffee, cleaned the kitchen, and headed for a Sunday sporting event. It was the season of basketball playoffs, Gail's favorite time of year. Attending Sunday games had become somewhat of a ritual whenever the city's sporting teams were in town. It had been a couple months since Dan and June wedded, and more time than usual had elapsed since the last time the four of them went out together. With June starting to show, she'd become self-conscious about going out so often. Gail understood, but Rodney felt conflicted about the newfound distance from his friend.

Rodney found that the time he and Dan used to spend together, such as after work or on weekends, became time the couples spent together. Basketball games, for one, used to be time for the guys. While Rodney thanked God that Gail enjoyed sports as much as he did, he missed hanging out with Dan like the old days. As time went on, Dan had become less involved with the "buddy" role, and more with the "husband, soon-to-be father" one.

The last outing the four had was baby shopping for the nursery at the hardware store. Dan had picked up painting tools and Rodney had assisted while Gail and June selected colors for the walls. If it wasn't decoration materials for the nursery, it was furniture, clothes, or toys. Everything revolved around the new addition. Gail was excited to become a godmother, and Rodney attempted to follow with comparable energy. It was nearly baby delivery time when Rodney received a call from Stanley and Starz. "Hi, Rodney," Starz said.

"Hey, Starz, how are you?"

"Doing great; California's still living up to our expectations. I wanted to speak with you again about the new project I mentioned. It's now a sure thing, and I just wanted to make sure your firm was on board."

"Tell me more."

"It's a great show about relationships, and a family. This story of an aunt–niece relationship will grab your heart. I mean, if I weren't a guy I'd cry at most scenes. It's an awesome story, and I want your group to create the marketing campaign."

"Really, this is welcoming news. When can I read the script?"

"You don't need to read it; we've already begun working on the production. Come and see the play rehearsal and talk to the advisors. I'm sure they will give you enough food for creativity. I have an idea, but I'd rather you work your magic."

"Well…" Rodney considered his schedule and pondered if Gail would be better suited to visit the set. "Send me the details, and I'll have a representative or myself attend."

Starz's tone hinted at his smile on the other end of the line. "Remember, there's no competition. It's the firm's job, as I loved the last campaign. The fountain idea worked and drew a lot of people in for the show."

"You made it work, I'm sure that's why the play has had so much success."

"I'm serious, and I want you to do this one, and time is of the essence. So, can we count on you to get things going? I'd like a confirmation."

"Give you a confirmation without sight or script…" Rodney thought for a moment. "Okay, we'll do it."

"Great! It's great working with you again."

"Same here, Starz. Oh, you might want to give Dan a congrats; he is now 'Mr. and Mrs.'"

"What? Who'd he marry?'

"A lovely lady named June. She and Gail are the best of friends."

"I remember her. She's a very nice woman. I'll give him a ring."

"Yes, please do, he would be glad to hear from you. Have a great day, Starz."

Gail and Dan were in Rodney's office shortly after Starz's call. Rodney looked at them both. "I spoke with Starz again about the campaign he mentioned on the firm's anniversary. He called and said they're going ahead with it, and he wants us to market his next production. I know it's going to be great. Since Stanley is gone, I think, Gail, you'll be our person in California." Dan and Gail didn't respond right away. Rodney noticed Dan sigh with disappointment. "You know I can't send you, Dan. June would kill me. You're going to be a dad soon,"

"I know," Dan said, "I'm not complaining, but pregnant women are tough."

Gail jumped in. "You should be over the hard part."

"The hard part?"

"Yes, at least now her cravings are down, and she's not having morning sickness as much anymore. You're on the way. Besides, I couldn't let you leave June at this moment. She needs you."

Rodney patted a quick drum roll on his desk. "Agreed, Gail is going to review the project and give us her ideas," He called his executive assistant and said, "Please coordinate travel for Gail to visit Los Angeles within the next few days." After receiving confirmation, he hung up the phone and turned back to Dan and Gail. "I'm open to anything on this project. I know we have to understand what we're marketing, but last time I had a theme idea before I even looked at product." He turned his desk chair towards the window and remembered when he met Gail in Calistoga and when he'd come across the fountain. He chuckled. "Maybe I should take a trip. Gail, I guess I'll have to take it while you're gone."

"Take a trip while I'm working, that's a good thing to do."

"He's always more creative on the road," Dan said. "Besides, you don't mind, do you?"

"Would June mind?" Gail frowned and stopped herself from saying another word. She reminded herself that they were in the office, and took a deep breath. "I apologize, Dan. It isn't my place in your relationship." Gail left, heading to her office.

Dan and Rodney waited for her to exit before speaking. "I guess you pissed her off," Dan said.

"I know, I'll talk to her later. I don't want her thinking I'm purposely leaving her out of my plans. I figured it wouldn't hurt while she was busy with Starz."

"Where are you headed?"

"I'm not sure. Why did you tell her I travel a lot?"

"It's not a lie. You actually return with great ideas when you travel. It's only been twice since we've been in business, but both times we delivered great campaigns."

"True enough, true enough. I'm not sure Gail can take that kind of spontaneity though."

"Remember, Rodney, you've only traveled twice in three years; *really* spontaneous," Dan said as he left the office.

Three days passed, and Gail arrived at the Los Angeles International Airport. Starz sent a limousine for her and had the driver bring Gail to the office. Gail, having visited Los Angeles before, didn't pay much attention to the scenery; she contemplated her involvement with the coming project. As the limo came to a stop, she noticed Starz's impressive new office building. She exited the limousine and saw that Stanley was waiting for her at the building's entrance. "Hi, Gail," he said.

"Hi, Stanley, how are you doing?"

"I'm doing well, thanks. I love working here with Starz."

"That's great." Gail smiled. "I'm glad to see it was a good move for you and your family."

"He gave me an offer I couldn't refuse. I love living on the coast. It's awesome, and the family likes the weather, people, and excitement." Stanley raised his arm, leading her to the conference room. "We're waiting for your arrival so we can get started. Can I offer you something to drink or direct you to the ladies' room?"

"No, I'm fine, thank you." Gail followed Stanley's direction. She entered the conference room and saw six people seated around the table. Gail spotted an empty seat and headed for it as she spoke to Starz. "Hi, Starz, you're looking great."

Starz rose to greet his long time friend and former employee. "Thanks, Gail, it's nice seeing you. How was your flight?"

"It was perfect. Thanks for sending the limo. I see you're still a classy guy."

"You know, treating people well is my thing."

"And you've always done such a great job making us feel that way," Gail said as she noticed four other people nodding their heads in agreement.

Just as Gail took her seat, Starz began his meeting with an introduction of all seated around the table. When he got to Sabrina, he directed his sight to Gail, and said, "Sabrina is actually the person that one of the main characters is based off of in the play. She is also from Richmond, Gail."

"Wow, small world. Nice meeting you, Sabrina," Gail said, "I'm sure we'll catch up after this presentation."

"Nice meeting you too. I'm sure we will." Sabrina smiled in response. Starz continued the meeting, explaining the plot of the show and the market he was expecting to capture.

Gail took copious notes and refrained from commenting on anything until Sabrina highlighted the fashion show. "Fashion show? Isn't this play a drama?" she asked.

"Yes, but we're going to incorporate Sabrina's clothing designs into the play," Starz said. "Part of the story is Sabrina's being a model and transitioning to a designer."

"So this story is your biography?" Gail asked Sabrina.

"No, well sort of, but not fully my story. It's a story including my aunt and sister."

"Sounds interesting enough," Gail said as she returned to writing notes on the production. Starz completed the conference presentation and had lunch ordered. He gave directions to the dining area just after informing the group of the afternoon's schedule. "Please enjoy your lunch, and I'll see you in the theater."

Gail and Sabrina strolled to the door. "This sounds like a great play," Gail said as they exited the conference room.

"I'm not sure how to answer that. Sometimes I think it is, but since it's so personal, it's hard for me to tell."

"Didn't you help write it?"

"No, I'm only an advisor. I added the fashion show and designed the clothes for the rest of the play, but it's only a small piece of the pie."

"It seems a very important piece."

"Are you into fashion?"

"What girl isn't?" Gail stopped talking to take a good look at Sabrina. "Excuse me, forgive my staring, but haven't I seen you on the cover of a magazine?"

"Yes, you have. It was a time before I married my husband—I'm sorry, soon-to-be *ex*-husband, James."

"James, James. Why does the name sound so familiar?"

"I'm not sure; maybe you've seen his work." *He probably screwed you too.*

"I remember, if it's the right James. He shot the poster images for a production a couple years ago when I was still working for Network Galaxy. Is he..." Gail described James's physical features so well it was as if she'd seen him the past afternoon.

Sabrina cut in. "Did he or didn't he?"

"Did or didn't he what?" Gail asked with a puzzled look.

"Sleep with you?"

"What? He was very nice looking, but I surely didn't sleep with him. I didn't have the time, nor the focus."

"I'm sorry, I shouldn't have asked."

"Sounds like you had a hard time with him."

"I thought everyone knew that he's a womanizer."

"I wasn't aware. But I can say, you'd know your guy better than anyone."

"I thought so, but I was wrong. Do you have a guy?"

"Yes, actually. He's adorable, loving, spontaneous, and all those explicit things a lady shouldn't tell." Gail grinned.

"You two just started dating?"

"No, it's been a little over a year and a half. It's great, and he's a very sweet guy. I began working for him when Starz moved to Los Angeles."

"It sounds as if you're getting serious."

"I hope we are. At least, I'm serious and want this to work."

"I wish you luck. The guy I should have stayed involved with, I let go."

"Good one got away?"

"Don't they usually?"

"Not this time," Gail said and repeated, "Not this time."

After lunch the group sat in the theater and were all focused on the stage. Starz welcomed everyone to the dress rehearsal, and as he took his seat the show began. It was just as he'd presented in the conference room. Scene after scene, multiple points hit home with Gail. Some scenes were so intense that she cried, hiding her tears from Sabrina. Sabrina's designs caught Gail's eye through the show, but the best designs were featured in the fashion show. When it began, Gail sat forward in her seat and awed at the impressive styles.

Sabrina took notice. "The right response."

"The clothes are lovely," Gail said.

"Thank you, I appreciate that; these are some of the outfits you'll help market."

Gail wrote a few lines in her notebook and then looked up at Sabrina. "Can we get together over dinner or drinks this evening?"

Sabrina looked at her watch, and hesitated for a moment. "If Starz has nothing planned, I'm game. Meet me in the hotel lobby at eight?"

"Good, very good. I'll see you at eight." Gail rose to her feet as Sabrina walked away.

Rodney left the office and ventured to the art gallery to think. Rodney strolled through the galleries and thought hard about where he should travel. His thoughts moved to Gail, and while observing a colorful pastel painting, he realized how different his relationship with her was from his last love. In comparison, Rodney realized, this relationship was so much more real. She wanted a serious relationship, and that was exactly what she was going to get, *I know she won't hurt me like Simone did after Ms. Marge's memorial cruise*, Rodney reasoned. He moved to the next picture and saw an airplane in the center of the canvas. Rodney exhaled, looked at his watch, and decided, *I'll do it.*

It was 6:30 p.m. after Gail finished her shower. She took advantage of the break after the show and worked out before meeting Sabrina for drinks. The room telephone rang, and Gail picked up the receiver with a towel around her body. "Hello," she answered.

"Hi, my darling woman!" Rodney said.

"Rodney! I was thinking of you. Are you traveling or still at home?"

"I'm traveling."

"Oh, where are you?"

"I'm in a sunny location. The water's just right, and the scenery is breathtaking."

"Oh, I'm jealous."

"Why? You're in sunny California."

"But this is work."

"As if relaxing isn't?" Rodney chuckled.

"Funny, really funny," Gail looked at the clock. "I have a lot to tell you, but I have to get ready for my meeting at eight. I just got out of the shower and need to get dressed. I'll call you."

"Wouldn't you rather tell me while you're dressing?"

"It would be easier, but you didn't call me on the cell, you called the room phone. Wait, I can call you on my cell and use the Bluetooth."

"I have a better idea. Why don't you open the door and tell me in person."

"What?" Gail dropped the phone and ran to the door. She opened it and there stood Rodney with a rose.

"I heard you had a long day," he said

"You heard right." Gail jumped into his arms. "I never thought you'd be here."

"I didn't either. No, who am I kidding? Of course I'd be here." Rodney kissed her. "Let me get my bag from the hall, and you can tell me all about your day."

Gail took a moment to gather her wits and blushed with excitement. She waited for Rodney to return to the room. Once the door closed, Gail faced Rodney, dropping her towel, and exposing her nude body. "First things first."

Rodney responded, moving towards her while removing his shirt. He grabbed her in his arms and kissed her deeply. It was a kiss full of meaning; Rodney hoped to relay the reason he'd flown to her. He whisked her up in his arms and placed her on the bed. While she lay in excitement, Rodney quickly stripped. "I love your reaction," he said as he moved onto the bed.

"It's genuine. What a wonderful surprise." She kissed him, pulling him closer to her. She ran her hands along his muscles, from the small of his back to the back of the neck. She pushed him, rolling him onto his back, and jumped out of the bed, heading for his wallet. "We don't have much time, so where is it?"

"They're in the toiletry kit."

Gail moved with haste and found exactly what she sought. She unwrapped the condom and returned to the bed. "Let's get you excited again," she whispered while laying her lips upon him. She tasted him, thrilling Rodney with the element of surprise and true seduction.

She rolled life's protection over the muscle of her affection, and then Rodney pulled her tender flower to him and said, "Two can play this game." In moments, Gail climbed the ladder of success, and continued her mission by stopping just before Rodney was about to explode. Rodney began to calm, but before he could regain his composure, she quickly took him for the full effect. She moved, they kissed, and without acrobatics, they both climaxed into a haze. Sweat was beading from both, and before Gail could catch her breath she said, "Time for another shower."

"I agree," Rodney said as he followed her to the bathroom. "I'm coming in with you."

"I wouldn't have it any other way." Gail entered the shower and reached for him. "I'm so happy you came."

"Me too, I hope you did as well. I think you did," Rodney

said with a smile.

"Yes, I mean, no, that isn't what I'm talking about. You come here, silly."

"I'm glad too," Rodney said as he washed her back while the water flowed down their bodies. "I needed to, because there is something I wanted to talk to you about."

Gail only partially heard Rodney's last comment. "I have to meet a lady in the lobby in twenty minutes, but you're more than welcome to join us. She's working with Starz on the play, and we'll be marketing her designs. I'm sure she'd love to meet you, but we've got to get going."

Rodney, baffled in her response, decided not to make that attempt again. He instead focused on getting showered and dressed for their dinner guest. Gail exited the shower just before he completed washing. She'd begun to get dressed when Rodney entered the room. Rodney began dressing too. "How did today go?" he asked.

"It was great. The play is really quite moving. It's dramatic and has shock and surprise. A very well-put-together play. I'm sure Starz will have another award winner with this one. Here's the special part: there will be real clothing designs on the cast, and a live fashion show. People can actually purchase the clothes at the show, or at any department store or outlet. I mean, I've never heard of such a thing. I saw the clothes, and those designs were good. I mean *really* good."

"Then it will be easy to market?"

"Easy in that the clothes will definitely sell well and the play is going to be a hit, but creating a marketing scheme that promotes the two together might be a challenge. I'm sure we can figure something creative out though. Isn't creativity your department?"

"A smart-ass question." He laughed. The two continued to dress and prepared themselves for their downstairs meeting.

As they left the hotel room and headed for the elevator, Gail grabbed Rodney's hand. "I caught up with Stanley during my trip too."

"Oh yeah?" Rodney said as they walked down the hall.

"I spoke with him when I arrived at the building. He's pretty happy. He said Starz's offer was one he couldn't refuse."

"I can only imagine. I bet his family loves it here."

"Yes, they do. He said that exactly."

"Good, I'm really happy for him, and he's a good contact to have in L.A. Just think, he'll continue to pass some work to us while he's out here. I'm not upset with Starz for taking Stanley. I got the better deal—I have you." Rodney smiled at Gail as the elevator door opened.

In moments, the elevator door reopened and they walked towards the lobby. Sabrina stood facing the lobby doors, as if expecting someone to enter from outside. Gail recognized her and approached. "Sabrina?" Gail asked as she stood next to her.

Rodney followed and heard Gail call out for Sabrina, a name he was familiar with, but he was still shocked when she turned around. Rodney opened his arms for a hug and exclaimed, "Oh, wow, Sabrina! Hi!"

Gail, stunned, moved to observe the two embrace.

"Rodney! Wow, it's been so long. How *are* you?" Sabrina asked.

"Yes, the last time was at the art gallery…you look marvelous," Rodney said as he stepped away from their hug and held her at arm's length to look. "You look really marvelous."

"You two really know each other," Gail said.

"Yes, we do," Rodney said.

"It's a long story," Sabrina said.

Gail raised her eyebrows. "I bet it is." Gail took notice of how Sabrina smiled at Rodney. "Was this a relationship or something between you two I should know about?"

"We're just friends," Rodney said, "I tried to date her sister. At the time, Sabrina was dating a guy too, I recall him being a medical resident, right?"

Sabrina nodded.

Rodney turned back to Sabrina. "Gail tells me you're a talented designer."

"Designer, yes, but 'talented' all depends on how you market the show and my products."

The three sat near a secluded location within the hotel lobby and conversed on Sabrina's vision of the play as seen by the public. "I want the image to stay classy but still become a common household name," Sabrina said. "This is a new venture, but I know it will succeed."

"Gail said she loves the clothes, and she'll be the one to drive the campaign. I'm sure we can market your product to the public. We've had success in the past and it will continue. Have faith in us."

"Rodney, I have no doubt you'll do it. I'm stressing the importance of the line's success. It has to reach a profitable level within two months of production."

"Immediate return?" Gail asked. "We can't guarantee an immediate return. There are too many factors to consider."

"If you can't do it, I'll have to suggest that Starz find someone else to do the job."

"Sabrina, when have we not completed a successful campaign?" Rodney asked.

"There is always a first time. I can't afford this to be your first." Sabrina continued, "This product line is very important to me. Perhaps we need two campaigns, one centered on the play, and one on the designs, instead of just one."

"We can do both, but it will cost you independent of Network Galaxy's fees," Gail said.

"I'm fully aware. You start planning and I'll get the clothing design documents." Sabrina stood up.

Rodney stood and raised his hand to Sabrina as a formalized farewell. Sabrina took his hand. "I thought we were having dinner?"

Gail said, "You thought correct," and rose to her feet, locking arms with Rodney.

"Oh." Sabrina noted Gail's prompt reaction. "All right, good, let's go. Who's driving?" The three exited the hotel lobby and stood next to the valet booth. Rodney requested his rental and, when it arrived, the three entered the car. Rodney suggested a lively restaurant bar, which neither woman rejected.

During the drive, Gail pressed them for more information on how the two knew each other. "You said Rodney dated your sister? What happened?"

"It didn't work. Rodney was the sweetest guy, but my sister wasn't as interested."

"Why wasn't she?" Gail asked.

"You'll have to ask her. I tried to fix them up, and when I tried, she flipped."

"Yes, I thought you'd sent me into a lion's cage." Rodney said to Sabrina. "It was a hard time."

"Is she married?" Gail asked.

"Yes, I mean no—it's a long story," Sabrina said.

"I hope she's happy, either way," Rodney said as he parked

the car. "We're here."

The three exited the car and the women followed Rodney to the restaurant. Gail observed Sabrina watching Rodney lead the way, and noticed her sizing Rodney up.

"Remind me, how long have you two dated?" Sabrina asked as she turned to Gail.

"It's been over a year and a half. It's going great."

"He's a great catch, I should know. I wish my sister had seen him as one."

"I'm glad she didn't," Gail said and passed through the restaurant door that Rodney held for them. The three conversed over dinner, more of business than history, but Sabrina and Gail both tried to slip in questions about personal history every so often. The women seemed on an information mission; Sabrina sought to find out as much as possible about the current relationship, and Gail pressured them about Rodney's history with Simone. Rodney felt the tension build, and at every opportunity, he directed the conversation back to the campaign and Sabrina's clothing line. Not once did Rodney contribute to their investigation by answering more than a simple yes or no.

19.
Fault Lines

LATER THAT NIGHT, Gail and Rodney found themselves back on the hotel elevator, finally alone. Gail embraced Rodney and leaned back. "Am I going to have to worry?"

"No, no worries," Rodney said. "No worries because I love you. You're my girl and I'm crazy about you."

"Are you sure you two didn't have anything?"

"I tried to date her sister, Simone. That was it. I told you, Sabrina dated a medical resident."

"I heard, but you didn't see her observe you, and I'm telling you, something is going through her mind."

"She's just catching up, think nothing of it. She's concerned because it seems that so much is riding on the success of her clothing line."

Gail exited the elevator just as the door opened, pulled out the room key, walked to their suite, and opened the door. She didn't wait for Rodney. "Then why didn't you tell me about dating Simone?"

"Oh, I see what this is about." Rodney tensed up. "I never asked you about who you dated or the kind of men in your life before me. I showed you Rodney and hoped for the best. No man in your past is here, and I'm confident you did the right thing. You're with me."

"I'm with you, the man I know as Rodney, but you have a different history than I was aware of. Do you have feelings for her sister? I sensed you limiting the response and changing the subject every time I got close to learning more information. Do you?"

"Why on earth would you ask such question? I'm with you, showering you with my love."

"I want to make sure. I can't have you when your heart is somewhere else. I want to make sure, Rodney, I'm not in this for a competition." Gail sighed and moved near the large glass window, staring at the city lights. "I realize now that I don't know everything about you—the women in your life, the failures. It never bothered me until now."

"It's because you have it all and still do. Why are you so concerned? Don't you feel loved, desired, and adored?"

"It's beside the point, Rodney. I'm not sure about Sabrina. She looked at you with determination. Trust me; I know there's more to this than what you see."

"I cannot help the way a woman looks at me, or even take notice. What I can help," Rodney said as he approached Gail, "is how you and I share in this relationship." He stood behind her and hugged her. "I really love you and want us to be comfortable in all situations."

"I am comfortable, but you know, a woman's intuition is always on point. There is more on her mind than marketing."

Sabrina closed the hotel room door and couldn't wait to dial Simone. It was seconds into her walk around the room when Simone finally answered. "Hey, sis," Simone said.

"You're not going to believe who I had dinner with," Sabrina blurted out.

Simone paused before responding, "I'd guess a popular actor, but there are so many."

"No actor but an interest of yours at one time."

"I'm not guessing. Who is it?"

Sabrina paused before answering, just to increase the suspense. "Rodney."

"Rodney? *My* Rodney?"

"Yes, one and the same," Sabrina said. "I know you've always wondered about 'if,' so here's your chance."

"Doesn't he have a woman in his life?"

Sabrina calculated her answer. "Yes, but I don't think they're married or serious. I think they're dating."

"Dating," Simone said. "Is Starz using Rodney's marketing firm for the campaign?"

"Yes, I didn't recognize the name until I saw him tonight. I don't know if he'll be totally involved, but I can find out tomorrow."

"Good, there are a couple other things you need to find out for me. I need personal stuff, history." Simone threw additional questions like "Is he in love? Was he ever married? And the big one, did he talk about me?" into the bunch just before ending the call. She lay in bed and before closing her eyes she thought, *I don't want him to get away this time. Look at the way he's built his firm. If we were partners, life would be very different now. He can help me save this company, and I could truly have love.*

Sleep fell upon her and during the night Simone recalled moments with Mr. Witherspoon. *Simone wore her favorite blue dress. It was snug and revealing, just enough to make a man swoon with excitement. It was a night waiting for Rodney, sipping wine, and feeling nervous... Rodney and Simone on the carriage ride around the park, and Rodney dancing with her. And then the cruise, where Mr. Slocum identified Rodney as the person who'd found Aunt Marge on the street.* The night continued with Simone in a deep slumber.

Sabrina and Gail were sitting together in the theater before Rodney arrived. Rodney took a detour when he saw Starz and Stanley. The three men greeted each other and began to catch up.

Sabrina, remembering the information Simone wanted, and Gail, being inquisitive about Rodney's past relationships, both took the opportunity to inquire to one another. "So, are you two serious?" Sabrina asked.

"I'd say we are," Gail said. "I am smitten with him, he's going to be my husband one day."

"Oh really? I gather Rodney hasn't asked you," Sabrina said. "You know, he's a great guy and you better get moving if you're going to keep him."

"Get moving?" *No, she didn't say "get moving," how dare she!*

"Of course, good men don't come by often. If Rodney is anything like he was before, you'd better snatch him off the market."

"Trust me, he's off the market. Tell me about before though. I'd like to know, because Rodney doesn't share much about his past relationships with me."

Sabrina realized her answer could help get Rodney back on track with Simone. She just knew he must still harbor feelings for her sister, because of his serious chase years ago. "He loved my sister," she began. "When a man like Rodney loves someone, it's not just a thing, he *really* loves. The two were an item for a moment, but it didn't work for whatever reason."

"It was your sister and not you, right?"

"Not me. At the time I dated a guy named Lorenz, a handsome, great, loving man."

"I guess he's not with you. Weren't you two married?"

"No, I married James, remember?" Sabrina frowned and crossed her arms.

"I remember, I'm sorry for reminding you of James. But what happened to Lorenz, why didn't you marry him?"

"I'll have to share that story with you another time. Why don't you tell me about you and Rodney? Where did you meet? How did you get serious?"

Gail took the chance to share her and Rodney's history and how they'd met. It was a chance to share more of their relationship in hopes of discouraging Sabrina from questioning it. Gail stressed Rodney's promise for a future together. Sabrina took Gail's explanations in stride and saw through Gail's insecurity. Sabrina made mental notes, planning to brief Simone on what she was up against.

After the three watched the rehearsal, Rodney suggested meeting in the hotel to review Sabrina's clothing line in greater detail. He offered Gail's room as a meeting spot and Gail nudged him with her elbow.

"Actually, uh, nevermind, I think it's better we meet in the lobby," he said.

"How about my suite?" Sabrina suggested. "It's large enough, and has separate areas."

Rodney didn't know how to answer; he looked at Gail and paused before answering.

Sabrina saw his hesitation. "She doesn't mind, do you dear?" she said, looking at Gail.

"Ah, no, it's okay," Gail said. "What time?"

"Seven, just like the last time. I'll have room service deliver dinner."

The three left the theater going separate ways. Rodney and Gail walked towards Stanley's location. On the way over, Gail gave Rodney a sideways glance. "What was that about?"

"What? You mean working on the clothing line with Sabrina?"

"Why did you invite her to our room and fell for going to hers?"

"It's business and there isn't anything to it otherwise. You were there."

"I know, it's why I'm asking you, what the hell?" Gail frowned and as Stanley approached, she headed towards the ladies' room.

"What's going on with her?" Stanley asked.

"If I really knew I might answer," Rodney said. "Sometimes you have to just let things fester until they surface."

The men looked puzzled. Both men stood there until Stanley broke the silence. "You weren't upset, right?"

"No, I'm baffled."

"Baffled? It was an offer I couldn't refuse. My family loves it here, my wife is happy, the job is fun, and I'm pretty content. I love my home and the life style here."

"Oh, of course, I thought you were talking…nevermind. Yes, I mean no, I wasn't upset when you left—I told you that Starz wanted to hire you before he did, remember? I think it was a great move for you. I knew if anyone saw your skills, I'd lose you. I'm happy Starz hired you."

"I appreciate your understanding. I enjoyed working with you though and always remember how you kept us involved as a team. I'm trying to do the same here."

"You're doing great. I just know it. I'm not upset and wish you the best of luck. Just don't forget your roots." Rodney patted Stanley on the back. "You can call me anytime."

"Good deal, I don't mind calling. As a matter of fact, Starz is looking at your firm for a long-term marketing partnership. As in, every new production will have your firm involved. I'm drawing up the terms of the contract now."

"Wow, that is great news!"

"I'm happy for you. I know he has plays in the pipeline for the next two years."

Simone and Sabrina spoke on the phone while Sabrina traveled back to the hotel. She explained Rodney's situation and her assumptions about Gail. "She's really an insecure woman."

"This isn't a game, Sabrina, it's Rodney."

"Exactly!"

Dinner arrived at Sabrina's suite as scheduled. The order was a combination of dishes that Rodney enjoyed. Sabrina had asked Simone to recall what Rodney cooked at their first dinner together. Despite her hopes for Simone, Sabrina kept conversation focused on business. It was why the three met, and of course, her intention to investigate and spark Rodney's interest in Simone was Sabrina's secondary mission.

Rodney and Gail examined Sabrina's clothing styles and ideas and listened to her objectives in regards to selling the designs in national department stores. She conveyed the importance of having a very successful marketing campaign. Sabrina took her clothing line seriously, but each time Gail added some input, Sabrina acknowledged it with a short response and turned her conversation back to Rodney.

It was an hour and a half into the discussion when a knock sounded on the door. Sabrina opened the door, and the bellhop pushed in the dessert table with covered dishes. The only immediately recognizable items were coffee and tea. "I took the liberty of ordering dessert for us," Sabrina said as she returned to the easel and turned the page. The bellhop left and Sabrina continued making her final point. "This is where we are today. With that said, let's see what we have for dessert."

The three moved towards the table, and Gail lifted the first cover, "Mmm, chocolate cake," she said as she replaced the cover and lifted the next top. "I have no idea what this is."

"Let me see." Rodney moved for a closer look. "Wow," he said as he recognized the dish as one he'd made for Simone years ago. He turned to Sabrina. "How did you get this?"

"It's your recipe, right?"

"Are you *serious*?" Gail glared at Rodney and Sabrina.

"Don't get mad, Gail, I remembered that Rodney liked this. We were friends before you came along. I just recalled his favorite dish."

"It wasn't my exact favorite, but I use to make this whenever I had guests over," Rodney said to settle Gail's inquisitive nature. "It was something I'd forgotten over the years."

"Did I remind you of something you'd rather forget?" Sabrina asked.

"No, it's fine," Rodney said as he took the plate and a cup of coffee. "Gail, darling, would you like to try this?"

Gail gave Rodney the eye. *We'd better go.*

Before she could say anything, Rodney pushed a taste of

the dessert in front of her mouth, "Here, it's good, trust me." He smiled and moved the fork closer.

Gail opened her mouth to catch the dessert before the fork hit her face. She chewed and couldn't help but be delighted by its taste. "Oh my, it's wonderful. You made this when?"

"For his special occasions and dates," Sabrina said.

"I did, I took pride in this dish."

"Why haven't you made it for me?"

"I'd forgotten about it. I guess I don't cook as much anymore, and we haven't entertained together just yet."

"We've been together for almost two years, and you cook a lot. I'm not sure what you mean by entertain." Gail rose from her seat. She looked at Rodney sitting there with a dumbfounded look on his face. "We should go," she said.

"Okay, we shall."

"No, please don't leave just yet, I have one more thing to share with you," Sabrina said.

"We should go; we can talk about it tomorrow. Rodney, are you coming?" Gail asked as she held the suite door open.

"I'll be right there, let me finish this. I haven't had this in forever."

"No, Rodney, let's go."

"Why not let him enjoy it? He won't take long."

"I'll be in my room, Rodney." Gail left the suite and slammed the door.

Gail and Rodney landed in Richmond on separate flights from Los Angeles. They finally met at the luggage claim. "How was your flight?" Rodney asked.

"Good. I thought about the other night in Sabrina's suite. I'm sorry," Gail said. "I guess I got jealous."

"No apology needed. I know I wasn't quite receptive to what you thought went on. She's just an old friend."

"I know, Rodney. I should be confident about us."

"I'm okay with us being as we are. If I wanted another woman, I'd go out there and make it happen. Have I done anything to give you a suspicion?" Gail paused before responding and when she saw her bag rotate on the luggage claim track, she moved without answering.

Rodney looked at her surprised. "You aren't going to answer?"

Gail responded with her bag in hand, "Nothing, Rodney, you've done nothing."

"I'll get the car."

"Aren't you waiting for your bag?"

"I traveled with a carry-on. I'm going to go get the car." Rodney walked out of the airport doors.

Gail moved her luggage to the exit and positioned herself in a clear spot on the sidewalk where Rodney could pull the car in. She waited and thought about Sabrina's actions the other night. *I can't believe her dinner and dessert was just a friendly gesture. How dare she go after my guy?* A car horn blew and the noise pulled Gail back to reality. She looked left and saw Rodney walking up to her for the bag. "I didn't see you," she said as Rodney arrived.

"It's okay," he said. They loaded the car with luggage and started the quick drive home. Silence fell upon them during the drive; Rodney wanted to say something but felt it was more important to be quiet for now. Gail was tempted to start her inquisitive venture into Rodney's history again but decided the drive wasn't the time.

Finally, after both had changed and sat down in the living

room she asked, "What kind of relationship did you have with Sabrina?"

"We were friends. I tried to date her sister Simone," Rodney said. "I thought I told you this while in Los Angeles."

"Yes, but you didn't exactly tell me about it."

"It was a time when I thought Simone was for me. It didn't work and I moved on."

"End of story?"

"End of story."

Before he could prepare a glass of wine, Gail asked another question. "How many dates did you go on with Simone?"

Rodney finished pouring his glass of wine and took a sip. "Actually it was only one date, but a lot of other interactions."

"Was there any sexual activity between you two?"

"Why on earth would you ask such a question?" Rodney asked as he moved to the couch. "How important is it, knowing my sexual history?"

"I don't want to know your sexual history, just want to know if you had sex with her."

"You are really digging for information about Simone. Why are you so interested in her? You haven't even met her."

"I met someone better. I met her sister and she wants you two to explore something."

"How on earth did you come up with that conclusion?"

"It's a woman's intuition. Trust me."

"What about my intentions? I'm here, loving you and only you, showing you more of us, and…" Rodney moved closer to Gail and touched her face gently with his hand. "…hopefully you see how I want a future for us." He placed his lips gently upon hers and crossed his fingers for a response, a positive response.

Gail, responded but not as he expected; she kissed him and moved back. "I'm not finished."

"Finished?"

"You better be careful, because Sabrina is up to something. I know it, and if it has an impact on us, you'll see the bitch side of me."

"I can feel the anger," Rodney said as he nearly put his foot in his mouth. *The same bitch I see now.*

Simone hugged Sabrina after her return home. "Well," she said, "the board is pleased with the projected numbers. All we have to do is get the marketing campaign in front of them, and we'll get their support for an added extension."

"Good, I'm happy for the business. I told you we could do it."

"You did, little sis, you pulled it off. Aunt Marge would be proud of us right now."

"Yes, she would. But hey, are you ready to see Rodney?"

"I'm ready to cross paths with him. Tell me, how much has he changed?"

Sabrina explained her observations: his attitude, his behavior, and the competition. "He's serious about Gail. I don't think you're going to break her."

"Just a challenge; she'll fall like the rest of the women who got in my way."

"He's in love, so you may not have a chance."

"Remember, he loved me first." Simone smirked. "He'll remember once he's reminded."

20.
The Kettle

A FLORAL ARRANGEMENT was delivered to the marketing firm. When the receptionist passed them onto Rodney's office, the rumor mill started. Rodney wasn't in the office when the receptionist delivered them. He was meeting new clients and reviewing contracts with lawyers. It had been a busy day for Rodney, and he was so busy that he had not found a chance to see Gail. The day ended and Rodney was last in the building besides the cleaning crew. It was then, when he walked into his office, that he noticed the floral arrangement. He went up to it and pulled the card from the stems.

Thanks for the memories.

There was no signature, and Rodney thought simply to contact Gail and thank her. Before he dialed Gail's number, he sat in his chair and pondered, *What does she mean by "memories"?* He sat there in the office while the vacuum cleaner buzzed away in the hall. He realized he should tell Gail thanks, even if the floral arrangement was her way of saying good-bye, but he decided not to call and hoped that Gail would contact him. On his way home, Rodney's phone, which was sitting on the passenger seat, began to ring. Thinking it was Gail, Rodney picked it up without checking the caller ID. "Hey," he answered.

"Hi, Rodney, it's been a while," Simone said.

"Yes, it has … Simone," Rodney said as he recognized the voice. "Nice hearing from you … how are things?"

"Things are well, thanks. I'm calling you to see if you're available to meet with Sabrina and me tonight. We have to make a decision on the wardrobe that will affect your campaign. Can you see us tonight?" Simone heard the dead air. "Are you still there?"

"I'm here," Rodney said. "Where would you like to meet?"

"Let's meet at the restaurant on the corner of Fifth and Broadway. I'm sure you know the place."

"I know the place well. What time?"

"Thirty minutes?" Simone covered her smile with her hand.

"I'll be there," Rodney said and ended the call. He dialed Gail to inform her of his meeting right away but got her voicemail.

"This is Gail. Sorry I missed your call. Leave a message … *beep.*"

Rodney decided it would be better to leave a message than to say nothing. "I'm going to the Cloak Room with a client, I'll be home later. Don't wait for me to have dinner. I love you, and thanks for the floral arrangement." Rodney drove to the restaurant and waited in the car a few minutes. This was the place he and Simone had went on their only date. At the time, he'd taken extra steps to impress her. *I'm not too sure about this.* Rodney shook himself to loosen up. *Get a hold of yourself, man. It's work. It's work, it's just work.*

Moments after he entered the restaurant, someone tapped his shoulder, "Hey," Simone said. "Oh my goodness, you look really good."

"Hi…uhh, thanks." Rodney reached out his hand for a handshake, but Simone pulled him in for a hug.

"Nice of you to come on such short notice," she said. "Sabrina isn't coming."

Rodney coughed. "Um, oh. Really?"

"Yes, she isn't coming for whatever reason."

"Then you feel comfortable talking about the marketing campaign?"

"Of course I do. It's still my company we're talking about. I have a stake in the success of the campaign. I know you can pull it off," she said as they walked to a table.

As soon as they sat down, Rodney asked, "What's on your mind?"

"Well, this campaign is really important; we need it to go well to help save the company."

"Save it? I read in the paper that Willingham Corp. was having some issues, but I had no idea it was that serious."

"It's pretty bad."

"I see. I promise to put my best foot forward and make this campaign an award winner."

"I'm more worried about profits than awards, Rodney. We're sinking and without you we haven't a chance to survive," Simone held her head in her hands. "Oh, it's just *terrible!*"

Rodney stared at her for a moment. *If I fall for this, I'm the fool. Too bad that I don't have Gail with me.*

When Rodney didn't respond, Simone peeked at him through her fingers. She looked up and shook her head. "It's hard doing this all alone."

"Doing what alone?" Rodney asked, as he knew Sabrina was helping Simone get the company back on its feet. "You have a smart group of people in your corner. I'm sure they advise you at each turn."

"It's not just business. I need a friend who I can share my frustrations with."

"What about your sister?"

Before Simone could respond, the waiter walked up to the table and served two glasses of water. Then he asked them for their dinner orders.

"Just the water is fine, thank you," Rodney said.

Simone looked at the waiter. "Well, I'm going to have salmon for dinner. Rodney are you sure you don't want to order?"

"I'm sure. This is work, strictly work."

"We are working."

"You seem to be asking for more than a business relationship."

"I want friendship, but the marketing campaign is essential. I really need your help here."

"You'll get my best. You'll get my best crew on it."

"Does that include you, Rodney? Will you be my contact through this?"

"You'll have a direct contact and someone who'll keep you on board with our efforts. She's a good person, you'll like her."

"Are you speaking of your girlfriend?"

Rodney stiffened. "My firm hires highly experienced people. She will do well with your account. She's totally involved and knows your product line."

"Are you involved, Rodney? I want you involved."

"You can contact me if there are any problems."

"Good, because I know you have an excellent work ethic. I have no idea about hers."

"Trust my judgment on this. I know she'll deliver, and I'll be around if necessary." Rodney stood and placed his napkin on the table. "Thanks for inviting me, but I have to get home. From now on you can call me during office hours." He turned, walked towards the restaurant exit, and didn't look back.

Rodney arrived at home and saw Gail sitting with her laptop. "Hello, Rodney," she said without looking up.

Rodney hesitated before answering. "Um, why the cold greeting?"

"If you didn't want me on this campaign you should have told me. I heard through the grapevine that you're taking over."

"What on earth are you talking about?"

"Sabrina called me and said you were meeting them and going over the details of the campaign tonight. You met them; they were the client dinner you referred to on your message."

"Yes, I met…" Rodney cringed but hoped Gail would be happy to hear he'd left without eating. "I met Simone. She tried to get me to be the one on the campaign, and I told her no and that I support you and am confident in your efforts."

"You met Simone? I thought it was over between you two," Gail said. "She must have her claws out, ready for a fight."

"Fight? What fight? I told her you were the one, not me, and said only to contact me during office hours."

"Yeah, I heard you, but those two are up to something. Why did Sabrina call me and then you only spoke with Simone?"

"Don't worry about it, we'll get this campaign over with and then we'll have our distance from them."

"I worry, not because of your actions, but more because

they disrespect me as your woman. Rodney, we have to announce something more soon. It's time we make a serious
commitment and announce it to the world."

Rodney moved to the kitchen, got a drink, and returned
to the living room. He sat across from Gail and said nothing.
He watched her stare at him, he looked into her eyes, and he
observed her facial features. He sat there in silence and waited
for another question he could honestly answer. Gail closed her
laptop and leaned forward towards Rodney. She clasped her
hands, locking her fingers and asked, "Are you committed to
this relationship?"

"Yes, I am, more than you realize."

"So why is it so hard for you to tell everyone?"

"Believe me, everyone important knows. That is, everyone
important to me."

"I want strangers to know we love each other."

"And our love shows whenever we're together."

"So why not make it official?"

Rodney returned to silence. *Why not make it official? That's
what she wants and I thought about asking her earlier anyway.
Why not get married?* Rodney shook his head. He couldn't ruin
something so good by having it come from such an ugly conversation. "I'll ask you in my time and not before," he said. He
rose from his chair and walked to the bedroom.

Gail followed him and didn't say anything until he changed
into gym wear. "Where are you going?"

"Where does it look like I'm going?"

"It's late, Rodney. You shouldn't go out to run."

"I'm going to the gym. I'll return soon. I have some thinking to do."

"Marrying me is still something you have to think about?"

"I have some thinking to do."

"I may not be here when you return," Gail said and she moved aside to allow Rodney to leave. As Rodney left the room, she called out to him. "I didn't send flowers!"

It was miles into his run when Rodney thought of Gail's response to his honesty. He thought about the time Gail had been in his life, the challenges he'd overcome, and the time it had taken to arrive to a point of trusting another again. He remembered the first time they'd made love and how he'd felt free to let go. He recalled their endeavors at the office, how he'd been so impressed with Gail's motivation. Rodney ran and ran, and for an hour and a half, the treadmill moved. He let the adrenaline surge through his body until the emotions went numb, and he concentrated solely on the sound of his feet pounding on the circular track. After two hours, he finally stopped.

He returned home and found it empty; Gail wasn't there. He called her cell phone and didn't get an answer. He called June, and Dan answered, saying that June wasn't feeling very well, but that they hadn't heard from Gail. Rodney didn't know what to do, so he left the condo and ventured to Gail's apartment. He knocked on the door and there was no answer. He didn't see Gail's car, so he left. He drove to their favorite locations throughout the city and still didn't see any sign of Gail. He called her four times, but it always went to voicemail. He left messages asking her to return his calls. After three hours of searching and trying to contact her, Rodney gave up for the night.

It was 8:00 a.m. and Rodney arrived at the office to find

everyone celebrating. He walked through the lobby in a haze (he'd barely slept the night before), and didn't notice the pink balloons and sheet cake that read "Congratulations, Dan."

As Rodney passed Dan's office, Dan stepped out into the hall with a big smile. "She's here, man!" he said.

Rodney's heart skipped a beat. "Where is she?"

"Well, she's not *here* here. She's still at the hospital with June. They're resting, so I figured I'd come into the office to settle a few things before I had to go back."

"Hospital! What happened?"

"Rodney, where have you been through this entire conversation? June had the baby last night! Sorry I didn't tell you sooner, but it was a quick delivery. I only just arrived at the office a little bit ago."

Rodney's eyes widened and he spread his arms wide for a hug. "The baby! Wow, congratulations, bro!" The men patted one another on the back and stepped away from one another. "Hey, sorry for the confusion," Rodney said. "After what happened with Gail last night, I've been out of sorts."

Dan and Rodney entered Rodney's office. "Oh yeah, I'd already forgotten about your call last night. What happened?" Dan asked as he moved close to Rodney's desk.

"Well, we had a fight. I was honest about the dinner meeting request I received from Sabrina and Simone, and Gail didn't like it."

"You saw Simone last night! After all this time, I thought you'd be over her."

"I *am* over her. So I told Gail the truth about meeting Simone, and then Gail pressured me to ask her to marry me."

"Pressured you? You told me you were going to ask her soon anyway," Dan said. "Why didn't you ask?"

"You know that's not the way to ask a woman for her hand in marriage. Even though I was, or am, going to."

"She doesn't know it. So when she comes in, you'll figure it out and settle this. Ask her, Rodney. She's a catch and you really love her, so ask her."

"I'll ask. As soon as she comes in I'll make dinner reservations and settle this."

The morning passed into afternoon and there was no sign of Gail. After lunch, Rodney's executive assistant tapped on his door. "Sir, you have a Simone Stephens on the line."

"Please take a message," he said. Rodney didn't want to talk to her without sharing his heart with Gail first. He wanted Gail, and it was all he could think about. He yearned to ease the friction between them.

Dan entered the room without knocking. He had a long face, which was strange for a man whose wife had just given birth. Rodney knew it must be for his benefit, and about Gail. "What is it?" he asked.

"June called and said Gail paid a visit to the hospital. She wants a hiatus from the job."

"What? Just because I didn't ask her to marry me last night!"

"Apparently so, she can't face you. Not now."

"Will she ever?"

"I think as soon as she calms down she will. She does love you."

"I never doubted her love, just the intent on being married. I guess she's heartbroken that I haven't asked yet."

"Simone being in your life doesn't help."

"I'm over her, I told you that. I told Gail that too, and the truth about the dinner last night. This is what I get for being honest."

"We have another thing to consider with Gail's absence: the campaign. We don't have anyone else, other than you, to cover it. No one I'd like to entrust with such a big project."

"I guess I'll have to step in."

"I'd love to help, but with the new addition I can't travel as much. Are you sure you want to do it though? I mean, we can have another team member take on the project if we have to."

"No, Starz is considering taking the firm on as his sole marketing group. We can't afford any mistakes on this one. We told Starz we would have our best on the project. I'll step in."

"I hope Gail comes back soon."

"As far as the project goes, we can't afford to wait and see. I hope she returns, not for the firm, but for me."

Unable to focus on work, Rodney decided to take his lunch break early and left the office. He ventured to a local coffee shop, one he'd visited many times when he needed invigoration. He wanted to create and strategize ideas for the new marketing campaign, but his mind kept wandering. He sat in a lounge chair in the corner, watching people come in and out of the shop. He thought of his fight with Gail, and then he thought about the cause of it—his dinner with Simone. Why had she been so interested in speaking with him? It seemed she had popped back into his life just as he'd begun to forget about the heartbreak she'd caused.

After two hours and three cups of coffee, Rodney decided to leave. He headed towards Gail's apartment and stopped at a floral shop along the way. He purchased a bouquet of day lilies, Gail's favorite flower, along with a single rose to remind her of their recent trip to Los Angeles. When he arrived at her apartment, he knocked on the door, but there was no sign of life, no sign that anyone had been there since his visit the night before. He placed the floral card on the door just in case Gail decided to return. With a sigh, Rodney returned to his office.

Five days passed, and Rodney couldn't afford to push things off. He had to communicate with Simone and Sabrina in order to continue working on the fashion and production campaigns. Although he would have preferred to keep his distance from Simone, Rodney jumped into the campaign with vigor. After reviewing Sabrina's designs and the way they fit into Patricia's script, Rodney went to work with his imagination and created a scheme to impress.

After eight days of vigorous work, he called Dan and one other staff member for a review. The three worked through a full day refining Rodney's ideas into a great presentation. It was like old times for Rodney and Dan, reminiscent of their beginnings. Towards evening, Dan stepped back and surveyed their materials: sales projections, plans for magazine ads, television commercials, storefront displays, and more. "I guess you're ready for the ladies," he said.

"I think so. I don't really want to do this. Are you up to it?" Rodney asked.

"No way, we both have to be there like we would for any other presentation. I have to be neutral in this or June would kill me."

"It's only work."

"Yes, but it's my wife's best friend."

"And we aren't best friends? Come on, Dan, we've been through harder times together," Rodney said.

"I..." Dan paused. "I don't know how to explain it, but

June and I are united now. I have to keep the home front warm and cozy, especially with the little one. I'm not stepping out on you, just maintaining a good environment."

"Yeah, I get it, it's the way I thought Gail and I would end up."

"You still can, I think you still can."

Rodney straightened up and his eyes darted towards Dan. "Have you heard from her?"

"No, neither June or I have. But we think she is cooling down from her disappointment."

"I was going to ask her, you know."

"I thought you would, honestly I thought you would," Dan said as he left the office.

Rodney's executive assistant confirmed before leaving that his meeting with Sabrina and Simone was set for noon on Thursday. As everyone left for the night, Rodney closed his office door and remained inside. He sat in the room preparing for a business meeting with his lost love, while pining for his current one.

He was determined to harden his emotions and deal with business, which had never disappointed him the way women had. Marketing was his love, his life, and his partner that never bailed. He meditated on his return to his previous mind-set and practiced the presentation as if he'd never faced the sisters on any occasion. After a few hours, Rodney felt better and completely prepared for the meeting. He would return to the routine that had sustained him before Gail had entered his life. Leaving the office, he visited the gym, purchased groceries for his dinner, cooked, relaxed, and read.

21.
Desire Revisited

FOUR DAYS LATER and halfway into the workday, Rodney's executive assistant announced that the lunch delivery and the conference room were ready. He didn't jump to leave the office for the meeting; instead, he stood by the large office window and reflected on his morning conversation with Dan. Rodney couldn't believe Gail still hadn't reached out to him. Dan told him she had conversed with June. She had no message for Dan to pass along, and June told Dan not to say anything more than to let Rodney know that Gail was physically okay.

Rodney couldn't believe how distant Gail had became so quickly, especially when he thought he'd done the right thing. He continued to look out the window when Dan appeared at his office door. "Are you ready?" he asked.

Rodney turned and stood up from sitting on the edge of his desk. "Yes, let's do this." The two approached the conference room and took seats at the far end of the table.

"It's nearly ten after. I thought these ladies would be on time," Dan said as he remembered the last time he saw them together in a business environment. It had been at Phil's office when Dan and Rodney won their second account with his law firm.

Rodney looked at his watch. "I guess they are being fashionably late."

"I hope not, but just in case, I blocked off my schedule for the entire afternoon."

"So did I," Rodney said as they waited.

Soon after, the two ladies arrived. Dan directed them to two seats in the middle of the conference table. "Sorry we're late," Simone said as she took her seat. "My last meeting ran a bit long."

"It's okay," Rodney said.

"Still the gentleman, I see." Sabrina smiled as she took her seat.

"I hope you two didn't have lunch on the way," Dan said as he pointed to the spread. "We took the liberty. Please help yourself, and we'll start when you're ready."

"Thank you, I'm famished." Simone moved to grab a plate. Sabrina followed suit. "It looks great."

The four took time creating their lunches and began to eat. After a minute, Simone turned to Rodney. "So, I understand you have something to show us?"

"Yes, I do." Rodney clicked the remote and the overhead machine flashed while the lights dimmed. "Let me say I'm happy to have your business, and from this point forward, I'd like to explain the marketing program in depth." Rodney started the presentation.

Sabrina was particularly impressed with his attention to detail. Her eyes misted as she began to see her dream taking shape, but she retained her composure. It was an hour into the discussion when she received a text message. "I have to take this," she said and left the room.

Rodney was going to continue with his presentation, but

Simone held up her hand. "Let's wait for Sabrina's return. She's driving this effort."

"Sure," Rodney said and took his seat.

In an attempt to fend off an awkward silence, Dan turned to Simone. "So, how's business since the investigation?" he asked.

"It's moving and we're surviving. With this clothing line we should be ahead of the game soon after the launch."

"Great news, I bet. I mean, after all the turmoil your husband left."

"You read about the investigations?"

"Yes, we read about the investigation and hoped you would find a way to pull ahead from it."

"I guess Dan speaks for me too," Rodney said.

"I know you two have been pals and partners for years. I think it's wonderful. Had I known better, I'd say you were more than mere friends. I'd call you brothers."

"That's a serious compliment, Simone. Thank you," Dan said as he tapped his fingers on the table. "I wonder what's taking Sabrina? We still have more to review and I have to feed my kid tonight."

"Kid?" Simone turned back to Dan in surprise.

"Yes, Dan has a little one and a wife," Rodney said.

"Big change from the single life." Simone stood to peek on Sabrina. Seconds later she came back to the conference table. "I think we'll have to continue on our own. I'll take good notes."

Rodney stood and continued the presentation. Twenty minutes later, Sabrina returned to the conference room. After she sat down, she fidgeted and looked in all directions, paying little attention to Rodney's words. "Excuse me, Rodney," she said. "I hate to stop you again, but I need to talk to my sister." Sabrina turned to Simone. "Sis, can I see you for a moment?"

"Of course, what's wrong?"

"I'll explain outside." They walked out to the hallway. Once the conference door was closed, Sabrina took Simone by the hands. "I got a call from James, and he's coming to town. I tried to keep him away, but he isn't buying it. So, I have to get things together. He'll be here in a few hours. Can you take over for me?"

"I think I can handle it. Are you going home?"

"I am going to find a place for us to talk. I don't want him at your house."

"You can have him there, you know. He is still your husband."

"I know, but not there, not right now. I'll be somewhere else tonight."

"Are you sure?"

"I'm sure. I'll call you later," Sabrina said.

Simone returned to the conference room. "Well, guys, it's just me. Please continue."

Twenty minutes before the end of the business day, the presentation was nearly complete. Dan stood, looked at his watch, and tapped it with his index finger. "I'm afraid it's time," he said.

Rodney looked at his watch. "I guess you're right." He turned to Simone. "Do you have any questions or added comments?"

Simone looked around the room. "I might," she said, "but I guess Dan has to get going."

"Yes, I do," Dan said while he moved towards the

conference room doors. He stopped when he reached Simone and shook her hand, "It's been a pleasure seeing you again."

"Yes, I'll have to meet your family soon."

"One day soon, you will," Dan said and left the room.

"Shall we finish now?" Rodney asked.

"We can finish over drinks, if you don't mind." Simone moved her chair closer to Rodney.

Rodney looked at his watch again, searching for an excuse. "Well, maybe the next time."

"Rodney, I know your girlfriend isn't here, remember? If she were, she would have delivered this presentation herself. I know you have time, and besides, you can give me a ride home. That is, if you're still the kind gentleman I recall."

Rodney thought for a moment. He sighed. "Sure. Let's go get a few drinks, and then I'll take you home."

By 9:00 p.m., the bar was hopping and the two were on their third round of drinks. "Are you serious?" Rodney asked.

"Yes, I am very serious," Simone said. "You were just too good to be true back then."

"How can anyone be *too* good?"

"Easily, you were there and you found Aunt Marge when she fell in the street. You were at the hospital the second time she got sick. And you were there when she passed."

"I think those were just coincidences, and under the circumstances, I shouldn't have been around."

"I know Sabrina didn't encourage you not to visit. She had good intentions that night."

"I had good intentions." Rodney smiled and squinted at Simone. He thought of the night Simone had shared a dance with him in the park. He closed his eyes and saw the blue dress she'd worn for him on date night and remembered how he'd felt for her. "Yes, I had great intentions." Rodney stood and looked at her from head to toe. "You still have it."

"Thanks, and so do you. Actually, I think you've added a few muscles or two."

"*No way*," Rodney flexed and looked at his own arms. Then, he signaled the bartender for another round of drinks.

"I think we may have to take a taxi."

"I think you're right. Let's finish these drinks first though."

"I think we'll need to get to my place." Simone leaned toward Rodney.

"Your place it is." Rodney smiled and accepted the round of drinks the bartender placed in front of them. "Last question for the night: why didn't you accept my heart when you had a chance?"

"Rodney," Simone said as she reached and touched his arm, "hindsight is twenty–twenty. But actually…" Simone attempted to straighten and pointed an unsteady finger at Rodney. "But actually, after evaluating the scenario over the years, the sight is actually twenty–fifteen."

Rodney nodded solemnly and then grinned. "Clear view now."

"So clear and without excuse," Simone said as she leaned over and kissed him. It was the first time Rodney had gotten close enough to enjoy a kiss from her. It was smooth, as he'd envisioned years ago, and his heart thumped hard with intention and anticipation.

Simone sat next to the far door of the taxi and Rodney scooted in after her. He announced his condo address as the destination, but Simone changed his directions and gave the driver her address instead. "You'll have to stay with me tonight, Rodney."

"Sure thing. I hope this is what you want."

"It's what I want, wanted for a long time. We would have already been something had I listened to Aunt Marge."

"I agree, you should have listened," Rodney pulled Simone over to kiss him. After what seemed like seconds, the driver announced the arrival and the cost. Rodney paid the man. "Keep the change."

They entered Simone's house and she grabbed him and led him to her bedroom. She pulled him closer. "It's our chance," Simone said. "It's our chance to love."

Rodney didn't respond with words, he responded with actions. He disrobed and stood nude in front of her. His excitement announced his intention to indulge in her offer. He helped her undress and tossed each garment on the floor. Then he lifted her in his arms and placed her on the bed. His imagination ran ahead of his actions as he fumbled kisses from her lips to her breasts.

"Uhm," Rodney moaned. It was his moment to explore the one that had gotten away and to fulfill his desire. She lay under him, allowing his tongue to touch any part of her body. Rodney took control and explored every bit of Simone. He continued kissing her, moving down to kissing her erogenous lips, and further down to her thighs and ankles. He flipped her onto her stomach and continued kissing—kissing her back, kissing from her buttocks to the small of her neck, visiting her shoulders, and caressing her as he roamed her body. He took notice and enjoyed her every curve; he smiled as he touched her in places he'd only imagined.

Simone rolled over and reached into her drawer. "It's time

you put this on. I don't think I can wait much longer."

"I'll be glad to." Rodney applied the condom and within moments he hovered outside her moist entry. He fell for the moment, seizing an opportunity he'd considered missed and off-limits, and finally plunged, bringing Simone to a loud moan.

"It's been a while," Simone whispered as she felt Rodney's goodness fill her with joy. She placed her arms around Rodney and danced with his movement. Rodney moved without rhythm; he moved in whichever direction struck him and found her pleasure points along the way. Simone breathed with rapture. Beads of sweat lined her neck and shoulders, and soon after, she couldn't move from the climactic adventure. Rodney lay beside her, silent, looking at the ceiling. He didn't move as Simone maneuvered to lie closer to him. Rodney didn't move. *Just like a man, falling asleep*, thought Simone. She allowed herself to slumber. Rodney eventually fell asleep, but not without feeling pain in his heart.

Rodney woke with sun's first light. He looked at Simone. *This is where I wanted to be years ago.* He observed her features as she slept, and he realized he saw her differently than he had before. He took in the image of the woman he'd fallen for years ago. This woman, who had crushed his heart and rejected his multiple efforts to love, lay next to him. She was just as beautiful, but he started to wonder how he'd ever arrived at such an intense desire without ever getting to know her.

He felt the urge to leave without saying a word. He rose from the bed and went into the bathroom. He dressed and pulled out his phone to call a cab, as he remembered he'd left his car at the bar the night before. He looked around before leaving the bedroom and walked downstairs. Sabrina was leaving the house gym. "Good morning." She smiled.

"Good morning," Rodney said as he began to dial for the cab. He looked up at her. "What's the address here?"

"Why? If you give me a moment, I'll drive you," Sabrina said.

"Wouldn't that be out of your way?"

"Not at all. I have to go in anyway, so why not be early? You know what they say: the early bird catches the worm."

"True, so true."

"If you'd like coffee, there's some in the kitchen. Help yourself. I'll be right back down."

Rodney found the kitchen after wandering around the huge house. He couldn't believe the place. It was nothing like Aunt Marge's simple house. *The girls have done well, very well*, he thought as he found cups and coffee in the kitchen. He poured a cup, sat at the counter, and caught his reflection in the window. *Oh my god, what am I doing? Why did I do this?* He didn't have an answer. He sat there immersed in his own thoughts until he heard his name.

"Rodney, good morning," Simone said as she walked into the kitchen. "I see you found the coffee."

"Yes, thanks to Sabrina," he said.

"Good. If you are hungry, I'll cook breakfast for you."

"No, thanks, I need to get my car and head in."

"When I didn't see you next to me when I woke up, I figured you'd left the house already. I didn't even get a morning kiss from you." Simone moved over towards Rodney and leaned in for a kiss. Rodney touched her lips with his. "Is that it?" Simone asked.

"Morning breath."

"As if that matters." Simone poured herself a glass of orange juice. "So, what time are you off today?"

Rodney intended to avoid seeing Simone in the near future, despite the campaign. His idea was to finish the campaign planning as quickly as possible and finalize whatever was needed to get the program started. "I'm probably working late today."

"How late?"

"Let's just say that your marketing campaign has priority—that late."

"Oh, a lot of catching up to do since Gail left. I see. Well, I'm sure we can do something another day. You catch up. I'll be in touch."

Rodney felt as if he'd escaped an unwanted commitment with Simone, another unexpected experience. He finished his coffee just in time for Sabrina to arrive. "Ready?" she asked.

"Yes." Rodney followed Sabrina out to her car.

Once inside the vehicle, Sabrina turned to Rodney. "My sister's happy you spent the night. I haven't seen her in such a great mood for a long time."

"It was nice." Rodney managed to answer without elaboration or revelation of his thoughts.

"She likes you, Rodney, she knows her mistakes now."

"Don't we all? I mean, we learn from our mistakes."

"Yeah, you're right. We learn a lot from mistakes." Sabrina drove into traffic. "I should really know better."

"What happened to you yesterday?"

"I talked to my soon-to-be ex-husband."

"Trouble?"

"No, but I let Simone think so. She wanted you and I helped."

"Bad girl. It's just like a loving sister."

"It worked, and I'm not ashamed I did it."

"Honestly, for your sister, I'd say you shouldn't be. But for me, it may be a different story."

"What does that mean?"

"I may not have been ready, but it's water under the bridge now."

"You aren't over your girlfriend. I get it, she left you and you're sunken. Poor Rodney."

"How did you know Gail left me?"

"Well, she was the main person working on the campaigns, and all of a sudden you're scheduling the presentation? It wasn't that hard to figure out; you two do work together after all. There's no such thing as actually keeping work and your personal life separate when you're seeing someone you work with."

"So when you agreed to come over for the conference, you knew I'd go with Simone?"

"It was a chance."

"What a setup. I'm that easy."

"No, you're just a man, Rodney. A good guy and one my sister should have gotten involved with long ago."

"That's what she said last night."

"She means it. I'm not sure you understand the troubles she's had in life."

"I'm not sure I want to know. As a matter of fact, I don't want to know. Turn right at the next light, the bar is on the hill."

"You think about it. I want her happy. She's done a lot for me, so I have high hopes we'll do this for each other. You know, the marketing campaign for me, and my sister for you."

"I'll keep my bargain to deliver the campaign."

"And I'll get you closer to my sister," Sabrina said as she stopped the car. "Deal?"

"I'll get back to you on the sister thing." Rodney exited the car. "Thanks for the lift."

Sabrina drove off and looked at him in her rearview mirror. *He'll come around soon, I know he will.*

Rodney drove to his condo, went inside, and looked at the answering machine. There were no messages. He walked around the condo, jumped in the shower, and prepared for the day. He called Dan and asked if June had heard anything new from Gail. Dan answered with the same answer as he had each day before: "Nothing."

Before leaving the condo, Rodney called Gail's cell phone for what seemed like the hundredth time since she'd left. "Please, Gail, give me a call. We can talk this through. I love you." Rodney drove into the office and, once there, focused strictly on his work. He dove into the two campaigns with a tremendous focus. He called Starz and set up his review in Los Angeles, and then coordinated his travel plans.

Rodney thought a trip west could be uplifting. He looked forward to getting away from Richmond for awhile, where there seemed to be memories of his life with Gail all over the place. Everywhere he turned, he thought he could see her from a distance. Rodney needed to clear his head. He knew a business trip would be just what he needed to encourage his continued concentration on the project and, of course, seeing an old friend always helped.

Sabrina and Simone got wind of his trip and coordinated their adventure to Los Angeles. Simone suggested that Sabrina attend the meeting, and Sabrina suggested that Simone tend to Rodney. They deceived Rodney's assistant into giving them Rodney's travel information and coordinated their arrangements to match his. They even reserved a room at the hotel he'd booked. It was a perfect setup for Simone.

A week after he'd scheduled his trip, Rodney arrived in Los Angeles. He took a day of leisure to review the campaign and prepare for his meeting with Starz. Later he took a drive along the Pacific Coast Highway, and soon his mind and heart returned to Gail. He fought back the emotions and stopped at a coffee shop when he reached Palos Verdes. It was a quaint place with a fantastic view of the beach and ocean. Rodney ordered a small cup of coffee and a pastry, and took a seat at a small table outside. He gazed at the view and allowed his mind to wander.

He placed his emotions on hold as best he could until he saw a figure running along the beach. He couldn't believe his eyes. He thought for sure it was Gail. Rodney jumped from the table and ran down the trail to the beach for a closer look. "Gail!" The person didn't turn. Rodney continued his pursuit. "Hey, Gail!" The woman continued running, and her figure disappeared as she rounded the beachside cliff. *Get a hold of yourself, man.* Rodney slowed to a stop, turned, and dejectedly returned to the coffee shop.

Rodney arrived back at the hotel in time for his evening run. His exercise routine helped him combat stress and prepare for upcoming challenges. Foregoing the hotel gym, Rodney ran on the sidewalks that lined the city streets. After two and a half miles, he circled back towards the hotel. As he approached the tall building, he noticed the two ladies, Simone and Sabrina, exiting a black car and handing their keys to the valet. He couldn't believe his eyes—they were standing in front of the same hotel where he was staying. Rodney approached with caution and tried not to attract their attention; he slowed his pace and waited for the women to enter the hotel. Not quite sure if they'd cleared the lobby by the time he reached the doors, Rodney entered the hotel and moved quickly to the elevator. As soon as the elevator doors opened, he entered and pressed his floor number and the close door buttons.

He thought the coast was clear until he arrived on his floor. Leaving the elevator, he noticed Simone standing in front of his door. Rodney almost jumped back in and pressed the elevator doors closed again, but he realized it would be use-less. She already knew where he was staying. Rodney wiped his forehead and stepped into the hallway. "Looking for me?"

Simone looked down the hall and saw Rodney. "Why, yes, I am." She smiled and waited for him to approach. "I heard you were in town and thought you'd like to do something this evening."

"I'm not up to it right now. I had an idea to rehearse my presentation for Starz and take in a nice quiet evening."

"We can do that too. I have time for us to rekindle things the right way."

"Rekindle things?" Rodney asked as he opened his room door.

"Our night together was wonderful, but I thought we'd add a little romance to the mix here in Los Angeles."

"I'm not sure I'm up for that," Rodney said as he walked into his room.

Before he could close the door, Simone followed him inside. "Of course you are, Rodney. I haven't forgotten how strongly you felt for me. You sure reminded me the other night. Why do you hesitate? Is it that woman you were dating? Is she still in your life?"

"Yes, she is," Rodney said. "She's definitely in my life."

"Are you meeting her here?" Simone moved to the window.

"Well, not exactly."

"Rodney, what woman has a man of your stature waiting? It's not like you need her in your life."

"Actually I do need her, more than I care to admit."

"Then don't admit it and move on. We can have so much together, the two of us."

"No, not really, I know what type of men you like in your life. I don't fit the bill."

"Then why did you stay with me the other night?"

"It was a dream of mine at one time, and the other night I got carried away. It was something I'd wanted for so long that I didn't realize until too late that it was a dream of the past."

"It *was* like a dream, wasn't it? Let's go back to that so we can enjoy each other again." Simone moved closer to Rodney.

He backed away. "You have to leave now so I can shower." He walked to the door and held it open for Simone.

Simone hesitated. "You sure you don't want me to join you?"

"Tonight isn't good for me." Rodney waved his hand from Simone to the door's opening. Simone reluctantly moved; she walked to him and paused before exiting to touch his face.

"You'll change your mind. I'm in suite 945." She left the room and Rodney closed the door.

22.
The Confrontation

GAIL HAD BEEN in California for almost four weeks; she was staying in a beach house not far from where Rodney had stopped for coffee. She always had access to Starz's guesthouse and found it a cozy place to rediscover herself.

She couldn't explain why she'd left so suddenly or why she wouldn't talk to Rodney. Even though she'd received multiple calls, emails, and text messages from him reaching out to her about his desires, it still wasn't enough to spark a return. She immersed herself in the solitude and closed herself off from the outside world. Aside from her daily phone call to June, she left her phone in the guesthouse kitchen unused.

It wasn't until Starz spoke to her explaining Rodney's visit for the campaign that she realized she needed to reach out to him. She knew it was him that she wanted. She loved Rodney.

With a newfound excitement, Gail called June to confirm what she'd learned about Rodney's upcoming trip. She had the idea that she'd tell him of her hope to return to her life, her friends, and hopefully her love in person instead of over the phone. She wanted to look in his eyes and feel his arms around her when she told him she was ready to come home.

Gail discovered the name of Rodney's hotel and decided to plan a visit. On the day she planned to surprise him, she found herself packing to leave the house as if she wouldn't be returning. While packing, she found a poster of Starz's last campaign that she and Rodney had worked on together. The production was now touring the country. She recalled the events, multiple dates, and interactions leading to the campaign's launch. Gail remembered the times she'd spent dining, dancing, and laughing with Rodney. The memories engulfed her, crashing over her one by one. They were thoughts that hadn't yet surfaced.

For weeks, she had only thought of ways to avoid Rodney, the rejection, and the fear of never being married. All her life, she'd promised herself that she would have it all by the time she turned thirty: a wonderful career, husband, and family. She wanted more out of life, and when Rodney didn't seem to reciprocate her desires, she was heartbroken. Gail had fallen into old patterns and had run the instant her beloved had resisted commitment. Her understanding of love and relationships stemmed from depictions in movies and magazines, not from real-life experiences. She wanted the fairytale. After listening to Rodney's heartfelt messages, she just knew he'd changed his mind.

Gail felt her anticipation grow as she drove into Los Angeles. She hardly took in the scenic views, as her mind was focused on one thing: seeing Rodney. She was about to burst with excitement, so she stopped the car to call him. Just as she was about to dial his number, she thought of their last trip to Los Angeles. *Rodney surprised me at the same hotel, and what a surprise was that! Better to return the favor than to call him now.* She giggled and decided to call June instead. June picked up after two rings. "Hey, Gail."

"June, I'm going to see Rodney. I found out he's in Los Angeles—I'm going to go see him right now!"

"That's great, Gail. Really great. Let me know how it goes, okay?"

"I will. Have a good night, June."

"You too."

Gail got back in her car and continued driving to Rodney's hotel.

Meanwhile, Rodney was in the middle of reviewing the first scene of a commercial for the production campaign with his firm. He was pleased to find that his L.A. office had continued to run smoothly in his absence. When Rodney focused on work, it was just that. He hated interruptions and would rarely answer his cell phone during the workday. He'd managed to avoid Simone, with work as his cover, though it seemed she was after his every free moment. Rodney worked himself through most of the day. Once it began to get dark, he decided to leave the office, find a few moments of fresh air, and grab some dinner and a relaxing drink before heading back to his hotel room.

Simone dialed Rodney's room and cell phone throughout the day but failed to connect with him. As night settled, she paced the floor of her hotel room, searching for ideas to interrupt Rodney and get his focus when he returned after a hard day at work. She knew he'd have an excuse, but that didn't discourage her. She was motivated by her memory of how sensitive and attentive Rodney had been years ago. *He danced with me, chased me, was there for me, and I ruined everything... well, not this time*. She wanted Rodney, and she wasn't going to make the same mistake of letting him go twice.

In light of the investigations into her company and her ex-husband's deception, she knew her heart needed a sensitive soul. Simone was determined, and didn't plan to acknowledge any obstacle that stood in the way of her intentions. So far she'd done everything possible to remove any obstructions, and yet it wasn't working. Simone decided to meet Sabrina in the lobby and rethink a new strategy.

Gail arrived at the hotel's guest services desk and asked the clerk for Rodney Witherspoon. The clerk dialed Rodney's room and explained that the line was busy. In an effort to avoid Simone's calls and messages, Rodney had left the phone off the hook, even when he wasn't at the hotel. "I can try again in a few minutes," Gail said. She attempted to convince the clerk to provide Rodney's room number but was unsuccessful.

Gail decided to wait in the lobby in the hope that the clerk would soon get through to Rodney. After a few minutes, she felt someone tap her on the shoulder. "Gail, is that you?" Sabrina asked.

Gail was shocked to see Sabrina standing before her. "Sabrina, what are you doing here? I thought you were still in Richmond."

"I'm here working with Starz. My sister came along too, since we've made a lot of progress on the marketing campaigns. Speaking of the campaign, where have you been? I was surprised to learn you'd disappeared in the middle of a project."

"Yeah, I am sorry about that. I've been around. I just needed some time."

"Not to worry, Rodney's been working very hard on the

campaign."

"Really? I was actually hoping to find him here…"

"Oh, don't worry about it. Rodney has everything under control now ,and I'm sure he's busy. Like I said, he's been working hard."

"I know he's busy, but this isn't about the campaign."

"Oh, you're here for personal reasons? Come on, Gail, let him get over you and move on."

"We aren't over…"

"Of course you are, you two haven't spoken for a month. You had your chance with him. Besides, what man will wait for a woman who's not speaking to him after so long?"

"Rodney, that's who."

"Don't be so sure."

"I am sure."

Sabrina stood before Gail and said nothing. Gail's jaw clenched. "Is there something you want to share?"

"He didn't wait," Sabrina said. "He and my sister are—"

Simone walked up to the two women. "Are what?" she asked.

"Hey, I was just explaining to Gail that you and Rodney are an item."

Rodney walked into the hotel lobby and saw Simone and Sabrina standing with their backs to him. He moved to get to his room before they noticed his arrival but stopped short when he saw Gail in front of them. His heartbeat increased and his feet compelled him to move in their direction. A smile spread across his face at seeing Gail.

Before he reached them, he realized their conversation had become heated. He saw Gail take a step back and cover her mouth. Simone smiled as she watched Gail's response. He realized with regret what the sisters had told her. *Oh no, they got to Gail before I could explain.* Rodney realized he had to interject soon, or he'd lose his chance. He walked to Gail's side and touched her on the shoulder, interrupting Sabrina and Simone.

"Hey," Rodney said as he looked at Gail.

Simone beamed at the sight of Rodney. "Hi, darling."

Sabrina smiled. "Nice seeing you, Rodney."

Rodney looked into Gail's hurt eyes with an equally pained expression. He was at a loss for words and shuffled his feet. "I guess it's a bad time."

"Not for me, I know you two have business to discuss, but we're heading out for dinner and drinks. You should come with us and catch up with Gail in the morning," Simone said.

"No, I need to talk to Gail, if that's okay with her?" Rodney searched Gail's expression for any sign of affection.

"I think you should go to dinner," Gail said. "I've heard enough from Sabrina to understand you are now a part of their lives."

"I'm what?" Rodney shot a glare at Simone and Sabrina. "Gail, we should talk."

"Talk about what, Rodney?" Gail asked as she shook her head.

Rodney picked up Gail's overnight bag off the ground. "Excuse me, ladies," he said to Simone and Sabrina. "Gail and I have some important things to discuss."

"But, Rodney, what about dinner?" Simone asked.

"I didn't have any intention of going to dinner with you two from the beginning. Have a good night," Rodney said as he encouraged Gail to come with him.

Gail stood her ground for a moment. She took in Simone and Sabrina's reaction to Rodney's stern words. They didn't seem as convincing as they had during their discussion before Rodney appeared. Gail decided to walk with Rodney but with doubt. She walked away from Simone and Sabrina and stopped short of the elevators. "I'm not going with you. We can talk here in the lobby," Gail said. "I just found out enough from the sisters. What the hell, Rodney?"

"I'm sorry you found out that way."

"You mean it's all true?" Gail frowned in disgust. "How could you do this to me?"

"Do this to *you*? I'm confused."

"You shouldn't be confused. I thought you loved me."

Rodney saw that other hotel patrons were beginning to take notice of them. "We should talk upstairs. Not here."

"Here is fine, Rodney. What makes you think I'd go upstairs with you?"

"Okay, I'm not much into scenes. I'll catch you another time when you're ready to talk sensibly."

"This is the time, Rodney. If we don't talk about this now, there's not going to be a later."

"Then later isn't an option?"

"Why? Because we should do everything on your watch, right? You haven't learned anything." Gail walked towards the hotel exit.

"Running away again?" Rodney asked. He watched Gail exit the door and felt a sharp pain in his chest. It was a reminder of his love for her, the pain he'd tried so hard to suppress hit him twofold.

She's doing it again. Rodney ran to catch up with her. "Hey, will I at least get a call from you? Will you answer the phone for me?"

Gail didn't respond. She didn't even look at him. As she

got into her car, she locked the door behind her and started crying. Her idea, her surprise, her imagination of a joyous return was all crushed. She drove off the lot and watched Rodney standing there in her rearview mirror.

Rodney stood there and watched Gail drive away. He stared after her as the car got smaller and smaller, farther and farther away, and prayed that she'd turn the car around. Gail's car reached the top of a hill, and just like that, her car disappeared behind it. She was gone.

Before he could walk down the street to the nearest bar, Simone and Sabrina pulled up next to him in the parking lot. Simone rolled down the passenger window. "Hey, you should come with us."

"No, thanks," Rodney said.

"She's not coming back, Rodney, I'm sure of it." Simone beckoned to him to enter the vehicle. "Come on, what can it hurt now?"

Rodney stood at the car, contemplating his next move. He looked behind Sabrina's car and saw that another group was waiting for them to get out of the way. "What did you tell Gail?" he asked.

"Get in, I'll tell you about it on the way."

Rodney opened the car door.

Gail arrived at the airport only to learn that the next flight to Richmond wasn't until the next morning. She'd cried the entire drive to the airport, so she booked a room at the nearest hotel she could find and crawled into bed. Gail tossed and turned and finally decided to call June. She dialed June's number and the phone rang.

"Hello?" June answered.

"You are not going to believe this," Gail said.

"Believe what? Gail, it's eleven thirty here."

"I'm sorry, but I need to talk to you. Rodney has another woman. The jerk slept with another woman."

"Gail," June said as she sat up in bed, "you need to hear this. I'm not going to let you lose out on a good guy."

"He's not so good." Gail sniffled. "He's like all the rest."

"What happened? I thought you were going to see him."

"I got there and was cornered by his new girlfriend and her sister. They filled me on what happened between them. When I tried to talk to Rodney, he wouldn't talk to me."

"They 'filled you in'? What did they tell you?"

Gail explained what Simone and Sabrina had related to her and described how Rodney hadn't tried to deny anything, and instead had pushed her away. She sobbed. "June, how could I have been so stupid? I went to that hotel thinking he loved me."

June listened intently, but stopped Gail with her last comment. "Now, Gail," she said, "you have got to calm down. Those girls knew exactly what to tell you."

"They told me the truth."

"Probably so, according to them; but here's what I know: Rodney loves you, he's been moping around for weeks. He's thrown himself into his work. We haven't seen him with anyone, he doesn't come out with us much, and he's taken everything you were doing for the job into his focus. Does that sound like a guy who's out with those sisters?"

"Yes, you just don't see what he's doing."

"Oh my, you're hurt and not seeing through the forest. Open your eyes Gail, come on, and open your eyes."

"I see everything; it's quite clear."

"Do you really see it? Gail, what did you expect Rodney to think? You weren't speaking with him."

"It was a lesson he needed to understand. I wasn't going to wait around forever."

"Seems like you got the lesson," June said. "This is the first he's heard from you in a month."

"I needed him to see what he's lost or losing. I know he realized it, because he called me nearly five times a day for the first couple weeks. Just yesterday he sent me a text. He claimed he still loved me, and then I return to him to find this."

"Find what? Two women leading you to believe he's not for you. If he isn't for you, then who is he for? Can't you see what they are doing?" June asked.

"I know he isn't for me. They can have him."

"Gail, you're talking nonsense. Think about what you're saying. You don't mean that, I know you don't."

Gail sobbed again. "No, I do mean it. He's not for me. I can do without Rodney. I can do without him."

Rodney closed the car door. "In retrospect, I'd better not. Thanks for the offer." He returned to the hotel and sat at a couch in the hotel lounge. When he was on his second drink, Simone tapped him on the shoulder.

"Hey," she said, "you look really sad."

"Actually, I am," Rodney said. "I'm nothing like you left me, I learned from that experience, but I'm pretty much hurt over this."

"Like I left you?"

"Yes, remember you slammed me during the memorial

cruise. I did nothing to deserve it, and you let into me."

"I wasn't thinking right, Rodney. I was mourning Aunt Marge."

"I understood, but it was still a horrible event. I never fully lived it down."

"I didn't mean to be so hard on you," Simone said, "You caught me at a terrible moment. Plus, I thought you were my stalker until Sabrina told me she invited you."

"Stalker? How could you call me a stalker when I didn't force myself on you?" Rodney frowned.

"You were everywhere I didn't want you to be at the time. But you're here now. I like you being here now. You shouldn't worry about Gail. She'll get over it."

"Gail, you mention the woman I love."

"Love! You actually love her?"

"Yes, I love her and would have asked her to be my wife if she hadn't left." Rodney took a sip of his drink and waved at the bartender to send another.

Simone hesitated. *I still have a chance.* "You need to let her go, Rodney. She left you again. I see a cycle. If she really loved you, she'd not have left. You two could have talked things over."

"Talk things over, yes, that's a novel concept, isn't it?"

"Maybe, but still, she's not interested. You need to open your eyes. I've been where you are."

"As if I haven't been in this position before? You don't seem to remember our past."

"It's not the same, nothing near the same. We never got as far as you two, and Gail isn't trying."

"Maybe she is, and I didn't give her a chance."

"What? I'm not buying that, Rodney. I know you gave her

a chance. You need to just sit back and allow me to show you how a woman treats her man."

"You?" Rodney laughed. He grabbed his cell phone from the coffee table and dialed Gail. There was no answer, and the phone went to voice mail. Rodney didn't leave a message; instead, he ended the call.

"Still no answer?" Simone asked.

"None."

"Open your eyes, Rodney, please open your eyes." Simone rose from the couch and stood over Rodney. "Pay attention, look at who is here for you. I am and will be in the future. You need to pay attention." Simone picked up her purse and began to walk away. "Call me when you see things clearly," she said as she stormed out of the room.

Gail arrived home after a long day of traveling. She entered her place in a haze; her eyes were dry from crying most of the day. She washed her face and decided to watch television, a movie, or anything to help her escape. After surfing channels for ten minutes, she decided she should just go lie down again. Before settling into her bedroom, Gail walked back to her front door to lock the dead bolt. It was then that she saw a sealed envelope that had been slid under the door. She opened the envelope slowly, and sucked in her breath when she noticed Rodney's handwriting:

My darling Gail,

It's been weeks since I've heard from you and my heart aches. I know you're in good health, and that is the only thing keeping me sane. I'm saddened about our time apart. Gail, you waltzed into my life when things were blurry from a broken heart. I tried to recover without anyone or any help. I put so much into bouncing back; it nearly pushed you away from me from the time we first met. Yet, you fought with persistence to pursue me, create us, and love. You came to me full of energy and dreams, which were the keys to my heart. You sparked inside me the passion I'd once lost. Today, you spark within me the music of sorrow. I miss you every day. Please, come back to me.

I dream of our life together each night, and wake in your absence feeling as if you'd returned. My heart pounds as excitement fills my soul, only to come to the reality that you're still gone. So I call, and text, and write you throughout the day in hopes that you'll respond. Each day, the only thing I pray for is your response.

Evenings are the worst. I remembered our day's end routine, where we'd catch up and cook dinner together. We got into such a habit of love and living, something I'd never experienced. Now my days end with me trying to cope with the sadness in my heart. Dinner is just another moment of missing you, and nothing is clearer to me than how much I love you.

I need you, Gail, and whatever it takes for me to find you is my mission in life. Love came to me and I didn't jump. I'm not letting it escape me, not this time. Whatever it takes, Gail. I will do whatever it takes to make things right between us.

I love you, Gail.

Forever,
Rodney

Gail's eyes filled with tears, and she reread the letter as soon as she'd finished to grasp every word Rodney had said. She stood up, grabbed her unpacked suitcase, and headed back to the airport.

23.
Try, Try Again

THE NEXT NIGHT, Rodney again sat in the hotel lounge. He sat, brooding. *Why wouldn't she talk to me in private? Why did it have to be a scene?* He thought over the events of the night before. *I'm glad Simone left. At least I don't have to deal with her right now.* After Simone had walked out of the lounge, Rodney had continued to drink until he passed out in his hotel room. His intention was to do the same tonight. He lifted his phone from the table in hopes of finding a message from Gail, but there was still nothing. Rodney thought about dialing Gail's number but resisted. He couldn't allow himself to be vulnerable any longer. He needed to accept the heartbreak and move on. He sat for another hour before moving into the night. Going amongst a crowd was better than sitting in silence.

Simone and Sabrina sat in Sabrina's room eating take-out. Between bites, Simone rose from the couch to grab a bottle of water. "Sis, he's not going to give up, and he will not see she's not the one. A blind man could see it, why can't he?" Simone returned to the couch.

Sabrina moved towards her sister. "Because, maybe he

loves her, Simone. Let's face it, remember when he seemed to love you or was so infatuated with you, he did everything possible to get you? He took all sorts of punishment back then, just for trying. You have got to remember, he's an emotionally driven guy."

"I remember, and that's why I know I made a mistake being with Stefan. He didn't love me, and Rodney did. I ended up with a bad man, an embezzler con artist."

"Don't beat yourself for being deceived, just move forward with the knowledge you have now. If you want Rodney to love you again, go fight for it." Sabrina urged her sister to stand up. "Knowing Rodney, he won't be in his room long. Why don't you get cleaned up and wait for him in the lobby? Don't be a bug, just be nice and ask if he'd like company."

Simone rose from the couch and walked to the door. She stopped just short of leaving. "I guess you're right. It's been a long time since I've tried to land a man."

"You'll be fine. Have fun." Sabrina closed her door as Simone exited.

Gail drove from the airport in her rental car. She'd returned to Los Angeles in haste, but now she was thinking about her argument with Rodney. *I can't believe he slept with Simone! And why didn't he try harder to talk to me?* Then she remembered Rodney's letter and softened. *Perhaps I jumped to conclusions. I know things can work between us now that I've learned of his feelings. I need to make up for that horrible, childish scene.*

Gail continued driving towards Rodney's hotel. When she stopped at a red light, she looked to her left and saw a flower vendor with displays along the street. She stopped to purchase a rose, the same type that Rodney had given when he'd surprised her two months before. The rose reflected her desire to make peace with Rodney and finally get her life back. *Four weeks is a long time for silence, but it worked. I know he'll marry me now, I just know it.*

Rodney had returned to his room and fallen into an alcohol-influenced slumber, not moving from his chair.

Simone went to her room to freshen up, to change into something more seductive, and to think about her strategy. She contemplated how to win Rodney's affection without resistance. She thought about Sabrina's advice and remembered how Rodney had tried to capture her heart years ago. She smiled and added more lipstick. It wasn't long before she left the room and headed for the elevators going down to the lobby in hopes of catching Rodney on his way out.

Gail arrived to the hotel again, and this time, she was successful in her flirtations with the desk clerk. He winked at her as he provided Rodney's room number. Gail grinned in response because she was on her way to reconnecting with her love. Gail stood at the elevators waiting for the next available lift. She couldn't believe her eyes when the elevator doors opened. Simone stood there as dolled up as Gail had ever seen her.

Simone saw her as she stepped out of the elevator and met Gail's gaze with an icy stare. "I don't think he wants to see you."

"This isn't your business, Simone. I suggest you stay out of it."

"That's where you're wrong, Gail; it's my business because he's my guy. I dated him years ago and now we've reconnected. He loves me. Always has, always will."

"Simone, you have got to be kidding. Stop fooling yourself.

I was the one who walked out on Rodney, and he pursued. I didn't speak to him, and he pursued. I know he loves me; he wants me more than anything in the world."

"You're so naive. You don't know Rodney and I have plans tonight, I'm here waiting for him. You can't ruin this, you're an emotionally challenged girl trying to play a woman's game. It's time you realize that you're through."

"I'm through? Well, let me tell you, Simone, he's my man, my guy, my love. I hadn't figured it out before, but you are the woman who hurt him so badly. You are the woman he tried telling me about and the reason he kept his distance from anyone who could get close. If his love for you were real, why is it he's not here? Rodney would never have a woman wait for him. Obviously, you're hallucinating." Gail pressed the call button for another elevator. "I suggest you make other plans." Gail entered the elevator and pressed the close door button. Simone walked to the hotel's lounge and ordered a stiff drink.

Gail walked to Rodney's room door and knocked. She waited and nothing happened. She knocked again, but there was still no answer. It wasn't until the third knock that she heard Rodney. "Who is it? Simone?" he called. "Simone?" *She was right, he does seem to be interested in her*, Gail thought and began to walk away. Before she got far, she heard Rodney through the door again. "Simone, I told you to leave me alone. I'm not interested." Gail smiled and knocked again, with enthusiasm. Finally Rodney opened the door and saw Gail. She held out the rose. "Peace offering," she said.

Rodney rubbed his eyes. "Oh, it's you," he said as he walked into the room.

"What kind of greeting is that?"

"It's the kind where I've waited for weeks to talk to you. When I finally see you, you give me hell and cause a scene." He sat back in the chair he'd been sleeping in.

"That's a warm welcome after not seeing someone for a long period, Rodney."

"I'm not sure what to think or say at the moment. I poured my heart out to you for weeks, and nothing. Once you finally see me, I get thrown claws and fangs. I'm not excited; I'm on the defensive."

"As you should be, but I know you love me."

"I never denied my love for you, but I'm not ready to accept another situation where I lose again. I've lived it once already, I fought to heal for over a year, and finally when I gave you my heart, you ran."

"You didn't ask me for my hand."

"Is that it? Think about why I didn't. Or are you seriously that psycho?"

"'Psycho'? I'm psycho now?"

"Ask any psychologist about your running away—anyone would confirm that you were crazy to leave like that and not call me for a month." Rodney poured another drink and took a sip.

Gail sat on the couch and watched Rodney drink; it was the first time she'd seen him partake in straight liquor.

He poured more whiskey into his glass. "I am not going through this again. I don't think I'll ever survive the stupidity."

"Now you're calling me stupid?" Gail's voice rose with anger.

"No, I'm calling your actions stupid."

"I had to do something, you rejected me. I'd given my all to our relationship. I've worked by your side and pushed us to excel. We made a good team, and I thought marriage was the next step."

"The next step."

"Yes, you know I want a family. You know my intentions, and they are not to simply play house."

"You have a strange way of showing it. Leaving me for weeks and not saying a word. Well, now I'm the one at a loss for words. Why don't you do your magic trick again and disappear?"

"You don't mean that, Rodney."

"I mean it, I mean it. You're no different from Simone. You both are horrible women. You have no idea what you have in a man until he's gone. Do as she did and leave me alone."

Gail sat in shock. This wasn't exactly the response she'd expected. The rose, the excitement, and the desire, all seemed like wasted thoughts. She remembered the letter, his profession of love and missing her, and wondered at how such strong emotions could have dissipated; she hoped they hadn't. Gail waited for another comment from Rodney while deciding her next move. *Should I go or stay?* She looked at Rodney as he sat staring into space. "Are you sure you want me to leave?" she asked. Rodney didn't answer. "Rodney!" He turned to look at her; his eyes were glossed over. Gail leaned forward. "Are you sure?"

"I expect you to," Rodney said and closed his eyes. Gail had never seen him in such a state. She decided to let him sleep and be there for him in the morning when he was over his inebriated condition.

It was early, around 6:00 a.m., when Rodney woke in the chair. He woke with such a headache and thirst that he immediately went to the bathroom for water. On the way, he noticed a purse on the nightstand. It wasn't one he recognized. In the bathroom, he went through what he recalled from the night before. *The last thing I said to Gail was to leave. Did Simone come to my room? God, I hope not.* He turned to look at the clothes in the chair, and rubbed his face. Rodney moved to the chair and opened the window shades; the rising sun peaked through the glass with its warm light.

"Good morning," Gail said as she rose from slumber.

Rodney sighed with relief. He turned to face her and hardened his expression. "Nice seeing you here. I thought you left last night."

"I decided you had no idea what you were telling me." Gail smiled and stretched. "I'll have to let that night be one of our past."

"I know what I said, but I didn't expect you to be here this morning."

"Are you surprised?"

"Yes, totally surprised you didn't leave when I asked you to." Rodney moved to the bed. "I'm not asking for forgiveness, and I don't regret what I told you last night. Why are you here?"

"I'm here because I love you."

"You have a hell of a way of showing it."

"Look, you have a right to feel upset, but you could have prevented all of this. You didn't ask me to marry you when I wanted you to."

"I think you need to get dressed and go about your business."

"Rodney, you are my business. I know how you feel about me."

"Do you really? I'm not convinced. You come back, I try to

talk to you about us, and you'd rather make a scene. Then you show up here out of the blue and expect me to smile and be excited to see you. How dare you?"

"I know you love me, Rodney. I read your letter."

"My letter?"

"The one where you professed your love for me and told me that you miss me terribly. I know our last conversation was rough, and it may have taken me two trips across the country to realize it, but I know you love me."

"You went all the way back to Richmond? That letter wasn't the only sign of my love for you, Gail. Why didn't you just answer the phone over those long weeks? You've shown you're good at disappearing, so why don't you do it again? I'm going to take a shower. When I come out, you should be gone."

"I'm not leaving until we settle this."

"Oh, it's settled all right. I'm not letting you in. Not this time. I trusted you, and you've proven to be no different."

"Different? Let me tell you different. You slept with Simone, and now she has the idea that you two can rekindle whatever you had. She is determined to win you over. And with the help of Sabrina, she may just do that."

"Don't you realize I let her go the more I opened up to you? I guess you were too selfish to see it. I didn't rush into this relationship for a reason, but I guess all you can recall is my reluctance to rush."

"I knew you weren't in any hurry. It's why I was patient. But my patience ran out when Sabrina came into the picture and you did nothing to stop her advances."

"I didn't stop her advances? There was no advance from her. She tried to encourage me to see her sister. For your information, I stopped the advance from Simone the night I came home and spoke to you about the business meeting. Yes, I fell short one night, and I admit to sleeping with her. But that was after you'd broken my heart and disappeared. I didn't hear from you, Gail. There was nothing—no message saying that you'd be coming back, no message saying you'd found another, no message telling me that we'd be able to fix things in time. What was I to expect? You did a pretty good job convincing me it was over between us."

"I wanted you to learn a lesson."

"Here's a lesson, don't play games with the one you love. I'm not going on the emotional roller coaster with you again. I can be Rodney for another woman."

"You're just angry. I know you love me."

"Yes, I'm angry. I'm hurt, upset, and pissed the hell off. I'm taking my shower and when I come out I don't expect you to be here." Rodney walked into the bathroom and closed the door behind him. Gail sat on the bed, looking out the window. *This sure didn't go as I thought it would.* Gail rose from the bed and moved to the bathroom. *It's all or nothing,* she thought as she dropped all her clothes and entered the shower with Rodney. Rodney turned in surprise when he saw her curves. His mind flashed to memories of many nights holding her, touching her, and enjoying her goodness. He fought the logic as his will to indulge battered his heart's uncertainty. He moved, touching her shoulder with his hand and pulling her closer but was reluctant to be aggressive. He felt as if it had been years since he'd been with her, and he recalled his many dreams of this moment.

Slowly, he pulled her face close to his and allowed his body to touch hers. He recalled the memory of her smooth skin, and felt the sweet feeling he'd longed for. She obliged him in her response, falling into his arms for the kiss, the seductive moment she'd dreamed of once again enjoying. He touched her lips with his under the smooth stream of jetting water. It was a sparked memory, sending a message to his heart and a reminder of what he'd missed.

Gail felt the passion she'd felt from Rodney before. She pulled him closer and grabbed his buttocks, pressing him towards her. Rodney began to explore her entire body. He touched her, curve after curve, and explored the erogenous zones he knew well. As he was about to lift her and find entry to their fulfillment, he paused and decided not to follow through. He couldn't break the pledge he'd made to himself; he couldn't risk getting hurt again. He allowed her to stand. "We can't do this," he said. "We can't take chances, not now." Rodney turned and finished washing his body. He turned back and saw her disappointment.

"I'm not afraid to start a family. I'm afraid you may decide I'm not moving fast enough, and then you'd leave me again."

"I told you last night, I left to teach you a lesson."

"Some lesson, I think that's why I told you to leave. I didn't see the point in going over everything when my mind was made up, but since you're here, we might as well continue."

"Yes, let's do that, Rodney. Let's continue, starting with Simone."

"I am sorry I slept with her. But I did and I'll admit it. I had no idea if you were leaving for good. You wouldn't talk to me. You totally shut me out of your life. Is that some lesson of love or a test of stupidity?"

"There you go again calling me stupid," Gail said as she exited the shower.

"I didn't call you stupid. Again, the actions were stupid.

Besides, if I'd left you for that long, and not spoken to you at all, you'd think we were over."

"No, I wouldn't. I'm not that easy to give up on someone I love."

"Then please, explain your lesson."

"You missed my presence in your life and realized how important I am to you. Now you're ready to move forward. You said so yourself."

"I admit, I thought of it many times over. And for your information, I did wait for you. After I slept with Simone, I realized my mistake and I pushed her away. But you'd not know this. After all, you never answered my many phone calls or even listened to my multiple messages."

"I heard them at first, but it was hard listening to them so I stopped for awhile. They came less frequently over the weeks. If I hadn't flown home, I'd not know how you feel today."

Rodney began to towel himself dry. "You should leave, really leave, and let me go on with my life."

"I thought you loved me, really loved me, Rodney."

"I love you, yes, but I don't know that I can trust you not to walk out on me again. You should go. Call June and have Dan tie up any loose ends with you at work, then you're out."

"Rodney, don't do this. You love me, need me, and want me in your life. It's why you wanted to ask me to marry you."

"I wanted to, but not now, no way. I want a woman who would be with me through thick and thin. You showed me it's not you."

Gail dressed and grabbed her bag. She walked to the door. "It's not over, Rodney."

"Great, another woman dictating. Good-bye, Gail."

24.
A Dose of Wisdom

SIMONE AND SABRINA met Starz, reviewed the last of the advertisement plans, and agreed upon which ad best represented the show. "I knew Rodney's group was talented," Simone said as she looked at the ratings chart that Starz had shown her from the last production.

"When do we launch the commercial?" Sabrina asked.

"Dan said the group is set to shoot the ad tomorrow, so after some quick editing they should be able to get it out next week." Starz looked through his folder. "The show hits Northern California first, then moves east. All the other advertising materials have been finalized, so our marketing campaigns will set the trail, and I suspect with the added media exposure for your line, we'll do even better with this play than the last."

"Our stockholders will be happy to hear this," Simone said.

"Can't we push national all at once with the clothing line instead of releasing it in increments regionally?" Sabrina asked. "The clothing line will be in some stores long before the show arrives."

"Good point. I wonder if Rodney considered that."

"I know Rodney, he thought of it," Stanley said as he walked in.

"Good morning, all," Rodney said as he appeared behind Stanley. He entered and took a corner seat. "Stanley's right. Sabrina, if you turn to page four of your booklet, you'll see there is a stand-alone advertisement that we've already created for your clothing line. We're going to put out nationally next week. I wanted to talk to you guys about launching it separately, but never got a chance. There is an additional cost associated with the individual launch. The ads for the clothing will precede ads for the show, but they will be connected by featuring the same models."

"Thank you," Starz said. "I hope it answers your question, Sabrina."

"Yes, it does. Sounds great, and I'm anxious to see it."

"I have a copy of the edited advertisement with me today. Would you like me to play it?" Rodney held up the disc.

Sabrina nodded.

"Yes, let's play it now," Starz said. He took the disc from Rodney and placed it in the player. As he took his seat, the video started. It featured three thirty-second versions, which showcased the clothing line and highlighted the department store availability.

Sabrina's eyes were glued to the screen. "This is amazing, Rodney."

"It's what you envisioned. There's nothing like a good campaign to get things moving."

"No, there isn't," Sabrina said as she eyed Simone, who had missed the entire ad because she'd been watching Rodney. Sabrina turned to Rodney. "I'd say this calls for a celebration."

"No, thanks," Rodney said. "I'm not sure it's a celebration until it's totally launched."

Starz stood. "I agree. We'll celebrate after the launch. Have a great day, everyone." He exited the room.

Simone stood and moved close to Rodney. "One day you'll learn to smell the roses. I'll be there when you do." She left the room as Sabrina followed.

Rodney took a seat and placed his head in his hands. Stanley rose to exit the room. As he passed Rodney, he patted him on the back. "She'll be back," Stanley said. "Gail is a real trooper. She'll be back."

Rodney remained silent until he was alone. "I hope so," he whispered.

Gail found herself again at the airport; she'd made it in time to catch the evening flight east. She figured Rodney wouldn't make an effort to see her before heading home. It was an easy flight, without incident, and when she arrived in Richmond, June picked Gail up from the airport. Gail entered June's car. "Hey, it's nice seeing you again." She reached across the seat and embraced her friend.

June reciprocated the embrace. "Glad you're back. Where's Rodney?"

"I don't know," Gail said.

"I thought you two would be together after you told me you were headed back to Los Angeles so soon."

"No." Gail buckled her seat belt. It didn't go well. I'm so pissed at him. He just doesn't get it, not at all. After all that, he still doesn't get it."

June continued driving to Gail's apartment. Silence fell in the car as they drove through the city. After a few minutes,

June broke silence. "What if he asked you to marry him tomorrow? Would you answer yes?"

Gail didn't respond right away as the question had caught her off guard. Marriage was her objective, but her anger prevented her from jumping to reply. She waited a few moments before responding. "Not today. I wouldn't today."

"Then explain to me, why the anger?"

"Because he didn't wait for me, and he didn't react the way I expected him to after showing him how important I am."

"I love you, you're my best friend, and I'm always in your corner, but you have got to be out of your mind. I've wanted to say this since you stormed to California over a month ago. I held my thoughts before, but I'm fed up with your silly ideas. What on earth did you learn from your hiatus? Rodney is a great man, and you do what? Instead of talking to him and sharing your fears, you give him an ultimatum. Instead of working through the problems, you run. I know we deal with things differently, Gail, I understand, but this was a bad decision. You are a great businesswoman but horrible when it comes to love. What would you do had he left you and didn't speak to you for weeks?"

June stopped the car in front of Gail's apartment. She waited for a response as she parked the car and faced Gail. "Come on, please tell me what would you have done had he done the same to you?"

"You know, I never thought of it. I guess I'd be on my way in trying to get over him. But I'd still feel something when he returned. I'd…oh my goodness," Gail said, "I really messed this up, didn't I?"

"I'd say so. Now what are you going to do?"

"I'm calling him. I'll give it another try. I can't believe this, June. Why didn't I see it sooner?"

"You didn't want to because of your pain. It's understand-able, but your lesson may cost you the love you've always wanted. It may have backfired, so you'd better try real hard to get your man back."

"I will, I will," Gail replied as she exited the car and grabbed her bags. She waved at June. "We'll talk later."

June waved and drove away.

After the meeting, Sabrina spent the rest of the afternoon walking the Malibu beach boardwalk, enjoying her last day in Los Angeles. She'd scheduled a flight on the red-eye for later that night and decided to watch the sun set on the ocean ho-rizon one more time before heading to the East Coast. As she walked, she noticed a woman sitting on a bench up ahead who looked too thin for her own good. As Sabrina approached, she realized she knew this woman. She was a model Sabrina had worked with years before. "Hey, Gina," Sabrina said as she walked up to the woman.

Gina turned and squinted at Sabrina. "Hey, umm—"

"Sabrina, we worked together a few years ago."

"Oh, yes. Now I remember. How are you?" Gina smiled.

"I'm okay. How have things been going for you? It's been years since we last talked."

"I'm doing okay. I'm actually here trying to unwind. There was this shoot I was hoping to get, and during the audition the designer said I was too frail for his vision. The nerve of him. I look too big now."

"Well, you know the industry is hard. Why don't you con-sider his feedback? It seems like more designers are looking for models with more curves these days."

"As soon as I gain weight, the next one will say I'm too

large. Damn, it's frustrating, and I need the work. I'm not getting younger, and those younger models are always getting the jobs."

"Have you thought of doing anything else?" Sabrina asked.

"I have, but I love what I do. I wasn't fortunate like you, inheriting funds and finding Mister Right."

Sabrina shook her head. "It didn't turn out as great as you'd think, but I understand what you're saying. Hey, would you want to come have dinner with me? I have a flight later tonight, but I'm free till then and should probably eat something."

"Actually, I have to get to my next audition. I'll catch you later."

"Okay, well at least take my card, call me, and let me know how it goes. You know, we have to network." Sabrina handed Gina the card as she watched the waif-like woman turn and wave farewell. *Wow, first Patricia, and now Gina. It's a shame that these girls would jeopardize their health just to be thin.* Sabrina continued her walk and began to contemplate her next move.

It was an exhausting flight for Rodney. He'd caught the red-eye; there was no reason to stay in L.A. any longer. His presentation and execution plan for the marketing campaign went well. It was a coincidence that Sabrina was at the airport when he arrived in Richmond. Rodney stood at the curb waiting for the parking shuttle when Sabrina pulled up to him in her car. "Need a ride?" she asked.

"No, my car is in parking. But thanks for asking."

"We'll come back for it. I have something to show you."

"I'm pretty tired; can I take a rain check?"

"No, this is pretty urgent and has to do with our future."

"Our future?" Rodney turned away and rolled his eyes.

"Business future; you need to come with me now because, as they say, it's all in timing, right?"

Rodney stood for a moment, pondering what he had to lose or gain. He picked up his bag, opened the car's rear door, and secured his bags inside. He took the front passenger seat. Once he'd buckled his seatbelt, Sabrina took off in the opposite direction from town. "Where are we going?" Rodney asked.

"Someplace where I'll be able to show you what I mean about the future," Sabrina said. She focused on driving. She drove into the foothills and pulled in when they reached a large building. The sign outside read: "Le Grande Hotel."

"What the hell, Sabrina? I thought you were taking me someplace for business?" Rodney asked. "I don't have time for this. Take me back to my car."

"Man, you are hard, aren't you? What happened to Rodney, the sweetest man any woman would love to meet? Where is he? I know you, Rodney, and this person isn't you. We are honestly here for business, and Simone isn't here. Relax, and let me show you something."

"Okay, okay, I'm here, let's see what you have in mind."

The hotel was situated on a hill that overlooked the mountain range. It was a two-story building, with multiple rooms, and it appeared to have been built in the early 1900s. The two approached the front doors and walked in. They saw the lobby, decorated with antique furniture. Sabrina looked around. "Wow, this is ideal for my next project."

"Your next project?"

"Yes, my next project. Last night I found out that this place is for sale, and my source told me it was perfect for what I had in mind. I haven't seen the place yet, but I thought it was worth looking into. Aunt Marge always said to give back to people;

I want us to open a center for women with eating disorders. I'm not sure how, and thought you'd be interested in helping." Sabrina walked around the lobby and soon the clerk arrived at the front desk. Sabrina walked up to her. "Do you have rooms available?"

"Yes," the clerk said. "How many nights?"

"None, we would like to just see a room. Any room will do," Sabrina said.

"Hmm, any room…" The clerk reviewed the list of available rooms. "Here you go, ma'am." The clerk handed Sabrina a key. "Room 234—it's on the far wing and has the best view."

"Thank you so much." Sabrina headed in the direction the woman pointed as she looked at Rodney and signaled for him to come along. They walked upstairs and observed the long hallway, and décor. Sabrina arrived at the door to room 234 and unlocked it. She entered and looked around. "Wow, what a lovely room."

It was a suite filled with antique furniture. The room featured a French balcony with double doors, which opened up to reveal a spectacular view of the mountains and city. It was perfect for an escape. Rodney watched Sabrina's reaction to the building as he tried to interpret her motives. He looked at the view from the French doors. He stopped near a chair and took a seat, continuing to examine Sabrina. "Are you serious about this, or is this a plan for your sister?"

"My sister doesn't know about this. Not yet. I'm doing this on my own. It's what I want, and I know she wouldn't approve. Not now, not until our business rebounds. But the sale is silent. What do you think?"

"I'm not sure; I'll have to really give it a look over. I mean, it's going to take some investment for the type of business you want, for renovations and the works. My first impression is that it's a lovely place, and I'd rather keep its charm."

"I thought about it, but I'm not excited about the hotel business. I think it would be perfect for a nonprofit. I think we could manage to hold onto the charm of this place by making sure to avoid the cold, clinical atmosphere. Of course, eating disorders are a medical condition, so we'd need to have a doctor or two on staff, but there's also the psychological aspect to consider. In that sense, this environment would be perfect for rejuvenation and a new beginning for women."

"You have to be serious if you're going to renovate this into that kind of facility. Since I'm a marketing guy, how do I fit in your equation?"

"Rodney, you are visionary and I thought you might be able to see what I see. Look at the opportunity, and maybe partner with me in the effort."

"Do you really think it'll work; us being partners?"

"Look, you can get a crowd of people to recognize the potential in anything. I'm learning the ropes on running a large business. I'm sure we can make this work."

"Let me think about it, since this is still a far cry from my usual business ventures," Rodney said as he rose from the chair. "It is a lovely place, I'll give it that. It's outside of the city, so clients will be secluded from the general public. It's an idea. I think it's a very good possibility."

"I'm glad you think so. I'm going to ask you one more thing." Sabrina smiled.

"And what thing is that?"

"Please don't share this idea with anyone. I'll let you know when the ball gets moving, and at that point you can give me your thumbs up or thumbs down to your involvement."

"Okay," Rodney said.

Sabrina drove Rodney to the airport parking lot and finalized her idea along the way. She was excited at the thought of Rodney joining her in her efforts. They both had reservations about hiding the idea from Simone, but Rodney actually felt more inclined to partner with Sabrina on the venture knowing that Simone would not be involved.

Rodney finally drove home after a long, physically and emotionally exhausting trip. He arrived at his condo, entered it, and was surprised to see a large floral arrangement and bottle of wine on the dining room table. *What now?* Rodney dropped his bags. Rodney ignored the items and continued to walk through his place. As he approached his bedroom, he noticed a trail of flower petals on the floor. His heart pounded. *It's got to be Gail, she's the only one who knows where I hide the spare key.* Rodney continued following the path to his bedroom, pushed the cracked door open, and saw a body in his bed.

"Hi," he said. No one answered. "Hey, are you awake?"

Still, the person didn't answer. He moved closer and just as he placed his tie on the dresser, Simone sat up in a see-through negligee. "Welcome home," she said.

Rodney stepped back. "What on earth are you doing here?"

"I'm welcoming you home, like a woman should for her man."

"You aren't my woman. I'd like you to leave."

"I'm not going anywhere." Simone moved from the bed and grabbed Rodney, indicating her intent. "You know, it's even better the second time."

"I don't think so. Not now, not ever."

"You're still confused. Think about what you're saying. I'm not the enemy here; I'm showing you love and how you should be loved."

"I tried with you before, you know, and it got me nothing but heartache. I'm not going there again, so I suggest you leave." Rodney pushed her away and heard his doorbell ring. "I'm going to answer that. I suggest you get dressed and leave."

"I'm not going." Simone sat back on the bed to demonstrate her determination. "You'll change your mind after you get rid of whoever."

The doorbell rang again, and this time the doorknob turned. Rodney glared at Simone. "No, I think you'll leave. If not, I'll have to call the police to escort you out."

"Do whatever you have to do, I'm not leaving."

Rodney ran to the front door just as it began to open. "Can I help you?" he asked before the person entered.

"It's me, Gail," she said as she entered the condo. "I came by to talk."

"Can we do this another time? I just got in."

"No, I need to talk to you now. I'm not waiting any longer, I waited too long before because I didn't understand how you felt, and I think it's important now."

Rodney eyed his bedroom door in alarm. "Well, I don't think now is a good time. I'll call you."

"Rodney, are you coming to bed?" Simone said loudly enough to carry to the front door.

"Oh, you have company, and it's that woman," Gail said and passed Rodney to walk towards the bedroom. "I'll settle this." Rodney followed behind her. "She's leaving too."

Gail continued walking to the bedroom with persistence.

Before she arrived at the door, Simone opened it and exited the bedroom. "I thought you'd left."

"You are leaving, get dressed," Gail said as she pointed towards Simone's bag in Rodney's room.

"Yes, get dressed, I'm not telling you again," Rodney said. He turned to Gail and pointed towards the door. "You get out too."

"I'm not leaving," Gail said. "Not until we talk."

"We had multiple times to talk, Gail, and I'm not interested at the moment. I'll talk to you later."

"I'm not leaving."

Simone walked out to the living room in her nightgown. "Well, I'm not leaving; I was here first—on both occasions."

"I don't care what either of you do at this point. I'm tired, want to settle in, and just have some peace and quiet," Rodney said as he walked into his bedroom. He slammed the door, leaving both women in the living room. A second later, he opened his door again, but only enough to throw Simone's clothes out of his room. He locked his door, leaving both women to fend for themselves.

Silence fell as both women stared at each other. Gail stood with her hands on her hips, her eyes locked on Simone. Simone went to pick up her clothes and got dressed. She looked at Gail. "You just had to come here tonight. After weeks of not speaking to him, an argument in L.A., and stressing out one of the better men I've come across, you still weren't finished. You just had to mess things up for us tonight."

"You are really imagining things." Gail laughed and shook her head. "You have no idea about Rodney. He's over you."

"I had Rodney years ago, and I'll have him today. You help;

every time you do something, you push him right to me. Keep doing what you do, and I'll be Mrs. Witherspoon before long."

"Over my dead body!" Gail moved towards Simone.

"You don't have to get violent. All you have to do is leave him to me and life goes on."

"Listen, Simone, he's my guy. My love, from every angle you can imagine or even dream of exploring. I'm not going to let you have him without a fight. And, I suggest you get ready. I'm not a pushover, especially in regards to the man I love."

"As if I am?" Simone passed Gail and approached the front door. Simone opened it and turned to face her adversary. "Get your game together because I love competition."

"I'm sure you do," Gail said. She walked behind Simone, and as Simone stepped out, Gail slammed Rodney's front door. She took a seat on the couch and decided to wait for morning. She'd talk to him then. Within the hour, Gail fell asleep.

The next morning, Rodney rose from bed. He began the day as he would begin any other when he returned from traveling, enjoying the comfort of home. He stretched, opened the drapes, and then meandered into the kitchen to make coffee. He walked out into the condo and saw someone sleeping on the couch. He shook his head and walked into the kitchen. After making a pot of coffee, he returned to his bedroom. Once there, he ventured to the master bath and jumped in the shower. It was home, and he enjoyed his specially designed showerhead jets, which gave him a full massage. As he turned, facing the steamed-up glass shower door, he noticed a figure standing on the other side. "Can I help you?" Rodney asked.

"Yes, can I join you?" asked a familiar voice.

"No," Rodney said. "I'd rather we talk out in the front room."

"Why can't we talk here?"

"I don't want the physical influence to be my weakness. I think we'll be better at focusing without the distraction."

"I'll wait for you," Gail said as she left the bathroom. Rodney continued his shower for a few minutes more. He stepped out of the shower and in front of the bathroom mirror with a towel wrapped around his waist. *I'm not going to do this,* he thought as he wiped the steam off the mirror for a better view. *I wanted to relax today, and now all it's going to turn into is an argument, just like in California. I just have to be up front with her and clear the air. I love her, but this isn't the way back.* Rodney dressed, went to the kitchen, and poured a cup of coffee. He looked at Gail, who was sitting in the living room. "Would you like some?"

"I have a cup, thanks," she said.

"Okay." Rodney walked to the couch and took a seat. "Look, Gail, I'm not sure what you want, how you want it, or if we'll arrive to where you'd like. Whatever it is, we have to clear the air."

"Rodney, I came here because I don't want you to give up on us."

"Give up on us? Isn't giving up what you decided for us by disappearing and shutting me out? Isn't giving up not talking to me in L.A. when you came to the hotel? Isn't giving up making a scene here with Simone? I'd say you gave up long ago."

"No way, Rodney, it was nothing like that. I said I'd never give up on us. I was clearing my head, trying to get control of my heart, and deal with the disappointment."

"Disappointment?" Rodney asked.

"Yes, and it got worse—you did what the average man would do. You slept with Simone and still have interest. I wasn't gone but a few weeks and you jumped into another woman's life."

"Gone but a few weeks; I called you multiple times a day, sent you dozens of text messages, and wrote you a hundred emails. I didn't get an answer. 'I'm like any other man and you left from disappointment'? Wow! For weeks I had no idea what to do, and wouldn't have known if you were dead or alive if it weren't for your good friend June. I'd thought you loved me, and instead you made me feel like I was…" Rodney paused. "Well, like I was nothing."

"I give you credit, Rodney." Gail moved closer to him. She reached her hand to his face. "You showed me how intensely you loved me at first. I get that, but what about later? Did you stop loving me that quickly?"

"Are you sick? Of course not! I never stopped loving you, and I still love you, but I'm not into this game, Gail. I thought you were better than this. I thought you were better than every woman I've ever dated. I thought you were my dream, my companion, my match in life."

"And now you don't?"

"I'm not counting on anything making it now."

"So, it's over?"

"I didn't say it's over. We just aren't where we once were."

"Can't we get there today?"

Rodney stood and walked to the door. "No, I'd like you to think things over and see if you can make up for the weeks of hell you put me through." Rodney opened the door. "You have to do it somewhere else. I'd rather be alone right now."

"So you want me to leave so Simone can return? I don't think so."

"Like I said, I'd rather be *alone* right now, and if you look around, nothing says Simone is returning for any reason. If she did, she'd have to leave as well."

"I'm not happy with this," Gail said, "I'm not happy with this at all."

"As if your leaving made me an ecstatic man," Rodney said. Gail rose from the couch and walked close to Rodney. She stood before him and moved to kiss him, but Rodney stepped back. "Gail, I think I've made it clear that I'm not ready for that; to be honest, I don't know when I will be. Please, just go." Gail walked through the doorway. He closed the door and returned to his coffee.

Gail returned to her apartment in tears. She cried as she pulled out her phone and dialed June's number. As soon as June answered the phone, Gail sobbed. "I can't believe it," she began, "he pushed me away again and rejected my advances."

"What did you expect? I thought you'd just talk to him."

"I tried, but Simone was there."

"What? Really?"

"Yes, she was in his bedroom, but it seemed like he was kicking her out. I had a few words with her. That bitch has got to back off and stay away from Rodney."

"Why would she? She figured he's available."

"I told her he wasn't."

"And your claim for Rodney is supposed to keep her away? I think you'd better make sure that claim is still valid. You need to work things out with Rodney."

"I tried!" Gail said. "What more can I do?"

"Just call him. I know he still loves you, but it's no surprise he doesn't trust you now. Call him again. Be nice when you do." June ended the call.

Gail placed her cell phone on the nightstand and rolled over in her bed. She looked at the ceiling in silence as if waiting for the room to give her guidance. She lay there for hours trying to make sense of her confusion, desire, and disappointment. She searched for solutions on how to reach Rodney, but she worried it was too late.

25.
The Two Again

IT WAS 4:00 P.M. when a call sounded in Rodney's office. It was Sabrina on the line. "Rodney, I wanted to talk to you more about the clinic. Have you thought more about my proposal?"

"I have, actually," Rodney said. "It sounds like an amazing idea, and there's a market for something like that in this area. This center would be the first of its kind here."

"Well, you know I was hoping to start it up as a nonprofit. After learning about Patricia's bulimia and then running into an old work acquaintance who was so thin, I just felt called to do this. I want models and women to balance their lifestyle with feeling beautiful and being at a healthy size. We have to get people back from the 'size zero' mentality and assist with the psychological and emotional battle they fight. I was so ill when I saw my friend, and especially after everything Patricia's work has done for us, I want to give back somehow."

"I know you want it to be nonprofit, and now I understand why. Your motives are admirable. When I said, 'market,' I just meant that it's something this area needs."

"Does that mean you're in?"

"I'm not sure, Sabrina. It's a great idea, and I'd love to help, but I'm hesitant to work with you, given everything that's gone on with Simone. I know she's your sister and you love her, but I'm in love with someone else now. I don't want our partnering on the center to jeopardize that."

"I understand what you're saying, Rodney, I do. But I think you're the right person for this. I can't guarantee that Simone won't be involved with this project on some level. We share assets. However, I can promise you that I will be the go-between when her involvement is necessary."

Rodney hesitated. After the recent scene with Simone, continuing anything that would keep him connected to her made him cringe. At the same time, he'd never had any problems with Sabrina, and this project was for a good cause. "All right," he said, "I'm in."

"Great!" Sabrina said. "What are you doing this evening, partner?"

"I'm headed to Dan and June's house after work," Rodney said, "but I don't have any plans after that. What do you have in mind?"

"How about a stroll in the park? I want to get your ideas on things."

"The park?" Rodney considered Sabrina's somewhat odd request.

"Yeah, why not?"

"Where and when?" Rodney asked. Sabrina explained the details, and they ended their call.

Simone and Sabrina sat at a coffee shop. Simone held her warm drink close to her mouth and looked up at Sabrina. "What are you up to tonight?"

Sabrina set down her sketchpad. "I'm meeting someone at the park."

"A date? Who is he?" Simone asked.

"No, nothing like that…" Sabrina paused. "I'm meeting Rodney. We decided to work on a new project together and were going to meet to brainstorm some ideas."

All Simone heard was "Rodney."

"Well," she said, "I think I should join you."

"What are you trying to do?"

"I'm going to win Rodney's heart."

"Sis, I love you, but I don't think you're going to do that right now. Why don't you give it a rest?"

"Rest?" Simone asked. "Rest? You mean after all these years of you pushing Rodney on me, now you want me to rest? I don't get it."

"Sure you do. Since you and Gail seem to both want to be with him, I'd back off so he can make a choice."

"Don't you know men need guidance in making a good choice?"

"No, not Rodney, I'm sure he's good at making the right choices. He isn't your average guy."

"I know he isn't, I finally see that." Simone smiled and shrugged. "He's amazing."

Sabrina looked at her sister helplessly.

Simone stood up. "Well, that settles it then. When are we meeting at the park?

"Just before sunset," Sabrina said.

"Romantic. Perfect."

"Okay, sis, see you tonight." She waved as she entered her car. The sisters left the parking lot and drove in separate directions.

Rodney placed the baby into June's arms as he spoke to Dan. "Nice, dude, you seem to be doing real well having a kid. It's like a mini you! I wonder how things will change as the baby grows. Are you ready for this?"

"I'm as ready as I can be at the moment. Who knows if they are ready or not? It's usually a huge change for everyone. I think it's more a question of who is ready to adjust. I think you'll be ready when the time comes," Dan said as he observed June and baby. Rodney watched June as she played peek-a-boo and noticed his friend Dan's look of adoration. Dan smiled and turned back to Rodney, "As for me, Rodney, I'm more ready now than ever."

It was near sunset. Simone, Sabrina, and Rodney all separately headed to the park.

Rodney arrived, just in time to see a couple with their young kids feeding the ducks. He observed how happy they seemed together. He thought of Dan and how excited Dan was about his new family. Rodney caught himself comparing single life with the idea of having a family. His heart swelled as he imagined himself with a wife and child.

Moments later, Sabrina appeared beside him. "Hey," she said. She motioned between Rodney and the family he'd been watching. "What a big smile."

"What do you mean?"

"I'm just saying I saw you looking at those kids."

"I thought we were meeting to walk around the lake?" Rodney asked.

"We are."

"Good." Rodney and Sabrina began walking. A paved trail

weaved through the park. When they reached the gazebo, Sabrina stopped.

"Are you tired?" Rodney asked.

"No," Sabrina said, "we have to meet someone."

"You said we were here to talk about your business idea. I'm not sure I want to walk around with a group of people."

"It's not a group." Sabrina nodded towards the direction they'd come from.

Rodney turned and saw Simone approaching. "You have got to be kidding me. What the hell, Sabrina? I thought we talked about this."

"I'm sorry!" Sabrina whispered. "I mentioned that I was going to the park, and she invited herself. What was I supposed to do?"

"Hey," Simone said as a grin spread across her face. "I didn't expect to see you here, Rodney."

"Neither did I," Rodney said as he moved to leave.

"Why are you leaving? We can still walk around the lake as old friends. Can't we?" Simone asked.

Rodney felt set up but had looked forward to walking around the park and tried to trust Sabrina's words. He knew from experience that Simone was not easily deterred. "I guess I don't mind a walk, it's good for the body and…well, we are old friends."

"Yes, we are," Sabrina said and stepped back towards the path. "Come on, sis." Sabrina motioned for Simone to move ahead of her. Sabrina turned back towards Rodney apologetically. "Sorry," she mouthed.

The three continued walking. None of them spoke as they trekked along the scenic path around the lake.

Simone broke silence. "Rodney, I saw Starz's numbers for the first show. Wow, he's good."

"Starz has a golden touch. I had no doubt it would be successful," Rodney said.

Sabrina nodded. "He's on top of the game. I'm sure our products will do well."

"That is exactly the forecast. We will do well," Simone said. "You did it, sis."

"We did it. And you know we couldn't have done it without Rodney." Sabrina tapped Rodney's shoulder in recognition.

"Hey, before you ladies get too far," Rodney said, "we've got to give credit to my team; I only presented the final touches."

"It was your leadership."

"You can't deny it."

"Okay, I see if I debate you two, it's a losing battle."

"Good, that's settled."

The three continued walking around the lake, observing people and their activities. They arrived at the bench where Aunt Marge had taken ill for the last time. Simone walked and sat where she'd last saw their favorite aunt alive. It was the first time either of the women had revisited this location. Sabrina started shaking as tears fell upon her face. Simone reached out to her sister as an invitation to sit on the bench. They embraced each other. "I'm so sorry, it wasn't a good idea," said Sabrina as she sniffled.

"It's okay, she's with us now," Simone said.

Rodney observed the girls with empathy in their time of pain. He walked closer to the water. *I shouldn't have come here. I should be with Gail right now. She's the one I need in my life.*

"Thanks, Rodney," Simone said as she approached him. "I never thanked you for saving Aunt Marge the first time."

"You don't have to. She was a very nice lady."

"One you didn't get a chance to know. She was our rock."

"I guess you are the rock now."

"Not really, not after what Sabrina has shown me. She's stronger than I ever realized. With her revenue creation, I'm sure things will soon be back to normal."

"I'm glad things are working out for you two. I wish you the best," Rodney said as he turned to leave. Rodney didn't want to make Simone believe he was there to console her. He remembered the last time he'd tried, and it had crushed his heart.

Simone watched him leave before deciding to speak. She was willing to abandon her pride in her quest for Rodney. "Hey!" she said. Her voice rose. "Where are you going?"

"Home," Rodney said as he walked away.

"Wait up!" Simone trotted towards Rodney. When she caught up, she put her hand on his shoulder. "Why are you leaving?"

Rodney continued walking towards his car, "Because it's better I left. I'm not trying to reminisce about what I wished for when your Aunt Marge was alive. I have other plans."

"Other plans?" Simone asked, even though she knew he was referring to Gail.

"Yes."

"If you truly have them, I'll be happy to support your decision. But not so fast—I'm the woman who could show you a wonderful life. I am the one who can match your creativity and entrepreneurial ego. I'm the one who can match your every need for love and affection."

"You make a strong case. The problem is, I'm not in love with you as I once was." Rodney stopped in his tracks and looked at Simone. "There was a time I wished for you. You wore a blue dress in my dreams. Your hair flowed with the wind, and your body curved like a cello. You were beautiful in my dreams, and I thought we'd make it one day. For so long, I held you close to me. I was crushed when you blasted me at Aunt Marge's memorial cruise. I allowed you too much power over my heart. After that, I worked very hard to become strong and to get back to being myself. I'll admit, it took a long time to get over you. Now, I'm here and stronger than ever. I'm over you, Simone. I can't do this anymore."

Rodney turned and walked towards his car again. He didn't wait for a response from Simone. He entered his car, and as his door slammed shut, it signified the parallel door to his past that he'd finally closed.

When Simone returned to Sabrina, Sabrina wiped her eyes and looked down the paved path. "What happened to Rodney?"

"He left," Simone said. Her palm rested on her forehead as she looked out at the pond. "I had no idea."

Sabrina took in Simone's anguish. "No, you didn't have any idea how much he wanted to be with you. It's partially my fault."

"No, it's not your fault. I knew he was interested, but I wasn't into him then the way I am now. I missed out on a great guy. It's over. Let him follow his heart, he deserves it." Simone looked in her hands as if searching for a message. "I had him here, right here in the palms of my hands, and now he's gone, like sand running through my fingers. Don't follow my example, sis. Don't you allow someone great to slide through your hands."

Sabrina looked away with pain in her heart, but she turned back to Simone and lifted her chin. "When opportunity knocks, I'll answer with a smile." Sabrina smiled.

Rodney drove home. He entered his condo and looked at the phone, but Gail had not called. He thought about calling her himself, but he had so much to say and didn't want to sound weak. He paced the condo, thinking about how to break the ice. He stopped in the kitchen to fill a glass of water, and continued his pacing, only pausing to sip from his glass. Rodney paced the floor for thirty minutes, going from one room to the other, and could not decide if he should contact her—he didn't even know what he'd say.

Rodney finally moved to his couch and sat in silence clearing his mind, trying not to think about Gail for a moment. He thought back to the park and his conversation with Simone. It had felt somehow freeing to be honest with her about his past feelings and to realize he no longer had them. He thought of the hurt she'd caused him what seemed like ages ago. Rodney had mourned for a lost opportunity, but now that Simone had offered it, he wasn't interested.

He thought over the other events of the day, remembering his visit to see Dan and his family at the park. He found himself envisioning his own children, and soon Gail entered his vision too. He saw Gail as the mother of his children. He'd seldom imagined himself with a child or having a woman by his side. Now it was all laid out in his mind; he could see it as if it were right in front of him. He'd kept Gail at a distance and pushed her away, but he realized suddenly that he'd been wrong to compare his relationship with Gail to his heartbreak over Simone. Simone had just been an infatuation. He remembered his many nights with Gail, their ease around one another, and most importantly, their love.

Rodney grabbed his phone and hit the speed dial for Gail, hoping she'd answer. The phone rang four times and went to voice mail. "Gail, it's me, Rodney," he said. "I need to talk to you, and soon. There's much I need to share, much my heart wants to tell you. Please, call me." Rodney ended the call.

He moved to the kitchen and thought more of his life with Gail. His thoughts brought him back to missing her. He felt empty again, exactly as he had when she first left. Rodney realized that Gail had approached him three times since her first departure, trying to mend what they'd had, and he had been the one to push her away. His heart fluttered with hope; she still loved him, maybe there was a chance. Rodney moved from the kitchen with a new optimism. He wanted to call Gail again but didn't want to be too anxious, so he went along with his day, still thinking of what he'd do and say when and if he heard from Gail. It was during Rodney's shower when a great idea entered his mind. He hopped out, threw on some clothes, and left his condo.

It was evening when Gail listened to her phone messages. Every day she'd hoped that Rodney would call. When she finally heard a message, a serious message from Rodney, her heart leapt and she sucked in a breath with mixed emotions. It was surely the message she wanted, but she was concerned about speaking to him on the phone, unable to gauge his sincerity.

Gail decided to think for awhile before calling him back. She wanted to be sure that she knew what she was going to say to him, after her last few failed attempts. She dressed for dinner and walked to her car. As she walked up to her car, she noticed a note on her windshield. She pulled the note from the envelope. It read:

Meet me where the stars are reflected upon a pond and the majesty of mountains sing a melody. Meet me where we once danced the night away, shared our secrets, and laughed away our tears. Meet me there in one hour.

Rodney

Gail knew exactly where to go. Rodney spoke of the restaurant they'd went to with June and Dan. Gail jumped in her car with enthusiasm. She drove while calling June to cancel their dinner plans. Of course, June encouraged her as a great friend would. When Gail approached the restaurant, Rodney stood at the door with a rose in his hand, dressed in a stylish shirt and slacks. Gail approached slowly, but her insides somersaulted with anticipation. "Hi," she said.

Rodney didn't say anything right away. He was hesitant with his response. "I give you this rose as an indication of peace, affection, and admiration." Rodney presented the rose to Gail.

"Oh, how nice," Gail said, not knowing how to respond.

Rodney raised his arm with his elbow bent to escort her into the restaurant. Once she grasped him, they entered the building. He moved his hand to the small of her back and guided her to a corner table with the very view he'd described in his note. A bottle of wine chilled at the table, accompanied by candles, and a wrapped box. Gail took one look at the elaborate setup and turned back around. "No, Rodney."

"No? It's not what you think," Rodney said. "Give me a chance, just a few moments. I know you came for a reason."

"I'll give you a chance, but only to talk."

"Talking is exactly what I wanted to do."

"Then why all this?" Gail asked. "Why such a romantic effort for a conversation?"

"Please, Gail, sit down." Rodney pulled out her chair. "Nothing in life is ever a simple conversation. I'm not changing the way I feel about you, nor am I jumping into a fiery storm. I'm simply appreciating you, and this is how I wish to show you my appreciation and admiration. I was hoping we could talk."

"This is talking?"

"It's a start. Don't you think?"

"I don't know, this seems like it is a distraction."

"I understand your fear, but trust me, that wasn't my intention." Rodney paused. "I think it's best I get to the point. Open the box."

"I don't know if I should."

"Come on, open it. It's nothing to be afraid of."

Gail took the box and pulled the bowstrings. She closed her eyes as she reluctantly pulled to remove the top. Rodney grabbed her hand just as she removed the cover and said, "Open your eyes."

Gail followed instructions, and looked down. The box was empty. "What?" Gail asked.

"I filled this box with an intangible gift, giving you what I think most important. It's something you can't touch, but something you feel. It's something you can't wear, but something that surrounds you. It's something that shines brighter than any jewel or stone. It's my love for you, Gail. I'm giving it to you."

Rodney took a breath while waiting for a response. Since Gail didn't say anything, he grabbed her other hand and looked into her eyes. "I came to a decision, a final decision to love you. I loved you before our misunderstanding, and I love you more now. I want to love you for the rest of my life. I hope you'll work with me to create a better life for us. I mean, we were working well along the way, and I flinched when you needed me most. I'm not flinching anymore."

Gail looked at him, gazing with excitement and fear. It was what she'd wanted him to say for weeks. Now that he was professing his love, she worried it was too good to be true. Gail continued sitting in silence, thinking of how to respond. "I'm not so sure, Rodney. It's hard believing you after your actions the other night. When you had a chance to profess love for me in front of Simone, you didn't. How do I know you aren't with her and trying to have both worlds?"

Rodney was taken aback by her response. He straightened and let go of her hands. "I'm not so sure you want to go there. I'm actually sitting here, forgiving you for your actions, and sharing my heart, when you left me in a state of confusion. I didn't give up on us, even when you were out of touch for weeks. I hadn't given up on us, even when Simone came into the picture, I pushed her away. I never stopped thinking of you. Now you want to question my intent here today? I should ask you the same question." Rodney sat forward in his chair moving closer to the center of the table. He looked into her eyes again. "Why should I believe you won't leave me when things don't go your way? Why should I give my heart to a woman who continually walks away from the man who loves her?"

"I knew you loved me, Rodney, but not as much as I

thought. When you didn't ask me to marry you, I thought it was just a game to you."

"Gail, I showed you more love in the time we were together than I've shown any woman."

"How am I to know? When Simone threatened us, I couldn't help but take offense."

"Offense? I hadn't shown Simone any interest and always placed you first and foremost in my life. When you gave me the ultimatum, I already had plans to ask you to marry me. When you wanted me to ask right then, it was like forcing me to choose to ruin the romantic proposal I had in mind. That night, I went for a walk, and I realized you should at least know how much I love you. When I returned, you were gone and wouldn't return my calls."

"I needed time to get my head together. I gave you my heart, my partnership, and trust. I need a man to stand next to me at all costs, on all occasions, especially when I feel threatened."

"I didn't think you were threatened."

"It wasn't about you, Rodney, it was about me."

"I gathered, and I now know how you respond to things. It's part of learning, understanding, and embracing you as the woman I love. But, instead of running, we have to meet each other halfway. It's why I'm here and why I asked you here. I'd rather talk things over calmly when issues arise."

"I tend to speak my mind with passion. I don't like holding in my feelings."

"This is something we have to work on if we're to move forward with us."

"I agree, we need to work."

"Does this mean you're accepting my gift?"

Gail looked at the empty box and considered what it represented. She smiled without looking at Rodney and kept her eyes down facing the box. She didn't notice Rodney had poured wine for them. "Well? What's the verdict?"

"We can work on this relationship, but only with one stipulation."

"Stipulation?"

"Yes, we have to tell Simone we're together.'"

Rodney felt conflicted at Gail's request. In his last conversation with Simone, he'd felt as if he'd already closed that chapter for good. "Consider it done," he said. The two tipped their glasses and toasted on the agreement.

26.
Love Has It

GAIL AND JUNE WALKED around the park with June pushing the stroller. It was a sunny, refreshing day, and the women enjoyed the chance to catch up with one another. Gail related the details of her night with Rodney to June. She explained how she'd been caught off guard by Rodney's apparent remorse, and she also expressed her own remorse at having left for weeks after hearing Rodney's response. She admitted that leaving had been a bad decision. "June, do you believe a man can change?" Gail asked as they turned onto another path.

"Sure I do. Look at Dan. He's changed and now he's a great husband and father," June said. She walked on, waiting for a response, but when one didn't come right away, she asked, "Why do you think Rodney needs changing?"

"I can't tell you how nice it was to hear Rodney profess his love last night, and I'm hopeful, but that doesn't change his actions. I want his actions to parallel his words."

"He made a mistake when he'd thought you'd left him, Gail. When you two are together, you're great, right? Isn't that what you talked about last night?"

"Oh, it was a great conversation. It was intimate, and we

didn't get any sleep. We cleared up everything and anything we thought could come between us."

"Even the things that have happened since you left?"

"Yes, I think we both understand where the other person was when we each made our mistakes. But even though we've talked through those things, we can't take them back; you know, it's not the same as before." Gail frowned. "I guess I'm just cautious."

"Did he say anything to indicate that he doesn't want you in his life?"

"No, he said exactly the opposite."

"I think you need to trust his intentions then. Look, he came after you for weeks trying to connect with you, and you were the one running."

"I wasn't running."

"Yes, you were running away from being hurt since he didn't do what you wanted."

"What if this is just a rebound attempt and we don't go back to the way we were? What if we *do* go back to the way we were, where things are great, but when it comes down to it, he won't commit?"

"Gail, it seems you aren't listening to me or yourself. What are you fighting? For years you told me about Mister Right. Now he's in front of you, and you're going to give up on things before they've even begun again. What gives?" June stopped the carriage to readjust the baby's blanket. "Are you listening to yourself?"

"I hear you. I guess I'm afraid of being hurt or giving so much again."

"Weren't you happy with him?"

"Yes, except it was time we took the next step."

"Then it's time you let go of the past few months and move forward. He seems to want to, so give it a chance. Take a few months to rekindle every emotion you had and live each day at a time. What is there to lose?"

"Lose?" Gail asked. "I'd lose myself and my self-esteem if it fails."

"You'd win if you open your eyes. Stop with the fear; it's self-inflicting."

They continued their walk in silence as June allowed her last comment to sit on Gail's mind. As they approached the path's end, June spoke. "I hope you think of tomorrow and the way he makes you feel instead of worrying and sabotaging your chances to fix things. Rodney's a great catch; there is a reason why Simone would do anything to have him. Don't lose the man you love because you're afraid to take a chance." June walked to her car and began securing the baby in the car seat. When she closed the door, Gail moved closer to June.

"Thank you for being my best friend," Gail said.

"You know I love you, and always have your best interests at heart. Go get your guy. He's waiting."

The two embraced for a moment. June released and entered her car, snapped her seat belt, and pressed the ignition. She waved at Gail, smiled, and took off on her way home.

Gail settled into her car and prepared to drive home. She pondered her conversation with June. *There is a reason someone else wants Rodney. Those qualities are hard to find. He's surely a catch, and he did nothing to provoke my running away. He's still professing his love for me after all this time. I need to welcome this second chance.*

As soon as Gail arrived at her condo, her cell phone rang.

She looked at the caller ID and was pleased to see it was Rodney on the other end of the line. She answered the call. "Hey, you," she said.

"Hello, love," Rodney said. "Do you have plans for tonight?"

"No. Well, I didn't, but I think I do now."

"Good. I'll pick you up around six thirty"

"Six thirty? That sounds pretty early for dinner."

"Dinner is included."

"What else do you have in mind?"

"I don't want to disclose all the facts, just say you'll come."

"Okay, I'll be ready."

"Great," Rodney said. "See you tonight."

Rodney stood at his office window and gazed at his watch. He was shocked to see how late it was already; he realized that if he were going to execute his plan effectively, he'd better get moving. Rodney shut the office down and ended his workday. He waved at Dan as he exited. "I'll tell you all about it tomorrow."

Dan knew Rodney well enough to know he had something up his sleeve. He called June. "Honey, have you spoken to Gail today?"

"We went for a walk together earlier, why?" June asked.

"I don't know, just got the feeling Rodney's up to something."

"I heard about their dinner last night, but that was the last I'd heard. Knowing Rodney he's got something romantic planned. What time are you coming home?"

"The usual. Would you like me to bring something home?"

"Yes, whatever you'd like for dinner and a bottle of our favorite wine would be great."

"Oooh, sounds like a lovely evening. I'm leaving sooner now," Dan said.

Rodney arrived home and changed into an impressive outfit: slacks, a collarless shirt made of fine fabric, and a sports coat. He took extra effort in getting ready so Gail would be pleased by his appearance. He drove to Gail's apartment and arrived exactly at 6:30 p.m. She opened the door and smiled as Rodney approached the door. "I love them!" Gail said as she opened her arms to greet him.

Rodney was happy to hear the roses had arrived to the house without issue. "I'm glad you do," he said as he gently kissed her. "Are we ready? We have to stick close to the clock."

"I'm ready. Let me grab my sweater."

"Wow, you look wonderful," Rodney said as he watched her walk further inside the apartment. "That dress looks amazing on you."

"Thank you. What time are we to be where?"

"It's the first part of our night. Just come along and enjoy."

The two jumped in Rodney's car and Rodney drove to the local airfield. "Rodney," Gail said, "where on earth are we going?"

"Someplace very special."

"Are we coming back tonight? I didn't pack."

"Yes, we'll return tonight."

When Gail reached the plane, she noticed the leer jet was luxurious. "Sit anywhere you like," the first mate said.

"Thank you," Gail said as she took a seat.

"It's great seeing you, Rodney. You have a great guy there, young lady," the pilot said. "If you'd like anything to drink, please help yourself; you know where things are." The pilot returned to the cockpit.

"Thank you, Jeff," Rodney said as he buckled in next to Gail. Within a few minutes, the flight was airborne.

"You and the pilot know each other?" Gail asked.

Rodney answered as he placed his belt across his lap. "We had a campaign together. I helped his business grow with a few ideas. It was an amazing growth opportunity; just played his cards right."

"I'd like to hear how that happened."

Rodney waited for the plane to settle before he answered. "Jeff's business was failing, and he needed a pitch to increase his revenue. We focused on idea after idea and nothing hit. One day, we were both sitting in his office and an elderly man walked in. He wanted to hire Jeff and rent a plane for an afternoon. The man said, 'I want to fly my wife to the beach, have a nice walk, and return home. I think four to six hours would do. You know, we haven't any children or family left, and she's not well enough to ride in the car or travel on a regular flight. It would be great if I can get her back to the beach, one more time. Seeing her smile again...' the man paused a moment as he placed his hand on his heart, '...she would really appreciate a walk on the beach.' Jeff nearly fell to tears listening to his story. Jeff was so touched that he agreed to take the couple at no charge. That's how it all started."

"Started?"

"Yes, it started. Jeff devised a day-trip business model that centered on taking the elderly from the city to a small beach town. The idea took off. He collaborated with a transportation service to get passengers from the airport to the beach, and with a beachside restaurant to provide a romantic lunch. They offered the trip as a package deal, and I helped market it. The elderly man's touching story prompted Jeff to offer four seats a month to those senior citizens who couldn't afford the trip. The campaign was extremely successful, and Jeff was able to purchase two additional leer jets from the increased business. We're flying in one tonight."

"Wow, that's so touching. How wonderful that Jeff continues the tradition in their honor."

Rodney smiled. "Do you want to see their beach?"

Gail nodded.

The flight headed to the bay as the sun began to set. Gail sat next to the window looking out. "What a lovely view," she said as she pointed out the window to Rodney.

Rodney continued looking at Gail. "Yes, a lovely view indeed." Gail blushed.

The pilot suggested that Rodney and Gail take their seats and secure their seat belts. During the descent, the two held hands and relaxed, and within minutes, the plane landed. Gail and Rodney exited the flight and stepped into a waiting taxi. "Wow," Gail said, "you didn't forget a thing, did you?"

The cab drove for ten minutes and stopped at a pier. It was the next step in Rodney's plan. He and Gail walked down the pier and stopped before a docked yacht. "Is this for us too?" Gail asked.

Rodney nodded as he pulled out his cell phone. He called the ship's captain. "Steve, hi. We're here, we're coming aboard."

"Sure thing, welcome aboard," Steve said as he came above deck. He and Rodney reached for Gail as she stepped on the yacht with her heels. On the deck was a table, with a bottle of chilled wine and a mixed floral arrangement of roses and lilies.

Gail smiled at the arrangement and took a whiff of the flowers. "Oh, how lovely," she said and embraced Rodney, throwing her body into his arms. "I'm such a lucky woman."

Rodney placed his lips upon hers. He broke the embrace, grabbed her hand and said, "Follow me." He led Gail on a quick tour around the yacht. As the two returned topside, the boat had begun its trip into the bay. Rodney poured glasses of wine and handed one to Gail. "A toast." He raised his glass and waited for Gail's response. She followed suit, and they held their glasses at the same angle. "To a night to remember, a love I wish you to enjoy, and a life I'm eager to share."

Gail smiled as she tapped Rodney's glass before taking a sip. "I really don't know what to say. I'm lost for words, really lost for words."

"You don't have to say anything at all. Why don't you take a seat, relax, and enjoy this wine? We'll be there in about twenty minutes."

"How did you get this yacht to taxi us to wherever we're going?"

"Another favor called in. I don't have much of a story on this one." He reached for her and received her soft hand, which he held as the yacht rocked from side to side.

"Is it always like this?"

"No, but hang in there, we'll be at our destination soon."

Soon after, the yacht approached the dock. "What did you think of the ride?" Rodney asked.

"We're here?"

"Yes, we are." Rodney pointed to the dock up ahead. They'd reached a small island. Bamboo tiki torches lined the path from the pier to a building at the top of a hill. The vessel docked and the two debarked onto the pier, following the lit path. Rodney interlocked his arm with Gail's and held her hand. "Are you hungry?" Rodney asked.

"After all this travel, I'm famished."

Rodney walked Gail through the restaurant and out the back door. "We're not eating here?" Gail asked in confusion.

Rodney led Gail outside. "Do you think you can find our table?"

Gail looked, and down the walkway to the beach, at the edge of the water line, was another table adorned with lilies and roses. More tiki torches surrounded the table, which was set for two. Gail and Rodney took their seats. The waiter served lobster, crab soufflé, and turf selections, with sautéed vegetables. "This looks great," Gail said.

She was delighted that Rodney was showing his love, but as the night went on she began to question whether Rodney had bigger intentions for the evening. Gail fell silent and hid her mouth with the napkin. "I'm sorry, excuse me," she said as she rose from the table and went to the restroom.

Rodney stood and watched her dash away. "Are you okay?"

Gail didn't respond. She made it to the ladies' room and stood in front of the mirror. *Am I ready for this so soon after reuniting? Will I disappoint him after he's gone through all this trouble? I'm swept away with all of this but... but...* She pondered for a moment longer.

Rodney called to her from outside the bathroom door. "Are you okay?"

"I'm fine, be right out," Gail said. Rodney stood at the door and waited. Gail peeked one last time in the mirror before leaving. As she opened the door, she saw Rodney standing there. "Oh, sorry, I thought you were back at the table."

"I hope things are okay," Rodney said as they turned to

return to dinner.

"I just needed a moment."

"If you'd like to go home, I understand."

"No, no, no, not at all. I love what you've done. I love this, Rodney. No woman I know would ruin a romantic evening like this. It's wonderful."

"Was the dinner selection all right? I don't recall you being allergic to anything."

"I'm not allergic to anything, and it's perfect."

The two arrived at the table, and Rodney pulled out her chair. "Let's get back to dinner, shall we?"

"Yes, of course."

It was moments in the meal when Rodney spoke. "I was thinking, how about we take a stroll on the beach after we're done? We could take our wine with us, unless you want dessert."

"Dessert, no. Walking the beach sounds nice. It's a lovely night."

"Yes, I agree, it's a lovely night and perfect for us. I mean, this turned out better than I imagined."

"You do have an imagination. It's what I love about you, Rodney. Your imagination is superb, but the best thing is how you make it come to life. I knew you were romantic, but I never thought you'd go so far to sweep a woman off her feet."

"Not just any woman."

"You have done this for other women, right?

"Actually, you're the first."

"Really? I'm surprised."

"I enjoyed each person as she came through my life. But with you, this is different."

"Different. How so?"

"I actually love you. It's an emotion I thought I had before, but with you, it's greater than anything I've ever experienced. It is one heck of a feeling every time a thought of you comes to mind. My body and mind fills with excitement and my palms sweat."

"Very interesting, Rodney." Gail giggled. "You have a way of showing your love. I have no doubt you love me." Gail thought of how she'd expressed the opposite to June in the park just earlier that same day; Gail was astounded to find that she meant what she said to Rodney. *I'm admitting it now, really admitting it. If he asks me, I know I'll say yes.*

"Are you ready for that walk?"

"Sure," Gail said and pushed away from the table as Rodney pulled back her chair and reached out his hand to assist her. He kept hold of hers as they ventured along the beach.

"This is really nice," Rodney whispered.

"Yes, very. It's not often a girl gets to stroll along the beach in the moonlight with the man she loves." Gail moved closer to Rodney and placed one arm around his waist.

Neither spoke as the sound of the waves upon the sand became music to their ears. The distant sound of the melody, played by the restaurant's violinist, carried across the shore. Rodney pulled Gail closer to him, held her tight in her arms, and led her in a slow dance.

Gail relaxed her head against Rodney's chest as she followed Rodney's lead. She thought of Calistoga, when she'd met Rodney, then remembered their first date. She recollected the ensuing months, when they had grown closer and closer. Her heart filled with happiness, and in that moment she let go of her fears about Rodney's intentions. She knew he was committed to her. It was a night she'd never experienced with any man in her life. *A night to remember*, thought Gail.

Rodney pulled his shoulders and face back to look at Gail. "I am so in love with you. I hope this night is one you'll always cherish."

"A girl's dream is having at least one night like this," Gail said, "and tonight is my night."

"I hope I'm not setting a precedent I won't be able to live up to in the future. You know every night won't be like this."

"Rodney, you forget that I already know what it's like to live day-to-day with you. I liked our day-to-day life. It's just nice to know you have this kind of romance up your sleeve for special occasions."

"Babe, that was the right answer." Rodney smiled and looked down into Gail's eyes.

Gail returned his gaze. *This is it, this is the moment. Yes, yes, yes.*

Rodney leaned in for a deep kiss. When they parted, he looked at his watch. "We'd better start walking. It's almost time to get back on the yacht." He led her back toward the dock.

They returned to the yacht and found comfort holding each other as they watched the island disappear. Gail didn't say much during the ride. *I really thought after all this romance, he'd pop the question. Am I disappointed he didn't?*

Rodney continued whispering to Gail, telling her how he envisioned their life in the future. He mentioned work and asked her whether she would be returning to the firm soon. Lost in her thoughts, Gail missed the first part of Rodney's question. Two words brought her back from her reverie: "Will you?"

"Will I what?" Gail asked excitedly.

"Return to the office so I can work side by side with you again."

Gail deflated but smiled at Rodney. "Well, that's the plan. I've loved working with you, you know that."

"Good, it's settled."

The night ended when Rodney walked Gail to her apartment door. "It was surely a night to remember," Gail said, and she smiled as she held Rodney's hand.

"Yes," Rodney said and took her keys to unlock the front door for her. "I'll see you tomorrow. I don't want to rush things. I wish you a wonderful slumber. Thanks for a fantastic evening." He reached for her face and laid his hands on her cheeks, leading her lips to his. "Good night. And remember, I love you."

"I love you too." Gail watched him return to his car. She waved farewell as she entered her apartment.

27.
Visions for the Future

RODNEY WOKE EARLY the next day for his morning run. The events of the night before lingered on his mind. He reflected upon the image of Gail in his arms, and thoughts of their future together motivated him. He'd run for nearly forty minutes by the time he'd circled back to his condo. He completed the five miles in record time and knew it was his focus on Gail, her beauty, her excitement, and her mind, that had taken the time away. Energized, Rodney dressed for a day at work. When he arrived, he parked his car and peeked into Gail's office when he entered the building. No signs led him to believe she'd returned. He walked to Dan's office. "Hey, how are things?"

"The usual," Dan said. "What happened last night?"

"Awesome evening, I hope she enjoyed it."

"Dude, I know she did. She and June were on the phone this morning."

"That's great. Did she say she was coming in?"

"Not a clue. Was she supposed to?"

"Last night she responded as if she were going to."

"Well, no sign of her yet, but I can call to find out if she'd planned to."

"No, let's let her make up her mind."

"Okay, but you've been pretty patient. You have to make a business decision, Rodney. If she doesn't return, we need to fill her position. Remember, we lost Stanley and replaced him with Gail."

"I know, I know. That's why I asked her last night to return."

"I'm just advising, Rodney. We'll have a tough time delivering on the next contract we win if her position is still empty. We are short handed."

"Got it, Dan, I got it." Rodney headed down the hall to his office.

Only minutes into his workday, Rodney noticed an email from Gail. He clicked on the link and it expanded on his computer screen.

Rodney,

Last night was wonderful. You swept me away again and ignited wonderful emotions within me. I didn't sleep after you left, and while pondering our lives, it made me realize I want to give us the best chance possible. I want us to work, but after everything it's going to take a lot of time and effort to heal the damage we caused between us. Don't get me wrong, I love you so much.

I'm not coming in today; actually, I'm never coming back to work at the firm. You can use this as my resignation notice. We've worked well together in the past, but after everything I realize there's no way to keep our business and personal lives separate when I'm working there. So, please forgive me for agreeing to return last night. I didn't think it through before giving you my answer.

Today I made a decision, a very important decision to follow my heart. I'm not sure if you know I'm afraid. I'm very afraid, yet I'm sure about us. I don't plan on letting this love between us die. I'm yours in heart and mind.

Gail

Rodney was shocked and saddened at losing Gail, who'd been a vibrant and productive member of the firm. They'd worked well together, but at the same time, Rodney felt a sense of relief. He knew this would be best for their relationship, and she'd told him something he'd wanted to know: she loved him. He walked to Dan's office, took a seat, and asked, "Did you know Gail wanted to resign?"

"No. Did she?" Dan asked.

"Yes, she did. I received the email this morning. I guess it's a good thing."

"It probably is, especially since you two are working things out."

"Being together both here and at home would have likely led to a problem." Rodney leaned forward in his seat. "I feel good and bad, Dan."

"You should be happy she decided to give you freedom to focus here."

"What a way to put it. Freedom."

"Rodney, you know I didn't mean it like that—she's not a ball and chain. It's just that for the past couple months, everything's centered around your relationship with Gail. I get it, I'd do anything for June too, but I think the separation between work and home will be good."

"I agree, and I want to thank you for keeping things running smoothly while I tried to get things together. Only a best friend would look out for me the way you have. I appreciate you, Dan. You'll never know how much." Rodney stood and left the room.

It was mid-morning and Sabrina watched the multiple versions of her clothing line commercials. She smiled as she realized how her dream of designing was now her reality. *That Rodney is amazing*, she thought as the last commercial ended. Her motivation to see everything come to fruition led her to visit the nearest department store, looking for her clothing line display. She left the office and found herself at the local mall. She walked into one store and found her clothes displayed with care and set up exactly as she and Rodney had mapped out. She didn't want recognition, so she took a discreet position with a clear view of the designs. As the hour went on, she watched the consumers and was pleased to see the positive responses and sales. As her clothes flew off the rack, she knew the commercial campaign had worked.

Contented by the clear success of her designing endeavors, Sabrina left the department store and headed to the old hotel to check on the progress of her next project. She walked through the building with a contractor and building inspector, identifying the building's condition and discussing how they would address anything that needed repair. Her excitement grew as she recalled her motivation for opening the center. She thought of Patricia, Gina, and all the other women she'd known who suffered from eating disorder illnesses. As a model, Sabrina had seen her share of anorexic and bulimic women.

Once they completed the walk-through, the contractor stopped and faced Sabrina. "You are going to have to renovate this building to get it to code. It's going to be a major undertaking."

"I realize it's going to be a challenge," Sabrina said.

"Structurally, for its age, the building has been kept up quite well," the inspector said. "The current owners should be able to assist you with the few things I've checked off on my list as needed repairs."

"That's great, because I have a plan, and I want this location. Look at the view, and it's quiet. It's perfect for the women's health center I want to open."

"There will be some obstacles since we'll be working with an older structure," the contractor said, "but I think it's worth it, given the charm and craftsmanship of this building. If you want, we can discuss your vision, and I can bring in an architect to help with the renovations."

"Sounds like a plan. When can we begin working, and how long will it take once we start the project?" Sabrina asked.

"It depends on the architect and your vision. Can we meet in two days?"

"Sure, will you call me with a time?'

"No problem."

"Thanks for coming out, you two. I'll have ideas at the meeting, and I'll see you tomorrow." Sabrina jumped in her car and left the location. She looked at the hotel in her rearview mirror and envisioned the center. Sabrina picked up her cell phone and dialed Rodney. "Hey, what are you doing within the next couple days?" she asked.

"Nothing much, just the usual."

"I met with a building inspector and contractor for the health center. The contractor wants me to meet an architect so we can nail down what the clinic should look like. Would you mind coming to the meeting with me? This is your project too."

"Yes, I will come, but no surprises this time. I mean, it's strictly business."

"I know, strictly business. Nothing is planned. I promise not to do anything with Simone."

"Okay, what time is the meeting?"

"It's two days from now, but we haven't set a time yet. As soon as I find out, I'll send you a text or email."

"Good. Shouldn't you decide what you want first? You know, develop an idea before meeting with the contractor and architect."

"Are you contributing?" Sabrina asked.

"Well, I haven't much planned this evening. Gail and I could probably meet you for a dinner meeting."

"Gail? I didn't realize she'd be included on this project."

Rodney remembered Gail didn't work for him any longer. "She's not, force of habit, sorry. What time is good for you?"

"Seven o'clock?"

"That sounds good. We can talk over dinner."

"Great. Where would you like to meet?"

"Let's do one of my favorites. The Asian fusion restaurant on the hill. You know the place?"

"I know it. I'll see you then."

"Sounds good," Rodney said, ending the call.

Gail and June were heading out for the evening while Dan spent a night with his daughter. "It's nice getting out for a few minutes without the baby," June said. "Talk about a job."

"I'd love your job."

"I'm sure you would, and I wouldn't change it for the world at the moment."

"At the moment?"

"I read when the terrible twos set in, this is going to be really different."

"I bet it's all a scare tactic for new mothers."

"Probably, but it's working. I can barely get enough sleep now."

"Isn't Dan a big help?"

"Yes, I love how he's so involved. He takes the little one as often as he can."

"I hope Rodney is like that when the time comes."

"So you're definitely with him now?"

"I think so. No, I know so." Gail smiled as she glanced at June.

"I know that smile, and we haven't even had a drink yet."

"It's a good thing," Gail said as she turned into a popular pub's parking lot. The two exited the car and entered the building.

"Wow, it's crowded," June said. "I had a little more relaxing evening in mind."

"I agree. You know where you'd like to go?"

"Yes, I do actually," June said. "There's an Asian fusion restaurant in town that's just superb."

Gail handed her the car keys as they exited the pub and walked to the car. "I think I know the place, but just in case, you drive."

June took the keys and headed towards the restaurant. "I know this is a good spot to escape the noise," she said.

"I'm with you; I didn't want any guys approaching me either, so I'm sure this will be a better place for us to catch up."

"I'm sure it is." June pulled into the parking lot minutes later. "There's a nice bar inside. Do you want to sit there?"

"Sure," Gail said. The women entered the restaurant.

Rodney had arrived at the restaurant earlier and was well into dinner with Sabrina when Gail and June entered. He was discussing a review of the work he thought the old hotel needed to function as a health center. "I know we'll have to create some sort of medical screening room," he said.

"I thought the same thing," said Sabrina.

"You know, this is really a good cause. I've seen a number of people, especially young girls, develop eating disorders."

"It's pretty bad in the modeling arena as well. Competition is tough."

"In addition to the building, we need a resident doctor."

"You're right; I figured we'd worry about that once we have the building closer to finished."

"Yeah, at least then we can show the concept in motion when it's time."

"What about the living quarters? You know, the suites. How should we have the suites developed?"

Rodney looked around the room to gather his thoughts before answering. At that moment, he saw Gail and June enter the restaurant and sit at the bar. "Excuse me for a minute," Rodney told Sabrina as he left the table to greet Gail and June. He approached behind them and touched Gail on the shoulder. "Hi, ladies."

The women turned around. "Rodney!" Gail said. She gave

him a hug and a kiss on the cheek.

"Hi, Rodney. It's nice to see you." June said.

"What are you doing here?" Gail asked.

"I'm with Sabrina working out a plan for a new project."

"Seriously?" Gail asked.

"Don't jump to conclusions, Gail. Why would he blatantly tell you about it if he were up to anything different?" June said.

Gail stood quiet for a moment before answering. "Good point. You're off the hook, Rodney."

"Thanks, June, for making sense. As for you…" Rodney looked at Gail, "…I was never on the hook in the first place. Enjoy your drink." Rodney returned to his table and frowned along the way.

"You sure know how to keep a man in your life," June said as she took a sip of her drink.

"I know, I shouldn't have said that. But Simone and Sabrina, those two have tried every trick in the book to get Rodney."

"So you help?"

"Am I helping them?"

"You are, stop being so afraid. You just told me he's what you wanted. Now go apologize."

"Now?"

"Do you love the guy or what?"

"Of course I love him."

"Fine way for you to show it. Look, he comes to you at first sight. He's polite, loving in his approach, and you blast him for being honest with you."

Gail digested June's explanation. "Maybe you're right. Are you coming with me?"

June cocked her head and looked at Gail through the sides

of her eyes. "Be a big girl. You can handle it." June smiled as she watched Gail leave the bar.

Gail took a deep breath and walked towards Rodney as Sabrina. Sabrina watched Gail approach. "You have company."

"Rodney," Gail said and then looked at Sabrina. "Hi, Sabrina." Rodney rose from his seat as Gail moved to an empty place setting at the table. "Am I interrupting anything?" she asked.

"Yes," Sabrina said. "We were in the middle of planning."

Gail ignored Sabrina's tone and turned to Rodney. "I just came over to apologize."

Rodney reached over to touch Gail's hand. "I understand. Apology accepted. Can we talk later tonight? Sabrina and I really do have a lot of planning to do. There's a big meeting the day after tomorrow, and we need to be prepared for it."

"I guess so." Gail looked over toward June, who was keeping her eye on their table.

"Good. Thanks for the apology." Rodney smiled and winked. Gail returned the smile and walked to the bar.

Sabrina shook her head. "Man, you've got it bad."

"Actually, I...have it pretty good." Rodney shrugged and smiled again.

"I hope it's worth it. I really do, for your sake."

"She's really a great woman. Trust me."

"Uh-huh."

"Come on now, let's get back to what we came here for." Rodney directed his gaze toward the blueprints on the table.

"I like this." Sabrina pointed as she moved her hand over the building design. "If we place this door here, we could have privacy suites in one area."

"That would work," Rodney said. It was an hour into

their meeting when dinner arrived. The two consumed dinner and worked on their ideas. They took notes and created bullet points with questions to ask the architect and contractor.

Rodney looked over everything they'd planned out. "I expect some high expenses, but maybe the guys will give us a few ideas."

"Let's hope so. I'm sure we don't have the capital to cover it all."

Rodney stopped to think of how much he'd agreed to invest in this venture. "You're right, my investment will not cover this."

"Neither will mine, but maybe we can get Simone involved."

"I know it's your sister, and there's no question that she's great with money and running a business, but I think you have the wit and business sense to pull this off on your own. We can come up with a different idea."

"I did hope to do this one without her help—maybe just to prove to myself that I can. On the other hand, the cause is so important to me now that if it meant asking Simone for help, I'd do it."

"Sabrina, you have a good heart. I'd stay on course, and we'll figure how to raise more money if needed."

"Thanks, Rodney."

After another hour, they finally decided to leave. "Let me just tell you, Rodney, you're a great guy. I want you to know you can do better," Sabrina said.

"I thought we did pretty well. The building will be awesome if our plans work out."

"I agree, the building will be awesome, but I'm referring to Gail. You can do better."

"I'd have to disagree with you on that. Gail is a wonderful woman. Besides, I don't want to get into your views on my personal life. It's strictly business between us from now on, Sabrina."

"I didn't mean to overstep my boundaries with you. I mean, if it's Gail you're in love with, I'll respect it. But, just for the record, you could have done better."

"With your sister?"

"She comes to mind."

"I'll tell you the same as I told her. I love Gail, and she is my life now."

"Does she know it?"

"She will." Rodney pulled out Sabrina's chair as she stood up. "So, you'll call me tomorrow with the details?" he asked.

"I will," Sabrina said. She walked in front of him, exiting the restaurant. "See you soon."

Gail waited on her couch and watched her phone for a call. She picked the phone up a couple times but found nothing. Soon after, she heard a knock on her door. She jumped up to open it, and Rodney was waiting on the other side. "You didn't call," she said.

"I know. I missed you and just wanted to see you."

"I'm glad you came."

"It's nice being here." Rodney moved closer to Gail. "Listen," he said as he took her in his arms. "There is no woman on this earth that can have an impact on us. It will not happen, and I don't want you to worry."

"Me, worry!"

"Yes, you." Rodney laid his lips upon hers.

"I believe you," Gail said as the kiss weakened her knees.

"I'm in love with you. I wouldn't give you up for the world."

"I love you too. It just makes me crazy when I see another woman after you."

"You shouldn't get jealous. When I gave you my gift, my intangible gift, I meant it, for life. Nothing can take that away from us." Rodney kissed her again. He kissed her passionately, as if to instill his affirmations within her. "I'm in love with you, need you, and want you."

Gail felt every word as his arms embraced her, and his lips pressed upon hers. She melted with excitement. "Yes, Rodney, I love you too." She pulled Rodney into her condo.

Sabrina entered the office early, focusing on the plans they'd drafted the night before. She sat at her desk, adjusting the sketches. She aspired to make the center a classy but practical place. She wanted the decor to exude glamour and comfort. They'd planned to create this atmosphere throughout the building but reserved some rooms that would be medically operational. Sabrina kept working, and by the time she looked up from her focus, it was time to end her day. She called Rodney. "Hey, I finished the sketches. Everything's set to meet at my lawyer's office tomorrow. He's knowledgeable about the business and zoning laws in this area, so I thought it might be a good idea to include him on the meeting."

"Sounds like a plan."

"Okay, bye." Sabrina ended the call and packed the sketches in her briefcase. She left the office, headed for home.

When she walked through the front door, she moved into the living room and found Simone sitting in a chair in the corner with her legs up. Simone barely looked up when Sabrina entered the room. "Hey, sis," Sabrina began, "what's up?"

"Nothing, just remembering my life before everything went crazy. You know, even though he deceived me and I hate to admit it, losing my husband is still hard. They may have been insincere on his part, but I thought we had some good times here."

"Oh, Simone, I'm sorry."

"I guess I just kind of miss being married. I miss being in a relationship."

"Don't you wish for a better relationship than what you had?"

"At least I had one."

"Okay, what gives? I know you; you cannot be wishing to have that relationship back. What are you really feeling?"

"I fell for the wrong man, and now I see I'm paying dearly for it. I can't stop thinking of him. I can't get him off of my mind."

"Rodney is gone, sis."

"I know, he told me over and over again. I get the message. But I didn't expect it to bring up these harsh emotions. I don't love him; I just wanted to love him."

Sabrina moved closer to hug Simone. There were tears in Simone's eyes as she hugged her sister. "I'm sorry it didn't work. I thought you were going to win his heart," Sabrina said.

"So did I," Simone said, "so did I."

Sabrina broke the embrace and lifted the strap of the bag she carried. "Can I show you something? Let's go into the kitchen." Simone followed without saying a word. She moved at a slow pace as she followed Sabrina to the counter stools. Sabrina pulled out a picture of the front of the hotel and showed it to Simone.

Simone squinted at the picture. "Are you planning on taking a vacation or something?"

"No, but I'm buying the building."

"You're what?"

"Yes, I'm purchasing the building and turning it into a women's health center."

"A women's health center?" Simone pushed her head back to analyze all the sketches and paperwork that Sabrina was putting in front of her. "Why didn't you talk to me about this sooner or ask me what I thought about your idea?"

"I mentioned it a few days ago, when we met Rodney at the park. At the time all you heard was 'Rodney.' I didn't talk to you about it sooner because knew you'd analyze it to death and talk me out of it. I want to do this. I'm doing this."

"Good, you made up your mind. What's the plan, how are you going to do this?"

"Well, I want to renovate the building to turn it into a center for women with eating disorders. I meet, well, Rodney and I meet the contractor and architect tomorrow morning."

"You partnered with Rodney? What a way to drop a bomb."

"Like I said, I tried to tell you the other day when we went to the park. But please don't take it that way. You know I've always respected Rodney, and after the success of the marketing campaign, I couldn't help but think he'd be the perfect person to help me with this."

"So, let me get this right. You are creating a place to help people who are fighting those diseases. And you're partnering with the man I've been fighting to have in my life."

"I know it's hard because of the personal connection, but initially I thought that might not be such a bad thing; I thought maybe with time you two would sort things out. Besides, I was trying to make a smart business decision. You can't deny that Rodney is an excellent businessman and someone I can trust."

"Well, you're right about that."

Sabrina smiled as she pulled out the sketches from her briefcase. "Let's drop the emotional stuff about Rodney for a minute and look at how I see this place changing." Sabrina handed the sketches to Simone and waited as she reviewed them. "Do you like it?"

"I think it's going to cost a lot to change this place. Are you sure you want to spend that kind of money?"

"I would give my all to have this place come to life."

"That is exactly why I think you should have spoken to me first before buying this building."

"I am not a little girl anymore, and didn't I prove my business sense to you?"

"Well, yes, you did. I know you can do it, but there is a huge risk."

"Aunt Marge helped so many people. Why can't I? Patricia's work helped us stay afloat. I want to do this in her honor."

"Good point. All right, well I'm in if you need me." Simone smiled. She pointed at one of the drawings. "I like the entryway. It's lovely."

"Yes, it is. Let me show you the rest," Sabrina said with excitement.

28.
Rebuilding Love

RODNEY WOKE WITH his arms wrapped around Gail. It was a sign that the day had started out right. It was early, and he stretched and swung his feet over the bed to head out for his morning exercise. As he stood up, he realized he didn't have workout clothes at Gail's apartment anymore. *I guess one missed run never hurt anybody. I'll make up for it by going for a run tonight.* Rodney crawled back into bed with his love. He gazed at her as she slept, relishing the moment that he'd missed for so long. Finally things were returning to normal. Gail woke slowly, and Rodney pushed a tendril hair off her face as she opened her eyes. "Mmm, you're comfy," she said.

Rodney pulled her closer. "You are too." They held each other for a few more minutes. Rodney looked down at Gail. "Coffee?"

Gail smiled. "Yes, please." She looked at the clock and watched Rodney as he sauntered out of the room and headed into the kitchen.

Rodney started the pot and returned to the bedroom. Gail opened her arms wide, inviting him back to bed, but Rodney shook his head.

"Sorry, darling, I have to jump in the shower. I have that meeting at nine o'clock and have to get moving if we're to share morning coffee."

"Just a few minutes."

"It's nearly seven. You know I'd love to, but dear sweet woman, I'm still trying to run a firm. I can't hang out this morning. I have things scheduled."

"I understand. I really understand," Gail watched Rodney go into the adjoining bathroom. As he started the shower, she said, "Your toothbrush is still in the holder. I never threw it out. Why don't we have lunch today?"

"Lunch? I'm not sure. How about dinner?" Rodney's voice echoed off shower walls.

"Dinner? Well … if, and only if, I get to cook."

"You cook! Oh, heck yes, I'll be home around six o'clock at the latest."

"Well, I was thinking I'd cook here tonight," Gail said. She went into the kitchen and poured a cup of hot coffee. She sat near the counter, waiting for Rodney to appear. When he entered the room, she poured his cup and placed it on the counter. "Your cup is there, sweetie."

"Thanks. So, I'll meet you here tonight then?" Rodney smelled the coffee and waited for it to cool down a bit.

"Yes, I know we stayed at your place more before, but it will give me more time to prepare if I do it here."

"You're right, you wouldn't have as much time if you waited to start cooking until I got home. Maybe I should make you a key to my place so that you can get in there when you need to."

Gail beamed. "I'd like that."

Rodney leaned in for a kiss. "Okay, I have to get going now.

I'll see you tonight. I love you."

"Love you too," Gail said as Rodney left the condo.

Rodney arrived at Phil's office building and met Sabrina outside. "Good morning," he said.

"Good morning!" Sabrina said. "You ready for this?"

"Definitely."

"Good, me too. Before we go in, I should tell you: I spoke to Phil, and he agreed to contribute to the cause."

"That's awesome news." Rodney smiled as he remembered that Phil never allowed his investments to fail.

"Isn't it? I'm so glad to see this all coming together." They arrived at Phil's office in time and entered a conference room where the contractor and architect were already waiting. Phil walked in just as Sabrina and Rodney took their seats. Introductions went around the room and Sabrina passed the sketches to everyone attending. "These are my ideas for the building."

"I like them," Phil said, "but why so much glitz?"

"Because I want it to be less sterile. I want the women who come here to feel comfortable and not alienated," Sabrina said.

"Isn't it misleading to the patients?" Phil asked.

"I don't think so," Rodney said. "We will still have exam rooms in the building, but since the women will be staying long enough to get rehabilitated, we want the atmosphere to be inviting."

"Yes, he's correct," Sabrina said. "The idea isn't to boast or mislead but to make the patients feel at home."

"This we can do," the architect said. The contractor gathered the sketches and reviewed each one. "I can have a price estimate in a week."

"A week? Why so long?" Sabrina asked.

"I have to research the materials, shipment options, and of course it's dependent upon our architect's input on anything additional that we might need."

"Yes," the architect said as he grabbed a sketch, "Sabrina, you did a good job with these sketches, but I have to visit the site with these drawings and work out a plan."

"Well, will a week suffice for you too? Can you two both give us a full price within a week?" Rodney asked.

"Yes, I think we can."

The five sat in silence for a moment. Sabrina turned back to the architect and contractor. "Can you give me a ballpark on what you think this might cost, given your past experiences with building renovations? I mean, with similar objectives; you know."

The men looked at each other and reviewed the sketches. The contractor nodded his head after the architect spoke to him under his breath. He looked at the faces around the table and said, "Approximately three hundred thousand."

"Three hundred thousand?!" Sabrina's brow furrowed. "I can almost purchase a new building for that much."

"But look what you're getting," Rodney said to Sabrina, "location, charm, building, accessibility, and marketability."

"You have a point, but that is beyond our budget. That's only the estimate for the renovations, and we still have the purchase price, the interior, and hiring to consider."

Phil listened to Sabrina and Rodney. "We can discuss this without these guys. I know what it takes to renovate an older building. Remember, this is just an estimate," he said.

"I guess it was price shock," Sabrina said. "Thank you, gentlemen." She stood and reached her hand across the table toward the contractor and architect.

All stood at the table and exchanged business cards as the two exited the room. "What are we going to do?" Sabrina asked Rodney and Phil. "I don't think it's wise for us to up the ante."

"We may have to," Phil said.

"How about coming up with a way to gain other investors or contributors?" Rodney asked.

"This is a nonprofit effort, right?" Phil asked.

"Yes, that's what we were planning, but we hadn't settled on anything just yet," Sabrina said. "We were hoping you might be able to explain our options to us in that regard."

Phil closed the door and looked at his watch as he returned to his seat. "I have a half hour for this, so let me explain things to you." Phil took Sabrina and Rodney through every aspect of running a nonprofit versus a profitable clinic. When he finished his explanation, the three agreed to go ahead with the center as a nonprofit organization and decided to call it the Patricia Dugan Healthy Weight Center for Women.

Phil agreed to legalize the organization as soon as possible. As Sabrina and Rodney left the room, Phil said, "I'll call you when the documents are ready."

"Great," Sabrina said, "we'll be ready when you call."

"I should get back. I have other meetings to attend this afternoon," Rodney said as he and Sabrina approached the parking lot.

"Okay, thanks for taking the time to come to this meeting."

"I'm glad I could make it. Actually, I just had a great idea."

"Really? I'd like to hear it."

"You've done wonderful things in fashion. This is a fashion-stricken illness, and we need money."

"I see where you're going. I can call my friends and con-nections in the industry and ask for donations."

"Yes, but that wasn't exactly what I had in mind."

"What did you have in mind?"

"Ask for donations, yes, but ask for things we can sell to earn more. Maybe we can do a fashion show and auction to raise money?"

"That's a thought," Sabrina said as she climbed into her car. "Actually, that's a really good idea. Let me think this through."

"Yes, do that. I'll talk to you soon," Rodney said and left to go back to his office.

After work, Rodney went home and changed into his running gear. Although he'd enjoyed his morning with Gail, it wasn't like him to skip his daily workout. After running, he show-ered and headed to Gail's apartment. It was still early evening when he arrived. He approached her door, and the wonderful odor teased his senses and touched his stomach. Rodney had skipped lunch in a hurry to get back to the office, so he was very hungry. On the way to Gail's he'd stopped to purchase a bouquet of flowers and wine. Since he had no idea what was on the menu, he'd purchased a bottle each of white and red. He knocked on the door and waited.

Gail opened it. "Hey, you. Dinner will be ready in just a few minutes."

Rodney walked directly to the kitchen and placed the bags on the counter. He smiled as he watched Gail in her apron over the stove.

Gail looked at Rodney. "No greetings? No kiss on the cheek or 'hello love'? What's up?"

Rodney leaned in for a kiss. "I just thought you were busy,

and I can't wait to eat! I picked up some wine for us."

"That will be perfect," Gail said. "Go settle in, and I will have dinner ready in a few."

"Are you sure there isn't something I can help with? I can at least set the table."

"How about opening the wine and pouring me a glass?"

"I can do that," he said. "What type of meat did you prepare?"

"Lamb."

Rodney selected the red wine, opened it, and poured a glass for Gail. He set her glass in the kitchen and took his to the table. "Can I at least set up the table now?"

"We don't have to be fancy, just relax. I'm sure you've had a long day."

"Okay, let me know when it's ready, and I'll come into the kitchen." He took a seat at the table and couldn't wait to taste the food he had been smelling. "Dinner smells wonderful."

"I didn't know if you'd enjoy lamb."

"I'd enjoy anything you prepare."

"Are you saying you like my cooking?"

"Always have, and from what I can see, it's almost as good as mine," Rodney said.

"Sure it is. Next time you'll have to refresh my memory."

"I think I will," Rodney said as he returned to the kitchen. He grabbed Gail's waist. "Let me refresh your memory of this." Rodney kissed her, holding her tight.

Gail responded with a sigh once he released her. "Wow, I remember, but you better get the plates, dinner is ready. I almost decided to postpone dinner and move right into dessert!"

"Sure," Rodney said as he laughed. Following instructions, he grabbed two plates and helped Gail dish the food onto them. He then took the plates to the dining table. He placed one next to the other and waited for Gail to arrive. "I didn't know which plate you wanted."

"No problem," Gail said as she took her seat next to Rodney. "This is nice. I like seeing you at the end of your day."

"Me too, but I wanted to talk about your not working with me, if you don't mind."

"I mind. Next subject," Gail said.

Neither spoke for a few minutes until Rodney broke silence. "You did great with the lamb. I don't think I've had it seasoned like this."

"It's a simple recipe. I found it online, and it took no time to cook."

"We'll have to do this lamb thing again."

"Thank you, dear. You're a sweetheart of a man."

"I hope you think so."

"I know so. I have an idea for dessert."

"Dessert? I don't think we'll have room for dessert. You cooked enough to last us all week."

"Who said dessert was something you consume?"

"Oh, oh, oh." Rodney grinned. "In that case, I'd love some."

It was morning, and when Gail and Rodney woke up, they greeted each other with a kiss. Rodney went to shower, and Gail headed to the kitchen to make breakfast and coffee. Just as Rodney was straightening his tie, he heard Gail's voice from the other room: "Breakfast, dear?"

"On my way." Rodney walked to the kitchen. He grabbed a cup of coffee and took a seat at the counter. "I like this," he said while grabbing a plate of scrambled eggs, bacon, and toast from Gail. He kissed her on the cheek. "Thank you."

"You're welcome. I have plans for today. Is there something you'd like for dinner?"

"Where are we having dinner?"

"I was thinking your place, if that's okay. It's larger, and I like your kitchen."

"That sounds perfect," Rodney said as he pulled a brand new key out of his pocket, "because I was going to suggest the same thing. I want you to move in with me, Gail. I know it's going to take awhile to rent or sell your place, but there's no reason you can't start staying with me in the meantime. That is, if you're still thinking of being with me."

Gail inhaled and took the key from his hands. "Rodney, I love you. How can I not think of being with you?"

Rodney smiled. "I'm happy you still want to be with me and that we're finally back on track to where we were. I'd love moving forward, one step at a time."

"I'm so happy, Rodney."

"Great, I hoped you would be." Rodney placed his dish in the sink and grabbed Gail for another kiss. He said, "You have the key, and call me if you need anything today." Rodney left the apartment and headed to his job.

Gail left her apartment to meet June. June, Gail, and the baby shopped together. It was a girls' day as the three walked through the market. "June, I'm starting to like this," Gail said.

"Shopping?"

"The domestic life—not working. I think I can keep Rodney very content if I take care of him. Rodney asked me to move in with him today."

"That's wonderful, Gail! Do you really want to give up being in the workforce though?"

"I feel as though it would be good. I can do the wife and mom thing."

"Here." June handed her baby to Gail. "Start practicing."

"Oh, come on, June, it can't be that bad."

"It isn't bad; it's just harder than I expected. I miss not being able to just drop things and do whatever. I miss working at the travel agency. Sure, I'm still owner, but ever since I had the baby, my senior manager has handled everything. It's just not the same. Are you sure you want such a life?"

"I thought you enjoyed being a mother."

"I love my baby, but I miss being a career woman."

"What about marriage? Do you like being married?"

"That's the part I love the most. Dan is a wonderful husband, friend, and lover."

"Good, I have at least one thing to look forward to."

"You have a world to look forward to. Rodney is a wonderful man."

"It's nice being free of professional challenges. Besides, I'm ready to start a family."

"Then follow your dream and heart. Don't listen to my complaints. Everyone's different." June took her baby and placed her in the stroller. "I think you'll do fine either way."

"I think so too."

Sabrina arrived at the art gallery; she was meeting Simone, who'd asked Sabrina to come. As Sabrina entered, she saw Simone looking at a particular piece of art. "Hey," Sabrina said as she approached.

"Hi." Simone hugged Sabrina. "It's been a while since

we've come in here."

"Yes, it has. What did you want to show me?"

"This," Simone said as she led Sabrina to a large painting. "This is perfect for the women's center—doesn't it remind you of Aunt Marge?"

Sabrina looked surprised. "Yes, it does. It's the right color and size too. I think it would be great in the front entrance area."

"I thought the same. Besides, you'll want a piece of Aunt Marge at your clinic. I'm sure you'd enjoy having her insight with you."

"Her insight keeps me sane. I remember her telling us all the time to follow our gut instincts."

"Yes, she did." Simone sighed. "If only my gut had pointed toward Rodney sooner."

"You have to let him go, Simone."

"I know that; it's just going to take some time."

"You aren't depressed, are you?"

"Not depressed, just demoralized with my love life."

"We have to get you out."

"I will in time, but right now I need to find my own way."

Gail completed cooking dinner at Rodney's condo. Her confidence was boosted by Rodney's invitation to move in and June's suggestion for Gail to go for what she wanted. *Tonight he'll understand how serious I am about becoming his wife*, Gail thought as she placed candles around the condo. She put a red tablecloth on the dining room table, set white placemats, and lit two taper candles. She added two wine glasses, plates, and silverware to the table. In the center, she placed a floral arrangement with a love note to Rodney. Gail wore a seductive, form-fitting dress. As a final touch, she turned on the stereo, and soft, romantic music filled the air.

It was just after 6:00 p.m. when Rodney arrived. Once he unlocked his door and stepped inside, Rodney looked at the place and smiled. "Wow." When he looked to his left, he caught sight of Gail. He looked her up and down. "Oh my." Rodney set his briefcase on a chair and walked up to her. He grabbed her in his arms. "This is what a man likes when he comes home. You look absolutely stunning."

"Welcome home, baby."

"What do you have in mind?"

"Like you don't get the picture?"

"What can I do to help make this a lovely evening?"

"Well, take off your coat and sit here." Gail pointed. "Just enjoy."

"I can do that," Rodney said. He took the seat where Gail directed. She gave him the card just before going into the kitchen. Rodney opened it and read:

Tomorrow's dream began yesterday before the ups and downs. I'd like to live this dream we share, as I love you with all my heart. I am yours, Rodney, totally yours.

Rodney stood after placing the note back in the envelope. He went to the kitchen and helped Gail with the plates. They went back into the dining room and sat down. Rodney looked at Gail. "I'm glad you decided to love me again."

"I never stopped; it was just a misunderstanding."

"Are you sure?"

"I'm more than sure, Rodney. And I'm not going to waste any more time showing you anything different than a confident woman."

"I see, I really see how you love me."

"I want you to see and feel more. Let me show you. Let me love you. Let me—"

Rodney interrupted. "Be my partner."

"Yes, your life partner."

Rodney poured wine for a toast. "Here's to our lives together."

The two began eating. After their plates were almost empty, Rodney looked at Gail with love in his eyes. "Can I say welcome back?"

"Please do, Rodney, please do."

He stopped eating and rose from the table. He pulled out Gail's chair, and as she stood, he lifted her into his arms. Rodney carried her to his bedroom and placed her gently on his bed. "I'll never let a moment go by without thinking of you, never without a dream of holding you, and I'm not moving forward without making love to you."

29.
Funds, Renovation & Friends

"SUNNY DAYS ARE AHEAD." Sabrina smiled as she reviewed contractor estimates and walked into Philip's office. "You aren't going to believe this, but they saved us fifty thousand dollars."

"Fifty thousand, a great number, but that leaves us a lot yet to raise," Phil said.

"I know, Rodney and I were thinking about putting on a fashion show and auctioning the clothes for the cause. I've contacted some of my designer friends, and I've already received a good response. Of course, I'll add in some of my own designs too."

"Why don't we get together and talk this through. I'm sure we can create a plan with our combined talents."

"I'm open tomorrow afternoon. Are you?"

"Yes, I'm available."

"We can meet here again. Let me contact Rodney and let him know."

"Are you sure he won't be busy?"

"He might be, but he'll make it. See you tomorrow, Phil."

Sabrina exited Phil's office. On the drive to her office, Sabrina noticed Rodney leaving a jewelry store. She couldn't believe her eyes. Sabrina thought of her sister and wished Simone had played her cards right. Then she thought of Rodney's words about Gail and realized it was only natural for him to purchase a gift. Sabrina decided to not stop and speak to Rodney, but to call him later in the day to coordinate the meeting with Phil.

Rodney often explored during midday, especially when he had new clients. His creative flow excelled outside the office. His latest client was a jeweler with a chain of stores around the state. Today, research had taken him downtown to visit one of the franchises. He wanted to be knowledgeable about the product when he provided feedback and guidance for his firm on this campaign. When Rodney returned to the office, he saw that Sabrina had called and left a message. In the message, she mentioned that she and Phil wanted to meet again to discuss funding. Rodney called Sabrina. "Hey, I got your message. What time did you want to meet? "

"Phil is available tomorrow afternoon. We need to fill his appointment slot. Can you make it?"

"Let me see," Rodney said as he turned to look at his desk calendar. "I have a meeting tomorrow afternoon at three. I can get to you two right after lunch."

"I'll ask about right after lunch, but just in case, I'd open my entire afternoon."

"I can't afford to cancel my appointments. I have a business to run."

"You invested into this clinic. Don't you want it to open and to add your name to the operation?"

"I have a business, and I need to be around."

"Don't you have a great partner and good people around you? Don't you have Gail working for you?"

"Yes, I have great people, and no, Gail doesn't work here anymore."

"Wow, really?" Sabrina paused. "Is that why you went to the jewelry store today?"

"You saw me at the jewelry store?" Rodney asked.

Sabrina waited for him to answer her question.

"If you must know, yes, I did a little shopping. I looked at a few items for Gail, but you know, I should have had her with me."

"That serious?" Sabrina asked.

"Yes, it's that serious."

"Good for you, Rodney. You deserve a shot at being happy. I wish you the best."

"Thanks." He paused. "I'll be there in the afternoon. Let me know the exact time."

"I'll get back to you after I talk to Phil."

"Yes, I don't know about the entire afternoon, but I'll give it my best."

"Great. Thank you, Rodney." Sabrina ended the call.

Gail spent most of her day shopping. She went to a furniture store and then from store to store while she gathered her thoughts before making her final decision to purchase a new living room set. She wanted to add her touch to Rodney's condo. Rodney, being a classy bachelor, had nice things, but they were all his, and she wanted the condo to start to feel like their home together. She called Rodney once she found the set she liked best. "Hi, Rodney," Gail said when he answered.

"Hey," Rodney said, "how are you?"

"I'm okay. I'm out."

"Oh?"

"Yeah, I'm just calling because I was thinking, now that we're officially moving in together, I want it to feel like I contributed more at the condo."

"What do you mean? You do contribute; you're there, and you cook and clean. I would hope you feel at home."

"I mean, even though I'm moving in, it's still your place and not ours. I want to redecorate the living room."

"Why redecorate? You know it's perfect."

"Perfect for a bachelor's condo; you're not a bachelor anymore."

"Yes, we are together."

"Then I need to change a few things so I feel at home and that we've shared in choosing the décor."

"I can share, but I thought we'd do it together. I enjoy shopping and adding my taste to our selection."

"Rodney, I see your selection. I can do this quite easily if you let me."

"Okay, I see what you'd like to do. Send me pictures of a few items you were thinking about."

Gail smiled. "Why not just trust me?"

"I do trust you."

"I like the word trust. Don't you?"

Gail sure had a knack for getting her way. Rodney realized it was bound to happen in time, but when he'd asked her to move in, he never thought it would happen that quickly. Rodney sighed but smiled. "All right, I trust you; and yes, I like the word."

"Awesome. I'll see you when you get home. I love you."

Gail did exactly as she desired in redecorating. She bought

a couch, love seat, and chair combination, which matched the color scheme she had in mind. The furniture dealer was able to secure delivery for the same afternoon. Gail also replaced Rodney's coffee table and end tables but kept his expensive and unique vases scattered around the room. After the furniture arrived, Gail made a last-minute dash to a few stores, collecting pieces that matched her vision. When she returned to the condo, she put up the new window treatments she'd found and added the last touches for perfection. After a full day of hard work, she stood back, analyzed the room, and was pleased to see her vision come to life. *Perfect*, she thought.

Rodney drove to his condo at a slower than usual speed. He didn't want to seem overly anxious or too eager to view the changes Gail had made. When he finally walked into the condo, he was amazed. It was as if he'd opened a page to the latest decorating magazine. Rodney considered himself one of superlative taste, but Gail had hit a home run with the living room. He walked slowly around the room, looking at everything. She hadn't painted the walls or replaced any of his expensive paintings, and yet each of the changes she'd made were an improvement.

"What do you think?" she asked.

"I think you are beautiful."

"No, silly, the room."

"Oh, oh, yes, the room. It's worth a million dollars—right out of a magazine."

"You really think so?"

"Of course I do. My girl has talent. You surprise me the more I get to know you."

"Surprise you?"

"I'm extremely surprised; you did wonderfully, and to be

honest, I thought we'd have a few words."

"You didn't trust me?"

"Of course I trust you, I love you. I just worried that our tastes would clash. Turns out they complement one another quite well."

Gail beamed. "Just like us."

Rodney kissed her. "Yes, just like us."

Phil entered the conference room and introduced two phi-lanthropists. One was a wealthy elderly man who made his money building vending machines, and the other was a tech-nology banker. Both men had capital to contribute to Sabrina's clinic and were interested in doing so because of their personal connection to the cause. Both men had daughters who'd de-veloped eating disorders. One man's daughter had been so ill that he'd spent nearly a fortune helping her return to health. The second gentleman had lost his daughter to anorexia and vowed to get involved in any effort that would help others avoid his pain. It was moving, hearing their stories.

Sabrina passed estimate documents to the men, along with some of the sketches and blueprints. "It looks great," the elder man said, "can you explain the operation?"

Sabrina explained her goals and told them about how the center would look, operate, and become an inviting refuge for women who needed help. She went into detail about the reno-vation effort and introduced Rodney as the marketing guru. Rodney then explained his marketing concept and their plan on how to reach out to patients.

"How much funding do we currently have to support this effort?" the second man asked.

"We've covered the sale price for the building and have a

little less than half of what we need for the renovation. We've mustered up one hundred and fifty thousand towards that," Phil said.

The man nodded. "How much are you asking from us?"

"As much as you can spare to share," Sabrina said.

"Yes, we have some plans for raising funds, but there's still a lot more costs to consider. Every bit helps," Rodney said.

"I see," the elderly man said. "I can contribute fifty thousand."

"I'll match his fifty," the other gentleman said. "Now you only need fifty thousand more for the renovation. Can you handle that?"

Rodney smiled as he looked at Sabrina before answering. "Yes, we can handle it."

Sabrina smiled. "Thank you for your generosity." She looked at Rodney and Phil. "We're still going to have to find a doctor who will work at the center too."

"I know one who worked for nonprofits earlier in his career," the younger benefactor said. "He was instrumental in helping my daughter. If he'd started working with my Cynthia sooner, I think she'd be here today."

"We'll definitely have to look into that when time comes," Sabrina said.

"Yes," Rodney said, "I'll be glad to meet him when it's time. Right now, it's a little early, as we don't have the renovations in progress just yet. We're still focusing on fundraising objectives."

"That's a very important step we still have to achieve. Can you tell me more about what you have in mind, Rodney?" Phil asked.

"Sabrina and I discussed a fashion show and auction

fundraiser."

Phil looked around the room. "You gentlemen are welcome to stay and contribute. We'd love having your input."

Both men said they'd love to stay involved.

"Awesome," Phil said. "Go ahead, Rodney."

"Since eating disorders are often so closely related to fashion, it's a fitting way to earn money. We'll feature healthy models. The marketing options for this type of fundraiser are endless."

Sabrina indicated her agreement. "As I mentioned yesterday, I already have designers willing to participate, and I'll create some pieces to auction off as well."

"This sounds like a great plan," the elderly man said.

"Quite," Phil said. "If there isn't anything more, I think we can finish this meeting and let Sabrina and Rodney work their creative magic. We'll meet again next week and see what progress we've made."

Back at home, Rodney spent the evening thinking about the fundraiser. He wanted the clinic to be a success, and felt pressured to come up with a good plan.

Gail interrupted his thoughts. "Are you okay?" she asked.

"I'm fine, just thinking about a fundraiser we're planning for the healthy weight center."

"What center?" Gail asked.

Rodney realized he never explained the business behind his new partnership with Sabrina. He then continued to explain the concept and motivation behind creating the center.

Gail gave Rodney her undivided attention. When he was finished talking, she said, "I think it's a great cause. How much are you invested?"

"I'm one of five investors at the moment, and we still need to raise one hundred fifty thousand dollars to cover the start-up costs."

"Why so many partners?"

"Because it's a nonprofit, and it's for a great cause. I'd be happy if five more joined, and we didn't have to raise money."

"What's the plan?"

"You aren't upset I'm a partner with Sabrina?"

"No, I'm not upset." Gail moved next to Rodney and took a seat as she grabbed his hand. She looked into his eyes. "I love you, and no woman can impact how I feel about you. I trust you."

"I'm glad to see how far we've come, Gail, I really am. I love you too."

"Good, so what's the plan?"

Rodney explained their idea for a fashion show. He also gave his first ideas for possible marketing concepts. Gail, with her affinity for business, added her thoughts, and the two were on it. Gail jumped in as if it were a new assignment; she got on the phone with her longtime friend, Starz. She explained the effort, and Starz not only contributed ten thousand dollars but also agreed to produce the fashion show.

Rodney was amazed at the quick response. He and Gail continued working without missing a step. They fed on each other's ideas. Late into the night, Gail went into the kitchen to make a pot of coffee. Rodney was thrilled with the progress they'd made and picked up the phone to call Sabrina.

"Who are you calling?" Gail asked.

"Sabrina."

"Look at the time."

It was 3:00 a.m. Rodney had lost the track of time as he and Gail had brainstormed their marketing ideas.

"You know, you can wait until morning to call," Gail said. "We have it together, and I know she'll like it."

"Okay, we'll get a hold of her in the morning. Tomorrow we'll explain our marketing concept to her, under one condition."

"What's the condition?"

"You work the campaign as your objective. I'll support you, but you have to do it while I run the business. Can you do it?"

"It isn't a matter of can I, it's more a matter of will I."

"Will you?"

"If she agrees, I'll do it." Gail smiled.

"I'm sure she'll agree, we need as much help as we can get, and it's hard to plan this and work our regular jobs too."

"Good deal, I'll explain it to her tomorrow. Let's get back to work."

"I have a better idea." Rodney stood and moved closer to Gail. "I'm going to scoop you up and whisk you away."

"I just made coffee."

"It can wait, lovely lady." Rodney lifted Gail in his arms and took her to bed.

Two days passed before Rodney and Sabrina spoke. The days were hectic; their regular business events and challenges kept them occupied. Though the women's center was their dream, it seemed they didn't have enough time to do everything for it. Rodney thought it was perfect timing to pitch Gail to Sabrina as the lead marketer and manager for the fundraiser. He finally got Sabrina on the phone, "Ready for a meeting?"

"I'm ready, but don't expect too much. I didn't work on the fundraiser as much as I'd like."

"No problem, I have a solution to help with our busy schedules."

"You do?

"Yes, let's make Gail the lead on this effort. She's perfect for it, as she's done both production and marketing."

Sabrina sat quiet for a moment and remembered Gail's disappearance on Sabrina's last marketing campaign. "She's not going to bail, is she?"

"Of course not."

"Are you sure? She did it to us once."

"It won't happen again. She and I are dedicated now, and there won't be any emotional distress to scare her off."

"Emotional distress, is that what she called it last time?"

"Actually no, I did."

"Rodney, I trust your judgment, but we have to be realistic. Will she disappear this time?"

"No, but if you're worried about it, make her even more involved. Put her in your fashion show."

"Good idea. Okay, welcome her to the team. Ask her to join us today."

"Done. See you in a few hours."

30.
Old Enemies, New Friends

GAIL, RODNEY, AND SABRINA met at a local coffee shop. The three greeted each other in the parking lot and entered the small building. They found a table and took seats. Rodney went to the counter to place their orders. Gail and Sabrina sat in silence until Rodney wasn't within earshot of their conversation. "I know what you're doing," Sabrina said.

"I'm doing something to help my guy."

"You're doing it to keep your guy away from the likes of my sister. Anyway, I don't mind because you two make a nice couple."

Gail was surprised at Sabrina's last comment. She didn't know exactly how to respond. "Thank you, I think," she said.

"He really loves you. I can see that now."

Rodney returned with coffee for the everyone. "You ladies didn't start without me, did you?"

"No, not at all, we're just having girl talk."

"Glad I wasn't involved."

The three began their planning session. It was going to be

great: a fashion show, marketing event, and fundraiser all in one night. Gail and Sabrina fell back into the friendly interaction they'd had when they first started working together.

"Can I visit the building before renovations are complete?" Gail asked.

"Sure, I'll take you," Rodney said.

"Why don't you let it be a girl's trip?" Sabrina asked.

"Um, I don't mind," Rodney said. He thought it was strange how Sabrina and Gail were now chummy. "I'm sure Gail will share her input on your decorating plans."

"Decorating?"

"Yes, she's a pro."

Gail smiled. "He's just boasting because I'm his girl."

"No, really," Rodney said. He looked at Sabrina. "I'll send you a picture of the work she's done."

"I look forward to seeing it."

The three completed their meeting and headed for the door. "Tomorrow afternoon we can ride to the site," Sabrina said to Gail.

"Good, see you then!" Gail said as she and Rodney entered their car.

Once inside, Rodney looked at Gail with confusion. "What's that about?"

"It's a girl thing, Rodney. Don't worry about it, it'll be fine, trust me."

Sabrina and Gail took off the next afternoon. Sabrina handed the drawings to Gail while she drove and explained her ideas for the renovation. She explained how she wanted patients to feel the positive energy throughout the center, and that she wanted the building to not look like a traditional clinic but like an elegant escape. Her depth in explanation gave Gail multiple ideas to work with. It wasn't until they arrived at the building that Gail finally spoke. "This is gorgeous."

"Now you see why it had to be here. The building used to be a hotel."

"Wow, look at the view." Gail waved her hand in direction of the mountains, the green valley, and the view of the city. "Do you think seeing the city will tease your patients?"

"I don't think so because it's far enough away. It will be a reminder of what they're returning to." Gail followed Sabrina to the front entrance.

The contractor greeted them just as they entered. "Hi, ladies," he said.

"Hi," both girls said in response. Sabrina introduced Gail as her right hand going forward. Gail gave the contractor a firm handshake and took his card. She then followed Sabrina around while reviewing the sketches.

When they came to the first room, Gail saw a decorating opportunity immediately. She explained her thoughts to Sabrina, who found that Gail's ideas complimented the plans that Sabrina had already made.

They moved to the next room. "Queen Elegance," Gail said. She ran to each room announcing her ideas. Sabrina enjoyed her energy and took notes. At the end of the tour, Sabrina suggested they work together to decorate the place. Gail jumped at the chance and agreed with enthusiasm. It was the beginning of a friendship; the foundation was set. It seemed they'd forgotten the ill feelings and events that had transpired between them.

"Sabrina, what are you doing tomorrow evening?" Gail asked.

"I haven't decided yet. What do you have in mind?"

"I'd love for you to meet June, my best friend. I'm sure you'd enjoy her too; she's similar to us and such a free spirit. June married Rodney's best friend, Dan."

"I would enjoy meeting her. She married Dan?"

"Yes, it was a fluke. When she first started dating him, I didn't know he worked with Rodney or was his best friend."

"Wow, Dan. He was the wild one, and it surprises me he got married."

"People change when they fall in love."

"That's true. People change when the right person comes along." Sabrina stopped talking as she thought of Lorenz. "I had a perfect guy once, and I pushed him away."

"I vaguely recall you mentioning him before—'the good one that got away.' What happened?"

"I just wasn't very smart in my selection at the time. Boy, do I regret it now."

"You should reach out to him."

"I may, I just may, if I can find him. We lost contact when I married James."

"Well, good luck. Don't give up hope—after everything Rodney and I have been though, I know anything's possible."

The girls ended their work excursion with plans to meet the next evening. Both women left each other with a new perspective. Sabrina recalled her aggressive antics to help her sister with Rodney and felt guilty that she'd helped come between Rodney and a great woman. Sabrina called him on her way home.

"Hey," Rodney answered.

"She is beautiful, such an adorable woman."

"Now you know."

"Yes, I know and can understand why you didn't give her up."

"I almost gave her up after those weeks of silence."

"Well, I'm glad you two are working things out."

"You two must have had a great time reviewing the building."

"We had a lovely time. I didn't know she had such an eye for decorating."

"Neither did I until she redecorated my front room."

"She and I are going to decorate every room with a theme."

"Isn't that costly?"

"Not if we do it right. I'm sure she knows how to land the best deals."

"She lands them, trust me." Rodney smiled during his last statement. He remembered how she worked his firm during Starz's marketing campaign.

"I see why you care about her so much. Don't blow this, Rodney."

"I'd never think of it. She's going to be my wife."

"You were looking for rings the other day. I knew it."

"No, I was visiting a store owned by my new client."

"Interesting timing. So why would you lead me to believe you were shopping?" Sabrina recalled their conversation.

"Because you had insight to my true feelings, so I went along with it. I do plan on marrying Gail."

"She'll be a great wife. She shows her love for you. Heck, I can see it, and we just became friends."

"Friends?"

"Yes, friends. We're going out tomorrow evening. I like the idea, so please don't do something to cancel it."

"I won't do anything to cancel your evening."

"She mentioned that her friend June is coming along. I was surprised when she told me Dan is June's husband."

"Yes, she is. Dan is a happy guy. If you three head out tomorrow night, I'm sure Dan and I will be with his daughter."

"Dan, a father?"

"Yes, and a great dad too. I'm taking notes." Rodney smiled as he reflected on how he'd one day embrace fatherhood.

"You'll do well. I'm sure of it. You two are a great couple; I can see that now. I'm happy for you."

"Thank you. It's really nice hearing that from you, Sabrina. I appreciate the support." Rodney looked at the clock. "I've got to go now, but I'll catch you later. Don't get my girl into some wild situation tomorrow night."

Sabrina laughed. "Like she'd let me. Talk to you soon."

Gail thought of her day with Sabrina and called June. She explained what had occurred during their review of the building, the decorating ideas, and how they'd connected throughout the day.

June, always in support of Gail, wanted to make sure Gail wasn't being misled or conned by Sabrina. "Did she ask anything more in-depth about your relationship with Rodney? You know, searching for something personal she can later use?" June asked.

"No, actually she shared more of her past with me."

"Okay, well I just want to make sure you don't get hurt. By the way, Rodney told Dan about your decorating the living room. He was so impressed."

"It was fun. I didn't think he'd share it with others. He encouraged me to see the building with Sabrina too. I bet he knew I'd share my decorating eye with her."

"You know he did. Rodney is good at opening doors for others, according to Dan."

"I'm learning. I learn more every day about this sweet man; my sweet man." Gail smiled. "Hey, I wanted to invite you to come out with Sabrina and me tomorrow evening. Can you make it?"

"Sure, Dan wanted baby-and-dad time anyway. We can catch up."

"Great, I can't wait. You're going to like Sabrina, you'll see."

It was late afternoon when the girls showed up at a local pub. The pub was not typically what they would visit, but June had heard about it on a local television show and suggested they check it out.

"I don't know this side of town," Gail said as they reached the building.

"I used to come out in this direction during my younger years, but I haven't been back in awhile," Sabrina said.

Once inside, the women noticed how the outside of the pub did nothing in preparing you for the inside. The place was actually charming and seemed to cater to an upscale clientele. "Wow, I'm impressed," Sabrina said.

"It's very nice," June said as she chose a booth.

"Where did you hear about this again?"

"A local morning show had the owner as a guest. He impressed me, and now, looking around, I can see I was right."

The ladies continued observing the décor and mentioned where they thought the various pieces of art originated. "This one is South African," Sabrina said as she pointed. "I recognized it from my visits."

The women looked at another piece. "This one looks very

familiar, and it's local," June said. She thought for a minute and then snapped her fingers. "I know, it a picture of an apartment building not far from here."

"Oh my goodness." Sabrina covered her mouth in surprise. "Girls, that building is where I had a wonderful date with Lorenz."

"Lorenz? Isn't that the man you told me about?" Gail asked.

"Yes," Sabrina said.

"And you had a date at this apartment building?" June asked.

"Yes, I know it sounds strange, but it was one evening when Lorenz volunteered at the neighborhood clinic. He always found time for volunteering. I don't know how he did it while studying and being a resident."

"He sounds like a really nice guy," June said.

"He was, or is. I can't tell you right now; we lost contact. Anyway, the kids in the neighborhood got wind of our date, and they took off. They cooked, catered, and entertained."

"Entertained? Did they put on a skit for you?"

"No, they sung a few songs while they served us dinner. It was so cute. Fish sticks and macaroni and cheese, with chocolate Twinkies for dessert. It was on the roof top of that building."

"Why that building?" Gail asked.

"A lot of the kids that went to the clinic lived there. You know, that was one of the best dates I've ever been on."

"What happened next?" June asked.

"We dated longer, but when he graduated I decided to return to James, my ex-husband."

"James must have had your heart," Gail said.

"I think it was more the excitement. I was a model, he was a photographer. We were going to do great things together, or so I thought. I didn't have the insight to the future as I do now," Sabrina said. "You know, Gail, Rodney is a great catch. Whatever you're feeling now, is what you should follow as a signal for the future."

"I hear it all the time," Gail said as she looked at June. "June keeps me on track with the same message."

"Listen to June. I've known Rodney for quite a few years now. Believe me, they don't come any better. Flaws and all."

"What flaws?" June giggled. "The man's perfect."

"He has flaws," Gail said, "you just don't see them."

"He has workable differences, not flaws." Sabrina smiled. "To be honest, it's why I pushed my sister to be with him. But, I'm glad he followed his heart."

The three continued their conversation and ordered hors d'oeuvres, as they enjoyed their evening of fun. They ended the night well into the early hours of morning. June and Sabrina exchanged numbers before heading their separate ways, and Gail took a cab back to her and Rodney's place.

Rodney sat on the couch half asleep in the condo before Gail returned. He'd spent the last few hours relaxing and listening to music. When she got home, Gail touched Rodney on the shoulder as she took the seat next to him. "Hey," she said.

Rodney didn't move at first, but he felt her presence and opened his eyes. "Hey, sweetie," he said groggily.

"Are you ready for bed?" Gail asked.

Rodney opened his eyes wider and took in how beautiful she was. "I'm ready for you," he said and pulled her flat against him. They leaned on the couch, and he kissed her deeply.

Gail responded with an aggressive move. She reached into his pants, and once she found the love muscle, she pulled it as if pulling a cord. "Follow me." Gail led Rodney into their bedroom and stripped him of all clothing. She pushed him on the bed and stripped herself as he lay there watching.

Gail crawled into bed next to him and pulled his manhood again. This time she got the response she desired. She maneuvered Rodney into a position where she could take control. She moved on top of him, rocking back and forth. Rodney moaned and placed his hands behind his head, enjoying her assertiveness. It went on for minutes, and after Gail climaxed, Rodney stopped moving. Neither changed position, and they fell asleep in each other's arms.

Days later, Rodney walked to his car from the office. Earlier his team had finished presenting a campaign concept to the jeweler. As he walked to his car, he called Sabrina. "Hey, Sabrina, I have good news."

"Hi, Rodney, what's going on?" Sabrina responded.

"The jeweler agreed to donate one of their pieces for the auction if we feature their jewelry in the fashion show. I figured you'd need accessories for the models anyway, so I agreed on the spot. "

"Rodney, that's amazing!"

"I know, I'm thrilled. I'm heading to your office if you have time. We need to get things rolling, and I have a few more ideas I want to talk to you about."

"I have time to meet you now. Come on by."

"On my way," Rodney said.

Rodney and Sabrina sat in her office hashing out plans for

the fundraiser event. Sabrina told Rodney that she'd received commitments from talented local designers and also a few friends from her modeling days. Rodney secured catering from Panache, the restaurant he co-owned. The show transformed from a concept to a real plan for the future. Contact after contact agreed to some sort of commitment in support of the center or fundraiser. Gail had spoken with Starz, who committed to producing the show once it was outlined and models were cast. At the end of the day, Rodney and Sabrina had one heck of a show coming together. They continued outlining their plan and documented the commitments.

Before they were about to leave, Sabrina turned to Rodney. "Didn't you say you had some other ideas you wanted to talk to me about?"

"Okay, here it goes," he explained. "I need a few minutes set aside during the show. Gail's still on board to model one of the outfits, right?"

"Yes…"

"Do you have a model yet for the evening gown you're designing?"

"No, and I'm sure it would look lovely on her, but why do you need a few minutes?"

"Well, there's a piece of jewelry from the jeweler that I really want to showcase." Rodney smiled.

"You're going to…" Sabrina's eyes were wide.

"Yes, I am. In my meeting with the jeweler today, I mentioned my idea, and he loved it. It wasn't my intention, but he said he's willing to donate an extra ten thousand dollars if I do it during the show. He thinks it will generate even more business."

"Genius."

"So I have you on board?" asked Rodney.

"Of course I'm on board! Just make sure I'm at the wedding."

31.
Showtime

THREE WEEKS LATER, the fashion show was in its final rehearsal stages and building renovations on the center were going well. Sabrina was proud to see her vision become reality. She stayed in contact with her group of designers and models to make sure everything would be perfect come showtime. She'd completed the dresses she'd designed for the show a week earlier.

One day, Gail met with Sabrina to check up on the renovations. "Hey," she said as she surveyed the progress, "things are moving along pretty well here."

"Yes, but there's been a few setbacks too. Did you know the second floor has rotted wood?"

"No, I had no idea."

"It's quite a bit. I hope this doesn't slow us down."

"I know you want to open the doors within the next six months."

"Sooner, if it's possible."

"Let's not get ahead of ourselves. I mean, I have no doubt you'll be able to open on schedule, but we still have the fundraiser."

"Speaking of, I need you to swing by my office either to-night or tomorrow so we can do a final fitting on your dress. I can't thank you enough for being willing to model it in the show."

"I'm flattered you picked me for your design."

"Thanks so much. Now more about the building." Sabrina and Gail spoke in depth about the renovation project and their plans for designing the rooms. After they'd made some prog-ress, they headed to Sabrina's office for Gail's fitting.

Rodney was pleased with his idea and eager to make the event a sensation. Plus, he couldn't wait to see the look of surprise on Gail's face. On Saturday morning, he and Gail woke after a night of fun. "Let's go out for breakfast," he said.

Gail cuddled up next to him. "Why, when I can cook? You like my waffles."

"Yes, I do, but today we should go out. I know it's the weekend, but I was hoping you could take a trip with me to my jewelry client today to help me pick out some pieces for the fashion show. You've seen most of the designs for the auction, so I figured you'd probably do a good job picking out accent-ing pieces of jewelry."

"Sure, I can help with that," Gail said. "Where are we going for breakfast?"

"No place exact, we'll find somewhere along the way to the jewelry store."

"I have a taste for a large omelet."

"I know where we can find the best in the city. It's not quite on the way, but it's worth going," Rodney said as he walked into the bathroom. Gail followed, and they showered and brushed their teeth together. For them, living together had become the norm weeks ago. Gail had found her comfort zone, and the more she settled in, the greater the relationship developed.

It wasn't long before they were both dressed and headed out. Rodney drove directly to the restaurant without passing the jeweler's store. He wanted to take his time and took a longer route to distract from the jewelry store visit. Rodney knew if he rushed things, the visit would seem too planned. It was after breakfast when they arrived at the store. Rodney led Gail inside and, as they entered, a clerk recognized Rodney and greeted him. "Hi, Rodney, nice seeing you again."

"Hey, it's good being here. We're just here to pick out pieces for the fundraiser." Rodney smiled. He led Gail around the store, pointing at some items from the varied selection. He asked, "What jewelry would you like to see on the models during the fundraiser?"

Gail looked with great interest. Picking out jewelry to match the outfits was just like decorating; with both, you had to find pieces that complemented one another. Gail chose multiple sets, including pearls, sapphires, and diamonds. She chose a white gold set of earrings and diamond necklace to go with the dress Sabrina had designed for Gail to wear.

"You're doing a great job," Rodney said. He looked over the list of designs and saw that each was accounted for. "All we have left to pick out is the ring for the auction," Rodney lied. In truth, the jeweler had already picked out the donated pieces himself.

Gail scanned the showcases again, searching. Finally she stopped at an antique-styled ornate wedding set. It was beautifully crafted, with a teardrop center diamond and other smaller diamonds surrounding it. "I think this one would be perfect," she said. "It's unique, unlike anything I've ever seen." Rodney took note as she responded and nodded to the clerk to record the size when he asked her to try it on. "Gail, why don't you try it on?" he asked.

"Oh no, no I couldn't," Gail said.

"Sure you can, it doesn't give us bad luck."

"Well, I guess it can't hurt." Gail smiled as she tried the rings on her finger. "Oh, it looks like it's too big. Oh well, it's probably best that it's not a small size so that whoever wins it in the auction can get it sized to fit."

The clerk took notice that the size was a problem. "Here, let me see…" The clerk put a silver sizing ring onto Gail's finger. "Did you know you wear a size six?"

"No, I thought it was larger," Gail said as she looked at her finger. It was exactly what Rodney wanted to happen. As the clerk moved away to record Gail's size, Rodney moved in to gain her attention. "I think we missed picking out jewelry for one more outfit. What do you think of these?" He pointed to some gaudy earrings.

"No way. Not even." She laughed. "I swear, men have no idea about jewelry and clothing."

"It's exactly why I brought you with me," Rodney said. *This worked so well.* He led Gail to the car. "You have great taste: an eye for decorating, fashion, and construction."

"Construction?" Gail laughed, but she knew what Rodney meant.

"Yes, the renovation is going great, and I know you've been at the site to oversee it fairly often. You have to know something about it to run it so well."

"I knew about stage construction and some things but not to the extent of this renovation. The job is huge, Rodney; you can't believe how much these guys do to renovate an 85-year-old building."

"I thought it was older. You've started with the décor?"

"A few areas, but mostly we have to wait because of construction."

"Okay, I see," Rodney said as he continued to divert Gail away from his objective. It was a nice day and Rodney decided to take Gail shopping to continue to distract her. They spent two hours strolling through the downtown shops and managed to pick up a few things for the condo. At the end of the day, Rodney knew his plan had been a success.

The night before the show, they held one last dress rehearsal. They allowed the media a sneak preview, showcasing the donated clothing designs to the general public. It was great exposure for the show, and they hoped the additional focus would entice ticket sales and bids on the pieces.

One reporter interviewed Starz. "Starz, everything you touch seems to become golden. I hear you're volunteering your time and effort for this event," the reporter said. "Will all proceeds of this show go to the new Patricia Dugan Healthy Weight Center?"

"Yes, all proceeds will, as the show is strictly a fundraiser. It's going to be a great show; I'm very excited," Starz said.

After the media left, the rehearsal really began. Each model put on her donated design, and Starz instructed the group on timing, placing, and more. Gail was busy with the other models, but Rodney and Sabrina were free to oversee the progress and catch any last-minute problems. After a busy two hours, everyone headed home.

Gail and Rodney didn't feel like cooking dinner after

rehearsal, so Rodney decided he'd run to pick something up for them to eat while Gail stayed home and relaxed. By the time he returned to the condo and walked in, Gail had lit candles, started some slow music, and had changed into a seductive outfit. "Hi, darling," she said.

"Wow," Rodney said. "Is this real?"

"It's as real as it's going to get."

"I had no idea; no idea that coming home could be this exciting or surprising."

"I like to surprise you."

"Baby, I like it too," Rodney smiled as he placed things on the table and followed Gail into the kitchen.

She moved into his arms and gently kissed his neck.

Rodney couldn't help moving to the music, gently swaying in motion, and Gail followed, rocking along with him from side to side.

"You are my heart, my joy, my inspiration," Rodney said.

"And you are all those things to me," Gail said. "I am your partner."

"Partner," he whispered and touched her neck with his lips. "Partner," he repeated as he kissed behind her ear. "Partner," he said again and pressed his lips against hers.

Gail responded by pressing into him. "Does this mean we're having dinner later?"

"I'm having dinner now." Rodney moved his growing manhood into a massaging position, encouraging Gail's continued response. She moaned and moved her hips with a subtle rotation, inviting Rodney.

"Dinner is going well, my dear," Rodney whispered, "and dessert is first." He stepped back and lifted Gail into his arms, taking her to their chamber of passion. He placed her on the bed, peeled off his shirt, and kicked his shoes into the corner. "I've waited to be with you all day."

"I've never wanted a man so much." Gail reached for him and pulled him closer to her, leaning her body towards his. "I love you…I love you, Rodney." she said. She held him and felt his excitement knock on her spot of ecstasy. Gail used her legs to grab him around the waist and pulled him closer while she held her arms around him, "I need you," she whispered with a moan. She lifted her waist again, inviting Rodney's erection towards her.

Rodney couldn't get out of his pants fast enough after breaking Gail's hold on him. He returned without missing a beat in passionate moves. Rodney found himself engulfed in Gail's grip. She moved and he responded, pulling in and out, exploring the inner core of love. They sweated in the heat of the moment, pulling, pushing, turning, and stripping Gail's lingerie from her body. It was an hour into their session before both finally climaxed, calling out sweet names to one another.

They collapsed in the bed. "I do hope future desserts are as wonderful as this was. I'm so happy I have a sweet tooth." Rodney said with laughter.

"This is exactly how things should be," Gail said.

"And are we ready for dinner?"

"I'm really hungry now." Gail giggled as she walked into the bathroom. Rodney followed, they cleaned up, and both dressed comfortably. Gail went into the kitchen and put a few things together before they began to eat dinner. *One day,* thought Rodney, *one day we'll have four here at this table.* He smiled at Gail as she looked at him.

"What?" she asked. "Why are you staring at me like that?"

Sabrina and Simone decided to watch the news in their home Sunday morning. "There's the feature for the fundraiser." Sabrina pointed. "They did a very nice job."

"Couldn't be any better, especially since it's free coverage," Simone said. "You're doing a great thing. It's going well, and you have a golden thumb. I see it. Wow, little sister, you've grown up so well."

"Do you think Aunt Marge would be proud of me?"

"So would Mom and Dad, I'm sure of it."

"Are you coming tonight?"

"Wouldn't miss it for the world."

"Prepare yourself for the unexpected, okay?"

"Unexpected?" Simone asked as she watched Sabrina leave the room.

"Okay," Simone said.

Sabrina had promised Rodney she wouldn't share his plans with anyone. *I know she's over Rodney, or at least I hope so.*

Limousines stopped in front of the pavilion where red carpet flowed to the curb, meeting each exiting passenger. Photographers lined the walk, flashing at the celebrity entrance. Car after car, people entered on the red carpet, and shortly after the first wave, security opened the entrance to everyone. The pavilion was filled with onlookers for the fashion extravaganza. Lights dimmed just as the hour approached to start the event.

The bands started with high-energy music, and an announcer filled the air with welcoming messages. He explained the fundraising goals, the schedule for the event, and the bidding process. A glimpse of the healthy weight center flashed upon the screens, presenting the fundraising objective.

The master of ceremonies then talked about eating disorder illnesses and their impact on society. Moments later, music blared, cameras, and spotlights filled the pavilion. "Showtime," the host said. Curtains opened, and the first model walked the runway.

"Here's our first peek from designer Gloria Kurtz. It's spring fashion at its best," the man announced. Lights flashed as the model pranced the strip. She paused at the end of the runway, posed, and returned to the stage. The next model followed suit, and each performed well within sync, just as rehearsed and planned.

An entertainer sang in between designers, providing a well-rounded show. Starz had cameras focused on certain models wearing jewelry sponsored by Rodney's client. The master of ceremonies identified the jewelry pieces and explained that one lucky bidder would be able to take home a piece of the jewelry that night.

It was almost time for Gail to take her turn on the runway. Backstage, Rodney approached her, "Are you ready? It's nearly time."

"I'm ready, no sweat."

"Good, just remember this: I love you, and just imagine I'm right there by your side."

"I know, it's just as we rehearsed. I'm okay. You make it easy." Gail waited for her cue to step onto the runway. Her dress was dark blue, the color of the night sky. Small sparkles adorned the waist in a flattering pattern. The dress fit exquisitely, accenting her seductive curves. Starz signaled for Gail to step onto the runway. She turned to give Rodney a quick kiss. "Here we go," she said. She glided down the runway and stopped to pose at the predetermined spot. When she turned around, she was shocked to see Rodney behind her, standing there in his fitted black suit.

Rodney grabbed Gail's hand. "What are you doing?" she asked.

Lights in the pavilion dimmed, a spotlight flashed on the couple, and cameras projected their image on the large screens. Rodney dropped to one knee while he pulled a small ring box from his pocket. He looked at Gail as he kneeled, still holding her hand, and said, "My life has changed drastically since you've come into it. I finally realized the importance of following my heart, having a partner, and the definition of true love. Will you spend the rest of your life as my wife?"

Gail covered her mouth in surprise. She saw that the ring Rodney offered was the exact ring she'd tried on at the jeweler's store, just days before the event. "Is this for the show?" she asked in a whisper.

"No, Gail, I'm serious. I want to marry you, if you'll have me."

Again, she paused in response. June shouted from behind the curtain, "Say yes!" Sabrina smiled and winked at Gail. Starz moved toward the microphone and said, "You've waited for this day, Gail. Say yes."

Gail heard all three as she gazed at Rodney. She smiled. "Yes, I love you and will marry you."

Rodney rose from his knee and placed the ring on her finger. It was a perfect fit. He kissed Gail, and the crowd thundered their applause.

Amongst all that happiness, one onlooker rose from her chair and left the pavilion. A tear fell down her cheek, and she got into her car. Simone drove towards home. After a minute, her cell phone rang. Simone answered the call; it was Sabrina.

"Are you okay?"

"How did this happen, Sabrina? I was supposed to be happy... happy in love, business, and family."

"Look, sis, it's okay, your time will come, I just know it. You need to let your regrets go and move forward."

"Easier said than done."

"Maybe so, but we at least have to try."

Simone didn't answer as she drove her car to the side of the road. She parked for a moment before responding. "This hurts, Sabrina. This really hurts. It feels like I've lost."

"It's okay, sis. Remember, you said yourself you didn't truly love Rodney. It wasn't meant to be. Let it go, and drive home safely. I'll see you in a few hours?"

"Yeah," Simone said. "I'll see you when you get home."

Rodney smiled as he reflected on the night he'd proposed to Gail. He remembered how, in the beginning, he'd worked so hard at finding love, finding the right woman. He remembered those feelings he had for Simone years ago. He recalled going through the pain of not having her reciprocate his feelings and how he'd done everything he could to escape. Somehow, in the middle of all that pain, he'd met the love of his life, Gail.

Rodney stood in Dan's yard looking into empty space, deep in thought. He turned and saw Gail showing June her engagement ring. *Finally*, he thought, *finally a new chapter in my life*. Rodney walked near Dan, who stood over the grill, and asked, "Do you need any help, my friend?"

"Yes, can you push the little one around the yard? That will keep her busy."

"I'd love to," Rodney said as he moved to the toy car stroller. He grabbed the stroller's handle. "Zoom, zoom," he said as he pushed, mimicking a car's engine. "Uncle Rodney's taking you on a ride. Get ready, kiddo, hold on."

Five months later, everyone met in Phil's office to discuss the final steps that needed to take place before the healthy weight center could open. Phil opened a folder and scanned the page inside. "It looks like all the accounts have been settled," he said. "We're ready to get this thing going."

"Great." Sabrina smiled. "Gail and I have almost completed decorating. I think we're just waiting on that order of area rugs, right, Gail?"

Gail and Rodney, whose wedding was set for only a few months later, sat at the opposite end of the table. "Yes," Gail said, "I think that order is coming in later this week."

Everyone had taken on their own projects to help their planning come to completion. Phil had handled the legal aspects and the finances. Sabrina and Gail had continued decorating and setting up the center. Rodney had persisted with the marketing campaign to create support for the center within the community, and the two philanthropists had followed through on their promise to contact the doctor and find employees.

"That's good," Rodney said. "It seems like everything is coming together. I've drafted the press release for the grand opening, but I wanted to wait till after this meeting before deciding when to launch. Are we really ready to open?"

"If my calculations are correct, we're covered financially for the first year of operation," Phil said. He looked at the philanthropists. "Is the doctor you wanted accepting the salary number we offered?"

"Oh, yes," Rodney said. "Tell me about this doctor you've

approached with the offer. He's the only person we've recruited for the position, right?"

"Yes," the elderly man said, "He's very personable. He made a name for himself and has a strong reputation for giving back."

"He sounds perfect for the position," Sabrina said. "Well, don't keep us in suspense any longer, did he take it?"

"It's good news," the elderly gentleman said. "He indicated that he'll take the job. I knew he would."

The other philanthropist nodded. "Yes, and we told him we were meeting here today." He looked at his watch. "Actually, he should be arriving at any minute."

As if on cue, Phil's receptionist stepped into the room. "Hello, everyone. You have a visitor."

The man walked into the room. Sabrina looked up, and her heart skipped a beat as she locked eyes with Lorenz.